when
constellations
form

USA TODAY BESTSELLING AUTHOR
MICALEA SMELTZER

when constellations form

© Copyright 2017 Micalea Smeltzer

All rights reserved. This book or any portion thereof may not be reproduced or used in any manner whatsoever without the express written permission of the publisher.

This is a work of fiction. Names, characters, businesses, places, events and incidents are either the products of the author's imagination or used in a fictitious manner. Any resemblance to actual persons, living or dead, or actual events is purely coincidental.

Cover Design: Emily Wittig Designs

Edited by Wendi Termporado of Ready, Set, Edt

Photography by Regina Wamba at Mae I Design

Models Anthony Kemper and Hannah Peltier

one
...

thea

"I'M GOING to kill my husband."

My best friend, Rae, looks up from the box she's packing as I flop onto her bed with a groan.

"Why? What'd he do?" she asks, folding a shirt neatly before putting it in the box.

The four of us—Rae, her fiancé and my brother, Cade, and my husband, Xander, have lived together in this house since the summer before Rae and I started our sophomore year of college. That was three years ago, and in that time, so much has changed. Rae and Cade got engaged, my mom lived with us for a while, Xander surprised me with a car of my own ... So many more memories, but the four of us decided that with Rae and me graduating this year, there was no need to keep living here. Rae and Cade are getting married later in the year, and Xander and I are already married. In other words, it's time for all of us to move on.

"He just kicked me out of our room, because he needs to pack." I roll onto my stomach and lean over the bed to watch her.

"What's so bad about that?"

"Oh, no." I wave my hand. "Not pack our stuff to move—no, he needs to pack our stuff for the honeymoon we're going on."

"You're going on a honeymoon?" Her nose crinkles in confusion, and she sets down the shirt she was folding.

"Exactly." I snap my fingers. "Apparently, he planned a honeymoon, since we never had one, and now he has to pack my bag since this is a surprise and he doesn't want me to know where we're going. But you *know* how I feel about my clothes. He better pack the right things."

"I'm sure he'll do fine." She shrugs and resumes her packing, like my meltdown isn't important to her.

"He'll probably only pack lingerie," I grumble.

She laughs. "Like you'd complain about that."

I crack a smile. "True. I hate surprises, though. I wish he'd given me more warning, but we leave tomorrow after graduation."

"That's probably exactly why he didn't tell you—he knows you'd try to find a way out of it."

"But now I have to worry about all the things he might have forgotten to do. Like, what if we get to this mysterious destination and he's like, 'Oh shit I forgot to book the hotel'?"

Rae snickers and tapes up the box she's done packing. "This is Xander we're talking about. He's not like that."

"Ugh," I groan.

"You're being dramatic," she tells me. Which is true, I know.

"I just hate it when he springs things on me. I figured we'd spend the next two weeks before he goes off to training camp hanging around our house and getting everything unpacked. Oh, my God." I sit straight up. "Seriously, what the hell is he thinking? The movers are coming tomorrow after graduation and now he's telling me we're *leaving* then. Oh, no. Boy's about to give me a heart attack," I ramble.

I shoot up off her bed and scurry out the door then down the hall.

"Xander!" I burst into our room.

"Jesus Christ, you scared me." He jumps a foot away from the closed suitcase on the bed.

Prue, our dog, jumps up from her bed in the corner and growls. When she realizes I'm the cause of the intrusion, she sits back down.

"We can't leave tomorrow—the movers are coming to pick up our stuff and take it to the new house. They're not going to know what's ours and where to put everything." I can feel my anxiety building.

"Relax." He closes the distance between us and takes my hands in his. "I have it covered."

"What? How?"

"Jace and Nova are going to make sure everything is put where it's supposed to. It'll be *fine*. You trust me, right?"

I frown. "I do, but you're pushing your luck at the moment."

He chuckles and cups my cheeks. "I've got this. I've thought of everything, believe me."

I wrinkle my nose, not believing him, but I choose not to say that. "It just feels like bad timing," I argue.

He smiles, his eyes crinkling at the corners. "It's the perfect time. We *need* a break, Thea. We've been going non-stop since we got married. This is our last chance, since you're graduating and don't have class, I don't have training yet, and you haven't started a job."

"Don't remind me," I grumble. I'm not looking forward to job searching.

"If we don't do this now, then your five-year plan will kick in and we won't ever be able to do it." He eyes me, waiting for my response.

"I'm sure I could pencil it in somewhere," I mumble.

He raises a brow. "That's cute."

I fight a smile. "Okay, so *maybe* it'd be a tight squeeze."

His hands find my waist, and he pulls me into his body. "We're going on vacation, and that's final." He grins. "You know, you might be the only girl that'd complain about a spontaneous trip."

I wrap my arms around his neck. "I gotta keep you on your toes," I joke, and stand on my tiptoes to kiss him. He smiles against my lips and pushes away.

"Now *go*. Let me finish."

I sigh. "Okay, okay." I raise my hands in surrender and leave the room.

I head back down the hall to Rae and Cade's room.

Rae now stands, pulling the last of their clothes out of the closet to pack.

Tonight is both of our last nights in this house before we move on.

Cade and Rae got an apartment in the city, close to where Jace and Nova live, while Xander and I bought a house in the suburbs. We looked at apartments in the city but they were all so cold and not homey. The house we bought has too much room for us now, but I know we'll grow into it one day.

"You weren't gone long," Rae comments, laying a bunch of Cade's dress shirts on the bed.

I shrug. "He says he has it covered, so I'm letting it go and trusting him."

Rae looks at me in disbelief. "Good for you."

"Am I really that much of a control freak?"

She laughs. "No, you just hate surprises, which is understandable after everything you went through."

I sigh. "Yeah, *that*."

Having your dad break into your house, which subsequently resulted in your mom shooting him, would make anyone a little crazy.

"I can't believe we're graduating tomorrow." Rae changes the subject. She folds one of Cade's shirts and clutches it to her chest. "Four years of classes, and tests, and grades, and it's finally over."

"It's surreal," I agree, picking up one of the shirts and folding it for her. "It feels like we're finally grown-ups."

Rae places the shirt in a box. "I'm going to miss living with you and Xander. It's been nice having you guys around."

I begin to tear up. "Not as much as I'll miss you guys. With all the time Xander's gone it's been great to not be alone. Now..."

"Aw, Thea." Rae hugs me. "We'll always be around if you need us. You know that."

"I know." I nod into her shoulder, my fingers clutching her shirt.

I'm so lucky to have a best friend like Rae—and better yet, she'll soon be my sister-in-law, so she can never get rid of me. We're bonded for life.

I let her go and wipe my eyes. "Ugh," I groan. "This move is making me so emotional, I swear. I cried yesterday when Xander packed my shark slippers—like I know I'm *going* to see them again. I'm a basket case."

Rae cracks a smile. "I've cried a few times too. It feels like the end of an era."

"Exactly," I agree, placing the shirt I folded in the box.

"You'll have fun on vacation, though. You and Xander deserve some alone time. You haven't had hardly any since you got married."

I grab another shirt to fold it. "Sometimes I can't believe I'm *married*. Like, I married my dream guy—what kind of fantasy world am I living in?"

She laughs. "You guys are perfect together, so don't be so shocked."

"Speaking of married ... you're going to let me help plan

the wedding, right? Now that we don't have school, it's time to crack down on the planning."

"Sure." She smiles. "You're better at that kind of thing than I am."

I clap my hands together excitedly. "This is going to be fun. Have you set a date yet? I know you guys were talking about something before the end of the year."

"I'm not really sure yet. Maybe a December wedding."

"Ooh, that'd be fun." My mind wanders off, thinking of colors (pink!), cake, and décor.

"Hey, dinner's ready." Cade pokes his head into the room.

"You need a haircut," I tell him.

I've been telling him that every day for the last month, and so far, he hasn't gotten his hair cut. Brothers are jerks.

His light brown hair has grown out to nearly his shoulders, and with his heavy beard, he looks like a fucking lumberjack.

Cade runs his fingers through his hair and then flips it over his shoulder dramatically. "You don't like it?" He knows I don't. "I think it makes me look like Fabio."

I gag. "Who wants to aspire to look like that?"

"Do you want me to cut it?" he asks Rae.

She raises her hands in defense. "I'm happy if you're happy."

"See, she hates it," I butt in.

"What do you really think?" he asks her.

She shrugs. "I like it a little shaggy, but not like this."

Cade nods. "Consider it gone then. I was going to get it cut tomorrow morning anyway."

"And trim the beard," I tell him. "Who knows what's growing in that."

He laughs and rubs his beard. "True. There's probably some crumbs living in it."

I shake my head and look at Rae. "Are you sure you want to marry that? I mean, he's my brother so I *have* to love him, but you have a choice."

Rae grins. "Yeah, I'm pretty sure."

I sigh. "Well, I tried."

"Tried to get my fiancée to leave me?" Cade interrupts.

"Tried to help my friend," I correct, wagging a finger. "She can't be saved, though." I shrug in a whatcha-gonna-do-about-it way.

Cade laughs. "Come eat."

I salute him and hop off the bed. "Aye, aye, Captain."

Rae reluctantly leaves behind the last of the clothes she has to pack and follows me out of the room with Cade trailing behind.

The door to my room opens, and Xander pokes his head out. "Did I hear something about dinner?"

Cade chuckles. "Yeah, it's ready. Time to eat." He smacks his stomach dramatically.

Prue pokes her head out between Xander's legs, sniffs the air, and then takes off down the stairs.

I follow her down and into the kitchen. The dinner smells amazing, but I feel sad knowing that this is our last dinner together in this house. The kitchen is bare, save for the essentials since we knew we'd be eating dinner here tonight. But after tonight, everything will be packed away since we won't be eating breakfast here in the morning.

"This smells delicious," I tell Cade, inhaling the smell of a roast.

The four of us have always taken turns cooking so that it never fell on just one person to make the meals, and tonight happened to be Cade's turn. Luckily, all of us can cook, so there's never a night when the food sucks.

Xander heads for the garage door, towing my suitcase behind him.

"What are you doing?" I call after him.

He pauses and looks over his shoulder. "I'm scared if I leave the suitcase in our room you'll be tempted to peek. You're too lazy to trek out to the car to take a look."

"Smart man," I agree. "But what about yours? Can't I peek at that one?" I challenge.

He grins. "It's already in the car."

I sigh. "Of course it is."

And he's right, I'm too lazy to bother going out to the car to check it. Besides, tonight the only thing on my mind is the move and graduation.

I grab a plate of roast, potatoes, and vegetables, and sit down. The light above the table is on which only serves to illuminate how bare the house really is. There are no longer any photos on the walls, nothing taped to the refrigerator, and no knick knacks on the counters. This place has always felt like home, and all of a sudden it's *not*.

Xander comes back into the house and grabs a plate of food before sitting down beside me.

Rae sits across from me, conversing quietly with Cade.

"What if I fall?" I whisper to Xander.

"Huh?" He looks up from his plate of food with a forkful of food halfway to his mouth.

"Tomorrow. What if I fall when I get on stage to get my diploma?"

He lowers his fork. "You're not going to fall."

"It's possible."

He shakes his head. "Thea, you wear six-inch heels on an almost daily basis and you don't fall. I think you'll be fine."

"But this would be the one time I *would* fall, and it'd be in front of my whole graduating class. Talk about mortifying." I hang my head, my cheeks already flaming like I *did* fall.

Xander touches his fingers to my cheek then trails them down my neck. "Don't worry so much about stuff like that. So what if you do fall? You'll get back up and move on."

"You're right." I nod in agreement as his fingers fall away.

"How long are you guys going to be on vacation?" Rae asks.

Xander clears his throat. "A week."

"I still can't believe you planned a vacation by yourself," I mumble. "You *did* remember to book a hotel, right?" I can't help but ask—I mean, he *is* a guy, so it's a very real possibility that he forgot.

"Yes." He laughs, looking at me like I'm so cute. I'm dead serious, though.

"How about plane tickets? Did you get those?"

"We could be driving," he argues.

I narrow my eyes. "I swear to God, if you take me to the mountains on this 'vacation' I'm going to push you off a cliff."

He laughs. "I'm not saying."

I glare across the table at Rae. "It's the fucking mountains. I know it."

Xander snickers. "You can think whatever you want, but you're never going to guess."

I groan, my fork clanging against my plate. "Just tell me."

He smirks. "No, that ruins the fun."

"You know what else ruins the fun? When your dick gets bit during a blowjob." I level him with a glare.

He pales. "That's not funny."

I raise my hands innocently. "I'm just saying."

"Ew, can we change the subject. I don't need to hear this," my brother interrupts.

I sigh and smack my hands against the table in exasperation. "Oh, grow up, Cade. People have sex. It's a fact of life. Xander and I are married, so I assure you he quite enjoys putting his penis in my vagina."

"Oh, my God," Xander mutters beside me, covering his face with his hands.

"Oh, not you too," I groan. "You boys are ridiculous."

"He's your brother," Xander argues, keeping his face covered. "He doesn't need to hear about our sex life."

"I'm his sister and Rae tells me about theirs," I argue.

Rae's eyes widen like a deer caught in headlights when

both boys look at her. "I ... I ..." she stutters. "Only sometimes."

"I can't believe this," Cade mutters.

"I feel ganged up on," Xander says to Cade.

"These girls are going to be the death of me," Cade agrees.

I roll my eyes. "You boys are far too sensitive. Honestly." I sigh.

I've always been open about my body and sex, and I wish more people were too. You shouldn't feel ashamed to speak freely. It's a natural part of life.

I finish eating my dinner, and after we've all eaten, Xander and I clean the dishes and pack them away.

When we're done Xander lifts me onto the counter. I look around at the empty room and frown.

"I'm sad to leave," I admit.

"Me too," Xander agrees, tucking a piece of hair behind my ear. "We have a lot of good memories here, but we'll make more at our new home."

"I know." I nod, but I still feel like I might cry.

I wasn't sad when I moved out of my parents' house and into the dorms, and I wasn't sad when I moved from the dorms to here, but this ... this is breaking my heart. I'd think something was wrong with me if everyone else wasn't equally as sad.

He touches his fingers to my trembling lower lip. "Don't cry," he pleads.

I suck in a lungful of air, using it to help tamp down my emotions. "I don't know why I'm so emotional." I smile weakly.

He places his hands on either side of my waist on the counter. "It's a big deal," he reasons. "It's kind of crazy to think that we've been married for almost three years and we've never actually lived just the two of us."

"Whoa." My eyes widen. "What if you get sick of me after a week and want a divorce?"

He laughs and shakes his head, his shaggy black hair falling into his eyes. "Not a chance. If I've lived twenty-six years—twenty-three with you alive—and haven't gotten sick of you yet, then I think we're safe." He taps his finger to my nose. "Besides, I don't think there are any hidden quirks about to suddenly surface. I hate to break it to you, sweetheart, but I already know the good, bad, and the ugly."

I fight a smile and pretend to be mad. "Is that so?" I raise a brow. "And what exactly is the bad and the ugly."

"You forgot the good," he points out.

"Okay, the good too then."

"Well, let's see." He grins and holds up his fingers to tick them off. "Good—you have the kindest heart, you're funny, you like the same movies and shows that I do, honestly the good list goes on and on. As for the bad, you *hate* mornings, and that's annoying because I happen to love them. You also despise change and like everything to go according to *plan*." He slurs my five-year plan. "But plans make life boring." He lowers his head and brushes his lips over my cheek, moving to the shell of my ear so I shiver from his touch. "And the ugly —well, you're kind of terrifying when you wake up. Your hair's a mess and you kind of mutter like a monster until you get some coffee."

"Xander," I scoff, and swat at his arm.

He laughs and dodges me easily, not that it would've fazed him anyway. Xander's always been a muscular guy, but thanks to the last couple of years of playing professional football he's *really* bulked up now.

"Come on." He grabs my hips and hoists me off the counter. "We have to finish packing."

I wrinkle my nose in distaste. "Don't remind me."

Like Rae, all we have left to pack is our clothes. I would've already had it done, but since he kicked me out of our room, I couldn't.

He takes my hand and guides me up the steps. I frown at the bare walls that were once covered in family photos.

I know that the move doesn't undo three years worth of memories, but it still hurts. I'm thankful, though, that we lived with Rae and my brother—and my mom for a time. It brought me so much closer with them all, and taught me a lot about them and myself.

Xander leads me into our room and Prue trails behind us, her blond hair a shaggy mess. She needs a trim, but I prefer her fur long and fluffy.

She plops on the floor where her bed would normally be, but since it's already packed away, there's only a bare spot on the floor.

My mouth pops open. "Xander," I scold, "who's going to watch the dog while we're gone?"

"Relax." He fights a smile, bending down on the floor to

assemble a box. "Jace and Nova are handling the move *and* taking care of Prue. I would've asked Cade and Rae since Prue knows them, but considering they're moving too I didn't think that was fair. So she'll stay with Jace and Nova until we get back."

"Does Jace even know how to take care of a dog?" I wrinkle my nose.

Xander chuckles and flicks a piece of too-long hair from his eyes. "Probably not, but I'm sure Nova can handle it—besides, it's not *that* hard. I even wrote out strict instructions for them about what time she eats and goes out."

I inhale a steadying breath. "You really have thought of everything."

His lips tip into a smile. "Told you so."

I finally give in to the fact that we're leaving. Amidst the chaos of our lives right now it feels like the completely wrong time to uncheck from reality *but* when is the right time?

The summery royal-blue dress with yellow flowers I'm wearing for graduation hangs from the back of the closet door, ready for graduation tomorrow. I was ecstatic when I happened along the dress since it's our school's colors. It's cheesy, sure, to wear the school colors on graduation but I'm feeling nostalgic.

Xander's outfit for tomorrow lies folded on the floor along with another change of clothes for after.

"I'm assuming my dress won't be appropriate for travel?" I hint, and he nods. "*So*," I drag out the word, "would you mind giving me a hint as to what I *should* wear?"

He smirks. "Dress comfortably."

I groan. "Ugh, what does that even *mean*?"

He shrugs. "Wear sweatpants and a top."

I roll my eyes. "I can't wear sweatpants."

He chuckles, his lips tilting up in amusement. "That's what *I'm* wearing."

"Fine," I grumble. "I'll wear *sweatpants*." I spit the word like it's venomous—which to someone fashion obsessed like me that's exactly what it is. Don't get me wrong, I'm perfectly fine wearing sweatpants at home, but in public? No thanks.

I end up picking out a pair of yoga pants and a fitted black tank top. I figure it'll be comfortable and the pants make my ass look amazing—at least that's what Xander tells me. I add a sweatshirt to carry-on just in case it's cold on the flight.

I add my tennis shoes to the pile of clothing as well as a baseball cap.

Xander starts packing while I gather the last of the items I'll need to wear for graduation—a necklace, watch, and a pair of heels.

"Do you have everything you need?" I ask him, pointing to his pile of clothes.

He narrows his eyes on the items and then jumps up. "Shit, I almost forgot my watch."

He runs across the room to a box labeled *Dresser Items* and comes back a moment later with his black watch—a gift from his parents for his team winning the Super Bowl two years ago.

I don't think I've ever been more proud of him than I

was that day, as I watched the love of my life realize his dreams.

He adds the watch to the pile of clothes and sits back down on the floor.

"Hang on," I say, this time being the one to jump up.

I grab my laptop and bring it over to the floor. I bring up Netflix and the last episode of *Arrow* that we watched.

"Now this will be much more fun," I tell him.

As the show plays we work together to pack the last of our clothes—because I'm a shopaholic it takes quite a while. By the time we finish, it's late and I'm ready to fall over.

Xander carries the boxes over to the door, and I stretch out on the floor staring at the ceiling.

Once all the boxes are moved, he towers over me, fighting a smile.

"What'cha doin' down there?" he asks with a slight smirk, his full lips tilting on one corner.

"Too. Tired. To. Move," I rasp in a voice like I'm dehydrated then reach out with weak fingers.

He laughs and hauls me up. "Cute, Kincaid." He kisses my forehead.

I might never get used to him calling me *Kincaid*. In fact, I hope I never do because I love the fluttery feeling of butterflies I get in my stomach. When we first got married I didn't have that feeling, I was terrified since it was such a spur of the moment thing, but now I love it.

Xander turns back the covers and climbs beneath them.

I join him and roll to my side. A moment later, his arm

wraps around me, and I smile as he burrows his head into the crook of my neck.

"I love you." He kisses the edge of my jaw.

"I love you too," I say back.

I thought I'd be too keyed up to fall asleep, but my eyes grow heavy and sleep claims me.

two
...

thea

I SHOWER, curl my hair, and carefully apply my makeup before getting dressed.

I assess myself in the bathroom mirror, since my floor-length mirror is currently bubble-wrapped for the move. The dress fits me well, it's a flattering cut, and ends just above my knees.

I inhale a deep breath. In a couple of hours, I'm going to be graduating. I'll no longer be a college student. Classes, homework, and exams have consumed my life for four long years, and even though I'm beyond happy to be done, I feel a little lost. *What do I do now?*

The obvious answer is get a job, but that's easier said than done.

"Hey, you ready?" Xander asks, poking his head into the bathroom.

My stomach dips when I see him because he looks too hot for his own good. The boy *knows* how to wear a dress shirt. The white material clings to his defined arms and chest.

"We need to go," he continues, fiddling with his watch.

I look at the time and curse. He's right, we do need to go since the four of us are supposed to meet Jace and Nova for breakfast before graduation.

"Yeah, I'm ready," I say, forcing a smile.

I *am* ready, technically, in the sense that I'm dressed and my hair and makeup's done. But my mind? That's definitely not ready for today.

I don't remember being this nervous at my high school graduation.

I smooth my hands down my dress and then flick off the bathroom light before I follow Xander out of the room and to the car.

Rae and Cade are already in his Jeep, and we join them instead of going in separate cars.

"Hey, look at you, no longer looking homeless," I comment, buckling my seatbelt.

Cade had gone out and gotten a haircut this morning. It's still on the longer side, but now just past his ears which is a vast improvement and the rodent that was on his face is now gone.

Cade starts to back out. "Stop!" I cry and he slams on the brakes. "I don't feel so good," I mutter, reaching for the door handle. I push it open and tumble out of the car, running for the house. I don't make it far before I stop in the middle of the yard and throw up.

"Thea?" Xander calls worriedly, and a moment later his hand touches the small of my back. "Are you okay?" he asks, pulling my hair away from my neck.

I inhale a ragged breath, trying to calm my rolling stomach.

"I think I'm okay," I say after a moment. "Just nerves."

His brows knit together, and I can tell he's unconvinced.

"I need to go brush my teeth," I mutter, pulling away from him.

His hand falls from my hair and he follows me back up the driveway. Cade's already opened the garage door so I head right inside and up the stairs.

"Thea?" Xander probes as he follows me. "What's going on? I'm worried."

I flip on the bathroom light and grab my toothbrush and toothpaste—practically the only essentials left in the bathroom.

"I don't know," I tell him honestly. "I really think it's just the nerves," I explain, but I'm unconvinced, and I can tell he is too.

"Do you think it's that bug or whatever you had a few weeks ago?"

I shrug. "Idoubtit," I say, my voice garbled around the toothbrush. I spit and rinse my mouth. "I took antibiotics for it, so I doubt it'd come back, especially this soon."

"But you feel okay, right?"

"I'm a little tired, but that's normal." I wipe my mouth and reapply my lipstick.

"I just want to make sure you're well enough for the trip.

I don't want to be ..." he trails off, realizing he's about to spill too many details.

"You don't want to be *what*?" I pester.

He bites his lip. "I don't want to be out of the country with you sick," he admits.

I raise a brow, fighting a smile. "We're leaving the country?"

"Yes, but I'm not telling you *where*. Not yet, at least."

I turn the light off and we go through the whole process of leaving the house again.

When we slide into the car, Cade immediately launches into a tirade. "Are you sick again? Should we go to the doctor? You can skip graduation if you need to, Thea. Your health comes first."

Honestly, my brother takes overprotective to a whole new level.

"I'm *fine*," I assure him. "Jace and Nova are probably wondering where we are, so let's go." I wave my hand in a gesture for him to hurry up.

He watches me in the rearview mirror so I paste on a smile and that seems to make him feel better.

Honestly, I feel fine now, like I wasn't just sick. In fact, I feel like I could go run a mile. I better not get ahead of myself —I hate cardio, unless it involves sex with Xander then I'm *all* over that.

We arrive at the café and my stomach rumbles. It's nearly ten in the morning and I haven't eaten anything yet—which *might* explain why I got sick.

Jace and Nova stand outside his truck. She stands in

front of him and he has his arms wrapped around her from behind, his head ducked into her neck. He must say something because she laughs, smiling a big smile, which in turn makes *me* smile. Jace has always been a bit ... intense and broody, but Nova brings out the best in him and vice versa. I've never seen two people more well-matched ... except maybe Xander and myself, because we go together pretty damn well.

Cade parks the Jeep by the curb and we all hop out. Jace and Nova walk over to meet us and hugs are exchanged.

We head inside and get a table. A waitress immediately takes our drink order and then we all peruse the menu, trying to decide what we want for breakfast.

My stomach rumbles, and I eye the items on the menu. Everything sounds good, but I ultimately decide on the French toast.

The waitress comes back with our drinks and then takes our order.

When she's gone, Jace speaks. "Well—" he drapes his arm behind Nova's chair "—you girls are finally joining us big boys in the real world instead of playing at school."

Nova shakes her head. "I wouldn't call it playing."

Jace's lips quirk, fighting a smile.

"Yeah, it's a lot of hard work," I pipe in, sipping my water.

"I'm just glad Nova won't have to buddy up with Joel anymore. How is it that you're constantly partnered with that guy?"

Nova laughs. "Because, after being *forced* to work with

him, I found that I like him and he's my friend so we *choose* to work together now. Plus, we have a feel for each other's techniques and styles so it makes working together not a headache. Besides, you like him—admit it, he's not a bad guy."

Jace sighs heavily. "He's okay."

"He's more than okay."

Jace growls. "I wouldn't go that far."

"Okay," I interrupt, "I know arguing is like your form of foreplay, but we're at breakfast."

Jace chuckles and raises his hands innocently. "All right," he relinquishes and Nova blushes.

Xander tugs on a piece of my hair, garnering my attention. "How are you feeling?" he asks, still worried.

I shrug. "Much better, honestly. I'm hungry, though—I think maybe that, combined with my nerves, made me sick."

He nods, like that makes sense. "You'll tell me if it's something more?"

I nod, sure that he's worried about the possibility of ending up in some foreign hospital.

"I really think I'm fine," I assure him and lean over, kissing him quickly. I fight a smile and wipe the lipstick that smeared on his mouth.

"We need a toast," Cade announces.

Xander chuckles and raises his glass. "Hit us with it, brother."

Cade raises his glass and we all echo. "Here's to growing up, becoming better people, and the best year of our lives. Cheers."

"Cheers," we echo, and clink our glasses together.

I smile over at Xander. While I've been worried about the future, I know that as long as I have him by my side, it's going to be pretty great.

He leans over to kiss my forehead, and I melt into his touch.

I never believed I'd one day look at anyone—but especially him—and think *this is my person*. He completes me in every possible way. I couldn't have found anyone more perfect for me.

The nerves return when we arrive at my school. Xander kisses me goodbye before he and the other guys head off to the stadium where graduation is being held.

Rae, Nova, and I head into the school and to the front lobby where we were told to meet to pick up our cap and gown rentals.

"Hey!" Joel, Nova's friend, waves at us and makes his way through the crowd to us. Joel started out as only Nova's friend, but has since integrated himself into our main friend group, and even though Jace won't admit it, I know he kind of likes the guy.

"Hey," Nova greets, and then hugs him.

He's a good-looking guy. Tall, but not a giant like Xander or Jace, and not nearly as built as either, but he has a sweet face with dark hair that flops over his forehead messily.

He then hugs Rae and me. It hasn't been long since we last saw each other but I think we're feeling nostalgic.

"Come here, don't fight this line," he warns, indicating the main line. "There's another back here that people can't see. I'll show you."

He quickly turns and heads around the crowd and we scurry after him.

He's right, there is another line and it only has ten people ahead of us, which is *much* less than the other line.

Joel already has his blue gown on, with his cap clasped loosely in his hand.

He speaks with Nova as we move up in the line.

It isn't long before the three of us have our yellow gowns and then we move off to slip them on.

Everything becomes a flurry of chaos as we're organized into lines. Nova is sent to the front since her last name is Clarke, Rae's in the back since she's Wilder, and since I'm Kincaid now, I'm pretty much in the middle. Joel's last name is Whitaker so he ends up hanging in the back with Rae.

Our graduating class is huge and it takes us a while to be organized.

I don't recognize any of the people around me, but I notice I get a few looks, especially from the girls.

As Xander's football fame has grown, we've garnered more and more attention. Especially when the media caught wind of our Vegas wedding. That story broke almost a year after we were married, but people ate it up. I think the only reason it stayed buried so long is because we had a 'normal' wedding at the end of the summer so our family could be there, so a lot of people thought that was our actual wedding. But people have been fascinated by us—I think because we're young and fun. Plus, I have no filter, which makes things interesting. Girls, however, seem to be extremely jealous of me—I guess because Xander's hot, because it's certainly not like they actually know him. Honestly, I've never understood why people get jealous over other people's relationships. I've known Xander since we were kids, and I can't help that we fell in love.

They finally get everyone in line and we file outside.

I take a deep breath, holding my head high as I walk with confidence.

Right now, all my worries are fleeing and I feel silly for freaking out earlier.

We descend the steps into the stadium. I scan the stands for Xander, my brother, my mom, her boyfriend, and Jace, but I don't find any of them, which isn't surprising considering the amount of people in attendance, but I still wish I could spot them.

The line snakes around in front of the seats and we all stand until they tell us to sit.

The summer sun beats down on us, and beneath the cheap polyester gown, I begin to sweat.

Gross.

Several speeches are given, but I zone out for most of it. Sadly, it's not very interesting. Besides, my thoughts are occupied with daydreams of where Xander's taking me. Now that I've warmed up to the idea of leaving I'm actually kind of excited.

It's overseas—I know that much, since a passport is involved. Although, it could be Canada, but I find that doubtful. My guess is something tropical, perhaps in South America.

"*Go*," the person beside me nudges me with a disgusted hushed whisper.

I jump, realizing that everyone has stood and the line is moving. I hurry into action, holding my head high like I wasn't daydreaming.

The line snakes around and up onto the stage.

"Thea Elizabeth Kincaid."

When I get my diploma and my tassel is moved from one side of my cap to the other, I finally spot my family in the crowd. Xander stands, whistling, and clapping. I smile up at him and wave as I descend the stairs. It's funny, for once *he's* in the stands cheering me on. I kind of like this reversal.

I stick out my tongue and grin at him. He winks back and my stomach flutters.

I see everyone else with him and wave at them all before hurrying to my seat.

It takes a good while longer for them to finish calling all the names.

I fan myself quietly, drowning in sweat. My stomach rolls and I worry that *maybe* I really do have a bug or something. But I know in reality sitting in the sun, dehydrated, isn't the best idea and this is probably all tied into that.

Suddenly, caps are flying in the air, and I realize belatedly that I haven't thrown mine.

I'm not with it today.

I pretend to toss mine off, but I really just lift it off and drop it back in my lap.

Everyone stands and the crowd in the bleachers descends onto the football field.

I lift my head in search of Rae and Nova. I spot Nova headed back toward me from the front so I wait for her.

"We did it." She smiles widely and hugs me. She steps back, her brown eyes bright and her freckles standing out across her nose.

"We did," I echo.

"Let's find Rae." She loops her arm through mine and pulls me through the crowd.

We finally meet up with Joel and Rae, and then we all look for everyone else.

I spot Xander and take off running into his arms.

"Whoa." He chuckles, catching me.

He lifts me up and I take his face between my hands, the scruff rasping against my palms, and lower my head to kiss him.

"What was that for?" he asks, his eyes sparkling with amusement.

"Because I can," I answer as he sets me down.

He wraps his arms around me, and I turn to see Rae kissing Cade, and Nova and Jace going at it in a way that is *not* at all appropriate for the public. It makes me laugh, though, since those two were so anti-relationship, but now might be the worst of all of us when it comes to PDA.

I spot my mom and her boyfriend, James, hovering behind the group.

I was so happy for my mom when she finally started dating again. What she had with my dad was a toxic and unhealthy relationship and she deserved to find a good guy. I think James is that guy, but if he turns out not to be, I'll kick him in the balls.

My mom is in a better place now. She's not the same quiet and meek woman she used to be. She's absolutely radiant. She smiles and cracks jokes. She bakes us cookies and drops them by the house. She calls regularly. She's *there*.

I extract myself from Xander's arms and go to hug my mom. She squeezes me tight.

"I'm so proud of you, Thea," she whispers in my ear.

"Thank you." Hearing that means more than she'll ever know. My first year of college I had no idea what I wanted to do. I think that's true for a lot of people. It's hard to decide what you want to do for the rest of your life. But I finally decided that I wanted to help kids and women affected by domestic violence. Social work isn't the most glamorous of jobs. I know it'll be long hours and hard work for little pay, but if I can make a difference in only one person's life then I've done my job.

I let her go and hug James.

"Come here, little sis," Cade says, opening his arms.

I smile and dive into my big brother's arms. I might give him hell and vice versa, but at the end of the day we really love each other. I think our bond is even stronger for having lost our little brother. When you lose a sibling like that, and at a young age, it makes you band together more.

"I love you," he says, kissing the top of my head.

"I love you, too." I don't know what I'd do without my brother. He's the one person in the whole world beside Xander that I know I can count on.

I let him go, feeling overcome with emotion.

We're all about to go separate ways. I've known it for months, been dreading it for days, and now the time has come.

Xander's hand slips into mine and he lowers his head to my ear. "Are you okay?"

I nod, because if I open my mouth to speak I might cry, and I really don't want to hear Jace make a snide comment about me being emotional. I swear, I must be about to start my period because I'm not normally such a weak ass bitch.

Xander looks at his watch. "I don't want to rush you, but we need to go if we're going to make our flight."

"I'm ready," I tell him. There's no reason to linger.

"So, I don't get a hug? I see how it is," Jace jokes.

"Since when do you not cringe like you're being boiled alive when some tries to hug you?"

"I've never cringed," he defends. I tilt my head, looking at him like he's crazy. "Maybe a small cringe," he acquiesces. I open my arms to hug him and he holds up his hands. "I changed my mind. I don't want to hug you."

"Too late now, buddy," I say, wrapping my arms around him.

He laughs and hugs me back. He lets me go and I step back. "Thank you and you—" I turn to Nova "—for taking care of the move and Prue while we're gone. You didn't have to do that."

"We wanted to help." Nova smiles. "I hope you guys have fun. You deserve this."

"Thanks." I hug her, then Rae. "I guess we're out of here, then?" I ask Xander.

He nods. "Yeah, we have to go."

"All right, let's get moving then." Cade claps his hands together. "Come on, come on." He corrals us toward the stairs.

We return our gowns and then head out to the parking lot together. Jace and Nova make plans to meet up with everyone at a restaurant for dinner after Cade and Rae drop the two of us off at the house, since we need to change our clothes and get our car.

I hug my mom goodbye. "Have a safe trip," she tells me. "I love you."

I watch her and James head off toward their car.

Cade's Jeep appears in the distance and Xander places his hand on my waist, guiding me forward.

I can tell he's getting nervous, probably worrying about the traffic leaving the school, and then at the airport. I don't know exactly what the time our flight is, and I haven't bothered asking since he wouldn't tell me anyway. There's no point in wasting my breath.

Cade starts the Jeep and we pile inside.

By the time we arrive at the house, Xander is about ready to jump out of his skin. He all but pushes me out of the car with a grunt of, "Go, go, go."

I'd like to see him *go* in six-inch heels, thank you very much.

I stumble inside. "Hey, Prue," I greet the curly-haired dog who wags her tail happily when she sees us.

"No time. We have to go," he urges, pushing against my back.

"Xander," I groan. "I'm about to shove one of my heels in your eye-socket. *Chill*."

"We're going to miss our flight," is all he says in response.

I reach our room and start taking my clothes off to change. Since Xander's being a psycho I can't even enjoy the sight of him tearing at his buttons like a mad-man. Normally, that's a sight that leads to a whole heap of good things, but not today.

I change into my yoga pants and a tank-top, slip my feet into my tennis shoes, and pick up my sweatshirt.

"I'm ready," I announce.

Xander finishes tugging down his shirt. "Everything we need is in the car."

"Including passports?" I ask.

"Fuck," he curses, looking around. "Where the fuck are our passports?" He mutters to himself, opening the dresser drawers but of course, they're empty. He suddenly freezes. "They're in the car. I put them in the glove box."

I narrow my eyes. "Are you sure? That hardly seems like a safe place for our passports."

"I only put them in there a week ago. Chill." He takes a deep breath. "We have to go."

We hurry through the house, say a quick goodbye to Prue, and head out through the garage.

We pass my Mini Cooper, a birthday gift from Xander,

and head to his truck. He's had the same truck for years. He could upgrade, but he loves it.

He opens the passenger door for me, and I climb inside.

I check the glove box for our passports and they're thankfully there, so I pull them out and set them in my lap.

Xander starts the car and winces when he sees the time.

"Why'd you schedule our flight so close to the end time of my graduation?" I ask him. "It seems like you've caused yourself a whole lot of unnecessary stress."

"Because it was the last flight of the day for this location and there wasn't another one for two days—and if I gave you that long you'd think of some very important reason for us not to go and I'd give in. I figured the less time you had to make up an excuse the better."

My lips twitch with the threat of laughter. "That's funny."

"I'm serious," he says, speeding down the road.

"I know," I agree. "That's why it's funny."

Xander presses the gas down and drives way too fast than is legally safe, but we manage to make it to the airport in record time and without getting pulled over.

Xander pulls a blindfold from his pocket. "Sorry, Thea," he mutters, reaching to put it on me.

I smack his arm away. "Don't you *dare* come anywhere near me with that thing," I warn him.

He narrows his eyes. "Yes, because if I don't then you'll know exactly where we're going in about five minutes, and that's no fun."

I groan. "Honestly, this *honeymoon* is coming with way

too many stipulations. Give me the damn blindfold." I snatch it from his hands and his lips twitch with amusement. "You'll mess up my hair if you put it on me," I defend. I slip the blindfold on and frown at the complete blackness. "I swear to God if you let me run into a wall I'll not speak to you the whole vacation."

He laughs. "Like you could go that long without talking."

I hear him open the car door. "Fine, then you better learn how to give yourself blowjobs. I hope you're a contortionist."

He snickers. "I love you."

"Right now I hate you."

His car door closes and mine opens a moment later. I feel shaky as he helps me out of the car into the parking garage. It's disorienting not being able to see a thing.

"Stay here," he warns, and I'm sure he's holding his hands out in a placating manner.

"Xander?" I call out. "How are you going to guide me and wheel both our suitcases?" He's silent. "You didn't think about that, did you?"

"Of course I did," he replies, his voice spiking—a telltale sign that he's lying.

"I'm gonna die," I mumble to myself.

Finally, he says, "You're going to have to wheel your suitcase."

"What if I trip over it?" I counter.

"Your legs aren't tied together, Thea. You can walk fine." He sighs in exasperation.

I sigh too. "If I die, I want to be buried in that ivory dress I love and my six-inch black Louboutins? Okay?"

"You're not going to die. Don't be dramatic."

He takes my hand and wraps it around the handle of my suitcase. He then takes my other hand and entwines his fingers with mine.

"Walk slow," I warn him. "I'm not as tall as you."

He slows his steps to match mine.

Somehow we manage to make it into the airport without me dying.

"Isn't it going to be weird going through security with me blindfolded?"

"They've seen worse, I'm sure."

True.

Security doesn't take long, thankfully, since we're already running late, but the people working it get quite a laugh at me and my blindfold.

"All right, this is where we wait," Xander tells me. I let go of my suitcase and he guides me to a seat. "I'm going to cover your ears with headphones and turn on some music," he warns.

I groan. "Now you take away my hearing too?"

He laughs. "Yeah, sorry, sweetheart."

"Are you sure you love me, because this feels like torture."

"Yeah, I'm pretty sure," he replies.

A moment later the headphones slip over my ears and the music begins to play.

I don't know how much time passes before he taps my

arm and helps me to stand. It feels like forever, but since we were running late it can't be that long.

We board the plane and take our seats. I hope that Xander is finally going to remove the blindfold and headphones, but *no*, he's going to make me suffer.

I can feel him messing with a carry-on bag and then he buckles my seatbelt for me before plopping in the seat beside me—I have the window seat, which I can't even enjoy since I can't see.

Jerk.

I lay my head against the window and settle in for the ride.

Hours later, I wake up. I have no idea how much time has passed and at first, it's extremely disorienting to open my eyes and be met with the blackness of the blindfold. It doesn't take long for me to remember Xander slipping it on my head. The music continues to play in my ears.

I tap Xander and he jolts awake beside me.

He takes the headphones off my head. "What is it?" he asks, his voice groggy with sleep.

"I have to pee."

"Oh, okay." He undoes my seatbelt and helps me out and to the bathroom. We don't walk far.

"Can I at least take the blindfold off while I pee?" I ask, shuffling around.

He chuckles. "Sure. But it goes right back on before you come out.

I sigh. He's such a fun sucker.

I close the bathroom door and rip the blindfold off, promptly letting out a little scream because the sudden brightness hurts my eyes.

Xander hears and knocks on the door. "Are you okay?"

"Yeah, just fine," I mutter, but I can already feel a pounding headache emerging.

I pee and wash my hands, then unlock the door before slipping the blindfold back on.

"I'm ready," I say, reaching for him.

"That's my butt, Thea." I can hear the laughter in his voice. The fabric of his clothes rustles as he turns around.

"You have a nice butt, I can't help myself, I also *can't see*," I hiss.

He grabs my wandering hand before I can grip anything else and guides me back to the seat. "We have a layover soon," he warns me.

"Great," I mumble. I've already slept all I think I can sleep, and if he's got me blindfolded that means I can't even watch a movie, and there's only so much music I can listen to before I go crazy.

Maybe that's his plan—to make me go crazy. I'm already halfway to insane so it wouldn't be a stretch.

I lay my head back against the seat, and surprisingly, I fall back to sleep.

It isn't long until he's waking me up to depart the plane. I'm pretty sure I growl at him. I *don't* like my sleep disturbed.

Soon, though, another problem arises. My stomach rumbles angrily.

"I'm starving," I tell Xander. "We need to eat something."

"We will," he says. "Let's just find our gate first."

After he locates our gate, he promptly drags me away and into one of the airport restaurants. I smell cheeseburgers and my mouth waters.

Xander guides me to a table and removes the blindfold. "I'm putting this back on you before we leave."

I sigh. A small reprieve is better than none. "Fine," I mutter reluctantly.

"I'll order our food," he says, striding away. His hair is a mess from sleeping on the plane, but he still looks good to me.

He returns a few minutes later with our drinks and a slip of paper with our order number.

I sip at the soda, trying to ignore the rumbling of my stomach.

"How much longer until we get to where we're going?" I ask.

He shrugs. "A couple of hours."

"By a couple of hours, do you mean two or ...?" He looks away. "Xander," I whine.

"It's better if I don't tell you."

"Ugh," I groan, just as our order number is called. He goes to grab it and comes back with two cheeseburgers and two orders of fries.

I grab my cheeseburger and bite into it, suppressing a

moan. I must still make some kind of noise because Xander snickers.

"So hungry," I mutter. I haven't eaten since breakfast, and I have no idea what time it is. Frankly, I don't want to ask.

I devour my cheeseburger and fries in record time, but I *still* feel hungry.

"I'm going to go get a milkshake. Do you want one?"

He shakes his head. "I'll get it for you." He wipes his hands on a napkin and hops up to get in line before I can blink.

"I would've gotten it," I call after him.

"I know," he mouths.

It doesn't take them long to make my milkshake. He sets the cup down in front of me and I grab it like someone's going to snatch it from me.

He laughs. "Eager, are we?"

I smile around the straw.

He finishes his meal while I sip on my milkshake. He doesn't seem in a hurry to get to our gate, so I take my time. I end up only drinking half the milkshake and Xander finishes the rest.

Before we leave the restaurant he slips the blindfold back on, along with the headphones.

We wait outside our gate and board the second plane thirty or so minutes later.

I settle into my seat and hope that I don't die of boredom before we get there.

three

...

xander

THE PLANE TOUCHES down and Thea jolts awake, her hands reaching out blindly for something to grab onto. I take one of her hands in mine and she instantly calms.

I don't remove the blindfold or headphones. I know I'm dragging this out as long as possible, but she'll thank me later.

The plane taxis in and we wait to be able to deplane. When we finally can, I stand and grab my backpack, slipping it onto my shoulders, before helping Thea off the plane.

I guide her to the baggage claim and wait for our bags. I can tell she's growing more impatient by the minute, and I can't blame her. She's been traveling for approximately sixteen hours, but considering I took away sight and hearing from her, it probably feels much longer.

I finally locate our bags and we wheel them outside to the taxi line.

The man hops out to put our bags in and I help Thea into the car.

I take the headphones off her and she immediately asks, "Can I see yet?"

"Not yet," I tell her.

I'm aware she might kill me in my sleep for this, but once we get there I think she'll be too blown away to care.

She groans and crosses her arms over her chest. "How much longer?"

"Not much," I tell her.

The taxi driver gets back in the car and I hand him a piece of paper with the address for our hotel on it.

Once we get there, and to our room, *then* Thea can finally know where we are.

The driver takes off, speeding down the road.

The city is beautiful, and I'm almost tempted to take off Thea's blindfold and reveal our destination now, but I know it'll be worth it to wait. The view from our hotel is spectacular.

I booked the honeymoon suite, and from the pictures I saw online, it's worth the price tag.

I'm thankful to make the kind of money I do, that it can afford me the opportunity to do these kinds of things, but more than that I'm just happy I'm doing what I love.

Playing football for the Colorado Rebels is a dream come true.

I'd always dreamed since I was a little boy that I'd get to play professional football, but I knew the chances of making it there were slim to none.

But I did it.

And I couldn't be happier.

The taxi driver stops in front of the hotel and I slip the headphones back on Thea's head.

She frowns but doesn't say anything. I help her out while the driver sets our luggage on the ground.

A bellboy immediately runs over, gathering up our stuff and putting it on a trolley. He follows us inside while we check-in.

Once I have our room key we head to the elevator.

The doors ding open and we shuffle inside. I press the button for the top floor and the elevator soars up.

I wish Thea could see this—the hotel is beautiful, but I know she'll see it later.

Right now my goal is getting her into the room, and to a window, so she can finally see where we are.

We reach our room and I let go of her, swiping the key card in the slot. It lights up green and I swing the door open. I help Thea inside and guide her to sit on the bed.

"Don't take it off yet," I warn her, pointing a finger at her even though she can't see.

The bellboy unloads our bags and I tip him before he leaves. The door clicks shut behind him and Thea's hands twitch impatiently.

"Almost," I tell her.

I take her hands and urge her to stand then lead her over

to the French double doors that lead to a much larger balcony than you usually see at a hotel. Perks of the honeymoon suite, I guess.

I open the doors and the ocean breeze filters into the room, lifting her hair around her shoulders.

"I swear to God if you've brought me all this way to throw me off the balcony ..." she trails off.

I fight laughter. "If I wanted to get rid of you there are much easier, less messy, ways."

Her lips twitch. She won't admit it but she likes it when I play along with her dramatics.

"Close your eyes," I urge. "I'm going to take the blindfold off now, okay?"

She nods. "They're closed."

I slip the blindfold off and toss it behind me on the floor. I brush my lips over her ear and she shivers. "Open your eyes, sweetheart."

"Holy shit."

Her jaw drops and she takes in the view in awe. Even I have to admit it's breathtaking.

She steps forward, wrapping her hands around the railing. "The water ... it's so *blue*." She turns to me with tears in her eyes. "Thank you. This is amazing."

I smile. I knew the trip would be rough, trying to keep it a secret from her, but it was worth it for this moment.

She throws her arms around my neck and I jostle a step back before wrapping my arms around her. She's small in my arms, but she fits against me just right.

"I love you," she murmurs, gazing up at me like I'm

everything to her, and if that doesn't make me the luckiest man alive, I don't know what does.

"I love you too." I lower my head and kiss her.

She moans, her body arching into mine. "You're *so* getting laid tonight."

I laugh. "I didn't have to bring you all the way to Greece to get laid." I wink.

She narrows her eyes. "Don't get cocky on me now."

"Wouldn't dream of it." I grin back.

She turns back to the view, taking in the deep blue water of the Mediterranean against the cliffs and white homes.

"I don't think I've ever seen anything more beautiful," she breathes.

I step up beside her. "I have."

She turns and looks up at me. "Really? What?"

"You."

She tosses her head back and laughs. "That's the cheesiest thing I've ever heard."

I shrug, fighting a smile. "It's true."

She sobers, a blush staining her cheeks. "Thank you."

Sometimes it's strange to look at my life and realize where I've ended up—that I got everything I ever hoped and dreamed of. It's kind of crazy. I got my dream job, and the dream girl, and now I'm living the dream life.

"Do you want to rest for a while?" I ask her.

She shakes her head. "No, I got enough sleep on the plane. I'm hungry, what time is it?"

"A little after four," I answer.

"Let's get dinner then, and maybe we can head down the beach?" she asks.

I nod, smiling. "That sounds good."

She pauses and looks down at her clothes. "On second thought, shower first and *then* dinner."

I laugh. "Whatever you want."

"I can't be seen like this," she tells me.

"What's wrong with that?" I point to her outfit.

She breathes deeply. "I'm going to forgive you for saying that since you're a boy, but the answer is *everything*."

"Boy?" I narrow my eyes. "How about all man?"

She pats my stomach as she passes. "Don't flatter yourself."

I sweep her up into my arms and toss her over my shoulder.

"Xander!" she squeals in a high-pitched shriek. "Put me down!" she demands.

"Take it back, baby."

"Never."

I drop her onto the bed and she bounces before I jump onto the bed beside her, caging her in with my arms. "I'm about to show you how much man I am."

Her lips threaten to rise into a smile. "Is that so?"

"Mhmm." I tuck my head into the crook of her neck, brushing my lips against the spot where her pulse thuds. She jumps slightly, and I smile in satisfaction.

I glide my lips down her neck and over the curves of her breasts.

Her fingers delve into my hair, tugging slightly.

I inch my fingers under her top and push it up and then off. Her eyes darken as she watches me.

She wraps her legs around my hips and tries to tug me closer. I capture her lips in mine and she moans. I love all the little sounds she makes, and the fact that even after being together for years she's still affected by me. At times, I worried that maybe we'd grow bored, but if anything, the excitement has only built as we've grown older.

I pull back and glide my hand down her face, just looking at her.

She blinks up at me with wide hazel eyes. "What are you waiting for?" she asks breathlessly.

"Shh." I press a finger to her pink lips. "I want to look at my wife."

She shakes her head. "Why?"

"Because I can."

I don't think Thea's ever realized how hard it is for me to leave her again and again. There are times when I don't see her for weeks or even a month. Training season is the worst. She's my best friend as well as my wife, so I miss her like crazy when I'm gone. I miss her smile, her laughter, and all the crazy things she says. She keeps me on my toes and I love that.

She reaches up and touches her finger to the scruff on my cheek. "Are you done looking?" she asks a moment later.

I nod and scoop her up into my arms, carrying her into the bathroom while she laughs.

The bathroom is really nice with marble finishings, a soaking tub, and a walk-in shower.

I set Thea down on the sink counter and go to turn on the shower.

When I turn around, she's already removed her clothes and my heart speeds up. She stalks toward me like a lioness about to devour her prey and I know I'm in trouble. I always have been when it comes to her.

She grabs the bottom of my shirt, and I lift my arms so she can tug it off. I end up helping since I'm so much taller than her. The fabric falls to the floor and then she pushes my sweatpants and boxer-briefs off my hips.

I step out of them and follow her into the shower. The glass shower wall is already foggy from the steam.

Thea gives me a coy smile as she steps beneath the spray. I watch the rivulets of water course down her chest and stomach.

I stalk toward her and her body tightens in anticipation.

I pick her up and she wraps her legs around me with her arms around my neck. The water drenches both of us, the heat of it soaking into our skin.

I lower my head and kiss her, sinking inside her at the same time. She cries out softly. Her hands slide against my slick shoulders and her eyes are lit with fire.

She looks down, watching me move in and out of her and she moans. "Oh, God."

I press my forehead to hers, watching too, as her nails rake against my back.

"Xander," she moans. "Oh, fuck. Harder, please."

I press my face into the crook of her neck. "I love your dirty mouth," I murmur, happy to oblige.

Her breaths grow rapid and her eyes close. Her orgasm hits her and she shudders in my arms. I hold her, keeping her upright.

Her eyes slowly blink open. "That was intense."

Her body is still quaking with aftershocks, pumping around me.

We're both drenched from the shower at this point, and her hair sticks to her forehead.

She's still beautiful. She always is.

I take her hands in mine, pinning them above her head.

"Oh, my God," she moans when it changes the angle. Her head falls back against the wall and her eyes are at half-mast.

I kiss her neck, collarbone, and the tops of her breasts before swirling my tongue around her nipple.

"Are you close again?" I ask, feeling my own orgasm coming.

She nods. "So close. *Oh, God.*"

She shakes around me, her moans filling the room, and I fall right behind her.

Our hearts beat a mile a minute and she looks at me like she's in a fog. I lower her legs and she can barely stand, so I hold her hips.

"I feel thoroughly and completely fucked," she says with a smile.

I laugh. "Good. Now come on, let's get cleaned up and eat. I'm starving." She blinks up at me, lost. "Turn around," I command.

She does as I ask and I grab the hotel's sample shampoo bottle. I lather it into my hands and then into her hair.

She moans, leaning back into me. "Do you remember our first time?" she asks suddenly. "Well, our second time, I mean. I forget about Vegas since later felt more real." She laughs softly.

"Yeah," I remember.

"You washed my hair first, just like this," she says, and even though I can't see her I know she's smiling.

"I did," I agree.

"I love it when you wash my hair. It always reminds me of that time."

"Me too." I bend my head and kiss her shoulder before urging her back under the water to remove the soap. Thea closes her eyes and lets me rinse the shampoo from her hair before I add conditioner. Her hair is so long that I end up using the whole sample bottle of that—it's not like I need it.

I finish her hair and then do mine. While I do that she washes her body. I watch her, I can't help myself, and her lips tilt up in a pleased little smirk.

We get out and dry off before changing into new clothes.

"I have to do my hair and makeup," Thea tells me.

I groan. "You're going to take two hours."

"It doesn't take me *that* long," she defends.

It so does, I think to myself.

She commandeers the bathroom, which leaves the suite to me.

Our room is large with lots of white, gray, and a blue that

matches the color of the ocean. It's pretty nice, and I like that we have room to move around. There's even a small table and kitchen area, along with a couch, TV, and the bed, of course. I love that the bed is huge with a thick comforter. As much as I'd love to spend *all* our time in bed, we *are* in Greece.

I flop on the bed and grab the remote, turning on the TV.

I don't understand a thing they're saying, but it's better than nothing.

I hear the blow dryer turn on and I stifle a yawn.

I cover my face with the crook of my arm. A little nap never hurt anyone ...

"Xander?"

Thea shakes my arm and I come awake with a start. I look around wild-eyed, feeling lost.

She stifles a laugh. "Have a good nap?"

"Um, yeah." I stretch my arms and roll my neck. "Are you ready to go?"

"Yeah, but you're not."

"Of course I am." I look at her like she's crazy as I smooth my hands down my shirt. "I've been ready. I was waiting for you."

She snorts. "Have you seen your hair?"

"Obviously not. I was sleeping." I squint at her.

She tugs on my arm and I stand from the bed, following her over to a floor-length mirror decorating the room.

"Oh, shit." I blink at myself. "Yeah, that's bad."

Napping on wet hair was not a good idea. My hair's already a bit shaggy and unkempt but now it just looks like an animal tried to make a home in it.

"I'll fix it."

Thea drags me into the bathroom like an unruly child. She grabs her hairbrush and then motions for me to bend down.

She brushes my hair down, but it hardly fixes the problem. She dampens some spots with water and brushes some more. She then grabs her hairspray and works some more magic before stepping back.

"Much better." She smiles at my reflection.

I turn and touch my hand to her waist. "Thanks, babe." I bend and kiss her. "You look beautiful," I tell her. She's changed into a fitted white dress and heels, with her sandy-colored hair loosely curled.

"Thank you. You don't look too bad yourself." She winks.

"So, did I do a good job packing your stuff?" I ask.

She nods. "Surprisingly well. I was worried."

I laugh. "Don't you trust me, sweetheart?"

She rolls her eyes. "With my life, *yes*. To pick my clothes? Hell no."

I can't help it, I laugh, because it's such a Thea thing to say. I honestly shouldn't be surprised. She takes her clothes seriously and has a huge addiction to shopping.

She bounces out of the bathroom then—Thea rarely simply *walks*, she's too hyper for that.

She grabs her purse and heads for the door. "Let's go."

I shake my head. Something tells me I'm going to spend my whole life chasing after this girl, and I couldn't be happier to do it.

four
...

thea

"OH, my God. Oh, my God. Oh, my God." I clutch Xander's hand and jump up and down. "*Look* at that view." I point.

He laughs. "I see it, Thea."

"Wow," I breathe. "I've never seen anything like this before."

The restaurant we found sits right on the water. The sun is just beginning to go down, and I know watching the sun set over the water will be magnificent.

The hostess, or whatever you call them here, leaves the menus on the table and smiles as she leaves us.

I let go of Xander's hand and he pulls the chair out for me. "Why thank you, kind sir."

He chuckles. "You're welcome, madam," he says, playing along.

He sits down, smoothing his hands down his white shirt. He picks up the menu and looks at it. I do the same. I have a hard time paying attention to the menu, because the view calls to me. It's absolutely stunning. I thought Colorado was beautiful with its soaring mountain ranges, but it has nothing on this place.

The ocean breeze stirs my hair around my shoulders and I smile as I inhale the salty air. I wasn't thrilled about Xander's spontaneous honeymoon trip, especially with the move and graduation, but now that I'm here I'm so thankful. And honestly? We needed this. The past couple of years we've only gone somewhere if I happened to go to an away game with him, which was rare, and he was busy so it's not like we spent much time together then.

This ... this is nice.

Our waiter comes by and we both order a glass of water and Xander also requests a bottle of wine.

"Planning to get me drunk, Mr. Kincaid?" I ask, waggling my brows.

He laughs, crossing his fingers together and leaning across the table to me. "What do you think is going to happen if I do get you drunk, Mrs. Kincaid?"

"Well—" I blink innocently "—I seem to have an affinity for removing my clothes when I'm inebriated."

He cracks a grin. "You also ask me to marry you."

"Only the once," I defend.

His smile widens further. "Oh, you would've done it again if I hadn't said yes the first time."

"You seem pretty sure of yourself there," I comment.

He shakes his head. "No, sure of you."

"Is that your way of saying you know I love you?"

He chuckles. "I guess so."

Our waiter sets the glasses of water down along with two wine glasses and the bottle. He pours us each half a glass and then gets our order before leaving. We both order a seafood dish. I guess we decided it was better to play it safe and get something familiar.

I sip at the wine, enjoying the flavor. The sun sets over the water and the image is one I'll remember a long time to come. The riot of colors is beautiful. I feel Xander's eyes on me so my gaze slowly drifts back to him.

"You're beautiful," he murmurs.

I stifle a laugh. "I think you've already said that."

He grins at me. "And I'll keep telling you every day, for the rest of our lives, because you deserve to hear that. You're beautiful, inside and out, and I'm lucky that I get to see every side of you."

"You're not so bad yourself ... even if you do eat M&M McFlurrys and everyone knows Oreo is the best."

He laughs. "We'll have to continue to agree to disagree on that matter."

"I shouldn't have mentioned McFlurrys." I frown. "I really want one now."

"You'll have to wait until we get home." He takes a sip of wine. "Although, knowing McDonald's there's probably one around the corner."

I force the thoughts of ice cream goodness from my

mind. I don't want to get my hopes up no matter how good one might taste right now.

And a Big Mac. That'd be good too.

Damn, I *must* be starving.

I honestly can't even remember the last time I ate. My time is all mixed up from traveling and the time change. I'm lucky I can differentiate between up and down at this point.

The sun completely disappears, and I look around, noticing a bunch of string lights hanging above us with a warm glow.

The place has a cozy vibe despite us being outside in the open air.

I finish my wine and sigh. "I'm scared," I whisper to Xander.

He raises one dark brow. "Scared? Of what?"

"Everything," I admit. "The unknown. I'm scared I won't get a job, or if I do that I'll hate it. I'm scared of being unhappy."

He shrugs. "Then you'll quit."

I shake my head. "I'm not a quitter."

"Is it quitting if you're miserable? Wouldn't it be *bettering* yourself? Besides, you don't know anything yet."

"Social work isn't easy." I tap my fingers to the table. "Sometimes I think maybe I would've been better off doing something in fashion."

He shakes his head. "I don't believe that. You wanted to help people, Thea, and that's what you're going to do. It's going to be rewarding, but I doubt it'll be easy."

"You're right," I agree. He usually is, though I'd never tell him that.

I know being fearful of my future is normal and is probably plaguing most graduates. It's a scary thing to spend four years in college and then be thrust out into the real world.

Our meal is brought to the table and we thank our waiter.

"This smells so good." I inhale the scent of the food—dill and lemon and some other herb I can't decipher.

"Yeah, it does," Xander agrees and then tops off my empty wine glass.

I raise my eyebrows. "You're definitely trying to get me drunk."

He laughs. "You don't have to drink it."

"True." I pick up the glass and raise it to my lips. "But you know I will."

We finish our meal and pay before heading back to the hotel.

I hold his hand and lean against him as we walk. The cool night air brings a shiver across my skin.

"Cold?" he asks, pausing to look down at me.

I nod and he wraps his arms around me. Wearing a strapless dress might not have been my best idea, but it looks great.

We walk along the stone pathway, going slow since I can't navigate as well in my heels. Music drifts softly from one of the houses along the street and I smile. It's so different here than at home and this is only a small taste.

We finally make it back to the hotel and change into our pajamas before crashing into bed.

I snuggle close to Xander, latching my arms around him like an octopus.

"You're mine." I kiss his neck.

His chest rumbles with a laugh. "Is that so?"

"Mhmm." I nod, already falling asleep.

I feel him run his fingers through my hair and then trace my lips, and that's the last thing I remember, though I'd swear he whispered, "I've been yours forever."

five
...

xander

"WHY ARE you looking at me like that?" Thea asks, looking at me over the rim of her large sunglasses.

"Like what?" I counter.

She smirks. "Like you want to rip this bikini off and fuck me right here."

"Then you have it exactly right."

She frowns. "It's too bad we have company then."

I groan as I imagine peeling off her bikini and fucking her right here on the beach. Sure, in reality it'd probably be ... messy and not practical, but in my mind, it's hot as fuck. Unfortunately, the beach is covered with tourists and locals, making such impossible.

Thea stretches out on her towel. It's the middle of the day already, and it's *hot* as hell. We spent most of the morning lying in bed and gorging ourselves on room service. When we finally decided to leave the bed we both agreed that we wanted to sit on the beach.

"Forget this," I say suddenly and hop up, pulling her along with me.

"Xander, no!" she shrieks when she realizes what I'm doing.

"You're not a witch. You aren't going to melt if the water touches you," I defend.

"Oh, yes I am." She tugs on my hand trying to pull away in the other direction.

I shake my head and wrap my arms around her thin waist, hauling her to the water.

"Ahhh!" she cries, kicking her legs. Her efforts to get away are futile as I drag her into the water. It's surprisingly cool, but feels refreshing against my heated skin.

I toss Thea gently into the water and she drops like a rock. She comes up sputtering a moment later. "I hate you." She glares at me, her long hair hanging in wet strings around her face.

I laugh—I can't help it.

"That was uncalled for." She points at me like I'm an unruly child. "Now I'm soaked."

"At least you're cool," I counter.

She splashes me just to spite me, I know, and I can't help but laugh more.

I splash her back and then before I know it we're having an all-out war in the middle of the ocean. She begins to laugh and her enjoyment makes me happier than just about anything. Thea likes to pretend she doesn't like spontaneity but she'd be pretty bored if I didn't keep her on her toes.

Somehow our war ends and she ends up in my arms with her legs wrapped around my waist beneath the water. Droplets of water drip from her nose back into the water. Her skin glows with a slight tan and something else—something entirely Thea.

"Hey, you." I kiss her nose.

She wraps her fingers in my hair and tugs slightly. "Don't ever drag me into the cold water ever again."

I laugh. "It's not that cold."

"It's cold enough," she counters, looking down at her chest and pebbled nibbles.

I press my lips together, but my laughter erupts anyway. "Okay, so it's chilly," I concede.

She drops her legs from my waist and lets go to swim away. I grab her foot and tug her back.

"Xander!" She tries to sound scolding, but she's smiling and there's laughter in her voice.

"I have a question for you," I defend.

She raises a brow and her lips quirk. "What is it?"

"How are you feeling?" I ask her, grabbing a wet piece of hair from her forehead and moving it behind her ear. "You seem better since the other morning but I want to make sure that's true and you're not hiding something from me."

She laughs, returning to her previous position with her legs around my waist and her arms around my neck. "I think it'd be pretty impossible to hide it from you considering we were in close quarters on the plane and now the hotel. I feel much better, though. I'm sure it was just nerves. I was convinced something bad was going to happen."

"Well, it didn't." I lower my head and kiss her.

She hums softly at the touch, her fingers flexing against my shoulders.

She leans back in my arms so the back of her head touches the water. She then stretches her arms out above her head while I hold her waist.

"This place is pretty magical," she murmurs. "It's so beautiful." She sits back up. "What made you choose Greece?"

I shrug. "I don't know. I always thought it looked like a beautiful place. And while I figured you'd prefer somewhere like Paris, because of the shopping, I just wanted to go somewhere where we could lay on the beach together for a while."

She smiles. "You're too good to me. What did I do to deserve you? I mean, I'm kind of a bitch, and you're always so nice and thoughtful."

I kiss her and she smiles even bigger. "You're not a bitch," I defend. "You're passionate, there's a difference. And you're much more caring than you give yourself credit for. The way you care for your family and friends is one of the reasons I fell in love with you so long ago."

Tears fill her eyes. "I'm gonna cry," she warns. "I don't want to, but I'm going to dammit."

The tears spill forward and I wrap my arms around her. "Oh, Thea," I sigh.

"I don't even know why I'm crying," she mumbles into

my shoulder. "But that was really sweet and my emotions are all over the place with everything."

"I get it. I do." I rub her back, trying to soothe her. The last couple of weeks have been tough for her, I know. With her graduation approaching, and the move, mixed with no job lined up, then throw in my surprise vacation, and she's been a mess. She's so scared of falling, but what she forgets is that I'm always going to be right here to pick her back up. Besides, she's the strongest person I know. She doesn't give herself enough credit.

She pulls away, sniffling, and wipes her face with the back of her hand. I can't really tell what's tears and what's water from the ocean.

She clears her throat and cracks a smile. "I need a drink."

I laugh. "I think I do too."

We swim back and Thea drops down on her towel, wringing out her hair.

"I'll get our drinks," I tell her.

"I want something sweet but full of alcohol," she calls after me.

"You got it."

I shuffle through the sand and over to the bar that's part of the hotel. I squint against the grueling sun and curse myself for not grabbing my sunglasses.

I order a beer, and Thea their special—some kind of fruity drink that looks comparable to a Pina Colada. I doubt it really has *that* much alcohol, but it'll do.

I write my room number on the slip so they can charge it there and then carry our drinks back to our towels.

I hold Thea's glass out to her and she takes it, slurping at the hot pink straw before playing with the little umbrella stuck in it.

"Oh, this is good," she comments with a thumb's up, while I sit down.

I take a couple sips of my beer and then set it down, using the sand as a makeshift cup holder.

I turn to my side, watching Thea sip at her drink. I'm sure she thinks I'm weird for watching her all the time, but I can't help it. She's magnetic. I can't help but be drawn to her warm spirit.

After a moment, I turn back and grab my book. It's a book Jace recommended, and I figured while I had time I'd try to read it. Lately, I don't have time to read. I'm usually too exhausted at night from practice or working out, and end up watching TV before I crash.

Plus, Thea prefers TV, so we always have a current show we can't stop watching.

Right now it's *Scandal*.

While I read Thea sits beside me sipping her drink and flipping through a magazine. We're both happy being together, we don't have to say anything at all, and that's nice.

There's nobody I'd rather do nothing with—I guess that's how you know you've found your true other half. Cade and Jace like to joke that they don't know how I put up with Thea, since she's so loud, and vibrant, and just out there, but that's all part of the reason I love her. I love that she's wild and can't be contained.

I don't want to tame the storm, I want to be a part of it, a part of *her*.

six
...

thea

I FLOP onto the king-size bed with a groan. "I'm exhausted," I announce.

We spent the whole day outside in the Greece heat, sightseeing all the monuments. I mean, there's no way we could come all the way to Greece and not see the Parthenon, among other things. So, the day was definitely worth it, but now I want to take a hot bath and go to sleep. Okay, maybe not go straight to sleep, but we'll see how my energy levels are.

Xander takes off his sweaty shirt and tosses it near his luggage before dropping down onto the bed beside me.

"Me too," he agrees.

"How? Shouldn't you be used to strenuous activities in the heat?" I quip.

He chuckles and rolls over to face me. "Yes, but it's a lot hotter here than in Colorado—so that makes a difference."

"Ah, I see. I guess I'll give you a pass," I joke.

He sits up and stretches his arms. "You said something about taking a bath on the way back here—want me to go start it for you?"

"Yes, please. I can't move."

He heads into the bathroom and I finally gather enough energy to sit up. I rub my head, feeling a headache coming on and I'm sure it's from getting overheated today and not drinking enough water. Though, I kept stopping to drink. I rub my temples and get up in search of some Advil. I rifle through my makeup bag and finally find the small bottle I keep for emergencies such as this one.

I dump two pills into my hand and grab my bottle of water, swallowing them down.

"Are you okay?" Xander asks, concern leaching into his tone.

"Just a headache." I rush to assure him. "It's nothing to worry about."

He narrows his eyes on me, so I know he *is* worrying. I think the boy searches for something to worry about it. It's in his genes or something.

He finally shrugs, choosing to let it go. "The water is running," he informs me, which is unnecessary since I can hear it.

I nod. "Thanks."

I put the pill bottle away and grab some pajamas to change into—a pair of blue shorts with white lace trim and a matching top.

I set my clothes on the counter in the bathroom and then tiptoe back into the bedroom part.

Our room is gorgeous, with a large bed covered in fluffy white bedding with cobalt blue pillows. The rest of the room is decorated similarly with lots of white and blue, and expensive chrome accents. Even the floor is plush carpet instead of the normal hard stuff that's in hotels. Something tells me I don't want to know how much this hotel is costing a night. I certainly don't plan on asking.

I lean against the doorway, smiling at the sight of Xander stretched out on the bed with his arms crossed behind his head.

He's looking at his phone, not paying a bit of attention to me.

I smirk and remove my cotton dress, balling it up so I can toss it at him.

The fabric covers his head and he shoves it away, looking in my direction where I now stand in only my bra and underwear.

"Want to join me?" I ask.

He hops up from the bed so fast I'm surprised he doesn't get whiplash. He runs toward me and lifts me up, tossing me over his shoulder.

I scream with laughter.

He sets me down on the steps leading into the bathtub and reaches for the button on his shorts. I finish undressing, relishing in the way his eyes trail my body.

I shiver and he touches his hand to my waist as my gaze drops to the floor.

He grabs my chin between his fingers and lifts my head. "Don't get shy on me now, sweetheart."

I feel a blush stain my cheeks. I can't help it.

He lowers his head, brushing his lips over mine. Softly at first and then with more pressure. My eyes close and I hum low in my throat, my fingers splaying across his abs. I used to daydream about kissing him, when I was young and inexperienced and he was my brother's best friend. The fact that he's *mine* now never ceases to blow my mind.

He sweeps my legs out from under me again and carries me into the water, settling me between his legs. The water threatens to overflow and he quickly turns it off. He added enough bubbles that I basically disappear beneath them.

The hot water feels heavenly, though. After I spent the whole day sweating and walking, my muscles are aching like crazy. I *definitely* got my work out in today—which is a joke since I never workout. I just can't get into it like Xander does. I'm a couch potato. I'm blessed that I have a naturally thin frame.

Xander rubs my shoulders and I moan loudly. "That feels good," I tell him.

I roll my neck to the side, giving him better access. He pushes against my neck and I wince.

"Sore spot?" he asks, pausing his movements.

"Yeah."

He rubs it again but a little more gently this time. He then rubs my back and I basically melt into a pile of goo.

"I can't believe we've already been here five days," I murmur, as he moves his hand lower down my back.

"Me either. It's gone by too fast."

We spent the first day hanging by the ocean, the next day shopping, the day after that by the hotel pool, yesterday and today were both spent exploring. I know there's still so much more left to see of Greece, but I think I'd rather spend our last days just hanging around doing nothing. I know once we get home we're going to be focused on the new house, and then Xander will start his training camp next month, and I'll be left alone a lot.

I'm not looking forward to that.

But hopefully I'll have found a job by then, so at least I'll have that to keep me busy.

"What are you thinking about?" He presses his lips to the crook of my neck, his hands sliding around my front to wrap around me.

"Nothing," I answer.

"Nothing," he echoes. "I doubt that."

I tilt my head back to look at him, the bubbles sloshing around my chest. "Are you calling me a liar?"

He chuckles. "I'm just saying I know you better than that. Spill it."

"It's just life, I guess. It's passing me by so fast."

"Yeah, it does feel that way sometimes," he murmurs.

I twist in the water, turning around to straddle him so I can face him. My center presses into him and I moan, unable to bite back the sound.

"What are you doing?" he asks, cupping the back of my neck.

"It doesn't take a rocket scientist to figure out what I'm doing," I quip.

"That mouth of yours." He brushes his nose against mine. "Always such a smartass."

I wrap my arms around his neck, my breasts pushing into his chest.

I brush my lips over his ear. "You love my mouth and everything it does and says."

He smiles widely. "You're right, I do. I love that you always say whatever is on your mind."

"And now," I lower my voice, "I'm telling you to shut up."

I cover his smile with my kiss. His lips part and I slip my tongue inside, brushing against his. The pads of his fingers dig with a bruising pressure into the backs of my thighs.

I reach between us and wrap my hand around him before guiding him inside.

A moan passes between my lips and I lean my forehead against his shoulder.

He guides my hips, rolling them against him, and my eyes fall closed, happy to let him control the pace.

I feel my heart beating in an out of control rhythm.

He makes me crazy in the best possible way.

I lift my head and slide my hands from around his neck to rest on his chest. I find that his heart is beating nearly as fast as mine and that fact makes me smile.

His dark hair falls into his eyes and he flicks his head to the side, his eyes meeting mine.

His eyes flash with lust, and love, and something that

looks like appreciation before his lips crash to mine once more. Water sloshes over the side of the bathtub but neither of us pays it too much attention.

He pulls back and grazes his thumb over my lip before he cups the back of my neck and draws my forehead to his.

"I love you," he whispers.

"I love you too," I murmur back, and for some strange reason, this makes me feel like crying.

He kisses me again, sucking my bottom lip into his mouth.

I tug at his hair, silently begging for more.

He kisses his way down my neck before circling his tongue over each of my nipples.

My moans increase and my breaths become chaotic.

"Xander," I pant his name, my eyes rolling into the back of my head. "Oh, God."

His hands slide beneath the water to my waist, holding me to him as he comes.

He then wraps his arms around me, and I fall woodenly against him.

We both struggle to regain our breaths, and we seem content to stay there forever.

Except the water is getting cold.

I start to shiver and Xander reluctantly lets me go so I can climb out. I grab a towel and dry off and he lets the water out before climbing out and doing the same.

I change into the pajamas I had set out and Xander pulls on a pair of sleep pants and heads into the room.

I brush my hair and gather it back into a ponytail before flicking off the light and joining him.

When I jump onto the bed, I see that he already has Netflix brought up on the TV. I love the fact that we can get Netflix on the hotel TV. Feeding my addiction, even thousands of miles away from home.

Scandal begins to play, and I settle beneath the covers so we can watch.

I burrow against Xander, still cold, and his body provides much-needed warmth.

I start to drift off to sleep and I feel his lips brush against my forehead.

"Sweet dreams," he croons in a lulling tone.

And I do dream, but they're anything but sweet.

seven
...

xander

"I HAD A NIGHTMARE," Thea tells me, laying her towel down in the sand. She plops on it, stretching out her legs. She looks fucking amazing with her golden tanned skin and that little white bikini. It barely covers anything—which means several guys are staring.

Fucking great.

"A nightmare?" I repeat, sitting down on my towel beside her. I peer at her over the top of my sunglasses. "About what?"

I try to recall if she was thrashing in her sleep or anything like that.

"You were talking to my stomach." She gestures to her stomach like I don't know where it is. "And I was fat."

"Fat? You mean you were pregnant?" My brows furrow in confusion. "I'm missing the nightmare part here?"

She glares at me like I'm stupid. "I was *pregnant*. That's the nightmare. Can you imagine us with a baby?" She laughs like it's the funniest thing she's ever heard.

I wince, feeling kind of hurt by that. "You don't think we'd be good parents?" I know Thea has struggled with thoughts of motherhood in the past, and I get it, her parents weren't exactly great so she didn't grow up desiring a family like I did.

She shrugs. "I don't know," she answers honestly. "I know some girls only dream of the day they get married and start popping out kids but that's never been me. I do want a baby, one day, but not now."

"You'll be a great mom one day," I say honestly.

Thea doesn't see herself clearly. She thinks she has no heart to give, but she's the warmest and kindest woman I know. Any child would be lucky to call her mom.

"One day, far, far, *far* into the future," she intones.

I chuckle. "After your five-year plan?"

"Exactly." She nods, adjusting her sunglasses. She rolls over onto her stomach and props her head in her hands. "I'm only twenty-two. I want to live a little first."

I stare at her. "Let's not live *too* much, okay?"

She laughs and smacks my arm. "Not like that. I just mean, I want to enjoy this time. Being young and married. Doing things like this." She shrugs and motions around us. "This is nice."

My lips crook into a grin. "So does this mean you can fit more vacations into that plan of yours?"

She laughs and tosses sand at me like it's a snowball.

"Yeah, I think so. We need to take advantage of these kinds of things while we can. Not just while it's only two of us, but also while we have the money and whatnot."

I laugh. "You think the money is going to disappear?"

She smiles. "You know what I mean. You can't play football forever, so we have to be smart with our money, which will mean less of this."

"I know what you mean." I lean over and kiss her. "Let's not stress about the future right now." I point to our incredible view, the ocean and sweeping cliff side with homes. "We have to live in the moment while we can."

By some miracle, she doesn't argue. Maybe, somehow, someway, I'm finally getting through that thick head of hers but it's doubtful.

We arrive back in the states and Thea immediately falls asleep in the car. I feel like falling asleep too, even though it's three in the afternoon our time. It's been a long hard day of traveling and we're both exhausted. I want nothing more than to get home, shower, and fall into bed.

It's strange driving *home* to a home that hasn't actually been our home yet.

We haven't slept here, not once, but this is about to be our home.

The place I hope we're going to grow old in.

We could've bought something smaller, but I had the money and that felt silly. I wanted our *forever* home, not a *just right now* home. We looked at condos in the city, and while some of those were larger they were all so cold and impersonal. Not that there's anything wrong with them, but it didn't feel like us. So we finally decided to get a home. We ended up getting a house in the suburbs on a bigger space of land. I also liked the fact that the house came with a gate. The media likes us for some strange reason. I think it's because we're young, and also because Thea commands any room she's in. People can't help but be drawn to her. Including me.

But the house isn't *too* big, which we both liked. It's big enough for us to grow into, but not big enough to feel museum-like.

It took us a couple of months of looking to finally find this one. I think our realtor was getting put out with us, but we knew what we wanted and nothing she showed us was it, until this.

We reach the gates, and I push the button on the remote to open it. Thea's still passed out asleep in the seat beside me, snoring lightly. She doesn't think she snores, but she does. Luckily, they're soft cute snores and not loud and obnoxious ones.

The house is two-stories—well technically three, since there's a basement—with lots of awnings and stonework. We were both drawn to the front porch. It's small, but has enough space that Thea said she wanted to add some chairs and plants.

I laugh as I pull up the driveway and to the garage. Above the garage, our friends have hung a WELCOME HOME sign. It makes me smile. Thea and I are lucky to have friends like ours—friends that are more like family.

I push another button and open the garage door so I can park my truck inside. It's a three-car garage so there's plenty of room for Thea's Mini Cooper, my truck, and my motorcycle.

I turn the truck off and Thea continues to sleep peacefully. I set our luggage out before I wake her up.

She sits up and blinks around, looking at the unfamiliar garage.

"Where are we?" she asks, squinting her eyes at me as if I'm strange too.

I laugh. "We're home, sweetheart."

Her eyes widen in surprise. "Oh, right."

She slips out of the truck and I take her hand in mine, tugging her away from the garage door that leads inside.

"What?" She blinks up at me, confusion filling her hazel eyes.

"Let's go in the front door this time." I squeeze her hand in mine. "It's our first real time coming home, I think we should do this right."

She smiles, her eyes still slightly sleepy. "Okay. Lead the way."

I grin and guide her out of the garage and onto the path that leads to the front door.

Three steps lead up to the large dark wood front door

and we take them slowly. We pause outside the door and just stare.

I feel overcome by an emotion I can't describe. I think maybe it's pride—pride in myself that I've accomplished this.

"This is our home, Thea." I squeeze her hand in mine. It feels so small compared to mine.

She jumps up and down in place. "Open it," she squeals, like the door is a present we're about to unwrap. I guess, in a way, it is.

I dig in my pocket for the keys and locate the right one to open the door. I slip it inside and twist the doorknob.

The door swings open with a slight squeak of the hinges.

The floors are hardwood and shine like they've just been cleaned, which seems impossible with all the tracking that's probably been done with the movers. It makes me wonder if Nova didn't clean the place for us.

Thea lets go of my hand and gives me a coy look. "Race ya," she exclaims, taking off for the stairs to our right.

I tear off up the steps after her. Since I'm tall I'm able to skip a few steps so I catch up to her easily. I bump her hip with mine to slow her down and she laughs uproariously.

"That wasn't nice!"

"You don't play fair—so neither do I," I tell her, reaching the top of the stairs.

We fight to get down the hallway to our room, pushing and shoving like a bunch of little kids, both of us unable to stop laughing.

We push open the doors to our room and race to the bed. I grab her around the waist before she can pass me.

"Xander!" She squirms in my arms before I toss her on the bed. I jump over her and kiss her, silencing her giggles.

She places her hands on my shoulders and tries to push me away. "That wasn't nice."

I grin. "You fucking love it and you know it."

She smiles back and stops pushing on my shoulders, instead pulling me closer. She brushes her nose against mine. "You think you know me, huh?"

I nod, my hair brushing her forehead. "Oh, I know you."

"What's my favorite color?"

I snort. "Thea, I'm pretty sure all the lemurs in the world know your favorite color. It's pink."

She laughs, squirming beneath me. "What the hell? Why lemurs?"

I shrug. "It was the first thing that popped in my head."

I have no real good defense. I know it was random. But that's us.

I sit up and look around the room. All the furniture is in place, but boxes with our clothes and stuff litter the space, and I'm sure the whole house. Our bed is made, though, and I can't thank Nova enough for doing that. I sure as hell know it wasn't Jace. He doesn't make his own bed.

But this is nice, especially since we're both exhausted from the trip. Even now I can tell Thea is fighting not to fall back to sleep. I lean over and kiss her forehead.

"I'll go bring our stuff in. You get a shower or go to bed, whatever you want."

She nods, and that's how I know she really is exhausted.

Normally Thea would insist on helping me, and I would then insist that she didn't.

I hop off the bed and jog down the steps and out the front door—which we stupidly left wide open. I close it and lock up and choose to come in through the garage this time.

I set our bags inside the mudroom and shut the garage door. It whirs as it goes down.

The kitchen counters are covered in boxes and more boxes sit on the floor. I know it's going to take forever to put all this stuff away and I'm not looking forward to it.

I carry our suitcases to the laundry room and set them inside. I would start our clothes to wash, but Thea is very particular about her clothes and prefers to do it herself.

I head upstairs and laugh when I enter the room. Thea's already passed out asleep, her arms and legs stretched out across the bed, hogging the whole damn thing.

I shake my head. As much as I want to shower, a nap sounds pretty good right about now.

I move Thea so she's lying with her head on a pillow, and then I cover her with the blanket that was draped across the bottom of the bed. I pull my phone from my pocket and send a text to Jace—letting him know we're in, and asking if it's not too much trouble if they can bring Prue home in the morning. He texts back almost immediately and says it isn't a problem.

I yawn, looking enviously at Thea as she sleeps. I strip off my shirt and pants, leaving me in my boxers, and climb beneath the sheets. Thea stirs in her sleep, seeking me. I smile, pleased that even in her sleep she wants me.

Her hair tickles my nose when she gets fixed against me, but I don't mind. I like being close to her.

I know we have an endless list of things to do in order to get the house ready, but for now, it's going to have to wait.

eight

...

thea

I SLEEP through the whole afternoon and night. Sunlight is just beginning to filter in through the open windows when I wake up. Xander sleeps peacefully beside me, his arms wrapped around me. Somehow, I've ended up against him with my leg thrown over top of his above the covers. I smile when I notice he covered me with the blanket—I'd kicked it off at some point, though.

I slip from the bed and stretch my arms above my head.

I need a shower. Desperately.

The problem is all our shit is in boxes.

"Fuck my life," I mutter.

Thankfully, I was meticulous in my labeling of the boxes so it doesn't take me long to locate the one with our shampoos and body washes. I carry the box into the bathroom and set it on the counter so I can unload it. I go ahead and put all the contents of the box away—one down, a million to go.

I break down the box and set it in the room.

I need something clean to change into, so I start opening the boxes with all our clothes. I settle on a pair of jean shorts and a tank top with lots of straps. I figure we're going to be working today, so I'll probably get hot.

Xander still hasn't stirred in the bed, so I leave him to sleep while I shower.

I find the box with our towels and washcloths first and unpack them, setting one of each out, before putting the others away.

Once I shower and my hair and body are clean I feel almost human.

I dry off and brush my hair, gathering it up into a damp messy bun.

Xander pads into the bathroom, rubbing his eyes. His hair sticks up around his head and he stifles a yawn.

"Morning," he says, bending to kiss me.

"Ew, your breath stinks," I groan.

He grabs my waist and pulls me closer. "So does yours," he intones, and plants a loud kiss on my lips, which I dramatically wipe off with the back of my hand.

"You're gross."

He winks. "You love me."

I shake my head while he goes to pee.

"Where'd you put our suitcases? I didn't see them in our room."

"They're in the laundry room. Don't worry, I didn't put anything in the washer."

He knows me too well.

"I'll go start them."

"I'm going to shower," he tells me while he washes his hands. "Then I'll go pick us up some breakfast. So let me know what you want."

My stomach rumbles at the thought of food. "Will you judge me if I say I want McDonald's?"

He laughs. "You and McDonald's. I'll get you whatever you want, you know that."

"I want a sausage McGriddle and an Oreo McFlurry."

His brows furrow. "A McFlurry? For breakfast?"

"That's what I want." I frown.

He shrugs. "Okay."

"Thank you."

I flounce from the bathroom and downstairs to start the laundry.

Once the laundry is running I decide to start unpacking more boxes. I start with the kitchen, figuring that room will take the longest.

I'm thankful Jace and Nova were here for the movers and delivery people—since most of our furniture is brand new. It's obvious they directed them on where to place the furniture. Otherwise it would've just been placed haphazardly. As it is, everything is pretty much in place. There are a few things I'll probably ask Xander to rearrange but better a *few* things than *everything*.

I'm putting the forks, knives, and spoons away in the

drawer organizer when Xander comes down freshly showered and changed.

"Still want a McGriddle and a McFlurry?" he asks, laying his hands on the island counter and leaning across to me.

I nod. "Yeah, that's what I want."

"All right, I'll be back soon. Jace and Nova are going to come by at some point today to drop Prue off so if they show up while I'm gone don't freak out—since they can come right in."

He leans across the counter and kisses me before he leaves.

"Don't forget my McFlurry," I call after him, and I hear him laugh before the door to the garage closes.

I finish organizing the utensils, and then start putting away the pots and pans.

By the time Xander gets back with our food I've made quite a dent in unpacking everything for the kitchen. I can tell Xander is impressed when he takes in all the empty boxes.

Xander sets the bag of food on our new kitchen table, along with my McFlurry.

I rub my hand along the table before sitting down. "We owe Jace and Nova big for this."

Xander nods in agreement.

If it weren't for them, none of our furniture would be here. Most everything—except for our bedroom set—is brand new. Since we were living in the rental with my brother, most things weren't ours.

"I can't imagine if we'd gotten back and had no furniture." I laugh at the thought.

He pulls the food out of the bag and hands me my sandwich.

"I'll go grocery shopping today so that we actually have food in the house."

I unwrap my sandwich and hold it up. "This is real food." I take a huge bite, driving home my point.

He shakes his head. "Maybe to you, but not to me."

"Well—" I cover my mouth with my hand "—since I hate grocery shopping I'm willing to let you handle that while I continue to unpack."

He chuckles. "Now it sounds like you're trying to get rid of me."

I smirk. "Never."

"I'll help for an hour or two before I head to the store," he says, wadding up the wrapper from his sandwich and throwing it in the paper bag. "We should be able to put a dent in the unpacking in that time."

"It helps that we don't have much yet—like little knick-knacks."

He grins. "I'm sure you're excited to change that fact."

"Oh, you know it. Any excuse to shop." I don't even try to defend myself anymore. I'm aware I have a serious addiction to shopping. I still have rooms to shop for in the house —like the dining room and formal living room. We were more concerned about the family room and kitchen, as far as getting anything new.

I finish my sandwich and grab my McFlurry.

"Mmm," I say, swirling my tongue around the spoon. "It's as good as I remembered."

Xander busts out laughing. "As good as you remembered?" he repeats, wadding up the trash. "It's only been like a week since you had one. Two, max."

I shrug. "It could've changed," I defend.

He shakes his head. "You're insane."

"You married me," I remind him.

"And I married a psycho."

"Hey," I snap.

He chuckles. "A very cute—" I glare. "*Sexy*," he amends, "smart, psycho."

"If I'm psycho that means I could kill you and no one would ever be able to trace it back to me, so you better be nice to me." I raise my chin in the air.

"I'll try my best not to piss you off." He taps his finger to my nose as he passes, and I playfully go to bite his finger, but he's too quick and skirts away. "Finish your ice cream and I'll work on this." He points to the plates and glasses I have lined up on the counter to be put away in the glass cabinets above the sink.

I kick my legs up on the table and watch him while I eat my ice cream.

With his back to me he lifts the plates up into the cabinet, his shirt stretching taut across his muscles and I hum in appreciation. He looks over his shoulder at me with a smirk.

"Watching me work, sweetheart?"

"Yeah." I swirl my tongue around the spoon. "Enjoying my ice cream with a view. The perks of married life."

He laughs. "I hope you always feel that way."

"I might get bored eventually, but that's what sex tapes are for."

He chokes on a laugh. "I shouldn't be surprised by the things that come out of your mouth anymore, and yet I still am."

"I'm pretty sure keeping you on your toes was in our vows, if it wasn't it was an unspoken one."

He shakes his head. "Is that so?"

"Oh, yeah. I'm sorry you missed it."

He turns back and starts lining up the glasses beside the plate.

I finish my ice cream and gather up the trash and then realize we don't have a trashcan yet.

"You should add getting a trashcan to your to-do list when you get the groceries." I set the trash on the counter for now.

Xander finishes with the glasses and turns around. "Something tells me this list is going to be a mile long before the day is over."

I shrug. "The beauty of being homeowners. It's always something." I lean my hip against the counter. "You think you can handle the kitchen? I'll go back upstairs and start on our clothes. I think that's going to take the longest. We have a lot of stuff."

He raises a brow. "*We?*"

I lift my hands in surrender. "Okay, it's *me* that has a lot of stuff."

"Yeah, I'm good here," he assures me.

I leave him and head upstairs. I grab my phone from the

table by the bed and play some music, refusing to work in silence.

I grab the nearest box and rip it open and then begin laying the items out on the floor. I decide to unpack all the boxes and then start putting everything away, figuring it'll be easier to work if I can see everything.

After a while, Xander comes up to tell me he's leaving.

"I'll be back soon," he says, leaning against the door to our room.

"Can you bring me back a Starbucks drink?" I ask, brightening like a dog about to get a treat.

He shakes his head. "I didn't want to be gone forever."

"Please," I beg, holding my hands below my chin. "I'll be forever in your debt."

He sighs, but I know it's done in an effort to cover his laugh. "Fine," he agrees. "But you owe me."

"I'll make it worth your while. I know tricks." I wink and smile widely.

He chokes on a laugh. "Tricks, huh?"

"Oh, yeah," I say breathily. "They'll blow your mind."

He smiles and backs away. "Looking forward to it."

I hear him bound down the steps and it isn't long until the security system dings, alerting me that the door has been opened.

I hum along to the song while I work on putting away some of Xander's things in the dresser. We have a large enough closet for the both of us, but he says he prefers his things in the dresser, so who am I to deny him what he wants?

Okay, let's be real, he probably doesn't like how my clothes and shoes take over everything. It's not my fault they have a mind of their own and like to form an avalanche.

My phone vibrates and I stop what I'm doing to look at the text.

Nova: We're bringing Prue home. Do you need anything before we come?

Me: Thank you! We're good!

It doesn't take me long to finish putting all of Xander's stuff away in the dresser and then I decide to go back to the bathroom to start organizing there. I know it's going to take me *forever* to put my stuff away, so I need a change of scenery before I tackle that beast, even if it is the bathroom.

Luckily, our bathroom is beautiful. The floors and counters are a shiny white marble that gleams when the sun hits it. There's a walk-in shower, a *huge* bathtub, plenty of counter space, and a separate area for the toilet.

There are a couple of boxes I haven't opened full of bathroom stuff, so I do that and sit on the floor so I can organize everything into little piles so it'll be easier to put away.

I start with the rest of the towels. They've gotten jostled in the boxes so I end up having to refold them and the cloths. But I refuse to put them away haphazardly.

While I work, I think about how I want to decorate—different colors I want to incorporate, among other things.

I get the towels in order and then decide to start on our medicine kinds of things.

The door alarm system beeps, and a moment later, Nova calls out, "Hey! We're here!"

"I'm up here!" I call back.

I hear Prue's collar shake as she goes running through the house toward the sound of my voice.

I stand and hurry to meet her. She's quick, though, and bounds into the bedroom. I bend down and open my arms and she jumps onto me.

"Prue!" I shriek. "I've missed you, girl." I hug her to me as she licks my face.

I hear Nova on the steps and look up to her entering the room. "I think she missed you," Nova comments.

"I'd say so. She's going to freak when she sees Xander. He's her favorite." I rub her face and kiss her nose. "It's okay, he's my favorite too." I laugh when she licks my nose. "How was she?"

"She was a perfect angel. We loved having her."

"You guys need a dog,"

She snorts. "Jace can handle a dog for a week, but I don't think I can convince him for longer."

"Aw, come on, he's such a softy when it comes to you. He'd so give in."

It's true too. He acts all broody and tough, but one bat of Nova's lashes and the guy turns to mush. It's really quite comical.

Nova shrugs. "We'll see. Do you want any help while we're here?"

"You mean Jace isn't about to drag you back to your love den to ravish you?"

A stain creeps up from Nova's neck to her cheeks. "No," she squeaks.

"Well, if you guys want to help it'd be much appreciated. Xander was working in the kitchen before he had to go to the grocery store. Apparently, food that's not McDonald's is a necessity but I honestly don't see the problem." I sigh with a shrug. "I'm sure it'd be easy for Jace to do something there and you could help me with this." I point back to the bathroom, where she can see the mess through the open door.

"All right, I'll go tell him."

"I'm sure he'll be *thrilled*."

She laughs, sticking her hands in her back pockets and rocking on her feet. "He might act like an asshole ninety-percent of the time, but he actually loves all you guys and likes helping."

"I know, I just like to give *Jacen*," I yell his full name so he'll hear me, "a hard time."

"I think he hates that and loves that about you."

"I'm a hard pill to swallow," I agree.

I head back into the bathroom with Prue at my heels while Nova heads downstairs to speak with Jace.

"Why do we have so many bottles of Advil?" I mutter to myself.

There are five unfinished bottles. I know I'm the culprit for this, though. I always leave the bottles in the wrong place, which leads me to not find them the next time I need them, and then I end up buying another so I can start the whole vicious cycle over again.

Prue lies down in front of the bathtub with her head on her paws, watching me. Something tells me she won't be letting me out of her sight, for fear of getting left behind again.

"All right," Nova says, breezing into the room. "What do you want me to do?"

I point to the medicine. "Finish organizing that and put it there." I point to the closet.

Since Nova is taking care of that, I decide to put my makeup and toiletries away. Xander and I each have our own counter and sink, with ample drawers for storage. Honestly, this house couldn't be more perfect.

I take my time lining up my eye shadows and color-coding my lipstick—I'm psycho, remember. I put my hair accessories in the next drawer.

"Honestly, why do I have so much stuff?" I gripe, as I untangle my curling iron cord from my straightener.

Nova laughs. "Because you're a girly girl."

"True."

I've always embraced it, so I shouldn't start complaining now. There's nothing wrong with liking shoes, just as there's nothing wrong with a girl liking the stars or fighting. To each their own.

I open the third drawer and grab my tampons from the box.

I set them in the drawer and go to close it, but freeze.

"No."

"No? No what?" Nova stops what she's doing, her hands frozen in mid-air like I've scolded her.

I pull out the tampon box. "No, no, no no, *no*." I chant.

"Fuck, this can't be happening." I'm on the verge of tears now.

"What?" Poor Nova asks, still lost.

"My fucking period, that's what. She's MIA." I inhale a deep breath while Nova's jaw drops.

"Where's my phone?" I mutter, looking around on the floor for it.

"I think it's in the bedroom," Nova says helpfully.

I run from the bathroom, dropping the tampons on the floor in the process, and find my phone on the floor of the bedroom.

I drop to my knees and turn it on, flicking to the calendar.

I go back a month and …

My phone drops from my hands.

"Fuck my life."

"What?" Nova asks, picking up my phone and looking at the screen like it's going to answer her question.

"I have to go," I mutter.

"What?" She looks after me as I leave the room, but I can't even offer an explanation.

"You guys can go," I call behind me.

It's not fair for them to stay and unpack all our shit while I leave, but I have to go to the store *now*.

I need to get my hands on a pregnancy test.

I round the corner downstairs and Jace jerks back, surprised by my sudden intrusion.

"I have to go," I tell him. "You guys don't have to stay. Thanks for the help. Lock up on your way out." My sentences come out short and clipped because I can barely think straight.

I locate my keys and dash out the door.

There's a drug store not too far down the road.

I push the button to open the garage door and get in my car.

I grip the wheel and inhale a deep breath, trying to calm myself but it turns into a sob.

What if I'm really pregnant?

There's a chance I'm not, but what if I am?

I just got done telling Xander I wasn't ready to be a mom.

I cover my face with my hands. This should be a monumental moment in my life. A *happy* one. But instead, I only feel pure and utter terror.

I couldn't even keep a hamster alive so how was I going to take care of a *baby*?

"This can't be happening," I mutter to myself, backing out of the driveway.

I hope to God Jace and Nova are gone when I get back. I don't need anyone to be a witness to my breakdown.

I keep going over and over the dates in my head, willing them to change, but they *don't*.

My period is late, and I feel like an idiot for not realizing it sooner.

I should've started while we were gone and I didn't. It's easy to chalk it up to all the stress I've had, but my gut says I'm pregnant.

It's like I *know* on some instinctual level that there's a baby in me.

Holy fucking shit—there might be a little alien inside me sucking the life out of me.

Just great.

"Deep breaths, Thea. You don't know anything yet."

I grip the wheel tightly as I drive, so tight in fact that my knuckles turn white.

At the intersection out of the neighborhood, traffic seems endless.

"Get the fuck out of my way," I shout futilely at the traffic, waving my hand wildly. I can see my destination in the distance. So close, yet so far away.

"Don't pass out," I tell myself. "Do not pass out."

I'm finally able to pull out and drive across the street to the drug store.

I park in the nearest spot to the entrance and then hurry inside.

My heart is beating faster than it ever has before. My hands feel clammy with sweat, and I'm sure if I felt my forehead it would be too.

I head past the condoms—little late for those—and to the pregnancy tests.

"Why are there so many?" I mutter to myself out loud.

There are strips, and sticks, and ones with curved handles.

There are some with smiley faces and sad faces, plus signs and minuses signs, and some that flat out say PREGNANT and NOT PREGNANT.

I feel like screaming.

"Do you need some help?" I look over and find a woman, probably in her mid-thirties, looking at me with pity in her eyes. She can probably tell I'm close to having a nervous breakdown.

I nod, my lower lip quivering. "This is ... It's a little overwhelming."

She smiles. "I've been there. It'll be fine, sweetie. I'd recommend this one, they're pretty accurate." She pulls out one of the ones that digitally says PREGNANT and NOT PREGNANT. "They're a little more expensive, but they're worth it."

"Thank you," I tell her, taking the box and grabbing two more just to be on the safe side.

I take a steadying breath and head to the checkout.

"Is that all?" the checkout girl asks, and maybe I'm paranoid but I swear she's sneering and looking at me like I'm dirty for buying pregnancy tests. I know I'm young but I feel like waving my left hand in front of her face and shouting, "I'm married!" but I also know that shouldn't matter anyway.

"Yeah, that's all." I get my total and pay.

She hands me my change and I grab my bag, heading out the door.

The drive home can't be more than five minutes, but it feels like five hours.

Jace and Nova are gone when I get there, and Xander hasn't gotten back.

I know he can't be much longer, though, which means I don't have long to pee on one of these sticks.

I close the garage door behind me and run into the house and up the stairs.

I drop the bag on the counter in the bathroom and fumble to get out one of the boxes.

According to the directions, it's best to wait and pee first thing in the morning—but I don't have time for that, so I'm doing it now. Besides, I've never been very good at following directions.

I rip open one of the boxes and get down to business.

Only I don't have to pee.

"Oh, for the love of God. Come on, come on," I beg.

I've never wanted to pee so bad in my life.

"Stay calm," I tell myself. "You're never going to pee if you're freaking out."

I close my eyes, and take a few deep calming breaths.

Finally, thankfully, I begin to pee.

It's a lot harder to pee on that stick than you'd think, though.

I manage to do it, though, and finish up.

I lay the pregnancy test on the counter and wash my hands. According to the directions it can take three to five minutes to get results.

I pace the length of the bathroom and peek at the test, but nothing shows yet.

"Ugh," I groan. "Hurry up."

My chest feels tight and I feel like I might throw up.

"This can't be happening," I mutter.

The alarm on the door chirps and a moment later I hear Xander call out, "Thea! I'm home!"

"Fuck, fuck, *fuck*," I curse.

"I'll be down in a minute!" I call out, hoping he doesn't come up. I can hear him carrying bags in, so hopefully he has enough that he'll be occupied long enough.

I glance at the time on my phone.

Two more minutes.

I circle the bathroom again, rubbing my hands together. My nerves are through the roof.

I hear Xander and go back out and come back in. "I got your coffee!" he yells up the stairs.

"Thanks!" I say back, though I'm feeling anything but thankful at the moment.

If I'm pregnant, the boy might lose his life.

Or his dick.

I haven't decided yet.

I look at my phone.

Time's up.

I dash for the pregnancy test on the counter and in my haste to get it I knock it to the floor.

"Fuck!" I curse, diving after it and falling to the floor.

My fall causes a loud bang and Xander calls out worriedly, "Thea? Are you okay?"

I don't answer him. I slide across the bathroom floor, my knee screaming in pain from the fall, and my fingers reach out for the slender white stick.

I finally close my fingers around it and pull it to me.

I flip it around and in the little screen staring straight at me is PREGNANT.

"Thea?"

I look up and find Xander standing in the doorway of the bathroom.

His eyes roam over the scene—the bag on the counter, the boxes, and me on the floor with the pregnancy test in my hand.

"Thea?" he says again. "What's ... What's going on? Is that ...?"

I swallow thickly. I can't hide it from him, I mean, I'm sitting right here with the stupid thing in my hand and I'm freaking the fuck out.

Tears fill my eyes and I nod, holding the test out to him so he can see.

He takes it from me, shock filling his eyes. His lips part and he looks from it to me. "What? When? How?"

My sarcasm rears its ugly head. "Well, the how is pretty obvious."

"You're pregnant?" He looks from the test to me and back again.

"According to that thing."

He drops to his knees in front of me. The shock is still written all over his face.

"We're having a baby?" he asks me.

I nod, tears falling from my eyes.

He grins at me, and reaches out to place his hand on my flat stomach.

"Wow," he murmurs. "We're going to have a baby, Thea.

This is crazy."

His smile is huge. I can tell he's beyond happy. And me? I don't know what I feel. Not happiness. Instead, I'm consumed by an overwhelming fear. I can't take care of a baby. I can barely take care of myself.

I know it's wrong, but I almost feel angry ... No, not angry, but jealous that he's happy. This should be my moment, one of the best in my life, and I don't feel happy.

Does that already make me a horrible mom?

Have I already managed to fail at this parenting thing before it even starts?

Don't get me wrong, I'm not thinking of doing anything drastic, but I'm not ready for a baby. I'm not even twenty-three yet and now I'm going to be a *mom*?

I know plenty of people younger than me are having kids, but they're different from me. I wanted to wait.

I guess fate had other plans.

Xander wraps his arms around me and hugs me tight. I'm still stunned and don't move my arms for a minute, but I eventually hug him back.

He kisses me, and I'm wooden against him. Normally, I come alive when he touches me or kisses me, but I'm nothing but cold right now.

He cups my cheek, pressing his forehead to mine. "I know you didn't want a baby now, but something tells me this is going to be the best thing to happen to us."

I press my lips together. I hope he's right.

"I'm scared," I admit.

Terrified.

Confused.

Lost.

"I know." He kisses my forehead. "It'll be fine, though. I promise."

I close my eyes and let his words wash over me.

I don't feel any better, though. Anxiety builds in my chest as I think about a screaming baby and all that comes with it, and then shame for not being happy. I know someone would do anything for this moment, and I'm not even grateful for it.

Something is seriously wrong with me.

nine
...

xander

"ARE you seriously going to watch me pee?" Thea asks, her fingers curling around the pregnancy test box.

I cross my arms over my chest. "Yes, I wasn't here the first time, so I'm going to be here now." I stand resolute in the doorway to the bathroom. Nothing is going to get me to move from this spot.

Thea sighs and opens the box, pulling out the stick and handing me the trash.

She wanted to take another test this morning, since the box said it was more accurate then, but we both know the answer isn't changing.

Thea pees on the stick and then lays it on the counter so she can wash her hands.

"How long is it supposed to take?" I ask, peering at the stick.

"It can take five minutes."

It barely takes two.

Thea picks it up and shakes it, like that can erase the answer she doesn't want to see.

"Hey," I scold lightly, grabbing her hand in mine to still it. "It's going to be okay." I take her face in my hands, forcing her to look at me. I can easily see the fear in her hazel eyes.

I know she's scared, I am too, but I know this isn't a bad thing.

She breathes out a shaky breath. "What are we going to do?" she asks softly.

"What we always do," I reply. "Figure it out."

I'm not naïve. I know a baby isn't an easy thing. I know it means a screaming, pooping, living being, but I believe in us.

Unlike Thea, I grew up in a loving home, and even though I'm a guy, I always knew I wanted a family one day. A big one. If I'd had my choice we would've already had a kid, but I knew better than to broach the subject right now, and I understood.

Thea's young, she barely just graduated college, and she wants to live her life a little.

I respected that.

But shit happens.

Shit *did* happen.

I let my hands fall, and she forces a smile, always trying to be strong.

"Come here," I tell her, opening my arms.

She dives into them gladly, and I hold her tight, hoping that I can make her feel the smallest bit better.

I brush my lips against the top of her head. Her hair is soft and tickles my nose.

"I'll make an appointment with my doctor," she says, her voice muffled against my shirt. She steps back, wiping tears from her eyes.

"Thea," my voice cracks with worry.

She holds her hands out in front of her. "I'm okay." She forces a smile, her lower lip trembling. "I'm okay," she says again. "Oh, fuck it, I'm not." She finally gives in and breaks down.

I wrap my arms around her again, murmuring comforting words under my breath.

"I shouldn't be crying," she says against my shirt, the fabric scrunched between her fists. "At least not *this* kind of crying."

"This wasn't planned," I reason.

"Yeah, but you seem pretty jolly about this whole thing." She rears her head back to look at me, her face splotchy and red from crying.

I try not to laugh. "Did you seriously just use the word *jolly*?"

"Fine then, how about *joyous*?"

"That's better." I tap her nose. "And yes, I am happy."

She frowns. "But that should be *me*. I'm the girl and you're the guy, you should be the one freaking the fuck out and wanting to run."

I chuckle. "Sweetheart, when have we ever done anything the normal way?"

"True." She sniffles some more and backs away. "I'm

gonna go call the doctor now." She wipes her face with the back of her hands. "Hopefully, I can get in soon."

She leaves the bathroom in search of her phone. I throw the box away and follow her out.

Last night, we didn't get much else done the rest of the day. I think we were both in shock, but while mine was happy shock, hers was ... well, not.

It's still early so I head downstairs to make us breakfast.

I'm sure Thea will tell me she's not hungry, but she's eating for two now, so I'll force-feed her if I have to.

She sits at one of the barstools in the kitchen already, on the phone.

I leave her to it and pull out the eggs from the refrigerator.

I figure I'll make omelets, so I grab one of the mixing bowls we recently bought and set it on the counter.

When Thea finally hangs up the phone, I've already started cooking the eggs. She sighs heavily, laying her head in her hands.

"When can they get you in?" I ask, my back to her as I watch the eggs.

"Friday," she answers, her voice muffled.

Three days from now. It feels like forever, but I know it's probably sooner than normal.

"What's that smell?" she cries suddenly. "Oh, God." I turn in time to see her slap her hand over her nose and run from the room.

"Thea?" I call after her. I turn the stove off and rush after her, finding her heaving over the toilet in the downstairs powder room. "Aw, man, I'm sorry, baby." I crouch down beside her and hold her hair back. I rub her back with my other hand, trying to offer her as much comfort as I can.

She finally finishes and sits back, looking up at me with watery eyes. "I fucking hate morning sickness."

"Do you think that's what you had the day of your graduation?" I ask, remembering back to how she became so suddenly sick.

She nods and stands, going to the sink to rinse her mouth out. When she finishes she says, "Yeah, I think so. It must've been the start." She bites her lip. "I'm sorry, but can you not make the eggs? I don't think I can stomach the smell."

I raise my hands. "You got it. Consider them gone."

"I'll go up and brush my teeth while you get rid of them. I don't want to get sick again. I *hate* throwing up."

"Is there something you think you can eat?" I ask pleadingly, knowing she needs to eat something.

She shrugs. "Toast with butter maybe? I'm not sure I can keep much down—I don't know if that's actually morning sickness, or just sickness from *all* of this." She waves her hand through the air.

"Toast," I repeat. "I can do that."

"Thank you." She gives me a small, sad smile, and pushes by me to go upstairs.

I get rid of the eggs. As much as I'd like an omelet for myself, I don't want to risk her getting sick again.

I put a piece of bread in the toaster for her and make a bowl of cheerios for myself.

The bread pops up out of the toaster as she comes down

the stairs. I put it on a plate and set out the butter so she can put it on.

She slides onto one of the barstools and I hand her a knife before I sit down beside her.

She butters her toast and takes a small hesitant bite.

She chews slowly and swallows.

"Think you can keep it down?" I ask.

She nods. "Yeah, I think so."

She takes another bite, bigger this time.

She manages to eat the whole piece of toast. I wish she'd eat more, but I know better than to push my luck.

I finish my cereal and rinse the bowl out before putting it in the dishwasher.

"What do you want to do today?" I ask her.

We have a little more unpacking to do, but there really isn't that much. We actually need to go shopping to get things, but I'm a bit scared to use that word with Thea. I know if I broach the idea we'll be gone all day.

"I want to wallow."

I lean across the counter to her. "This isn't the end of the world, sweetheart."

"That's easy for you to say. You don't have to carry the baby for nine months. You have a job—a *career*—that you love, and I'm an incubator."

I try not to laugh, but it's futile, she's not amused, though.

"I'm serious." She glares at me for laughing.

"It won't be as bad as you think. We're going to have a

son or daughter, Thea. A little person that's half me and half you. Think about how amazing that is."

"Yeah, a little person that's going to scream, eat, and poop non-stop for the first year. *Then* it'll start walking and talking, and our lives will truly be over." She blows out a breath and it stirs the hair around her face.

I reach out and cover her hand in mine. "I know that this baby is going to change our lives, I'm not stupid, but I also think it's going to better us."

"How?" she asks, her lower lip pouting out a bit. I don't think she even means to do it, and I can't stop myself from rubbing my thumb over it.

"I think this baby is going to teach us to be more humble and responsible people."

She swallows thickly. "I'm really going to have to work on the swearing."

I laugh in agreement. I don't swear as much as she does, but it's enough. "We'll get a swear jar," I tell her, curling my hand into her hair. "A quarter for every time we curse."

"We'll be able to go on a month long European vacation in no time."

I smirk. "With your mouth—make it a whole year."

"Hey!" she cries in offense and swipes at me, so I jump away, pulling her hair by accident in the process. "Ow! Oh, it's on now!"

She launches off the chair and at me. I turn to run, but she launches at my back like a fucking spider monkey.

I'm not expecting it and I start to go down. I manage to

catch myself before my knees hit the ground, and I stand there with Thea hanging around my neck.

Here we are, having just found out we're going to be parents, and we both clearly refuse to grow up.

But I think it's that quality that'll make us amazing parents. I just have to get Thea to see it.

This isn't a bad thing.

Not by a long shot.

"You can let go now." But even as I say it, she's winding her legs around my waist from behind.

"You pulled my hair," she says in my ear.

"It was an accident."

She reaches up and tugs on my hair playfully—it doesn't hurt at all.

"Now we're even." She finally lets me go and drops down onto the floor.

I turn around and find her smiling, but it doesn't quite reach her eyes. I know she's scared, and worried, and a million other things right now, but I want nothing more than to make her feel better.

And I know just how to do it.

I sweep her legs out from under her and she screams in surprise.

"What are you doing?" she asks, her arms going around my neck.

"We're having a lazy day," I declare.

"But we have to finish unpacking." She looks to the stairs, where most of the mess is in our room.

She has *a lot* of clothes.

"It'll wait," I say lightly.

I carry her back through the kitchen and into the open family room. I don't sit her down until we reach the leather sectional couch. We only have one blanket for now, and I grab it from the back of the couch and drape it over her.

The box of DVDs hasn't been unpacked, but there's only one box and not that many in it so it doesn't take me long to find the movie I'm looking for.

"Want me to make popcorn?" I ask her as I kneel on the floor to put the DVD into the player.

She gags. "Um, no. I don't think my stomach can handle that."

"Fair enough."

I start the movie and join her on the couch. She snuggles against me, and I smile. I don't think she even realizes that she's done it and I love that.

The opening credits for *Jaws* starts and Thea smiles up at me.

It seemed appropriate to me, on a day when our lives are changing forever we should watch *Jaws*. After all, it also marks the moment I knew I loved Thea, and that too was a pretty big deal to me.

"I love you," I murmur, brushing my lips over her forehead.

Sometimes I love you doesn't feel big enough to encompass what I feel for her.

She's everything to me.

The sun and the moon and the stars. She's it all.

She smiles too, and this time it's genuine. "I love you too."

She turns back to the movie, wiggling against me, and I rest my head on hers.

We're having a baby.

It's a shock, that's for sure, but this isn't the end of the world like she thinks it is. Somehow, I'll get her to see that.

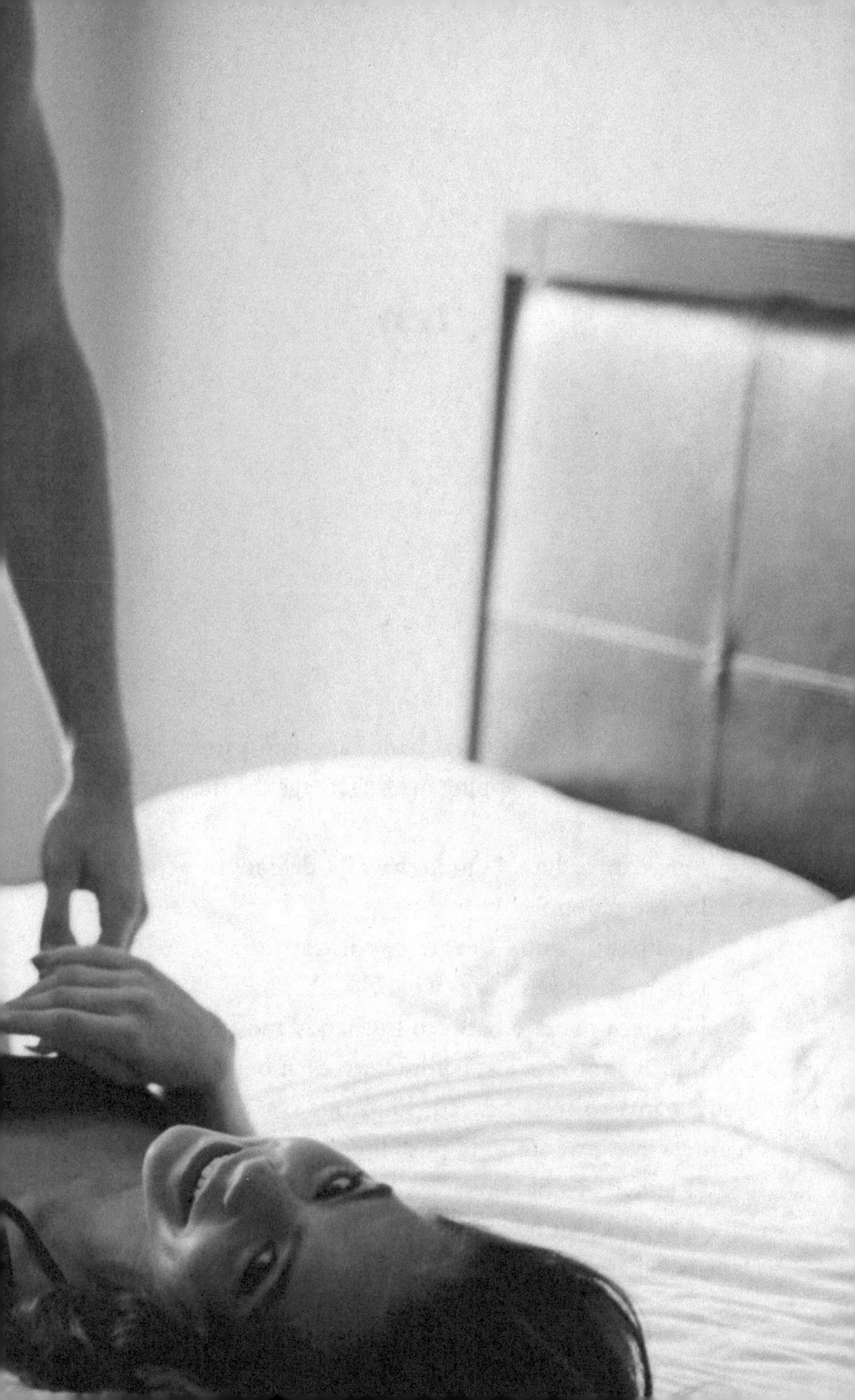

ten

thea

"STOP FIDGETING."

Xander grabs my restless hands and holds them between his to stop me from tapping my fingers against the wood arm of the chair.

I glare up at him. "I'm *nervous*," I defend my actions. "I need a distraction."

His lips quirk up. "I'm great at distractions."

I narrow my eyes. "Like what?"

He grabs my face between his hands and presses his lips to mine in a forceful kiss before I can even blink. At first, my body wants to melt beneath him, but two seconds later it registers *where* we are and I push him away.

"Xander," I scold under my breath, "we're in the doctor's office." I look around at the other expectant mothers and few fathers. Thankfully, they're all absorbed in their own conversations and not paying us any mind. "I can't believe you did that," I hiss, my cheeks heated with embarrassment.

Normally, making out with my husband would be a great thing, and usually lead to other, more fun activities, but now isn't the time or place.

"Just trying to distract you and it worked." He smirks at me, entirely too pleased with himself.

I raise a finger in warning, scolding him like an unruly child. "Xander Kincaid, wipe that smirk off your face or I'll enjoy shoving my heel up your ass." I point my extended finger at the four-inch heels I wear—it could be worse, they could be six inches.

He shakes with laughter, clearly not afraid of me.

I guess if I was a giant Viking I wouldn't be afraid of me either.

"Thea Kincaid?" they call out.

I stand. "That's me," I say unnecessarily to the nurse holding my chart.

Xander stands and follows me.

"How are you feeling, Mrs. Kincaid?" she asks, leading us down the hall.

I gag. "Call me Thea, please." I don't know why but I always hate the sound of *Mrs. Kincaid*. Don't get me wrong, I love being married—most of the time—but *Mrs. Kincaid* sounds so stuffy and formal, which is not me at all. "And a little nausea but other than that, I'm okay."

She leads us into an exam room. "You can sit there." She points Xander to a chair. "And you—" she turns to me "—can pee in this." She hands me a little cup with a green cap.

"There's a bathroom right across the hall, put the specimen in the silver door in the wall, you can't miss it. Come back here and take off your pants and underwear. There's a gown you can use to drape over you. The doctor will be in shortly."

She turns, her blond ponytail swishing, and disappears down the hall.

I give Xander a look. "I have to pee again? Seriously? We've already done two of these at home."

He shrugs. "I guess it's procedure. How would I know?"

I sigh and head across the hall to pee in the cup. I finish and set the cup where she told me and wash my hands before going back to the exam room.

"How long are we going to have to wait?" I ask with a groan. I'm not the most patient person on a good day, let alone when something like this is happening. "This all seems a bit unnecessary. I told them I took two pregnancy tests, and that they were both positive, and they were basically like, 'oh yeah, you're pregnant'. So what's with all this?" I wave my hands around wildly. "Can't we just get on with it?"

Xander stands and cups my cheeks. "Breathe, Thea. You're going to give yourself a panic attack."

I cover his hands with mine, and breathe out like he says.

"My heart is beating so fast. I feel like it's going to explode out of my chest. Why are they making us wait so long?"

His lips twitch like he's fighting not to laugh. "Thea, it's been like … five minutes since you peed, if that. Give them time."

He moves one of his hands to the back of my neck and his other rests by my leg.

I breathe in and out slowly, mirroring his breaths, and it seems to help.

After another minute, he sits back in the chair and takes my hand. It helps to touch him in some way. He centers me, like an anchor.

Doctors' offices are notoriously the worst for making you wait, so it's no surprise when a good thirty minutes pass before the door finally opens. I'm about to lose my mind, and Xander knows it.

Dr. Hawkins steps inside the room with a big grin lighting his bearded face. "Well, kids, looks like we're having a baby."

I was expecting this, and yet the words aren't any less shocking.

I look at Xander and he's smiling happily, clearly pleased that everything is as we thought.

I think a part of me was hoping the tests were wrong and we were going to come in here and they'd laugh at us and tell us the tests we used must've been broken.

"Why don't you lie back and we'll get a look at your baby?"

If I thought my heart was beating fast before, it's galloping now.

I lie back like he asked and prop my legs up. It's always unnerving being exposed like this, but at least Xander's here this time.

"Since you're probably pretty early in the pregnancy,

according to when you say you missed your period, we'll have to do a transvaginal sonogram."

I look from the doctor to Xander and back again. "That sounds painful."

He chuckles. "Nobody's ever complained too much. You'll be just fine."

He has a penis, so I don't necessarily believe him.

I lie back, taking a deep breath, and trying not to freak out too much.

He pulls out a wand looking thing and my eyes widen.

"Whoa, no, no, *no* you're not coming anywhere near me with that thing."

He chuckles, amused by me, but I'm not kidding. "You're going to be fine," he assures me.

I glance at Xander, begging him with my eyes to help me, but he just blinks back at me.

Husbands are fucking useless.

The doctor covers the wand thing in what looks like a condom ... and I think he adds lube.

"What the fuck is happening?" I mutter.

"Relax," he urges.

There's no chance in hell of that. I'm too wired.

I grab Xander's hand as the doctor eases the probe inside.

It's not that bad, but it does feel weird, and then ...

"Holy fucking shit is that the baby?" I ask, looking at the screen. "It looks like an alien! Or a blob! Is that even human?"

The doctor chuckles, pressing some buttons. "Yes, that's your baby. Right there." He points to the screen at the round bean-looking little shape. "You're measuring around six weeks pregnant." He presses a few more buttons and whooshing sound fills the room. "And *that* is your baby's heartbeat. Sometimes six weeks is too early to hear it, but the transvaginal probe usually can pick it up."

I look over at Xander, my stunned expression mirroring his.

Tears fill his eyes and slowly spill over.

"You're crying?" I ask stupidly, and then I begin to cry too, because holy shit that's our *baby*.

The doctor lets us listen for a moment longer and then takes some more pictures.

"There's only one in there, right?" I ask, the idea of twins suddenly occurring to me.

I can barely handle one baby, let alone two.

He laughs. "Only one. Looks like you're going to be due around the end of February. I'd say the twentieth. I'm going to print off some ultrasound photos for you." He smiles kindly.

I look over at Xander, and he's still staring in awe at the little bean on the screen.

That's seriously what it looks like—a bean. It's beyond me how that thing is a baby.

"When can we find out the gender?" I ask.

"Usually sometime between sixteen and twenty weeks you'll have an appointment and if the baby is cooperating the technician will be able to see. If the baby is being stubborn you'll probably have to come back."

Xander chuckles and squeezes my hand. "If the baby is

anything like you, it'll be incredibly stubborn and we won't know what it is until it comes out."

"It better cooperate," I mumble, looking down at my flat stomach. "I have to know what kind of clothes to buy and how to decorate."

Xander laughs, and stands up beside me, brushing his fingers soothingly through my hair.

"I can't believe that's our baby," I whisper.

The doctor pulls the probe from me and the image of the baby disappears.

"I should warn you, that you are still very early in your pregnancy and any number of random things could happen, resulting in miscarriage. Typically we look at twelve weeks as the all clear—something could still happen, but your chances drop significantly."

He hands me a stack of ultrasound photos.

"Those are for you. Do you have any questions for me?"

"Yeah." I clear my throat. "How did this happen?" I blush. "Okay, I know *how*, but ... we weren't trying and I'm on birth control."

"Birth control isn't one-hundred percent and can be affected by any number of things. Were you recently on antibiotics for anything?"

"Yes ... and the timing lines up perfectly."

He nods. "Antibiotics are known to counteract birth control. Your physician should have warned you, but ..." He shrugs.

Yeah, *but*.

He pats my knee. "You're going to be fine. You can get

dressed and check out—they'll make your next appointment there."

He leaves the room and I'm left alone with Xander.

"Can I see those?" he asks, holding his hand out for the sonograms.

I hand them over while I put my pants back on.

"I can't believe that's our baby," he murmurs. "It's so small."

"It looks like a bean." I peek at the photo.

"But it's *our* bean."

He touches his finger tenderly to the gray blob. I pause, watching him, with a small smile. While I have my doubts about my ability to be a mom, I have no doubts that Xander will be the best dad ever. This baby is lucky to have him.

We check out and schedule my next appointment for four weeks.

Once in the car, he asks, "When are we going to tell people?"

"I don't know," I hedge. "Maybe we should wait until I'm twelve weeks, like the doctor said, something could happen. It's still early."

His brows knit together, clearly not liking this. "So, what? If we lose the baby, we're supposed to just mourn to ourselves and not share that with people?"

I shrug. "I was just repeating what he said," I mumble. "How about the Fourth of July? That's in three weeks, and everyone will be together in one place, so maybe we can come up with some fun way to announce it."

He nods. "Three weeks feels like forever, but I can live with that."

"My brother is going to kill you when he finds out," I warn.

He shakes his head. "He'll be fine."

"Ten bucks says he at least tries to hit you," I challenge with a smirk.

"You're on," he agrees.

"I'm hungry—can we stop somewhere?"

"Sure, what do you want?"

"Um ..." I bite my lip, thinking. "Ooh, Italian."

"There's that place you love close to here," he suggests.

"Dominic's? Yes, let's go there!" I bounce in my seat, giddy at the thought of food. I could barely eat any breakfast, so I'm starving.

Xander turns off the highway and drives down the road then into the parking lot for Dominic's. It's packed and it takes him a minute of driving around to find an empty spot. When he finally does I barely wait for him to put the truck in park before I'm hopping out.

Food.

We head inside and the hostess takes us to a booth in the back.

I don't even look at the menu, since I know what I want.

When our waiter comes, I order a Sprite and Xander orders a water.

Xander continues to peruse the menu. He finally makes up his mind and lays the menu on the end of the table.

Our waiter returns with our drinks, complimentary bread, and takes our meal order.

I dig into the bread. "Oh, God," I moan. "That's delicious."

Xander's brow raises in amusement, his lips quirking. "That good, huh?"

"So good." I dip it in marinara sauce and take another bite.

He slides the whole breadstick basket over to me.

"Smart man," I remark, grabbing another breadstick.

I wouldn't normally be such a pig, but it's almost one and I've only eaten a couple of crackers today.

I finish the second breadstick and push the basket back to him. "Hide them from me," I plead with him.

He chuckles and takes the basket, placing it on the booth beside him.

"So," I start, sipping at my Sprite, "I guess we have a lot to talk about."

He sits back in the booth, stretching one of his arms along the back of it. The gesture stretches his ash gray t-shirt tight across his chest. I might drool a little bit, but *damn* the boy looks good.

"Things are going to change, that's for sure," he agrees.

"Prue's going to be a big sister," I joke. I play with my straw wrapper. "I guess it's a good thing we got the house and not a condo."

He smiles. "True. It wouldn't have been fun to have to move again."

"How are we going to tell everybody?" I ask, tapping my fingers against the table.

He shrugs. "I don't know. We'll figure something out."

"Your mom is going to freak."

He grins. "Oh, yeah," he agrees. "She'll probably try to move in."

I laugh. "That honestly wouldn't surprise me."

Sarah, Xander's mom, has been dropping hints for the last few months that she wants grandchildren. I was adamant in telling her that we wanted to wait a couple of years, so I could get established with a job. So this will be welcome news to her.

Our waiter brings our food to the table and I inhale the heavenly scent of the Alfredo sauce.

I dig in and it tastes as good as it smells.

Three bites in and disaster hits.

"Oh, no." I shoot out of the booth, running for the bathroom.

"Thea?" Xander calls after me.

The swinging door to the bathroom swishes closed behind me and I run for a stall, dropping to my knees. Normally I'd be freaking out about how unsanitary this is, but all I care about is making it to the toilet and not throwing up all over myself.

I empty the contents of my stomach, my body heaving.

The door to the bathroom swishes open. "Thea? Are you okay?"

A moment later Xander's there, gathering my hair away from my face and rubbing my back. He's been there every time I've gotten sick, refusing to let me be alone, even though I hate him seeing me like this.

I finish and sit back, looking up at him. I'm sure my mascara is streaked across my cheeks by now.

"Whoever called it morning sickness is a fucking liar. It's all day sickness and they know it. They lie to you, because otherwise no one would ever want to have a baby," I defend.

Xander chuckles and holds out his hands to help me up.

I take them, leaning against him. I feel exhausted. "Can you ask them to bag our food? Maybe I can eat it later, if I'm lucky. I just want to go home now."

"Sure thing, sweetheart." He kisses my forehead and leaves me in the bathroom to clean up.

Five minutes later I leave the bathroom. Our food is already packed in boxes and bagged away.

"I already paid," he tells me as I approach. "So we can get out of here."

I grab my purse and then take his hand, letting him lead me out of the restaurant. I feel embarrassed that all those people saw me go flying into the bathroom to throw up, but I can't help it. It is what it is, and I'm going to have to get used to it.

Pregnancy is definitely no cakewalk from what I've experienced thus far.

All those smiling and happy women on TV are a bunch of liars and should be sued.

We head home, and once we get there I head straight for the couch, curling up on it with Prue.

Xander fixes me a glass of ginger ale and then heads to his

home gym—I say *his*, because the idea of me ever using any of the equipment in there is laughable.

I wiggle around on the couch and get comfortable. I'm hungry, but I'm too scared to attempt to eat something, so I watch TV instead.

"Well, Prue," I sigh, curling my fingers into her fur, "it's going to be a long eight months."

She looks up at me with big brown eyes, and I swear she nods.

See, even the dog knows this isn't going to be easy.

eleven
. . .

xander

8 weeks pregnant

"Are you going to love me when I'm fat?"

I look up from my book and bust out laughing. "What the hell is that?"

"I know it's lumpy, but I had to work with what I had."

I shake my head. Thea has what looks like a sweatshirt wadded up into a ball and stuffed under her shirt.

"Now, I'm serious, are you still going to love me when I look like this?" She presses her hand to her fake round stomach.

My wife is a nut case, but at least there's never a dull moment.

"I'll love you forever, no matter what," I tell her honestly.

I've loved that girl for so long, even when I shouldn't have.

She sighs and sits down beside me. "I'm going to get so big." She frowns, looking down at her fake belly. "I won't be able to see my feet. I hope you'll help me put my shoes on."

I chuckle, setting my book aside. "I'll do whatever I have to do."

She rests her head on my shoulder. "It still doesn't feel quite real yet."

"I know what you mean," I agree. "We weren't exactly prepared for this."

She pulls the sweatshirt out from under her shirt, revealing her flat stomach. I reach over, placing my hand against her stomach. She puts her hand over mine and smiles at me.

"I wonder when we'll feel it kick."

"I don't know." I shrug. "Maybe we should go to the bookstore and get some books. I feel so clueless about this whole thing."

"Ooh, yeah." She brightens. "That sounds fun."

"I don't really like calling it an it," I admit. "That feels ..."

"Yeah, I know what you mean, it's weird." She purses her lips, thinking. "What about bean?"

"Bean?" I repeat.

She shrugs. "That's what it looks like right now."

I nod. "Bean ... I like it. Bean it is."

I remove my hand from her stomach and stand. "Let's go."

"Right now?" She looks at me incredulously. "I just sat down."

I tilt my head at her. "If we don't go now, we never will, you know how we are."

She laughs. "That's true. Give me like five minutes to change."

I groan, tilting my head back to the ceiling. "Five minutes—that's five hours to you."

"I won't be long, promise." She scurries out of the room and up the steps.

She's going to get all dolled up, like usual, and there I'll be in my gym shorts, t-shirt, and baseball cap.

I settle back on the couch with my book, because no matter what she says, she'll be at least an hour.

It's a fact of life.

Prue sits beside me on the couch, resting her head on my leg.

I pet her, smiling.

Sometimes I wonder what life would be like without Prue. She came to us accidentally, and now I can't imagine not having her. Everyone in our family loves her too.

An hour and five minutes later, Thea comes downstairs, with her hair and makeup done, and a dress with heels.

"Uh ..." I start. "Is it safe to wear heels when you're pregnant?"

She narrows her eyes. "As long as I'm comfortable, it's fine. Heels are my life, don't try and change me now."

I chuckle and raise my hands in surrender. "Wouldn't dream of it."

I let Prue run out back to pee before we go, and then grab a bottle of water.

We go in my truck—we always do when it's both of us, because I refuse to try and fit my giant self in her Mini Cooper. I'm a big guy, that's a small car, and I'm not going to hunch.

"We're going to have to get an SUV," I tell Thea as she climbs in my truck.

"What?" She looks at me like a deer caught in headlights. "Why?"

"Because, you can't be climbing in and out of my truck when you're nine months pregnant—and I don't think it's that safe for a baby, and your car is too small."

"We'll make it work." She shrugs, buckling her seatbelt.

Thea doesn't like me spending what she calls unnecessary money—for example, buying a new car. But I view it as a necessity. We have to have something family friendly, and neither of our cars is that.

"We can always strap the little bean to a buggy and haul it behind your motorcycle."

I narrow my eyes on her. "That wasn't remotely funny."

"It was hysterical." She smiles widely.

"This is serious," I defend, backing out of the garage.

"I really don't think it's that big of a deal," she mutters.

"We have room. Your truck is plenty big. It has a whole backseat for fuck's sake."

"Thea …"

"Shit."

"Aw, dammit, I did it again … and again." She slaps a hand over her mouth.

I smirk. "That's three quarters for the swear jar. At the rate you're going, you're going to pay for Bean's college education before they're even born."

"Stop." She lightly smacks my arm in jest. "I'm not that bad."

I raise a brow. "Really?"

"Okay, so I'm awful, but I don't mean to be so that counts for something, right?"

"Whatever you have to tell yourself so you feel better." I wink.

She pouts, looking out the window. I reach over and take her hand in mine. I bring her hand to my lips, kissing her knuckles.

I might pick on her for excessive use of swear words, and her overall dramatics, but it's one of the things I love the most about her.

She keeps me on my toes. There's never a dull moment.

I turn onto the next street and then into the strip mall complex that has the bookstore.

I park and Thea hops out. I meet her at the front of the truck and take her hand in mine. I glance down at her heels, shaking my head. I don't know how she wears those things, let alone walks in them. Girls are talented creatures who don't get enough credit.

We head into the store, and I ask one of the clerks for help.

Thea gives me a disgusted look, because she hates asking people for help. I, on the other hand, don't want to waste my whole day looking for what I need when someone could easily help me.

"Everything you'll need is here." The clerk smiles, pointing down an aisle. "Do you need help with anything else?" she asks, smiling pleasantly at us.

"No, we're good, thanks." She scurries away to another part of the bookstore and Thea and I are left alone.

I squat down, reading the titles. Thea scans some books a few feet away.

I pull a couple out and lay them on the floor. Thea grabs a couple and then we head to the checkout.

"Do you mind if we go to the furniture store next door?" Thea asks, biting her lip nervously like she's scared I'm going to say no. "We still need some things, and I'd like to look while we're out."

"Yeah, that's fine with me." I'll be bored out of my mind, but it's fine. "I guess we also have to shop for a nursery now." I hadn't thought about that. Babies are so small but they need so much stuff.

"Yeah, I've already been looking."

"Really?" I raise a brow as we move up in line.

She nods. "I won't get anything yet—not until we know

if Bean is a boy or a girl, but I wanted to get an idea of what I liked."

"And?" I prompt.

She shrugs. "It's all so cute. I want it all."

I chuckle. "Something tells me this baby is *not* going to help your shopping addiction."

"Not at all," she agrees.

I shake my head, and it's finally our turn so I drop the books on the counter with a thump.

The clerk rings it up and I hand my card over to pay. Thea eyes the magazine stand behind the checkout and I look at what she's looking at.

A blond, blue-eyed, baby drools on the cover of some parenting magazine and I see her cringe.

I hate that she's so worried about this, that she doesn't trust herself to be a good mom.

It's breaking my fucking heart.

I have to come up with some way to show her that this is going to be the greatest thing to ever happen to us.

I collapse on the bed, rolling to face Thea's laptop.

"What are you watching?" I ask her.

"YouTube videos of people revealing they're pregnant." She sniffles.

My head whips up to her, shock clouding my eyes. "Are you crying?"

She glares at me. "I'm pregnant, and apparently that makes you real fucking emotional, okay? I can't help it. I'm not normally so weepy, but this stuff is so sweet."

I clear my throat. "Quarter."

"Oh, shut up," she grumbles.

I grin slowly. It's hard not to be amused by her.

"So have any of these given you any ideas on how to tell everybody?" I ask, reaching over to tap the keyboard to pause the video so we can talk.

She shakes her head. "No—the crying started pretty much immediately so after that my only thoughts were, 'aw' and 'this is so sweet'. I wasn't really thinking about how it could apply to us."

I sigh, running my fingers through my hair. "Maybe we just tell them and don't make a big deal out of it."

Her mouth pops open and she looks at me, horrified. "No. No way." She shakes her head roughly back and forth. "We have to do *something*. I'm not saying it has to be extravagant, but I'm not just going to be like, 'Surprise, I'm knocked up!'."

"I didn't think we'd say it like that," I mumble, looking down at the bedspread.

She waves a hand dismissively. "We'll think of something. We have a week."

Prue jumps up on the bed and over my legs, so she can lie between us.

"Pretty soon it's going to be the dog *and* a baby in bed with us," I comment, looking at the empty space above Prue.

Thea's lips part in surprise, her hazel eyes wide. "That's

so weird to think about. There's going to be another *person* living here. Everything's going to change."

I reach over, touching my fingers to her cheek. "Nothing's going to change," I disagree. "Life's just going to get better and it's going to be amazing."

She smiles at me, her eyes trusting. "I hope you're right."

I grin back. "I know I am."

twelve
. . .

thea

9 weeks pregnant

I fix the bows on the gift bags—one for Xander's parents, and one for my mom—and step back, appraising my handiwork.

"You did good," Xander comments, stepping up behind me and winding his hands around my waist.

I lean against him, tilting my head back so I can look at him. "You think so?"

He nods, pressing his lips against my neck. "They're going to be shocked, though, that's for sure."

I came up with the idea to put baby things in a bag to

give them. I figured it was cuter than just blurting it out, and it wasn't too crazy.

"Are we taking Prue with us?" I ask, untangling myself from his arms and picking up the bags.

"Yeah, I think we should. It'll be a long day for her if we don't, and my parents don't mind."

Everybody is meeting at Xander's parent's house for the holiday. We thought about doing it here, but since we only moved in a few weeks ago, we chose not to.

"Come on, Prue," Xander calls out and then whistles.

Prue comes running down the stairs, her collar jingling.

She skids around the corner, her paws sliding on the hardwood. She runs straight toward us, then around, and stops outside the garage door.

"How does she already know?" I whisper-hiss.

Xander chuckles, pressing his hand to my back to urge me forward. "Because she's a dog. They know everything."

I move the bags to one hand and open the garage door.

I set the bags on the backseat and climb into the truck. I'm beginning to see what Xander means about needing a family car, even if the idea disgusts me. I love my little car, and he loves his truck, so getting another vehicle seems like too much. Who needs three cars? But the idea of climbing in and out of his truck when I'm hugely pregnant or having to squat to get into my small car, is *not* appealing in the slightest.

I climb in the passenger seat and buckle my seatbelt. Xander lifts Prue into the truck and she pokes her head in between the seats, licking my arm.

"Hey, girl." I laugh, petting her head.

Xander climbs into the truck and looks over at me. "Are you ready?" he asks, tilting his head.

I know he's asking me if I'm ready to tell them—not if I'm ready to go.

I nod, and smile, but I'm sure he can still see the tension in my eyes. "Yeah, I'm ready."

It's a lie, though.

I'm so not ready.

I still haven't wrapped my head around this whole thing and now we have to tell people. Up until now it's been something fairly easy to dismiss from my mind—to pretend it's not real—but now there will be no denying this.

Ready or not, here comes baby.

We pull up to Xander's parents' house and find the driveway already filled with vehicles.

Which means we're probably the last ones here, and I can't delay the inevitable.

I hop out and smooth my hands down my fitted white dress. Looking at me, you'd have no idea that I'm pregnant. It's proof that looks can be deceiving.

I open the back door of the truck and grab the two gift bags while Xander gets Prue.

The bags are blue and red for the Fourth of July. I didn't

want to do anything babyish that would give it away before they got to the contents of the bag.

Xander meets me at the other side of the truck, with Prue on a leash. He takes one of the bags from me and then holds my hand. He gives it a slight squeeze and gives me a reassuring smile.

"It's going to be okay. *Breathe*."

I do as he instructs.

He lowers his head, brushing his lips over mine, and when he pulls away, I laugh. "You have lipstick on you now." I move the bag to my wrist so I can use my fingers to wipe the red smear away. "Got it—but whore red is a *great* look on you."

He snorts. "Noted."

"I'll buy you a shirt." I grin at him.

"I'm sure you will," he grumbles.

"Gotta feed my addiction."

We head inside, not bothering to knock. The house is empty, so Xander keeps going, straight out the back.

We find everybody gathered around tables, or standing talking. Xander's dad, Cooper, is grilling, and his mom is chatting with mine. His sister, Alexis, and brother, Xavier, are bickering—because siblings never grow up. I spot my brother, Rae, Jace, and Nova at a table hanging out. Nova sits on Jace's lap and he sips at a beer. Cade and Rae sit side by side, Cade's fingers brushing against her leg.

"So," I hiss under my breath, "are we doing this now or waiting?"

"Uh ..." Xander pauses, looking around at everybody,

and I can finally sense *his* nervousness about this whole thing. It's nice to know I'm not the only one freaking out. "I think we should do it now. Rip it off like a Band-Aid."

I try not laugh and fail. "Did you just compare the revealing of our child to ripping off a Band-Aid?" I whisper so no one can hear me. Besides, they're all so absorbed in their own thing they haven't even noticed us.

"I'm nervous, give me a break," he defends.

I smile, pleased that his feathers have finally been ruffled by this whole thing. He's been so calm the last few weeks, taking the whole thing in stride while I've freaked out. It's nice to know he's not as impenetrable as he always appears to be.

"Hey, guys!" I finally call out.

"Oh, hi!" Xander's mom, Sarah, cries. She hops up, hurrying over to us. "I'm so glad you guys came. I know you're probably still busy with the move." She hugs me.

"It hasn't been too bad," I say with a smile. "We finished everything within the first week. We have some more things to buy so the house isn't so bare, but other than that it's done."

"Well, that's great news. Your dad will be done grilling soon and then we'll eat," she says to Xander, and pulls him into a hug. "I've missed you." She stands on her tiptoes to kiss his cheek.

"I've missed you, Mom."

"Come, come." She waves her hand "Get a drink and sit down."

"Oh," I say, holding out one of the bags. "Can we do gifts first?"

Sarah smiles at the bag. "That was sweet of you. You didn't need to get me anything."

"This is for you and Cooper." She takes the bag from me.

"And this is for you, Lauren." Xander holds the other bag out to my mom.

"Me?" She points at herself.

"Yes, you," I laugh.

She hops up, leaving James for the moment, and grabs the bag before sitting back down with it.

Cooper checks the meat and closes the lid on the grill before joining Sarah to open the bag.

Xander and I stand by our parents to watch them open the bags—everybody else is watching too, curious to see what we got them.

Sarah rips at the tissue paper, pulling it out and dropping it on the ground while my mom very carefully removes it.

Cooper peers into the bag but lets his wife have her fun.

She pulls out a binky and my mom pulls out a onesie.

"What?" Sarah looks in shock from the item in her hand, to us, and back to the bag. She pulls out a onesie too, shaking her head.

"Oh, my God," my mom says, it clicking into place for her.

Her words must break through to Sarah because she screams—like *screams* bloody murder, drops the bag and items, and runs at us.

"You're pregnant?" she asks me, looking from me to Xander.

I nod. "We're having a baby."

She screams again and throws her arms around my neck. "This is so exciting! Oh, my God! I'm so happy!" She hugs Xander next. "I'm going to be a grandma!"

My mom comes over and hugs us too, then Xander's dad. Even James, my mom's boyfriend, hugs us and offers his congratulations.

"Wait a minute," my brother calls out. "You had sex?"

I roll my eyes. "No, Cade, this was an immaculate conception." He tilts his head, wondering at my sarcasm. "Of course we had sex, you idiot. That's how babies are made." I look up at Xander. "Honestly, how am I related to him?"

Xander chuckles and turns it into a cough.

"This is fucking weird," Cade mutters. "I'm going to be an uncle. Whoa."

"Does *he* have to put a quarter in the swear jar?" I ask Xander.

He shakes his head. "Nah, I think that's just for us."

"Darn it." I snap my fingers.

We move further into the yard and over to where our friends and his siblings hang out.

"Congrats, man." Xavier claps Xander on the back.

"Hey, Xavier. It's good to see you. I wasn't sure you were coming back for the summer."

He shrugs. "I thought about staying on the east coast, but I missed everybody, so here I am." He spreads his arms wide.

Xavier has one more year of school left—and since he's a smarty-pants he goes to Yale. I've missed having him around. He's a lot like me, a jokester, and the life of the party. He keeps things interesting.

He looks a lot like Xander too, with the same mop of dark hair and olive skin. He's a little bit shorter, though, and not nearly as built. He's still a muscular guy, but Xander's on a whole other level—but with his job, that's kind of a given.

"So, I'm totally going to be the godfather, right?" Xavier asks, looking from Xander to me.

"Uh ..." I hedge.

"No, I am," Cade pipes up.

Xander shakes his head. "We haven't even talked about it."

"Sit down, you fucker, *I'm* going to be the godfather," Jace pipes in.

We all look at him, because Jace is *never* the person to speak out, and nobody expected it on something like this.

"What?" He blinks innocently. "I like kids," he defends. "I'd be the best fucking godfather ever."

Xander shakes his head. "Between Jace and you, this kid is going to be cussing before it walks."

Jace leans back in the chair he occupies so the front two legs come off the ground. "That sounds like the coolest kid ever. Do we get bonus points for making it more awesome?"

"No, no," Xander chants. "That would *not* be more awesome."

Jace chuckles and leans over to whisper something in Nova's ear.

"I'm really happy for you guys." Rae stands and hugs me.

"Thanks," I say, though the words are on the tip of my tongue to tell her *I'm* not happy.

Cade hugs us too, and then Xander's sister.

Once all the hugs and congratulations are out of the way, we finally sit down.

I let out a groan, already feeling exhausted and we just got here.

Xander finally lets Prue off her leash to run wild in the backyard, and she takes full advantage of the freedom. She runs around the yard, chasing butterflies.

Xander rubs my knee and rests his hand on my thigh. He watches me carefully, like he's worried I'm going to have an anxiety attack or something.

So far, so good.

It's weird, knowing that everybody knows now, but it also makes me feel better to have someone other than Xander to talk about it with.

Our parents drag the other table over to us so that it's almost like we're all sitting together.

Sarah makes sure her spot is beside me. Once she's settled, she says, "I'm so excited for you guys. This is the best news ever. I was worried you were going to make me wait a few years for grandkids."

I laugh lightly, but there's no humor in the tone. "Yeah, me too," I mutter.

Xander squeezes my leg lightly in warning. We never really talked about it, but it was sort of a silent agreement that we wouldn't tell our parents that the baby was an accident. We didn't want that fact to somehow diminish their happiness over the news—because we knew they'd be thrilled.

Unlike me.

I'm coming around to the idea more every day, but it still scares me.

I can barely take care of myself, let alone another human being.

"Have you thought of any names yet?" my mom asks, raising a glass of lemonade to her lips.

I shake my head. "No, not yet. We've only known for a few weeks, so we haven't discussed names. This is all still very new." I gesture with my hands.

"Wait." Nova snaps her fingers together. "Is that why you were acting funny the day Jace and I were over?"

I nod, tucking a piece of hair behind my ear. Xander moves his arm to drape over the back of my chair.

"Yeah," I answer. "I suspected, so when I ran out, it was to get a pregnancy test."

"Oh, wow." Nova shakes her head, her lips parted in awe. "That's crazy."

"I know," I agree.

That's what I keep saying about this whole thing, that it's crazy. Some days I feel like it's a dream, but then I get sick and realize it's real.

"How have you been feeling?" Sarah asks, her voice breaking into my thoughts.

I shrug. "I have good days and bad days."

"Mostly bad," Xander mumbles.

I laugh. "Yeah, mostly bad," I agree. "Morning sickness is no joke—and why do they call it morning sickness? I'm sick all day."

Sarah smiles and pats my hand. "I know what you mean—I only experienced the all-day sickness with one kid, and it was no joke. Any guesses which one it was?" she asks, her eyes sparkling with humor.

As a collective group we all turn to look at Xavier. "What?" He bats his eyes innocently. "I'm a perfect angel, I'd never do such a thing."

Sarah snorts. "My whole pregnancy with Xavier, I cursed Cooper and told him I hated him. I was miserable."

"And then she had him, and he never shut up," Xander pipes in.

Alexis laughs and looks at her little brother, ruffling his hair. "You cried *all* the time," she tells him. "I remember asking Mom if we could give you away."

"Hey," Xavier whines, ducking away from her hand. "You guys love me, and you know it."

"We do now," Xander chortles. "But back then? Not so much."

Xavier frowns. They always make fun of him, it's one of the many perils of being the youngest.

"When are you due?" Sarah asks.

"February twentieth."

"Oh, that's plenty of time to get things ready. Perfect." She smiles optimistically.

I, on the other hand, disagree. That feels much too soon.

It's crazy for me to think that in a matter of months I'll have a *baby*.

Xander rubs my shoulders, sensing the tension I'm feeling.

I look over at him, flashing a grateful smile.

He leans over and kisses the corner of my mouth. "Breathe," he reminds me in a hushed whisper.

Whenever I get nervous I have this bad habit of holding my breath. I don't quite understand it, and it sucks, but thankfully I have Xander to remind me to breathe.

"Food's ready!" Cooper calls out from the grill.

I'm thankful for the small reprieve from baby talk.

I'm sure most women would be *thrilled* to talk all things baby, but not me. It makes me nauseous.

Or maybe that's just my morning sickness rearing its ugly head.

Ah, shit.

I take off running for the house, but I know I'm never going to make it. I veer off for a bush, heaving over it.

"Aw, Thea," Xander murmurs, pulling my hair away from my face. "I'm sorry, baby." He rubs my back. I know he truly feels awful every time I get sick. I wish he'd leave me alone, so he didn't have to see me like this, but he insists on being there.

When I'm done, I stand up, tears in my eyes. "That was embarrassing," I hiss, glancing over his shoulder to see if anyone is watching.

They all are, of course.

"Don't be. It happens." He rubs my arms.

"Do you think your mom has an extra toothbrush I can use?" I ask.

He nods. "I'm sure she does, but I'll ask."

"Thank you."

I head inside while he goes to ask and get a glass of water, swishing the liquid around my mouth and spitting it out in the kitchen sink.

The sliding glass door opens, and Xander steps inside. "She said there are some in the guest bathroom."

He nods for me to follow him down the hall.

"I can't believe that happened," I mumble, following him down the hall past family photos. I stop, smiling at one of him in high school. He's in his football uniform with his arm slung around my brother. They look so young.

"Checking me out?" he jokes when he glances back and sees me staring at the photo.

I laugh. "You're my husband, I can look all I want." I stick my tongue out at him. I point at the picture. "I thought you were so hot—no lie, I used to doodle Mrs. Kincaid on all my notebooks."

He smiles crookedly. "I'd be lying if I said that didn't make me happy."

"I had the biggest crush on you. It was next level—like stalkerish."

He laughs, his brown eyes sparkling with amusement. "I lived across the street, so I don't think it counts as stalking."

My lips tip up in a smile. "My old self would never believe I got to the guy. Let alone knocked up by him."

"I don't think it counts as knocked up when you're

married to the guy," he reasons with a raised brow.

I shake my head. "When it's a surprise it does. Now get me a toothbrush." I wave my hand, urging him forward. "I don't like tasting my throw up. It's disgusting."

"You're the one staring at my picture."

"You're the one talking," I argue back.

"I can never win with you." He shakes his head, but he's smiling.

"I know." I grin back. "You should give up and accept defeat now."

He shakes his head and heads further down the hall and to his right.

I follow him and watch as he ducks down and opens the cabinet beneath the sink. He locates a toothbrush and toothpaste and holds it out to me.

"Oh, thank God," I cry and take both from him gratefully.

I feel like I've spent the majority of the last few weeks throwing up and brushing my teeth.

Wash, rinse, and repeat.

Xander leans against the wall, his arms crossed over his chest while I brush my teeth. I start to tell him he can go, but I know it's pointless. He's probably worried I'm going to get sick again.

I finish brushing my teeth and leave the toothbrush on the counter, in case I *do* get sick again and need to brush my teeth before we leave.

I'm kind of scared to go back outside actually—in case the smell of the food makes me sick again.

But I know I can't avoid food for nine months ... or well, I guess it's seven now.

Holy fucking shit—that's crazy to think about.

In seven months I'll have a kid.

A real, live, eating, breathing, sleeping, pooping, and puking baby.

I'm so not ready for this kind of commitment in my life.

People joke that it's eighteen years, but it's a *life sentence*.

"Hey," Xander murmurs, stepping away from the wall and grabbing my arms. "What's going on?"

"Nothing," I lie.

He raises a brow. "Don't lie to me, sweetheart. Something's bothering you."

I exhale a heavy breath. "It's just scary, that's all." It's the same thing I've already said a million times over. I'm terrified of this whole thing. Xander says nothing's going to change, but for once he has to be wrong. How can a baby *not* change things?

He cups my cheeks in his large hands, my face nearly swallowed whole.

"I'm scared too. This is a big change, but I know it's going to be okay."

"How?" I practically whine. "How do you know?"

He shrugs his massive shoulders. "I just do. We're not tasked with more than we can handle. This has happened for a reason." He moves his hand to my stomach.

I close my eyes, ducking my head as I exhale a shaky breath. I'm moments away from crying.

He grabs my chin and forces me to look up at him.

"You'll see," he murmurs softly, his eyes flicking down to my lips. "This is a good thing, Thea. I know it is." He cups the back of my neck and presses his forehead to mine. "You're going to be the best mom."

I wet my lips with my tongue. "How can that be true when I have *no* idea what I'm doing? I don't even know how to change a diaper," I cry, laying my palms flat against his shirt.

He chuckles, the sound laced with amusement. "I'll teach you."

"*You* shouldn't have to teach me," I whine. "You're the guy. I should be the one teaching you."

His lips tip up into a crooked smile. "Since when have we ever done anything the normal way?"

"True," I agree reluctantly. I sigh heavily and rest my head on his solid chest. I hear his heart thump against my ear and my eyes close. I already feel better. Something about the sound of his heart always manages to calm me. It's my favorite sound in the world.

"We're going to figure this out. One step at a time."

He lowers his head and brushes his lips over mine. The kiss starts out soft, just barely a press of lips, but then it grows more urgent. Both of us yearning for more. My hands scale his chest, seeking purchase around his neck, and his fingers press into my waist.

I let out a little sound and he swallows it with a groan, backing me into the wall.

"Hey, Mom wants to know—whoa!"

We jump apart like two kids caught doing something

they're not supposed to.

"Well," Xavier chuckles. "I know now why I'm becoming an uncle so young. Bravo." He claps.

My cheeks flame and I duck my head against his chest. Normally, I would come out with something flippant but I'm going to blame my sudden shyness on another side effect of pregnancy.

"Anyway," Xavier continues. "Mom wanted to know if you felt well enough to come out or wanted to stay in here?"

Xander looks down at me, tilting his head and allowing me to answer since I'm the one constantly puking my guts up.

I nod, pushing my hair out of my eyes. "I think I'm okay to go back out."

"Cool." Xavier backs away slowly and then pauses. "Is everything okay?" he asks.

"Yeah."

He eyes us, and I can tell he's unconvinced, but he finally nods and leaves us alone.

"Your brother is entirely too perceptive," I mumble.

He chuckles warmly. "He's a Kincaid."

I know we can't hide out in the bathroom forever so I reluctantly pull away from him and head down the hall and then out the back door in the kitchen.

Everyone is sitting around eating, and they look up when they hear the door slide open.

"Are you feeling better, sweetie?" Sarah calls out, shielding her eyes with her hands. I don't know why she doesn't just wear sunglasses.

When Constellations Form

"Much," I reply, and as of right now, that statement is true.

The only unrest in my stomach is from the turmoil of worry and nothing to do with actual sickness.

I grab a plate and make a burger with lettuce, tomato, onions, and mayonnaise. I add some chips and macaroni salad to the side.

Xander makes his plate of food and we sit down where we'd been before.

"So," Sarah starts, clearing her throat, "now that you're pregnant, are you still going to look for a job or stay home?"

"I'm going to work," I snap, horrified by the idea of being a stay-at-home mom. "I'd go crazy being home all the time, especially with Xander gone a lot."

"You might change your mind," she warns with a knowing look.

I snort. "Doubtful. I need to be out doing something. I refuse to stay at home as his little wifey, making dinner every night, and taking care of the kids while he goes off and works and provides for the family. I want to work too, I want us to be equal, I don't want—"

"She doesn't want to feel trapped," Xander finishes for me, giving me a knowing look.

I've never talked about this with him before, I don't think I really knew how to voice how I felt.

I glance at my mom sadly. "Exactly."

"I just don't understand." Sarah shakes her head, her brow narrowed in confusion.

"Sarah," my mom interrupts, "she doesn't want to end up like me."

Sarah's eyes widen in surprise and then horror as she connects the dots. "Oh ... *oh*. But Xander's not your dad. He'd never trap you."

"I know he's different." I look up at my husband and he smiles down at me. "Xander is kind and good and amazing, but that fear of what could be still lies there." I tap my heart. "I grew up seeing my mom not be able to do *anything* and I vowed to never let that be me."

"It won't be." Xander presses his lips to the side of my forehead.

I love that he understands me, and accepts me, even with all my crazy.

I know I'm not the easiest to love, but he makes it seem like it's effortless.

The conversation turns to football, for which I'm thankful.

After we eat, we all help clean up, and then the guys go to play basketball on the driveway.

I move down to sit beside Rae and across from Nova—leaving the parents to themselves.

"I can't believe you didn't tell me." Rae smacks my arm lightly in jest.

"I'm sorry," I apologize. "Xander and I decided to tell our parents first, and then we figured today would be best since everybody could find out together."

Rae nods. "Okay, that makes sense, but still—I'm your best friend, you should've dropped some kind of hint."

I laugh. "The next time I get knocked up you'll be the first to know."

"Hey, what about me?" Nova pipes in.

"I'll call you too—conference call style."

"You guys need to come over and see the condo." Rae brightens, her whole being glowing. "It's almost ready. Do you think you guys could all come over for dinner one day to see it?"

"Yeah, of course," I say. Getting out and spending some time in the city with my friends sounds great.

"That'll be good with us," Nova adds.

"Are you liking living in the city?" I ask, taking a sip of water.

"Loving it," she answers, tucking a piece of dark hair behind her ear. "It's so nice being able to walk out the door and having everything within walking distance. How are you liking your place?"

"It's beautiful ... but quiet."

Rae laughs. "It won't be quiet for much longer."

"That's true," I agree, wiping the condensation off my water glass. "We need to start pinning down wedding details," I remind Rae. "It's going to be here before you know it. Do you have a solid date yet? I'll start looking at venues if you do."

"We think December second, it's the first Saturday of the month."

"That sounds like a good date. I'll start looking at places and send you guys some options."

"Thanks—I'm excited, but wedding planning is

stressful."

"That it is," I agree. "What color are you thinking for bridesmaids dresses? Pink is a lovely color you know," I joke.

Rae laughs and shakes her head. "No, no pink. I was thinking maybe an emerald green or purple. I haven't quite decided yet. Why didn't *you* have pink bridesmaid's dresses?"

"Because my mom and Xander's planned our wedding within a matter of weeks and turquoise was apparently the only color they could get." I roll my eyes. "I don't buy that load of bullshit for a minute, though." I close my eyes and groan. Opening them, I say, "This whole not supposed to cuss thing is going to take some getting used to."

Nova laughs. "You *do* have a potty mouth—but it's one of the things I love most about you. You're always so pretty and put together, but with the mouth of a sailor."

"Um ... thanks, I think."

"It was definitely a compliment." Nova smiles, the gesture causing her freckles to spread out.

"We need a girls' day," I declare suddenly, and they both groan. "Don't even think about trying to get out of it. We haven't done anything together in a long time thanks to how busy we've all been."

"What do you have in mind?" Rae asks.

I shrug. "I'll think of something."

"Please don't say shopping or nails," Nova pleads.

My jaw drops. "But that's fun."

"Maybe to you."

I laugh. "Okay, okay—no to those things. I'll try to come up with something fun and different."

Surely, in a city as large as this one, there must be *something* we can do that we'll all love.

The guys come strolling back into the yard.

"It's starting to get dark," Xander observes. "Let's head down to the park."

There's a park a couple blocks away from his parents' house that sets off fireworks—like the good kind, not shitty ones.

"Do you want to walk or drive?" I ask.

"I think we should walk, if we drive we might have trouble getting out of the lot and it's not too far of a walk."

"When you're as out of shape as me, it might as well be five miles," I grumble.

"If you get tired I'll toss you over my shoulder." His eyes sparkle with amusement.

"Or you could pull me in a wagon," I reason with a shrug of my covers.

He grins and holds out his hands to help me up from the chair. "I prefer caveman carrying."

I place my hands in his and let him haul me up. I fully expect him to let me stand on my own two feet, but the jerk hauls me up and over his shoulders.

"Xander," I cry, kicking. "I'm wearing a dress," I hiss in despair.

"Don't worry, I'll make sure the goods are covered." He then uses his very large hand to cover my crotch and butt.

"Put me down," I plead.

"No, too late now."

"Xander!"

Our friends and parents laugh, completely amused by the whole thing and *no* help to me whatsoever.

Dickwads.

Xander carries me the whole way to the park, which is a good half a mile from the house, and the jerk isn't even winded when he finally sets me down.

"Whoa." I sway as the blood rushes back to my head.

He reaches out and grabs my hips, steadying me.

"You okay?"

I wait a moment, making sure the sudden influx of blood to my brain isn't going to send me puking up my guts again. When I think I'm in the clear, I nod, and he releases me, taking my hand in his.

We follow his parents through the park, my mom and James behind us, and Jace, Nova, Cade, and Rae behind them.

We reach the center of the park where everyone is gathered and find a spot to sit in the grass.

Xander's parents have brought a couple of blankets and they spread them out so we can all sit down and not itch to death from the grass.

Xander sits down and tugs me into his lap.

I giggle as he buries his head into my neck. I scream when I feel his tongue swipe against my skin.

"Ew, get away," I bat at him.

He chuckles, amused by me and not the least bit afraid.

I settle between his legs, turning to face away from him so I can see the fireworks. It's almost completely dark now and people begin counting down.

"Ten, nine, eight, seven," they chant.

We join in with, "Six, five, four, three, two, one."

Right on cue, fireworks shoot off and explode in the sky.

The red fireworks light up the sky, and before they completely disappear, more go soaring through the air, exploding in a shower of blue and silver.

"Wow," I murmur, the different colors dancing over our skin.

More shoot off and these are purple. They rain down, reminding me of a weeping willow.

The whole show lasts no more than thirty minutes and ends with an explosion of so many fireworks that my ears will be echoing for the next day at least.

The park begins to clear out and we stand up, gathering up the blankets.

We head back to the house, and Jace and Nova immediately say their goodbyes before leaving in his ancient truck.

My mom and James depart next.

"Do you guys want to stay a while?" Sarah asks us.

Xander looks at me, letting me make the call. "I'd love to, but I'm really tired. I just want to go home and go to bed."

She nods. "Understandable. Let me wrap up some leftovers for you. It'll just take a second."

"I'll be in the car," I tell her. "Thanks for having us today," I say to Cooper, giving him a hug.

Xander heads inside and returns a moment later with Prue. She runs out and jumps up at me, her tailing wagging.

"We love having everybody over." He hugs me back, squeezing me a little too tight.

"Bye, we need to do something soon." I hug Alexis. "And you." I hug Xavier. "You should come over when you can."

"I'll try to fit you into my busy schedule," he jokes, his brown eyes shining.

"Such a kidder." I pinch his cheek.

"Hey." He pulls away, offended by the gesture while I laugh.

I hug my brother and Rae next, and they get in his Jeep and leave. I climb in the truck and Xander puts Prue in, getting in the driver's seat. I'm buckling my seatbelt when Sarah comes back outside with a bowl of macaroni salad and chocolate pudding that we had for dessert.

I roll down the window for her and she lifts the stuff up for me.

"Here you go, sweetie."

"Thanks." I smile gratefully.

"I'll see you guys soon." She waves at Xander in the driver's seat.

"Love you, Mom." Xander waves back.

"Love you." She blows a kiss as we start to back out.

I watch Cooper come up and wrap his hand around her waist. She smiles and leans her head on his shoulder. He presses his lips to the top of her head and her smile grows.

I look over at Xander beside me.

I want that to be us one day, watching our child.

And that thought doesn't even make me want to throw up, so I really should get a sticker or a lollipop for being such a grown up about this whole thing.

For the moment, at least.

thirteen
...

thea

14 weeks pregnant
Baby is the size of a nectarine

I've officially reached the point where none of my clothes fit.

I know I'm lucky that it's taken nearly four months to reach that point, but I still find it to be a major fucking inconvenience.

I huff and groan, and make all kinds of noises as I try to button my jean shorts.

I flop on the bed, sucking in my gut.

"Come on, come on, I can do this," I chant.

"Hey, Thea," Xander calls out, padding into the room

and completely oblivious to my struggle to get my pants on. "According to this app, the baby is a size of a nectarine this week. It also says that at this point all the internal organs are formed and will continue to grow as the baby gets bigger. How cool is that?" He finally looks away from his phone and notices me red-faced on the bed. "What are you doing?" he asks, tilting his head to study me.

"What does it look like?" I snap. "I'm trying to put my shorts on and they don't fit."

"Don't you have others to wear?"

I sit up and look to the pile of discarded clothes on the floor. "These were my last hope."

"Well, shit."

I raise a brow.

"I'll put a quarter in the swear jar," he promises. "Do you have *anything* you can wear?"

"I probably have a loose dress that'll work, but I wanted to wear shorts—and they're all too small now." I pout. "I'm only going to get bigger. I need to go get some new clothes." I gulp. "*Maternity* clothes," I hiss, like it's something dirty.

He shakes his head. "Well, you go shopping. I have to go to practice."

"Right, I love you."

He closes the few feet between us and kisses me. "I love you too, I'll see you later for your doctor appointment. I'll let Prue out before I leave."

"You don't have to go," I call after him, because I want him to know it's okay with me and I understand he has other obligations.

"Not a chance, sweetheart," he yells back and I shake my head.

I hear him whistle for Prue and her collar jingle.

I hop up from the bed and shed myself of the constricting shorts, breathing out in relief once they're off. My waist is thanking me for the sudden return of blood flow.

I scour my closet and finally find a loose pale pink cotton dress. I slip on a pair of silver ballet flats.

I look at myself in the mirror, shocked by how much my belly has popped in the last week. What sucks is, I'm at that awkward stage where people can't tell if I'm actually pregnant or just gaining weight.

I poke at my stomach and make a face.

It's just weird to think that there's a baby in there. I haven't felt it move yet, and the doctor said I might be twenty weeks along or more before I feel the baby move. He said it would be a few weeks after that before Xander would be able to feel it and notice it on the outside. I think he was a little disappointed by that fact. I'm growing the thing, though, so I should be the one to feel it first, let's be real.

I think about calling the girls to meet me at the mall but I know they hate shopping, and they're both busy with work and photography.

I let Prue back inside and then I head out to the mall. There's one about thirty minutes away. There's a smaller one closer, but who has time for that? If I'm going to shop I want to do it right.

Finding a close parking spot proves to be a challenge.

I drive around and around until I finally catch someone

pulling out. I snag their spot, while someone honks at me, but I'm pregnant so I get dibs.

I grab my purse and head inside.

I have no idea what I'm looking for, so when I reach the store I ask for help. I have zero experience shopping while pregnant, so I figure it's best to leave this to the professionals.

A couple hours later, and loaded down with bags, I make my way back through the mall.

And then I have to go and pass the stupid fucking Pottery Barn Kids and see all the cute stuff through the glass.

So, I mean, of course, I have to stop and look.

An oval crib calls to me, and I walk over, admiring it. It's decorated with navy blues and grays for a boy, with a little, stuffed elephant sitting inside the crib.

I spot a pale pink and cream bedding set and something in my heart lurches.

One day soon I'm going to be bringing home a little baby boy or girl, to a room decorated like any of these little sets.

That's crazy to think about.

Emotion overcomes and I begin to cry.

"Ma'am, are you okay?" a worker calls out.

"Fine," my voice is thick with tears. "Hormones," I explain.

This has been happening a lot lately, at random times too. Like yesterday, I cried because Xander clapped at something on TV and it scared me.

He felt awful.

I felt like an idiot.

I take a few deep breaths and manage to calm myself. "I'm sorry," I say to the worker.

She smiles and holds out a tissue to me. "It happens more than you'd think."

I take the tissue gratefully. "Thanks." I dry my eyes.

"Can I help you find anything?" she asks.

I shake my head. "Not yet. I don't want to buy anything until we know if it's a boy or a girl."

"When are you due?" She smiles kindly, not at all bothered by my sniffles.

"February twentieth."

"Well, we'll see you soon then."

I thank her again and then I head out of the store with all my bags. I got enough clothes that it should do me for my whole pregnancy. They already had fall and winter apparel out, with the summer clothes on sale, so that was nice.

I head to the car and put everything in the trunk. I check my phone before pulling out and find that Xander's called me and left a message.

I put in my password to listen to it.

"Hey, baby, I just wanted to let you know that practice is running late. Coach is being a dick and drilling us hard today. We shouldn't be too much longer, and then I have to shower. I *will* be at your appointment but I might be late. Coach is yelling at me to get my ass back on the field—I love you, bye."

I shake my head. The silly boy. Don't get me wrong, I'd love for him to be there, but I understand he has to work and has obligations other than me.

I put my phone in the cup holder, not bothering to call him back since he's either on the field or in the showers.

I drive straight to the doctor's office, arriving twenty minutes early.

Go me.

I sign in and take a seat.

Ten minutes later I get a text from Xander saying he's just gotten in his truck and he's on his way.

"Thea Kincaid?" the nurse calls out.

"Here," I respond, tucking my phone in my purse and standing.

She leads me back to the room and over to the scale. "We'll weigh you and then I need you to pee in a cup for me."

"Pee? Why? I'm pretty sure there's a baby in there." I point to my stomach.

She laughs, amused by me. "It's just procedure."

She weighs me and then hands me the cup with the same instructions as before.

I do my business and wash my hands. She's waiting outside the bathroom and takes me back to my room.

"You can hop up there now." She points to the bed thing. "Just pull your dress up above your stomach and drape this over your legs." She hands me a sheet. "The ultrasound technician will be in soon." She smiles before leaving.

I look around the room, at the charts on the wall. There's one of a baby in the different stages of development. They change a lot in a week, it's pretty insane.

The door opens and I look up, expecting the tech, but I smile from ear to ear when I see that it's Xander.

"How late am I? Did I miss it?" he asks, shutting the door behind him. His hair is still slightly damp from a shower, and he's in clean clothes—a pair of khaki shorts and a white t-shirt.

I shake my head. "No, you're right on time."

He breathes out a sigh of relief. "Oh, good. I broke probably ten traffic laws trying to get here." He takes a seat beside me.

"Don't do that," I scold, reaching over to touch his face. "I'd rather have you in one piece than at my appointment."

"Noted." He rests his hands on knees.

"How was practice?" I ask.

"Exhausting," he replies. "Coach is drilling us hard, but hey, it's expected. He gets more determined every year, I swear."

"But you love it," I state.

"I sure do." He smiles up at me. "But not as much as I love you."

I push his shoulder. "Ew, stop."

He chuckles as the door swings open.

"Hi, how are you?" The ultrasound technician asks. It's a different one than I had last time. She has pretty red hair, freckles, and kind eyes.

"I'm good, how are you?"

"Just fine." She smiles. "How have you been feeling? How's the morning sickness—it's noted on your chart from last time that it's been really bad."

I wave my hand back in forth. "It's better, but I still have moments where a smell or something becomes too much.

I've had a couple days where I've felt nauseous all day, but thankfully that seems to have passed."

"All right, well lie back and we'll get a look at your baby, and if you have any questions after then we'll go over them."

At my last appointment, I was ten weeks, and the baby still looked like a blob with vague arm and leg-like features.

She squirts the goo on my belly and I jump, expecting it to be cold like last week but it's surprisingly warm.

She laughs. "I'm nice and warm it up for you."

She turns the computer screen to us and grabs the wand, pressing it to my stomach.

She moves it around and then the baby comes onto the screen.

"Oh, my God," I breathe, tears filling my eyes. "That's really a baby."

This week there's no mistaking the tiny human growing inside me. This is the first time I've really and truly been completely overcome by the sight.

She presses a button and the sound of the heartbeat fills the air around us. It sounds strong, and fast, and entirely precious.

I look over at Xander, and he has a hand pressed to his mouth, his eyes filling with tears.

"That's our baby," I whisper, not even cringing at the word baby.

His eyes drift to mine. "It's perfect."

"Look, Mom and Dad," the technician speaks. "Baby is waving at you."

I gasp when I look back at the screen, because she's right, it does look exactly like the baby is waving.

"Let me get a picture of that for you." She presses a few buttons on her computer. "Got it."

"That's amazing," Xander murmurs, looking from me to our baby.

She finishes up her measurements and the screen goes blank as she removes the wand, the sound of the heartbeat leaving with it.

She wipes the goo off my stomach and smiles kindly. "Do you have any questions for me?"

"Will we find out the gender at my next appointment?"

She nods. "You'll be eighteen weeks, so it's possible."

Excitement fills my belly. I can't wait to know if it's a boy or girl.

"Any other questions?" I shake my head and look at Xander, in case he has any. He shakes his head too. "Okay, then. You can get cleaned up and just head to the desk to make your next appointment."

My next appointment where I'll find out if I'm having a son or daughter.

Whoa.

She leaves the room, and I remove the sheet, pulling my dress down over my belly.

Xander sticks with me as I check out and make my appointment and then walks me to my car.

"See you at home." He bends and kisses my cheek before turning and heading for his truck.

Butterflies explode in my stomach.

We've been together for three years and my husband still manages to make me feel all fluttery inside.

"Shit," I say, suddenly. "Mommy didn't say shit," I add a moment later, looking down at my tiny bump.

But Xander and I totally forgot our anniversary. We always celebrate both—the one where we got married in Vegas, and then again in August when we got married in front of all our family.

With the excitement of the afterglow of our vacation, the chaos of the move, and then baby, it slipped both our minds.

Also, pregnancy brain is totally a thing because I forgot where I put my toothpaste the other morning.

It was in the drawer, where it always is, for the record.

I finally get in my car and head home. Xander has beaten me there, since I stood in the parking lot for so long. I head inside and find him out back with Prue.

"Hey," he greets.

I take a seat on the deck step, since we haven't gotten an outdoor set yet.

"We forgot our anniversary," I announce.

"No we didn't, it's August eighteenth."

I shake my head. "No, the other one."

His lips part. "Oh."

"Yeah," I grumble. "I feel better that you forgot too, because you never forget that kind of thing."

He chuckles and takes the ball from Prue, tossing it for her to catch. "We've had a lot going on. So what do you want to do for our belated anniversary?"

I grin. "Let's keep it simple—*Jaws* and McFlurries." I do a little dance where I sit, because McFlurries are the best.

He smiles, throwing the ball again. "Sounds good to me."

We've probably watched *Jaws* at least two-hundred times —at least it feels like it—but it never gets old.

"I'll get the ice cream," he says, taking the ball from Prue and starting back to the house. "You get the movie and popcorn ready."

I clap, excited. "I can handle that."

I hop up and follow him inside.

He grabs his car keys and heads out, taking Prue with him since she loves to ride in the car.

I put the popcorn into the microwave and get some drinks ready. By the time Xander gets back, I have our popcorn and drinks set up on a tray on the couch and the movie is ready to go.

Prue comes running in and jumps up on the couch.

"Hey, girl." I pet her head and she snuggles beside me.

Xander hands me my Oreo McFlurry and I eye his M&M one with distaste.

"Everyone knows Oreo's the best," I grumble, wiggling around on the couch. He grabs a blanket and drapes it over my legs before plopping beside me.

He flashes me a smile, his eyes sparkling with amusement. "We'll agree to disagree."

I pick up the remote and press play—a feeling of contentment washing over me as the movie starts.

You'd think I'd be sick of it, with as many times as I've watched it.

But it never gets old.

My ice cream tastes like heaven. I've always been mildly addicted to McFlurries but now that I'm pregnant, I want them all the time.

I've asked Xander to run out at least three times this week to get me one.

He never complains.

Xander finishes his ice cream and reaches for the popcorn.

"Mmm, you got this perfect." He points at the popcorn.

"Duh, because I'm perfect. I can do no wrong," I joke.

He smiles back and grabs another handful of popcorn.

"I'm sorry I forgot our anniversary," he says after a bit. "I feel like an ass."

"I forgot, too," I remind him.

He shrugs. "Yeah, but I'm me and you're you."

"Hey." I smack his shoulder and he laughs.

The movie is almost over, and when I glance outside, I realize the sun is beginning to set.

Xander reaches over, twining his fingers in my hair and drawing me to him.

"I love you, you know that, right?"

"Yeah, I know."

"You're supposed to say you love me too," he jokes.

I shake my head. "But you already know that."

He nods, his eyes flicking to my lips. "I do."

I don't know who moves first, I don't think it matters, but suddenly I'm in his lap and he's attacking my mouth like he hasn't kissed me in forever.

I moan and he groans low in his throat in response.

His fingers push at my dress, where it's bunched around my hips, and he lifts it up and over my head.

His eyes rake over me, from the curves of my breasts to the tops of my thighs. His eyes linger on the soft mound of my stomach.

"You're so beautiful," he murmurs, finally looking into my eyes.

"Please," I beg.

He touches his fingers to my lips. "Please, what?"

"Fuck me," I breathe the words. "And I swear to God if you tell me to put a quarter in the swear jar I just might poke your eye out."

He grins and then silences me with a kiss.

My fingers delve into his hair, tugging on the strands to draw him closer.

A little scream escapes my throat when he moves suddenly, launching me onto the couch and then diving on top of me.

My fingers fists into the fabric of his shirt, tugging it off as quickly as I can.

His warm, tan, skin comes into view and I skim my hands along the smooth planes of his chest.

His hips press into mine and my legs fall open.

He grabs the cup of my bra and tugs it down. I wiggle so I can sit up and take the cumbersome thing off.

He cups my breasts and my back arches off the couch. My boobs are incredibly sensitive right now. Not really sore, just tender.

He flicks his tongue over my nipple and my hips buck against his.

"Xander," I plead. "I need you."

His eyes flash with desire. He grabs my panties, pulling them roughly down my hips.

He stands and sheds himself of his pants and then settles between my legs. He guides himself inside me and I moan, my fingernails raking his chest.

"More," I beg.

He pushes in all the way and I gasp.

"Oh, God," I moan, biting my lip.

He kisses me, silencing anything else I might say.

Everything then fades away, and all that exists is him and me, and this, and us.

We might've forgotten our anniversary, but *this* is perfect, and I wouldn't have it any other way.

fourteen
...

thea

15 weeks pregnant
Baby is the size of an apple

"How's the job hunting going?"

"Just great," I grumble, propping my head in my hand.

I met Rae and Nova at a little café near where they live for breakfast.

"That good, huh?" Rae raises a brow and then slurps at her iced coffee.

I roll my eyes. "Everyones excuse is that I need more experience in social work, but *how* am I supposed to get experience if no one will take a risk on me?" I frown, honestly put out with the whole thing.

"Being a millennial sucks," Nova agrees. "Old people think we're lazy and don't want to work, but that's not the case at all."

"Amen," I agree. "How's the job hunting going for you guys?"

Rae shrugs. "I've booked a few weddings, and maternity shoots—you should let me do yours." She brightens.

I nod. "Yeah, I guess I should have that done in a couple months. I didn't even think about it," I grumble.

There's a lot to take into consideration when having a baby—things I didn't even know to think about.

Like the fact that you're not supposed to use bumper pads in cribs, because it can lead to SIDS. Or that your nipples can bleed if you're breastfeeding.

I do *not* want bloody nipples.

"So, what about you?" I turn the conversation to Nova.

She wipes the condensation from her cup of iced coffee and shrugs. "Joel and I are talking about teaming up, since we work well together, but I'm not sure exactly what we can do to make a *business*, since neither of us is interested in doing what Rae does. We prefer the art of it." She shrugs. "So for now, I dream and work at the record shop."

"Do you think you guys could come by for dinner this week?" Rae asks, looking from me to Nova and back again. "I know it's taken a while, but everything is finally in order and I want you guys to see the place."

"Yeah, of course," I say, picking up my cup of lemonade. "It's not like I have a job to worry about," I joke, because if I don't I might cry.

Nova nods. "Yeah, that's fine with me."

"Saturday night?" Rae suggests with a raised brow, opening her phone calendar app to add it in.

"Yeah," I say.

"Yes," Nova chimes in.

It'll be nice to spend the evening with everyone. We've all been so busy this summer so we haven't spent much time together. I've been shocked by how this whole baby thing has taken up so much of my time.

When I'm not looking for a job, I'm researching, and there seems to be an endless amount of things you need to know.

It's stressful. I feel like I need to take a test before they send me home with the baby.

Rae snaps her fingers in front of my face, bringing me back to reality.

"Yoo-hoo, Thea? Where'd you go?"

"Sorry, I spaced out." I shake my head, bringing myself back to reality.

"I asked if you guys had any suggestions for dinner on Saturday?" she prompts, tilting her head to wait for our answer.

"Ooh, I vote for Cade's scrambled eggs and your pancakes—I miss the breakfast you guys would make. Besides, breakfast for dinner is the best thing ever."

"That sounds good to me," Nova agrees. "Besides, she's the pregnant one so you should do what she wants."

I laugh. "I'm hungry all the time," I confess. "But I also throw up all the time, which means I try not eat. It's a vicious cycle."

"I don't envy you a bit." Rae shakes her head.

"You better watch out," I warn her, "or my brother will start poking holes in condoms."

Nova snorts at this and slaps a hand over her mouth, muttering, "Sorry."

"He better not even think about it." Rae laughs. "I know he wants kids—I've told him to give me a few years, though."

"I wanted to wait too, but apparently my husband has super sperm." I point to my belly for evidence to my proclamation.

Both the girls laugh, and I'm glad we can make light of the situation.

"You guys will be great parents," Nova tells me with a small smile.

"Thanks." I smile back at her, touching my fingers to my growing belly. I'm still in that awkward stage where people can't quite tell if I'm pregnant or just gaining weight—but another week, and I'll be completely rounded and there will no longer be any way to deny it.

This is happening.

"Xander's going to be a great dad," Rae adds. "He's going to be crazy about that kid."

Nova nods along with her. "You find out the gender at

your next appointment, right?" she asks, munching on a piece of pita bread and hummus.

I nod, tucking a piece of hair behind my ear. "Yeah, I can't wait. That's probably the most exciting thing about this whole process."

"Are you going to find out at the appointment or wait and do a reveal?" Nova asks, wiping some crumbs on a napkin.

"Uh ..." I pause. "We hadn't really talked about it. I'm not sure I have the patience to wait. This has already sucked enough."

"So," Rae begins, "what do you want? Boy or girl?"

"I haven't really thought about it," I answer honestly. "I'm super girly, so a girl would be fun, but a boy would be fun too. I'd love to see Xander teaching him to play football, but he could teach our daughter too." I shrug. "It doesn't really matter."

"Are we allowed to take bets?" Nova asks.

I laugh, taking a sip of my lemonade and shrug. "Sure, I guess."

"I vote girl," Nova chimes, raising her hand.

"And I vote boy." Rae raises her hand.

I shake my head. "I wonder what the guys think it is."

"We'll ask them." Nova laughs softly and shakes her plastic coffee cup. It's almost empty and her ice jingles against the sides.

"I'm curious now what Xander thinks it is. I don't really have any sort of maternal instincts that are telling me, oh it's a boy, or, oh it's a girl." I shrug, and pick up my cup. "Maybe I'm broken."

Rae laughs and shakes her head. "If I was pregnant I doubt I'd have any sort of idea on what I was having. Stop trying to make something out of nothing." She reaches over and pats my hand like a mother would.

Changing the subject, I say, "Did you and Cade like any of those wedding venues I emailed you?"

She sits up a little straighter in her chair. "We both liked the rooftop idea, but then we remembered the wedding's in December."

I smack my forehead. "In my defense, pregnancy brain is totally a thing."

She grins at me. "We both got quite a laugh about it."

I shake my head. "I'm such an idiot."

"It's okay. The historic hotel downtown you suggested is probably the best fit, if the date is still available."

"I'll check when I get home, if you're sure?"

She nods. "Yeah, go for it."

"I can't believe my big brother is getting married *after* me. I never thought that would happen." I shake my head.

Rae laughs. "That's what happens when you get drunk in Vegas and wind up asking your crush to marry you."

I blush. "You guys are never going to let me live that down, are you?"

She grins back. "Nope, never."

I sigh, resolving myself to the fact that they're going to bug me about this forever.

"Oh, shoot." Nova jumps up from her seat, nearly

knocking over her nearly empty coffee. "I have to go to work. I'm going to be late. I'll see you guys Saturday." She grabs her purse and then bends to hug us both before running out the door of the shop.

"Are you going to ditch me too?" I raise a brow at Rae.

She laughs and shakes her head. "Nope, you're stuck with me."

"Oh, good." I breathe out a sigh of relief. "I'm going to get a cupcake," I tell her, and hop up to go order.

It's liable to make me sick, but a cupcake is worth the risk.

I order my blueberry cupcake with lemon frosting and head back to the table. Lately, I've been craving lemons—of all the crazy things. I asked Xander to go out and buy me whole lemons the other night and then I proceeded to eat them like an orange. He looked at me like I was crazy the whole time, but I'm growing a human so I'm allowed to be insane.

I remove the wrapper from my cupcake and take a bite.

"Oh, my God, that's is so good," I mumble around my mouthful of cupcake. "Best damn cupcake I've ever eaten." I groan. "Text me to remind me I have to put a quarter in the Swear Jar when I get home."

Rae immediately picks up her phone to do just that. My phone chimes a second later with the reminder text.

Xander and I should be embarrassed by how full the jar already is. Well, *I* should be, because the majority of it is my quarters. He's maybe had three slips, while I've had dozens.

I can't be expected to change overnight.

Sometimes habits die hard.

And, apparently, this one doesn't want to die at all.

I finish my cupcake, and since it seems to be staying down I decide to order another one for later. Rae looks at me like I'm crazy, but, again, I'm growing a human.

Armed with my cupcake box and a refill of lemonade, Rae and I head outside in the summer sun. It's the third week of August, and I can't believe how fast the summer is passing. I'm glad that I'm not going to be hugely pregnant until the winter, though. I don't think I could stand the summer heat at nine months pregnant.

"Let's run in there." Rae points to a shop that's full of stationary.

I shrug. "Lead the way."

I follow her inside the store, and I'm immediately overwhelmed by the smell of paper. I throw down my stuff and slap a hand over my mouth, running back outside.

I manage to make it around the corner and to a bush before I empty my stomach.

Goodbye, cupcake. You were good while you lasted.

"Thea? Thea? Are you okay?" Rae calls, her steps thudding on the concrete behind me. She reaches me and touches her hand to my back. I wipe the back of my hand over my mouth and straighten.

"I'm okay," I tell her, my voice slightly shaky. "It was just the smell of the paper. It was too much."

"I'm so sorry. I should've thought."

I shake my head. "You never know what will trigger the

sickness. Don't feel bad. If it's okay with you, I just want to head home now."

She nods sadly. "Yeah, okay. I'll walk you to your car. Let me go back in and get your stuff."

I nod, smiling gratefully at her.

She returns a minute later with my stuff and we then walk side by side to my car.

"You need a new car," she tells me.

I laugh, placing my purse and cupcake on the passenger seat before turning around to face her. "That's what Xander says."

"Xander's always right." She grins, waiting for my reaction.

I rolled my eyes. "Don't tell him that—he doesn't need a bigger head than he already has."

"Xander's the least cocky guy we know," she counters. "Jace is the worst."

I throw my head back and laugh. "You have a point. We need to knock him down a few pegs."

"I notice you always seem to try to do that."

I wink. "What can I say? Some people have a talent, like playing piano, or making pottery, mine is deflating guy's egos. Someone has to do it." I sigh heavily like it's *such* a hard job.

"Bye, you nut." Rae hugs me.

I hug her back and then head around to get in my car. She waves from the sidewalk, the wind stirring her hair. Her dark brown hair is halfway down her back now.

I pull away from the curb and when I look in my

rearview mirror, I see Rae walking away in the opposite direction.

We're all going in different directions now, and it makes me sad.

I miss what used to be, and I'm terrified of what's to come.

fifteen
. . .

xander

15 weeks pregnant
Baby is the size of an apple

I walk in the house after practice, my body spent.

Everything aches.

Seriously, things I didn't know could ache, do—like my toenails.

"Something smells good," I call out, kicking off my shoes in the mudroom.

Prue comes running at the sound of my voice, and I bend to greet her. "Hey, girl." I kiss her head. She sticks her tongue out and licks my face.

"I made lasagna!" Thea calls back, and then I can hear her singing along to a song.

"I got you something ... Well, the baby something." I stand and round the hallway into the kitchen.

I smile when I find Thea in the kitchen, her hair clipped up, and wearing nothing but a pair of underwear and one of my white dress shirts.

Fuck, I'm the luckiest guy in the world.

It's moments like these that hit me the hardest, how lucky I am. It's not something I ever want to take for granted.

Thea smiles at me and it hits me like a ton of bricks.

I used to live for football, and even my grades—because fuck if I was ever going to fail—but now all I live for is that girl's smile.

"Hey," she greets me with a smile, swaying her hips to the song.

"Hi, beautiful." I lean against the counter, holding the gift in my hand. I asked the lady at the store to gift-wrap it, and when I did she asked me if the baby was a boy or girl so she could match the paper. I told her we didn't know yet, so she wrapped it in a pale yellow paper with green ducks.

"I missed you." She leans over to meet me and kisses me, before returning to what she's doing, which is covering bread with some sort of butter garlic sauce.

"Do you want to open your present?" I ask, tossing the small box from one hand to the next and catching it easily.

She stops what she's doing and flicks a piece of hair out of her eyes that's fallen loose from her clip. "I told you I didn't want to buy anything for the baby until we knew if it was a boy or girl. We have a couple more weeks."

I grin, undeterred by her words. "Trust me, this was perfect and you're going to love it for a boy or a girl."

"All right, if you say so." She stops what she's doing and cleans her hands on a striped dishtowel. She holds her hands out for the present and I hand it to her. "Something isn't going to jump out and scare me, is it?" she asks, raising a brow.

I shake my head. "I wouldn't do that to you, now please open it," I beg, impatient.

When I was in the city today I drove by a store with all kinds of baby things so I stopped and went inside. When I saw this I knew I had to get it. It was made for our baby—and I selfishly wanted to be the one to buy the baby's first anything because I know Thea's going to go crazy once she knows the gender.

She peels the paper back slowly, her lips lifting into a smirk, and I know she's messing with me—making this take as long as humanly possible.

"Thea," I practically beg and she laughs.

She rips the paper off then, revealing the small white box beneath.

"A box?" She mock gasps. "What could it possibly be?" She shakes it, and listens.

"Thea," I warn again, and her smirk grows.

The girl is evil.

She lifts the flap of the box and pushes aside the pale pink and blue tissue paper.

"Oh, my God." Her jaw drops as she removes the slippers from the box. "Xander," she barely whispers my name. "They're perfect."

I grin, pleased that she's happy. "I did good?" I confirm.

She nods, clutching the slippers to her chest. "They're perfect."

When I looked over in the store and saw the hand-knitted shark slippers, almost an exact replica of the ones I got Thea years ago, except baby-sized, I knew I had to get them.

Thea's lower lip begins to tremble and I'm shocked when I see a tear course down her cheek. "Thea?" I probe.

She sniffles. "I'm okay ... It's just ... this was really sweet ... and I'm pregnant ... and hormones." She shrugs by way of explanation.

I go around to the other side of the counter and bring her into my arms. She wraps her arms around my back, clutching at my shirt. Her tears dampen my shirt.

"I didn't mean to make you cry," I murmur, kissing the top of her head.

"S'okay," she mumbles against my shirt. "It was a good cry."

I step back and take her cheeks in my hands, rubbing my thumbs over her smooth skin. "I love you, and I already love this baby so much," I tell her honestly and her eyes lower. "This is going to be amazing," I whisper, my breath tickling her face.

Her hands move around to my front, pressing into my abs. "I hope you're right."

"I know I am, sweetheart." I kiss her nose. "Can I help you finish with dinner?"

She nods gratefully and wipes her eyes with her hands. "Can you pull the lasagna out of the oven? I'll finish with these and stick them in there for a few minutes to brown and then everything is ready."

"Sure thing." I grab an oven mitt and pull it out. It smells delicious, and I can't wait to dig in. I'm starving.

I set the lasagna on the cooling rack and Thea pops the bread in the oven, closing the door.

I wind my arms around her hips and pull her against my chest.

"Xander." She giggles, trying to pull away, but I don't let her.

Now that I've caught that girl I'm never letting her go.

"Dance with me," I whisper in her ear.

"Why?"

I brush my lips over the curve of her neck. "Because there's music and I want to dance with my wife." We're already swaying slightly back and forth.

She turns in my arms to face me, wrapping her arms around my neck. "Dance then, ball boy."

I shake my head. "Do you always have to make jokes when I'm trying to be romantic?"

She grins up at me. "You wouldn't have me any other way and you know it." She winks.

I smile back at her, because she's right. We move to the song, slow dancing in the kitchen.

I know it's a simple thing, dancing with my wife in the

kitchen of our new home, but this is something I'll never forget.

Especially her tiny little bump pressing into me—I definitely never want to forget the feel of that.

"Ugh," she says suddenly.

"What?" I ask, worried.

She clears her throat. "I just keep feeling this weird fluttering feeling in my belly. I think it's just gas or something—the joys of pregnancy."

I tilt my head, thinking over something I read. "Thea ... I think you're feeling the baby move."

She shakes her head, looking at me like I'm crazy.

"No, no way."

She stops dancing and backs away from me, getting the bread from the oven and setting it beside the lasagna. Prue watches us from the floor, hoping for a crumb.

She stands with her hands on her hips and looks at me. "Do you really think it's that?"

"I think so." I nod. "I read something that said a lot of women think it's gas when it's really the baby moving." She presses her hand to the small swell of her stomach. "Are you feeling it now?"

She nods. "Yeah."

"Can I feel?" I hold out my hands to her stomach and wait for her to nod. When she does I place my hands against the white shirt and feel. I don't feel any movement, just the heat of her skin. I frown, disappointed.

"You don't feel it?" she asks, and she sounds as sad as me.

I shake my head. "No, but don't freak out. I also read

that the mother feels it first before it's noticeable on the outside—so if that's what it is I should feel it a few weeks."

I keep my hand pressed against her stomach, hoping maybe I'll feel something. She places her hand over mine.

"This baby is so lucky to have you as a daddy," she tells me.

I remove my hand and cup her cheek. "And you might not see it, but this baby is incredibly lucky to have you as its mommy."

She looks away, like she doesn't want to hear my words—doesn't want to believe them.

I still haven't figured out a way to show her that she can do this, but I know I'll think of something eventually.

For now, all I have are words, and I'll keep telling her over and over again until she believes them.

"You're too good to me," she finally says.

I shake my head. "Just telling the truth."

She steps up on her tiptoes and presses a kiss to my lips before backing away.

"Let's eat, I'm hungry."

She doesn't have to tell me twice.

I cut the lasagna and set out our pieces on plates. Thea adds the bread.

She carries the plates over to the table and then I get us each a bottle of water.

"Thanks for making dinner," I tell her, sitting down across from her.

"You're welcome." She grabs a napkin from the basket in the center of the table.

I dig in and the food is amazing. After a long day of being in the gym and then a grueling practice this is much needed.

"Thank you for the baby slippers," Thea says around a mouthful of lasagna. "I can't believe you found ones that practically match mine."

I grin at her. "I'm magical like that."

"You're something, that's for sure," she agrees.

"Rae invited us to dinner Saturday and I said that was okay with us—it is, right?" She raises a brow, baiting me to see if I've made plans that extend beyond Friday—which is our second wedding's anniversary.

Three years, it's insane.

I wince. "Um, no."

"No?"

I shake my head. "No, because I made plans for us to leave Friday and go somewhere over the weekend."

"Humph," she harrumphs, obviously pleased to have pulled this information from me.

"I'm not telling you where we're going, so don't even waste your breath asking," I warn her.

"You're mean." She frowns.

After I forgot our first wedding's anniversary, I felt like shit, and I set about making it up this time around.

I booked us a three-day stay in a nice cabin up in the mountains. Just me, her, and nature. I know it won't exactly be Thea's kind of thing, but the place is nice with an amazing view and a great spa, so she'll survive.

"You'll let Rae know we need to reschedule?"

She waves a hand dismissively. "Yeah, I'll tell her."

We finish our dinner and clean up together. I let Prue out and Thea folds the blankets in the family room.

I come back in with the dog and grab Thea, tossing her over my shoulder.

"Xander!" she squeals as I run up the stairs with her.

I smack her butt and she laughs harder.

I push the doors open into our room and jog over to the bed, dropping her on it.

"You suck," she says, looking up at me with her hair fanned out around her head.

I lean over her, bracing my arms on either side of her head. "You love it and you know it."

I pull away from her and grab a pair of sleep pants from the drawer. I already showered after practice, so I change my clothes and climb into bed.

Thea changes into her pajamas and gets in bed too.

"We should talk about baby names," she prompts, grabbing the baby name book off the side table.

She picks it up and flips to a page. "I like Arielle for a girl."

"Like *The Little Mermaid*?" I wrinkle my nose.

She rolls her eyes. "That's Ariel."

"Hate it."

She sighs. "Moving on. What about Aiken for a boy."

"Are you going in alphabetical order?" I joke.

"Yes," she sighs. "It's easier. I have them all marked that way."

"Aiken is a no," I say. "It sounds like Anakin."

"Oh." Her lips part. "I didn't even notice that. Okay, girl name ... Brielle?"

I raise a brow. "Do you have a thing for names with *elle*?"

"Apparently so," she laughs. "Boy name, Caleb."

I shake my head. "It's not bad, but it's too plain. I can't see us as Xander and Thea with a kid named Caleb."

She crosses Caleb off her list.

"Eh—never mind."

I grin. "What was it?"

"Elle," she tells me, amused at herself. "Okay, what about Finley for a girl?"

"Eh." I wave my hand back and forth. "That's the best so far but I think there's something better out there. Something more ... us."

She presses her lips together thinking.

"Do you have any suggestions?" she asks, handing me the book.

I take it from her and flip through it. "What about Hank for a boy?"

Her mouth parts, horrified, just like I knew she'd be.

"Xander," she hisses. "We can't name our potential future son something that rhymes with stank, bank, tank, and God knows what else." She gestures wildly with her hands.

I laugh. "Okay, Hank is out. It was just a suggestion." I play like I was serious about the name.

I flip through the book and land near the end of the alphabet.

I scan the names and grin to myself.

"That for a girl, and that for a boy," I point to the two different names on the same page.

She looks from the names to me, and back again with wide eyes. "Those are perfect," she breathes.

"It feels right to me too," I admit. "Wow, I'm surprised that didn't take us the whole pregnancy," I joke.

"Now we need a middle name."

She takes the book from me and flips back a few pages.

She bites her lip as she scans the page and then a slow grin appears on her lips.

"This one for a boy, and that one for a girl." She points out two different names.

I think it over, putting them with the first names I picked. I smile from ear to ear at her. "It's perfect, Thea."

She tosses the book down on the bed and throws her arms around my neck.

I press my hand to her stomach. "Did you hear that, Baby Bean Kincaid? You have a name. Now we just have to find out if you're a boy or girl.

sixteen
...

thea

15 weeks pregnant
Baby is the size of an apple

"Holy shit!" Xander looks over at me with a little smirk. I roll my eyes. "I'll put a quarter in the swear jar when we get home, scouts' honor." I cross my fingers over my chest.

He chuckles, entirely amused. "So you like the place?" he asks as he pulls up the rest of the drive to the chalet.

The house is huge, much too large for two people to stay in for a weekend. The side of the house facing us is covered with windows, which overlook the stunning view of the mountains.

"It's beautiful," I say honestly. "Especially since there's no snow."

"We're coming back when there is snow—I want to go snowboarding. We should bring everybody."

"That might be fun," I agree. "But I'm not snowboarding."

He shakes his head at me and parks the truck. "You'd be eight months pregnant, so yeah, no snowboarding for you."

I look down at my stomach and mumble, "Sometimes I forget the thing is in there."

He laughs. "Thing?"

I wave a hand dismissively. "Thing. Alien. Bean. Baby. Whatever you want to call it."

"If anything or anyone is an alien, it's you," he counters.

My mouth pops open for a retort, but I have nothing, because he's right.

I'm definitely a species of my own, and I'm perfectly okay with that.

We hop out of the truck and Xander grabs our bag—he tried to get me to put both our things in one duffel bag so we wouldn't have to contend with an extra bag, but I'm a girl and I need options so I shot him down. So, instead, I have my suitcase and he has a bag.

I'm thankful he didn't try to blindfold me this time. I might've karate chopped the stupid thing out of his hand.

We head up the stairs to the front door and Xander mutters to himself.

"I forgot the code."

"Are we locked out then?" I ask.

He shakes his head, putting down our bags. "It's in my email on my phone. Give me a second." He pulls his phone out of his pocket and presses a couple of buttons. "Got it."

He pushes the numbers on the electronic keypad and the door dings before he swings it open.

He grabs our bags and steps inside. I follow, my head on a swivel with my mouth agape.

"This place is fucking amazing!" I cry, and he glares back at me.

"Quarter," I mumble. "You know, you can't expect me to change overnight. I'm an intelligent, classy, lady that says fuck a lot so give me a break."

He shakes his head. "You read that in a meme."

"Memes are my life," I retort, as he sets our bags by the stairs. "So are McFlurrys, Cheez-Its, Nutella, and currently lemons—please tell me we remembered to pack lemons."

He covers his face with his hands. "Dammit."

"Swear. Jar." I smirk, rubbing it in that he's not Mr. Perfect after all.

"I'll go get you some lemons," he mumbles. "There's a grocery store not far from here."

"I'll go with you." I raise my hand to volunteer like I'm in school and he needs to call on me to pick me. "I'm starving. Me and the soul-sucking life force inside me need to eat."

He gives me a funny look and then busts out laughing. "You're too much sometimes—scratch that, *all* the time."

I shrug. "I have to keep things interesting. Otherwise, it gets dull."

"I'm going to take our bags up to our room and then I'll

be back." He adjusts the baseball cap he wears backward on his head. He's dressed simply today, in a pair of basketball shorts and a t-shirt, but he still looks hot as fuck.

"Quarter!" I shout, but then laugh because I realize it was a *thought* and I didn't say it out loud, so it doesn't count.

Xander comes back down the stairs. "Did you say something?" he asks.

I shake my head. "Nope. Maybe the place is haunted," I reason.

He laughs. "Not likely. Let's go." He places his hand on my waist, guiding me back to the front door.

We get back in the truck and Xander turns it around, heading out of town.

I'm starving, since I couldn't keep my breakfast down this morning.

Xander's right, there's a grocery store close by. He barely has the truck stopped before I'm hopping out and running in, because *fooooood*.

I grab a shopping cart and wheel it through the sliding doors. Xander jogs up to me, not even out of breath a little bit. "Thea," he scolds. "Don't do that."

I shrug. "You caught up to me in like five seconds."

"The truck was still moving." He narrows his eyes on me.

"I'm *hungry*," I defend.

He shakes his head and quiets, accepting defeat.

I roll the cart over to the lemons and get twelve because I'm going to need them to make it through the weekend. From the lemons, we move through the store to the snack food. I grab a box of Cheez-Its and a bag of sour cream and onion chips, and then I get some kind of queso dip that looks good enough to dip my finger in.

"Ooh, you know what else would be great?" I ask rhetorically. "Pickles!"

I charge through the store and Xander groans, running to keep up with me.

I find the pickles and stop the cart, admiring the choices. I finally pick one and unscrew the lid, pulling one out and taking a bite.

"Thea!" Xander admonishes.

"Imsohungy," I mumble around the food in my mouth.

"We have to buy it first," he hisses, taking the pickle from me and returning it to the jar.

Some guy on the same aisle chuckles. "Pregnancy, man, it turns our wives into savages."

I hiss at him ... So, yeah, he's right. Total savage.

I finish chewing the pickle in my mouth and then ...

"No."

I take off running, my eyes scanning for the restroom.

I manage to spot it at the front of the store\ and push a poor little old lady out of my way to get there.

I push open the swinging door and burst inside the bathroom.

Thankfully, there's an empty stall. I make it just in time as the small amount of pickle I ate comes up. I'd felt fine and nausea came out of nowhere—like it usually does.

There's not much in my stomach, so it's not long until the heaving stops.

I stand and make my way to the sink, splashing some water on my face.

"Thea? Are you okay?" Xander pushes his way in the bathroom—not caring that it's women only.

"Get out," I hiss. "You're not allowed in here."

"You're my wife, dammit, and you just took off, and I had to make sure you were okay. So people can just deal with it."

A woman comes out of one of the stalls, she's a little older, probably in her fifties and she smiles as she goes to wash her hands. "My husband was just like that," she tells me. "They only get worse the further along you get." She points to my stomach. "Good luck." She offers us a smile before heading out.

I turn back to the sink and splash water on my face. Xander stands tall and imposing behind me, but he looks almost boyish the way he's dressed and with the baseball cap.

I bite my lip, looking at him in the reflection.

"Don't look at me like that," he warns.

"Like what?" I ask breathlessly.

His dark eyes flash in the mirror. "Like you want me to fuck you."

A little gasp escapes my throat. I can't find the words to remind him of the Swear Jar and our promise, because frankly, he's right, that's exactly what I want.

One minute I'm puking my guts up, and the next I want my husband to bend me over this counter and fuck me.

Pregnancy is weird, man.

My whole body tingles all over, my nipples tightening,

and then the door to the bathroom opens and a girl squeaks when she sees Xander and the spell is broken.

"You can't be in here," she tells him, glaring at him like he's personally offended her. "Wait ... Oh, my God, you're Xander Kincaid from the Colorado Rebels, right? Can I get a picture?"

I roll my eyes.

"Yeah, sure." He shrugs, because he's too nice to say no, like I would.

She pulls out her phone from her pocket and holds it out for a selfie. "Eh," she groans at the angle. "Would you mind?" She holds her phone out to me.

I raise a brow. "Excuse me?" I glare at her phone like it's contaminated.

I know I'm being rude, but I just puked my guts up in a grocery store bathroom, I'm *still* hungry, and this bitch wants a picture with my husband, so I can't seem to find it in myself to be agreeable.

"Here, I'll do it." Xander intercepts the phone and holds it out, smiling and snapping a couple of photos of them.

The girl takes it and hugs him, smiling from ear to ear before running out of the bathroom and apparently forgetting why she was there in the first place.

"Don't be mad," Xander pleads. "I can't say no to a fan."

"I know," I sigh. "I'm blaming my pregnancy hormones on this irrational bout of jealousy."

His lips lift into a small smile. "You're always jealous, Thea."

I frown, because he has a point there.

I shrug. "I don't like sharing."

He laughs, entirely amused. "You're *not* sharing. I'm smiling for a picture."

"Eh." I wave a hand dismissively. "Can we not fight about this? I'm still hungry."

"Aren't you afraid you might get sick again?" he asks, tilting his head slightly to the side.

I narrow my eyes up at him. "I sneeze and have to vomit—so I'm going to have to take the risk."

He laughs, pushing open the bathroom door. "Whatever you say."

"I really wish I could suck on one of those lemons," I mumble as we head back to our abandoned shopping cart.

"Not until we buy it," he warns.

I roll my eyes. "Such a spoil sport."

He grins back. "Someone has to keep you in line."

Sadly, he has a point there.

We arrive back at the cabin—as Xander calls it, but seriously it's a freaking mansion and calling it a cabin doesn't do it justice—and unpack the groceries we bought. We got way too much, considering it's Friday evening and we leave Sunday afternoon. Thankfully, we don't live that far away—about three hours—so we can easily bring whatever we don't eat this weekend home with us.

Xander unpacks the Cheez-Its and I grab them and the Nutella.

"What are you doing?" he asks, the bag crinkling as he unpacks the items.

"Watch and learn, kemosabe." I unscrew the lid and pull off the seal on the Nutella, then open the box of Cheez-Its and break open the plastic bag. I dip a Cheez-It in Nutella and moan. "So good. You want one?"

Xander gags and shakes his head. "No, thanks. That looks gross."

"It's not," I assure him.

"I don't trust your cravings." He shrugs and starts putting things away in the cupboards.

I shrug. "More for me," I mumble, and dip another Cheez-It in the mixture.

I sit on the metal stool in front of the island.

The kitchen is a modern marvel with stainless steel appliances and granite countertops. The cabinets are a dark wood, darker than the wood floors. The walls are covered in reclaimed wood and siding and the ceiling is open up to the second floor, where it's then tin with crisscrossing wood beams. The staircase is L-shaped and stands near the front door. Across from that is the family room, which has a stone fireplace, large couch, and two leather ottomans. There's also a wall in there of solid books. I haven't gone upstairs yet to check out the rooms, but I'm sure they're just as lavish. Right now my priority is food and hopefully keeping it down.

Xander puts all the lemons in the bowl on the counter

and then crosses his arms, bending to lay them on the counter. "You good here? I have to go check on something."

I nod, completely absorbed in my food.

He straightens and jogs for the stairs, and I hear him pound up them a moment later.

"Just me and my Nutella, just the way I like it," I joke to myself, scooping out a dollop on my finger and licking it off. I look down at my stomach. My bump is still pretty small, but it's definitely there—and the maternity clothes are *much* appreciated ... well, I didn't actually end up buying maternity clothes, I just got regular clothes in a bigger size because they were cuter. "You're going to make me fat," I tell the Bean. "And not just because *you're* going to get big, but because you make me eat all the things." I reach for another Cheez-It and pop it into my mouth.

I hop up and get a bottle of water from the refrigerator. It's still warm since it's barely been in there five minutes, but I'm thirsty so I don't care. I swallow down about half the water, and then I look for a knife so I can slice one of the lemons.

It takes a minute of drawer opening before I find one. I slice into the lemon and cut it into little quarters. I eat the insides like someone would an orange, moaning the whole time. I don't cringe a bit at the sourness. It tastes refreshing and delicious.

Xander bounds down the steps and into the kitchen and cringes at the sight of me. "How do you eat those?" he asks.

"I'm *pregnant*," I say slowly, like he forgot.

He shakes his head. "Well, when you're done, get your

pregnant ass upstairs." He points over his shoulder to the stairs.

"Quarter," I warn him.

"We're on a roll today—we're going to pay for kid two's college soon."

"Kid two?" I echo. "How many kids do you want?" I ask, my voice spiking.

I don't know why, but in the last three years the topic of how many kids we wanted never came up. Yes, we talked about kids, but it was always in the vague sense of somewhere in the future we were going to have *a* baby. Since we both knew we wanted to have kids someday, we never ended up talking about *how many*.

He pulls out the stool next to me and sits down. "I want five."

I choke on my tongue ... or maybe that was a bit of lemon.

"Five?" I shriek, trying to catch my breath. "No. No way in hell am I pushing out *five* kids from my vagina. Nope." I shake my head. "That's insane. Why would you want five kids?" I press a hand to my heart and find that it's racing. "I think I'm sweating," I mumble more to myself, and pull my shirt away from my chest, using it to fan myself.

He shrugs. "I like kids. I want a big family. I grew up with two siblings and ... I don't know, I always wanted more."

"You're insane," I squeak. "I think I might pass out."

"You're not going to pass out, Thea," he says sternly. "How many kids do you want?"

"One," I answer, and he frowns. "Two max. A boy and girl."

He raises a brow. "If you have two you could get two boys or two girls, you know."

"Well, then, at least they'll have each other," I reason.

He shakes his head. "How have we never talked about this before?"

"Planning to leave me so you can breed someone else?" I ask, picking up another lemon slice and raising a brow.

"God no, Thea," he snaps, clearly irritated that I'd say such a thing even though it was a joke.

"Good, because I'd cut off your dick and shove it down your throat if you left me." I wink, trying to bring some levity to the conversation.

He huffs out a breath, that I know is a laugh he's trying to mask. "We're going to have to learn to compromise on things, you know?"

"I know," I sigh.

"Four," he answers.

"What? Four kids instead of five?" He nods. "No way. Maybe three—*maybe*."

He smiles slowly. "How about, instead, we agree to make it through the first one and go from there?"

I bite my lip, thinking his proposal over, and nod. "Deal."

"Deal," he echoes, shaking my hand and grinning, his eyes bright.

I think I just got pregnant again from that look alone—five kids might be out of my control.

seventeen

. . .

xander

15 weeks pregnant
Baby is the size of an apple

We shake on it, and the deal is done.

Thea doesn't know it now, but I'm confident we're going to have to more than two kids. Once this baby is here, she's going to fall in love and want a house full of babies, I know it, and I'm going to be more than happy to give them to her.

She wipes her crumbs off her hands and stands up. "What's upstairs?"

I smirk, looking her up and down—because she's my

wife, and she looks cute in a pair of shorts and a tight white top that stretches over her growing belly.

"You'll see." I stand and lead her up the stairs.

Her eyes scan the cabin as we go upstairs—I splurged renting it for the weekend, but I wanted to check the place out, because I think maybe, if Thea's on board, I want to buy it.

I want a place for us and the baby to be able to go, and our friends and family too. Sometimes you just need to get away from the craziness and this place allows for that. It's quiet, and in the middle of the woods.

In the summer, there are pools and spas on the main property, and in the winter you can go snowboarding.

Sounds like heaven to me.

Normally, I'm the more practical one, while Thea's not, but I know in this instance, chances are she's not going to agree with me.

I lead her down the hall and to the master bedroom. It's large, not as large as ours at home, though, with an attached bathroom. It has double doors leading out onto a deck that looks out back to a lake. Thea hasn't even seen the lake yet.

"I'm getting spoiled. First Greece and now this."

I smile back at her. "My first game is soon, and this is our anniversary, so I just wanted to get away." I shrug. "Chances are, we won't get away again before the baby's born."

She inhales a soft little gasp. Anytime I mention the baby being born she does that. I think it scares her to realize how close we actually are to having a baby—she's still in the early part of her second trimester, which makes it seem like we have time, but when you start looking at everything, we really don't.

"Things are going to get busy soon," she says instead.

I wish she wouldn't do that—I wish she'd be honest about how she feels instead of bottling it inside. She's going to explode one of these days. But that's Thea, always thundering ahead.

I take her hand and lead her to the bathroom.

I don't turn on a light, because covering the bathroom floor and counters are hundreds of little candles.

They were a bitch to light, but seeing the look of awe on Thea's face makes it all worth it.

I wanted to curse and stomp around trying to do it, but I kept my cool so I wouldn't ruin the surprise.

It was worth it.

The look on her face is everything.

"Xander," she murmurs, looking around the space, her skin glowing from the reflection of the candles. "This is amazing."

Her eyes land on the bathtub, it's large, room enough for the both of us. I've filled it with warm water—but not too warm, since her doctor said that was a no-no—added bubbles, and peony petals on top. I know roses are the norm, but peonies are Thea's favorite. There's a small wooden table stretched over the bathtub and I've managed to sneak some snacks up here without her seeing. I even have a lemon and a knife to cut it. The rest of the snacks consist of cheese and crackers. Glasses of ice water round out the display, since

Thea can't drink and I don't like rubbing it in her face. Plus, she wouldn't take too kindly to it.

"I love you." She wraps her arms around my neck and stretches up on her tiptoes to kiss me.

"I love you, too," I whisper back, rubbing my nose against hers. My fingers graze her back where her shirt has ridden up and she shivers.

Her eyes are bright and happy as she looks up at me, and I feel an immense sense of satisfaction because *I* put that look in her eyes.

She bites her lip, nibbling on it, and I reach up plucking it from her teeth.

"Don't do that, you'll bleed," I scold.

"I can't believe you did all this," she breathes. "I don't deserve you."

I tuck a piece of hair behind her ear. "Don't ever say that."

"Why not?" she asks, her voice slightly breathless. Her eyes keep darting around the darkened bathroom like she can't quite believe what she sees.

"Because that makes it sound like you're somehow less than me, which is the furthest thing from the truth. I've never met anyone that's more my equal than you."

Her lower lip trembles.

"Are you going to cry?"

"Yes." She wipes a tear. "I'm pregnant—apparently that means you cry at everything." She looks up at me, her hazel eyes wide. God, I hope our baby gets her eyes and not mine.

They're exotic and beautiful, unlike my brown ones. "You make me happy."

That sends a pang to my chest. "You don't know how good it is to hear that, sweetheart."

I want to make her smile, and laugh, and for all her days to be filled with joy for as long as I'm alive.

Her laugh is music to my ears and I never want to live a day without hearing it.

I kiss her again, because I can't help myself.

Her lips are warm against mine, and slightly tangy from a lemon, which makes me smile.

Her hands creep under my shirt, pushing the fabric up and I lift my arms, making it easier for her to remove it.

It doesn't take long for all our clothes to be piled on the floor in a rumpled mess. I take off my hat and drop it onto the pile and slip into the tub across from Thea, our legs bumping, with the table between us.

She laughs, picking up a petal. "Did you murder a peony?"

I shrug and the water sloshes. "It died for a worthy cause."

She sighs and drops the petal back into the water.

"We find out the gender at my next appointment," she says, and I'm kind of shocked that she's bringing it up.

I nod. "Yeah." I pick up a piece of cheese and cracker and pop it into my mouth. I shouldn't be eating cheese, but fuck it.

"What do you want?" she asks, cutting up her lemon and adding some to her water.

"Huh?" I ask, confused by her question.

"Do you want a boy or a girl?"

I shrug. "I don't know. Either would be fine, I'm a guy so I see myself with a little boy. It's easier to picture what to do. What do you want?"

"I thought I didn't care, but last night ..." she trails off and the water sloshes as she rubs her small bump.

"Last night?" I prompt, trying to get her back on track.

She inhales a breath. "Last night, I had a dream and the baby was a girl—and now I really want a girl." She looks away, her eyes distant. "I want *that*." She puts emphasis on the last word, and I know she means more than a girl.

"You want what?" I urge her to tell me.

She slowly brings her eyes back mine, and the sadness in them guts me. "I want what I didn't have growing up. I want to be a mom who plays dolls, and does her kid's hair, and plays dress-up and make-believe games. I want to go to dance recitals and games and encourage them to try new things. I don't want to be a failure like mine." She wipes away a tear. "Things are good now, but she wasn't always there. I want our kid to know I'm always there."

"Oh, Thea." My heart breaks. I wish I had some way to get to her, and hold her, but I can't. "I've tried to tell you, and you don't want to listen to me, but you're going to be an amazing mom. There's no luckier kid on the planet."

Her tears fall and she tries to hide them, but it's pointless.

Besides, there's nothing wrong with tears. Tears show you care, and that's never a bad thing.

"You're already a good mom, Thea," I tell her and she wipes her tears away.

"How?" she asks. "All I do is complain about being pregnant, eat, throw up, cry, and complain some more."

I laugh, because she's right. "That's true, but for you to say what you just did, you already care and love this child. That's what tells me you're going to be a good mom."

She mulls over my words and nods. "But it's still scary. I don't know what I'm doing. I've never changed a diaper, ever."

"Ever?" I ask, trying to think of some time growing up when she must have. "Didn't you babysit?"

She shakes her head. "No. My dad wouldn't let me."

I press my lips together, forcing back the not-so nice words I want to say.

Malcolm Montgomery tore his family apart piece by piece and he didn't even care.

I hate that all those years that I was close with them I had *no* idea, because I would've put a stop to it. Told my parents. Something. Cade and Thea shouldn't have had to grow up in that.

All I can say is, at least the man is gone, and things are good now. Thea and I have each other, and Cade has Rae.

"I guess it's not too late to babysit," I joke.

Even though I say it as a joke, it gives me an idea.

I think I finally have a solution to the problem, but I'm not saying anything to Thea yet. Over the years I've learned it's better to do and not ask.

So I don't say anything to her about my idea.

I grab her foot beneath the water and begin to massage it. Her eyes fall closed and she moans.

I work my way up her calf, getting dangerously close to her center, before moving my hand back down.

"I'm going to fall asleep," she warns.

"Do it," I tell her. "I'm not going to let you drown."

She smiles at that, her eyes still closed.

She trusts my words, and they're not a lie. I'd risk my life for hers, and now our child's. Call me crazy, but that's what love does to you.

eighteen
...

xander

15 weeks pregnant
Baby is the size of an apple

"We're lost," Thea announces beside me.

"We're not lost," I groan.

"We're lost," she says again, looking out the window. "Totally, and completely lost."

"No, we're not," I counter.

"Yes, we are," she argues. "I don't know about you, but all I see is trees, trees, and more trees!" She grows shrill at the end.

"Recalculating," the navigation system announces.

Thea gives me a pursed lip look. "See? We're lost. We're going to die out here and all they're going to find is our vulture-eaten bones and maggots covering our clothes. Let me tell you, my dress and Louboutin heels are not going to look good on a skeleton. I better text Rae my back up." She types furiously on her phone.

"We're not going to die, don't be dramatic, we're just a little turned around."

"Which is code for lost. Uh-oh."

"What?" I ask, stopping so I can mess with the navigation system. I'm not worried about stopping in the middle of the road, since so far there's been nobody but us. I guess in hindsight, that's not a good thing. At least if there were other people we could ask for help.

She wags her phone in front of my face. "I lost cell reception."

"Recalculating," the navigation system interrupts again.

Thea gives me a look that says she's not impressed. "We're lost, and now we have no phones, or navigation system."

"All right, so we're lost," I finally agree, letting out an aggravated sigh.

Someone told us about some natural spring that exists out in the woods of the complex our cabin is a part of, and we both wanted to check it out. Unfortunately, the directions they gave us were the shittiest directions known to man.

"It's okay," I say, remaining calm and in control of the situation, since neither is something Thea's capable of. "I'll just turn around and head back the way we came."

She eyes me. "How? It wasn't really much of a road and more of a path through the forest."

"It should be easy enough to follow my tire tracks."

"Whatever you say, Indiana Jones."

I shake my head and back up the truck to turn around. The road is narrow, only one lane, with lots of trees like Thea said, so it takes me a while to turn around without hitting anything.

Once I'm turned around I start the slow drive back to where we started.

Thankfully, I make it there without incident. There's a road that leads back to our cabin, and another that leads to the resort.

"Where do you want to go?" I ask, putting the ball in her court.

"Would you hate me if I said I wanted to go back to the cabin and watch movies?"

"We can do that at home," I tell her.

"I know." She shrugs. "But it's my favorite thing to do with you ... besides the obvious."

I grin slowly. "What's the obvious?"

She rolls her eyes, fighting a smile. "Sex, of course."

"Ah." I nod, fighting a smile. "Of course," I echo, matching her tone.

I turn to head back to the cabin. Considering we're spending the weekend away, I think we should go do *something* but if Thea wants to sit around and watch movies, who am I to tell her no?

I park the truck and we head inside. I got popcorn when

we went to the grocery store, so I start popping it while Thea selects a movie.

"How do you feel about *Dirty Dancing*?" she asks.

"I guess that depends—is anybody naked? Because it sounds like they're naked," I joke.

The family room is open to the kitchen, and she launches the remote at my head. I duck behind the counter and it bounces off the top, where it would have missed me anyway.

"You need to work on your aim," I tell her.

She makes some high-pitched noise, mocking me. I end up laughing harder.

She starts the movie and I finish with the popcorn.

"You want any snacks?" I ask.

"Just some lemons," she replies.

I shake my head. "Those can't possibly be good for you."

"I *want* a lemon." She gives me a look that says if I don't bring her a lemon she's either going to cut my dick off, or my neck—depending on if she wants me to live or not.

"Okay, okay." I raise my hands in surrender and slice her a lemon, placing the pieces in a bowl.

I'm learning quick that when your wife is pregnant, you'll do just about anything to keep her sane. Thea's crazy, on a good day—but pregnant, she's certifiable.

If that means she wants lemons—she gets lemons.

Sometimes, it also means I have to drive thirty minutes to the 24-hour McDonald's to get her a McFlurry. That's only happened once so far, so I'm not going to complain.

But something tells me the further along she gets, the crazier and worse she's going to get about things.

And I get it.

She has a baby inside her, and that baby is going to get big, and she's going to be miserable.

She's never going to want five kids.

Having a family wasn't something I thought about or obsessed over. I'm a guy. I had school, football, and family. But I knew I wanted a big family one day. Once I married Thea, I just started thinking we'd have five kids. That's probably something I should've thought to tell her, but it never came up—I knew she wanted a family some day, and I didn't take it further than there.

I carry the popcorn bowl and lemons over to the family room and settle on the couch by Thea.

"I miss Prue," she says. "She'd normally be cuddling with us."

"I miss her too," I agree.

She's staying with my parents for the weekend, since I didn't feel right asking Jace and Nova to watch her again.

"I guess, in a way, she's like our first baby." Thea wiggles around on the couch, trying to get comfortable.

I'm not sure she realizes she does it, but every time we watch TV or a movie, she spends a full minute wiggling her ass around until she makes a nest. Her nest usually involves me, a pillow, and a blanket.

Today is no different. She fixes a pillow behind her back and drapes the blanket over us before lying against my side.

The movie starts and she snags a handful of popcorn, smiling up at me.

If we would have actually managed to find the natural spring, that would've been nice. So would have the spa.

But this is my most favorite thing of all.

Just being with Thea.

"I want to buy this place," I say suddenly, blurting the words out in a horrible case of word vomit.

"Huh?" Thea says, thinking she hasn't heard me right.

"The cabin, this place is for sale. I want to buy it."

She sits up, looking at me like I'm crazy. I probably am.

In fact, I know I am.

But this place, and what it could mean for our family in the future is what spurns me on. Not just *our family*, but our extended one as well. Rae and Cade will be married soon, and I'm sure they're going to start popping out kids. Even Jace and Nova make comments here and there about kids.

One day, I want us all to be staying here with our kids running around together.

Even though not all of us are related by blood, we are still family, and I want our kids to grow up like cousins.

"Are you insane?" she shrieks. "A place this nice must be a million plus. It has six bedrooms."

"More," I say.

"More what?" she snaps, the blanket falling to her waist around her small bump.

"It's two-point-two million."

"Oh, my God." Her eyes are wide and she looks like she's going to pass out. "We can't afford that. We just bought a house."

"Actually we can. We can afford much more."

"Are you insane? No way!"

"Thea, we lived cheap for the first three years of our marriage. Almost one-hundred percent of what I made went straight into the bank. We're more than fine."

She inhales a shaky breath. "This is crazy."

"I want this for us." I take her hand. "Us, the baby, and the rest of our family. I want a place for everybody to go where we can just let loose and hang out. We might all be moving on and going in different directions, but I want a place we can all come back to that's ours. A place that's home."

Tears fill her eyes. "You're going to make me cry." She grabs her stomach suddenly and makes a muffled cry. "The baby kicked." She laughs. "I think the baby is saying they agree with daddy."

Thea smiles and I grin back.

"We're buying it?"

She giggles, rubbing her stomach, and nods. "Yeah, we are."

I grab her face and kiss her dramatically, which only makes her laugh more.

"We're insane," she says through tears of laughter.

"We might be crazy, but at least we're happy."

As long as we're happy, we have everything, so I'd say our life is pretty fucking full.

nineteen
. . .

thea

17 weeks pregnant
Baby is the size of a pear

Xander's gone to practice, so he'll be missing for the bulk of the day.

Which means I'm bored.

I spend ninety-nine percent of my time bored.

That's what happens when you can't get a job and you're stuck at home.

I let Prue out and then I head into town. I need *something* to do, so I might as well shop.

I head downtown, into the city, and park on a side street.

I pull my phone out of my purse and text Rae.

Me: Hey—I'm in town, can you do something?

Rae: No, sorry, I'm working.

I text Nova next.

Me: I'm hanging out in town today—are you free?

Nova: Sorry, I'm out with Joel. We're photographing the art museum today for their event next month. They wanted new photos for their fliers.

I groan and smack my hand against the steering wheel.

All my friends have jobs or things to do and I'm just pregnant.

My phone beeps again.

Nova: Jace is home. He doesn't work until evening. Ask him.

Am I literally so desperate to hang out with someone that I'd ask Jace?

The answer is yes, yes I am.

Me: Hang out with me.

Jace: No.

Me: Yes.

Jace: NO.

Me: Please. I'm bored. Xander's gone all the time and it's just the dog and she likes him more so when he's gone she sits by the door and cries all day.

Jace: Ugh.

Me: I'm near your apartment. You can meet me at a café or something. We'll get lunch, my treat. And then walk around for a while. I just need to be out, and I'm pregnant, so being out by myself makes me

lonely and then I cry. You don't want me to cry in public do you?

Jace: Ugh.

Jace: Text me where you are. I'll be there in five.

Jace: But you're buying me the most expensive burger ever.

Me: Deal.

I look where I am and text him the address and then sit in my car to wait for him to meet me.

It doesn't take him long to get there. I see him striding up the road. He's really tall so he stands out. He's much leaner than Xander, though. His blond hair is longer on top and shorter on the sides and he has it shoved back, like he's been running his fingers through it a lot.

I hop out of my car and meet him on the streets. "Thanks, Jace." I smile at him—and he should seriously know how thankful I am since I didn't call him Jacen. I know he hates his first name, so I like to constantly use it to make him mad. Making Jace mad is a hobby of mine, because he never gets raging mad, and just gets this disgusted look on his face like he tastes something sour.

He shrugs like it's no big deal—but a few years ago, before Nova, no convincing on my part would've gotten him to come out with me.

"Where do you want to go?" he asks.

"I have no real agenda. I just had to get out, so I left."

"Smart. You did remember to close the door?" he jokes.

"Yes, I closed the door." I roll my eyes. "I am kind of hungry. Where do you want to eat?"

He shoves his hands into the pockets of his light wash jeans. "How about W.T.F.?"

"But you work there, don't you want to go somewhere else?"

"They have the best fucking food in the city."

"All right then. Lead the way." I swish my hand and he starts walking. Three strides and he's half a block away from me—or so it seems. "Slow down!" I call after him. "I can't walk that fast and you know it."

He grins at me over his shoulder. "I was hoping to lose you."

I roll my eyes. "I'm not so easily shakable."

He slows down and I catch up and then we head the couple of blocks over to W.T.F.

They do have great food and an amazing atmosphere. The bar and restaurant is more upscale, but not too snooty—or, let's face it, Jace wouldn't work there. I've met the owner, Eli, a few times, and he's young and eccentric.

We turn left and head down the street, past Jace and Nova's apartment, and keep walking. W.T.F. is down the street from where they live so it doesn't take long to get there.

We arrive and on the door is inscribed:

W.T.F.
What the fork.

(Did you think we meant something else)
Restaurant & Bar
Est. 2013

Jace holds the door open for me and my mouth falls open in shock.

Wow, the boy's learned some manners.

The hostess starts to say something to me, but then Jace walks in, grabs two menus, and keeps walking.

I shrug at her and then run after him. Thank God I wore flats today and not heels.

Jace picks a table by the windows overlooking the street. I slide into the booth.

"Why'd you bother to get a menu?" I ask. "Shouldn't you have the thing memorized since you work here?"

"You're buying so I'm planning on getting at least five things—I don't know the prices so I have to see what's most expensive." He grins at me, his green eyes light and playful.

Joking with Jace. I never thought I'd see the day.

I pick up my menu and scan the items. I've been here a lot over the years, but this is one place that there are several different things I love to get, so I never know what I want.

I finally decide on the B.L.T. with truffle fries.

I lay my menu aside.

The waitress comes up to our table and smiles. "Hey, Jace." She smiles flirtatiously.

"Hey," he replies, not looking away from the menu.

"What can I get you guys?"

"I'll have water with ice," I say.

"Coke," Jace says, still not looking at her which I can tell pisses her off. "And cheese fries for an appetizer. Extra ranch."

"Are you ready to order?" she asks.

"Give us a minute," he tells her, holding up a hand.

She turns sharply, blond ponytail swishing and disappears to get our drinks. I hope she doesn't spit in our drinks for him ignoring her.

"She likes you," I state.

"Who? Mindy?" He finally looks away from the menu.

"The girl that was just here, so if her name is Mindy, then yes."

"Ew." He makes a face, brow wrinkling. "That's fucking gross she's like twelve."

I laugh. "She looks a little older than twelve, but at least I know you don't have a wandering eye."

He drapes an arm over the back of the booth, his eyes boring into me. I've always gotten the impression that Jace sees more than he lets on. He's definitely not a dumb guy, that's for sure.

"Trust me, Nova's all I want and will ever want."

"Good." I nod. "You guys are great together."

His lips tip up in a half smile. "I think so too."

Mindy comes back with our drinks and takes our order. I tell her mine and then Jace orders.

"I'll have the cheeseburger with fries, nachos, uh ... and the filet salad."

"You seriously want all that?" Mindy looks at him in disbelief.

"Yes." He nods. "She's paying," he says by way of explanation.

"I'll get that in." Mindy turns and heads over to one of the computers to enter in our order.

"What happened to ordering the most expensive items?" I ask.

He shrugs. "I decided to get what sounded good." He looks out the window.

It's a nice day, and hot, for early September. You wouldn't believe fall is just around the corner, but it'll get cold soon. Much too soon in my opinion. Sometimes I wish Xander would get traded somewhere warmer, but then again, staying near our friends and family is a whole lot more appealing. Especially with the baby to think about.

Mindy brings us the order of cheese fries. I'm starving so go to grab one and Jace smacks my hand away.

"Hey," I defend. "What's that for?"

"These are mine." He points at the fries.

"Are you going to deny a pregnant woman fries, Jacen?" I glare.

He narrows his green eyes on me. "Are you going to call me Jacen all fucking day? 'Cause I can leave and take my fries with me."

I sigh. "Fine. Can we call a truce?" He nods and lets me continue. "I'll stop calling you Jacen, for the day, at least, if you share your cheese fries with me."

His lip curls, clearly not pleased with this proposal, but, finally, he nods and agrees. "Fine. Deal."

He moves his hand and lets me grab a fry. I dip it in the

ranch and try to suppress my moan. I ate a piece of toast with jam for breakfast, but that was hours ago.

I grab my fork and end up shoveling half of Jace's cheese fries onto the small extra plate Mindy dropped off.

Jace glares at me. "Did you have to take all my fucking fries?"

I point at his plate. "You have half. This is called sharing, *Jace*." I put emphasis on his name since I didn't say Jace*n*.

"That's called, you stole all my fucking fries and I want them back."

"You ordered like three meals," I defend. "I'm growing a human, what are you doing?"

"I'm fucking hungry and that's my food."

I pick up a fry and make a big show of eating it. "Don't make me tell Nova you were mean."

He narrows his eyes. "You wouldn't."

"I would, and you know she'd choose my side in this situation."

He shakes his head. "You're as crazy as they come."

I smile widely at him. "Thank you."

"It wasn't a compliment," he grumbles.

"I know." I smile like a shark.

Jace reluctantly shuts up and I can finally enjoy my—*his*—fries in peace.

Mindy comes by at one point to refill our drinks and tell us the rest of our food will be ready soon.

"Are you gonna steal the rest of my food too?" Jace asks, fighting a smile.

I shrug. "Depends on if it looks good or not."

I'm surprised when that gets a gruff laugh from him. He's not a big laugher. Jace is kind of ... intense.

Our food arrives and Mindy clears away the empty plate of cheese fries.

My B.L.T. looks delicious, and despite the fries I just ate my stomach rumbles.

"So, I know I must've been your last resort to hang out with. I'm surprised you didn't go by yourself."

I frown, growing serious. "I've been spending a lot of time on my own lately. Xander's tired, or at practice, or the gym—and his playing season is going to start soon, so it's just going to get worse. I get sick of being in the house by myself all day long, since nobody wants to hire me, and now I'm pregnant so they *really* don't want to hire me. Rae's busy working, Cade too, and even Nova. While I'm just cooking a baby. It sucks. Is it bad that I miss living with Rae and Cade? At least then people were running in and out of the house all the time. Now that it's only Xander and me it's so ... quiet."

Jace doesn't come back immediately with something snarky like I expect. Instead, he stares at me, his head tilted to the side like he's studying me.

"I get that," he finally says.

"You do?" I ask, my voice small.

"Well, sure." He wipes his fingers on a napkin. "Right now, Nova's gone a lot. She has work, and her and Joel are trying to start a business together, so that's her focus. I work most evenings. It's hard to see each other. The apartment is quiet a lot and it sucks. So yeah, I get it."

"I guess you do," I sigh. "I don't know if it's the pregnancy or what, but I feel really emotional about it, which I hate."

"Right now is a big transition for you," he reasons. "You're not in school anymore, you don't have a job yet, you're in a new house, and your husband is gone. It's a lot of new and different things. I think it's perfectly reasonable for you to feel emotional or off balance about the whole thing. I don't think it's because you're pregnant."

"Hmm." I sit back in the booth. "You know, you're actually kind of smart."

He laughs fully at that. "Don't tell anybody. I have to let them think I'm just a pretty face." He rubs his jaw and smirks.

"I can't believe summer is over," I mutter, looking out the window.

"Winter's not so bad."

"Bleh." I gag. "It's cold and wet, and did I mention cold?"

He chuckles. "It's not that bad." He picks up his burger and takes a bite, making a big show of chewing.

"Is it good?" I ask.

"Fucking fantastic. So, what's new with you?" he asks.

I raise a brow. "Are you seriously asking me about my life?" I have to bite my tongue not to call him Jacen.

"I'm *trying* to be nice. You make it difficult."

I laugh. "Well, we bought a house."

He groans. "I fucking knew that. I've been there."

"No, we bought *another* house. Xander calls it a cabin, I call it a mansion. It's like a getaway house. He wanted some place for all of us to be able to go and hang out. He's really excited for the winter when you all can go snowboarding."

"No shit. That sounds fun." His eyes widen, clearly impressed.

"I'm excited about it. I wasn't at first, but once he told me why, I understood."

"So what the fuck is up with this dinner at Rae and Cade's place? It keeps getting canceled and it's pissing me off."

"I don't know what's going on. Maybe she's pregnant too," I joke.

Jace laughs. "That's all we need, two of you pregnant at the same time. Though, I doubt any one of them would be as psycho as you."

"You say psycho, I say ... nope, I'm psycho."

We finish our meal, and Jace ends up asking for a box to take the rest home with him for Nova.

"Are we done now?" he asks when we exit the building.

"No, I want to shop a bit."

An inhuman growling type noise escapes him. "No."

"Yes." I grab his arm and tug him in the direction I want to go.

There are all sorts of stores, so this could take hours.

I smile to myself at that.

Jace might lose his mind by the end of this, but oh what fun I'll have.

"For the love of God, let me walk you back to your car," Jace groans, tilting his head back dramatically. "I only have two hours before I have to go to work."

"One more store," I plead. "Just one." I hold up a finger and wiggle it around.

"Fine," he reluctantly agrees, weighed down with my shopping bags.

For the record, I didn't ask him to carry them, he offered, and he's probably really regretting that now.

We enter a cute little boutique. It's full of unique clothes and I immediately eye a pretty boho chic dress.

The walls of the store are painted yellow and around the top are little plaques with quotes.

It's a really cute little store.

"Can we go now?" Jace asks.

I glare at him over my shoulder. "We've been in here five minutes. *Chill*."

He groans. "I'm never, ever, for the rest of my life, answering a fucking text from you, ever again."

I hold up a hand. "Silence."

He groans and rolls his eyes.

I move further into the store and Jace hangs back. Good riddance.

I browse their jewelry and pick up a bracelet with a dainty moon and various stars.

"Constellations," I murmur to myself.

"Hi, can I help you with anything?"

"Ah!" I jump back, startled by the salesgirl since I didn't see her. "Um, hi. Yeah. I want this." I point to the bracelet.

"Is that it?" she asks.

I nod. I've done enough damage today.

Apparently, shopping is my form of therapy.

I follow her to the checkout and notice a sign proclaiming WE'RE HIRING.

I point at the sign. "Do you have an application?"

"Yeah, sure. I can stick one in your bag?" she asks and I nod.

Working in a cute boutique like this is about as far as you can get from my degree, but I think I'd like it.

"Did someone ask for an application?" another voice calls from the back room behind the register.

"Yeah," the girl checking me out says back.

A woman appears, she's probably in her forties, with dark brown hair, and kind brown eyes. They're slightly crinkled at the corners like she's spent a lot of time smiling.

"Are you interested?" she asks.

I nod enthusiastically. "I really need a job, and your store is beautiful. I think I'd be happy somewhere like this."

"You're hired," she says.

My jaw drops. "Are you serious?" I feel like I'm being Punk'd.

She nods. "Yeah, I'm sure. We need the position filled, desperately, and you look nice enough so you're hired. Can you start Monday?"

"Yeah, absolutely."

She holds out her hand for me to shake it. "You're hired."

I pay for my bracelet and head to the front.

"You look really fucking happy about something," Jace comments, holding the door open for me.

"I just got a job," I tell him.

His eyes widen, impressed. "Good for you."

"It's not social work, but I think I'll like it. I mean, I love clothes so it should be a good fit."

Jace walks me back to my car and helps put the bags away.

"See you later," he calls, walking away. "And never text me ever again."

"I'm calling tomorrow, honey pie!" I call after him.

He gives me the finger. "Blocking your number, psycho."

I get in my car and text Xander.

Me: I got a job.

I'm surprised when he texts right back.

Xander: Really? Good for you? Where?

Me: A little boutique downtown. It's called Sunshine's.

Xander: Cool.

That one word tells me all I need to know. He's not happy about this.

But I need to get out and have my own life. Can't he see that?

twenty
...

thea

18 weeks pregnant
Baby is the size of a sweet potato

I leave work early and head straight to my doctor's appointment.

My heart is racing in my chest, I think it's excitement, but maybe it's fear. I can't really tell anymore.

Today, we find out if we're having a boy or a girl.

It makes it all the more real, because now, instead of some vague shadowy creature that I see in my head it's going to be a real person.

Not that the baby wasn't real before, because I know it is,

and there's no denying the kicks I now feel—Xander still hasn't been able to feel one—or the outrageous morning sickness I'm still dealing with.

My phone rings and I press a button my steering wheel to answer. "Yeah, hello?"

"I'm almost to the doctor's office, are you there yet?" Xander asks.

"No, I'm on my way, though."

He breathes out a sigh of relief. "Okay, good. I might beat you there, then. I'm close. Coach was being a pain in my ass and didn't want to let me leave practice early."

"Xander," I sigh. "I don't want you to get in trouble in work."

He growls over the phone. "This is one appointment I'm not missing. Don't even try to argue with me about this."

I laugh. "Okay, okay. I *want* you there, don't get me wrong, I just don't want to put you in a bad place."

"It's fine, Thea. I'll see you in a few." His tone softens.

"Bye." I hang up and exit off the highway.

Ten minutes later I pull into the lot of my doctor's office and park by Xander. He's already standing outside his truck, leaning against the door.

I hop out and meet him. He bends and kisses me, smiling.

"How was work?" he asks.

"Fun. It's only been a week, but so far I like it. Laurel, the owner, is really chill." I shrug. Xander I haven't really talked too much about my job. He's been busy with football season and tired when he's home, and, frankly, I know he's not too happy about my working so I think he's choosing to keep his mouth shut because he doesn't want to piss me off. He understands why I want to work, but he also wishes I didn't want to.

He puts his hand on my waist and guides me inside. I sign my name to check in and we sit down.

The sight of all the pregnant women and baby-covered magazines doesn't send me into a frenzy anymore, so at least I'm making progress.

"Thea Kincaid?" they call, and we hop up.

We follow the nurse back to a room. She takes my blood pressure, checks my weight, and makes me pee in another dang cup. Seriously, what do they do with all the pee they collect?

Once all that's done, we wait for the doctor.

I touch my hand to my chest. "My heart's beating so fast," I tell Xander. "I'm so nervous."

He grabs my hand and holds it in his. "Don't be."

There's a knock on the door and then Dr. Hawkins steps inside. "Howdy, kids. How are we today?"

"Good," I answer.

He sits down in his swivel chair and looks over my chart. "How's the sickness?"

"Still pretty bad," I answer. "In a way, it's better, because it's not as often, but it happens at the most random of times. I notice lately it's more related to smell than food. Like, the other day I sprayed my perfume and it hit me wrong."

"Hmm." He clucks his tongue. "If it gets much worse I

can prescribe you something to help with the nausea, but if you think you can do without it, that's better."

"I'd rather not take it if I can help it," I tell him honestly.

He nods. "Is there anything else you'd like to discuss before we start?"

"I think I've been feeling the baby kick for about two weeks now, but Xander still can't feel it. Is that normal?"

"Yeah, it's nothing to worry about. What you're feeling is probably like little flutters, right?" He waits for me to nod. "So, it'll probably be another week or two before they're solid kicks and then he'll be able to feel it on the outside. Don't stress about it. Every pregnancy is different." He claps his hands together. "All right, lie back and roll up your shirt."

I do as he says, revealing my rounded stomach. It's still small, but there's definitely a baby in it. Xander, unable to help himself, reaches over and rubs my stomach. His hand is large and when he spreads his fingers he's able to cup almost my entire stomach.

His dark eyes flick up to mine and he smiles.

I smile back.

I wasn't on board with this whole baby thing. Heck, I'm still scared. But seeing my husband look at me like this makes me fall more in love with him and gives me hope that this is going to be okay.

Dr. Hawkins squirts the goo on my belly and pulls out his magic wand.

At least that's what I call it.

He flips the screen toward us and the baby looks back at us.

"Look at the little legs." I point, and you can see the baby kicking them around.

The doctor takes some measurements and snaps some photos. He presses another button and the heartbeat thunders through the room. It's so strong and fast sounding.

I glance over at Xander and he has his left hand pressed to his mouth, looking in awe at the screen.

I thought, maybe by now, it'd get old but it still feels awe-inspiring each time.

"Is it a boy or a girl?" Xander asks, looking from the screen to the doctor. "Do you know?"

Dr. Hawkins smiles. "You want to know? I can tell you."

"Yes!" we both shout simultaneously.

I hold my hand out to Xander and he takes it, squeezing it.

Dr. Hawkins smiles. "It's a girl."

"It's a girl?" I gasp. "Are you sure?" Tears begin to fall, and I'm helpless to stop them.

"I can tell you with one-hundred percent certainty that it's a girl. Look right there." He points at the screen between the legs. "That right there means it's a girl."

I glance at Xander and find that he's crying too. "Xander," I breathe. "We're going to have a daughter."

He leans over and cups the back of my neck, drawing my lips to his. He kisses me deeply, our tears mingling together.

"This is real," I tell him.

He wipes my tears away and smiles. "So real."

We're having a little girl.

I would've been happy with a boy too, but a girl ... I don't know, it feels right.

Like she was always meant to be a part of our family. This wasn't how or when I wanted to have a baby, but things don't happen unless we're ready for them, and we must've needed this little girl.

"Thank you," Xander murmurs, rubbing his thumb over my forehead.

"For what?" I ask as the doctor finishes.

"For making us a family."

My throat closes up.

A family.

Our family.

Xander, Baby, and me.

twenty-one

. . .

xander

18 weeks pregnant
Baby is the size of a sweet potato

We head out of the doctors' office, both of us still kind of in awe.

I've known for weeks, two months, actually, that I'm going to be a dad. But it's one thing knowing that and another actually visualizing your child.

A little girl.

A little girl who can be and do anything she wants to do.

It's a beautiful and amazing thing.

I walk Thea to her car. "Do you have to go back to work?" I ask her.

She shakes her head and pushes a piece of light brown hair out of her eyes. "No, Laurel gave me the day off. What about you?"

"Coach gave me the rest of the day off." I shove my hands in the pockets of my jeans, looking down at the glossy ultrasound photo Thea holds. It has an arrow pointing between her legs saying IT'S A GIRL. "Should we go around and tell everybody?" I ask. She shakes her head and I raise a brow. "No?"

"Well, I mean, I want to tell them, but let's make it fun."

I tilt my head to the side. "What do you have in mind?"

"You'll see."

Twenty minutes later, I find myself at a party supply store, strolling the aisles, while Thea calls everyone and begs them to come over to our place for dinner.

She hangs up from her last phone call and looks up at me. "Everyone can be there by seven, so we'll reveal the gender and have dinner."

"And what kind of dinner are we having?" I ask, raising a brow. I doubt we have enough food for a meal that feeds all of us.

She waves a hand dismissively. "We'll order pizza. It'll be fine."

I nod along with her idea. "Pizza works."

It's easy enough to feed a bunch of people pizza. Everybody loves pizza.

"Okay, so what are we doing?" I ask, leaning against the cart as I push it.

"I think we should get one of those really big black balloons and fill it with pink confetti and pop it."

I think over her idea. "Yeah, that sounds cool and easy enough."

"I thought so too. It's too short notice to do like cupcakes or something, and I don't want to wait." She vibrates with excitement so I believe her. She's smiling from ear to ear. It's the first time through this whole pregnancy that I've actually felt like she's happy about it.

We head to the counter and order a gender reveal balloon.

The guy working the counter looks like he's barely in high school. He's tall and scrawny with acne. He moves in slow motion and it's obvious he hates his job.

After a ridiculously long amount of time, we finally get our balloon, and I'd be praying it was indeed filled with pink confetti if I hadn't seen him do it, but it's a miracle he didn't mess it up. The kid acts so flustered about everything.

We head out of the store and kiss goodbye, since we're in separate cars and head home.

We still have hours until dinner, which sucks, because I just want everyone to know.

I'm going to have a daughter.

It's so fucking crazy and exciting.

I can't wait to be able to hold her, and tell her I love her, because I do.

It's so crazy to me that I can already love someone I can't see. It doesn't matter, though. She's half me and half Thea, so she's already perfect.

We arrive back at the house and Thea immediately grabs her laptop and blanket, getting fixed on the couch.

"I want to look at nursery ideas," she tells me.

"What do you have in mind?" I ask, Prue jumping up and down in front of me, trying to get my attention.

"Pink, duh." She rolls her eyes, and I chuckle. I should've known.

Thea loves pink the way some people love coffee—like it's necessary to her existence.

While she daydreams about cribs and who knows what else, I head outside with Prue.

I jog down the deck steps and into the yard, with her bouncing at my heels. I find her ball and start throwing it back and forth so she can run and burn off some energy.

I haven't been playing with her enough, and I feel bad about that. I've been tired after practice—Coach is playing us hard. He's determined to get a Super Bowl win this year since we didn't make it last year. I get it, we all want it, but the work to get there is tiresome. And soon, I'll have to travel for games and I'll be gone even more. I love what I do, but for the first time in my life, I have a reason to want to stay more. Not that Thea wasn't enough of a reason before, but it was different. She wasn't alone then. Now she is, and pregnant. It worries me, which isn't good. I need to focus on the game, and that's going to be difficult.

After about thirty minutes of playing, Prue is tired. We head inside, and she jumps straight up on the couch, curling up beside Thea. Thea reaches over and absentmindedly rubs her head. I smile to myself, because that's two of my three girls. I'm surrounded by girls now, and I couldn't be happier.

I grab a bottle of water and sit down beside Thea.

"I've already ordered ten outfits," she tells me.

I raise a brow. "Seriously? That many?"

"I can't help myself, everything is so cute." She shrugs. "Plus, I got a onesie that says Tutus and Touchdowns for her to wear to your games so she can support her daddy, so I was totally thinking of you while I was shopping," she reasons.

I clear my throat, a little hung up on the word *daddy*. Hearing it come out of Thea's mouth is strange, but I love it.

I'm a dad now. It's pretty crazy to think about. For years, I only had to think of myself, then Thea, and now this little girl is going to be dependent on us to take care of her.

"Look how cute this is." She points to a crib on the screen. "I love everything. I don't know how we'll ever decide."

"I'm sure you'll figure it out eventually." No way in hell am I picking out that stuff. She'll tell me I got the wrong thing. This is all her.

"There's so much we have to get. It's insane," she rambles. "We need a crib, and a changing table, a rocker, stroller, car seat, and oh, my God, the diapers. We're going to need so many diapers."

I lean over and kiss the side of her head, closing her laptop as I do.

"One step at a time, just breathe for now."

She smiles up at me gratefully and leans her head on my shoulder.

"We're really having a baby," she whispers. "This is happening."

"Yeah, it is." I move my hand to her stomach and I feel a little jolt like a tiny heartbeat.

"Did you feel that?" she asks.

"Yeah." I nod, my eyes meeting hers.

She grins up at me, tears in her eyes. "That was the baby. She's kicking."

My mouth parts in shock. "Are you serious?"

She nods again. I roll off the couch and drop to my knees, cupping her stomach in both hands.

I feel the little bump again and I grin up at Thea. "That's amazing. Wow."

Nothing, no experience, compares to this one. This right here is what life's all about.

"Hi, baby." I lean forward and press a kiss to Thea's stomach and look up at her. "Are we going to tell them the name?"

She shakes her head. "No way. They'll hate it, and then we'll doubt it, so we're not telling them until the ink on the birth certificate is dry."

I laugh, she's right though, I'm sure they'll all hate it. The name we picked is ... different, but it's us.

The doorbell rings and I reluctantly pull away from

Thea. I just want to stay here all day feeling the baby.

I head to the front door, Prue barking at my heels. I open the door and let Thea's mom and James in.

"Hey, Lauren. James." I hug Lauren and shake James' hand, and then guide them into the house. "Thea's in the family room." I point.

Since they've arrived I decide to go ahead and order the pizzas, figuring it'll take at least an hour for them to be delivered.

I make the call and it isn't long until Rae and Cade show up.

"Hey, man." I greet Cade with a handshake and fist bump.

Cade and I were inseparable growing up. Always running around, playing football, and getting into trouble. Now we barely see each other. That's life, though. You grow up and move apart. I married his sister, so it's not like I can actually get rid of him.

Not that I'd want to.

Soon, everybody's arrived—Jace and Nova, my parents, and even my sister, Alexis. My brother, Xavier, is already back on the east coast finishing up his last year at Yale. The smarty pants.

"Is the pizza here yet?" Thea calls out. "I'm starving. Growing a human is hard."

"Should be here any minute," I call back, opening the refrigerator so I can get everybody drinks.

My mom sneaks up behind me. "Is it a boy or a girl? I promise to act surprised."

I shake my head. "Nice try, Mom, but you're going to have to wait."

"Ugh," she groans. "I'm your mom. I should have dibs on knowing what my grandbaby is." She frowns, truly put out.

"Yeah, if I tell you Thea's going to make me sleep on the couch for the rest of my life."

She waves her hand dismissively. "That's a small price to pay."

"Easy for you to say."

The doorbell rings again and I go to get the pizzas.

It should be said that ordering enough pizzas to feed this many people is an expensive business. We should've just gone out for that amount.

"Food first, and then we'll pop the balloon," Thea tells everybody, pointing to the black balloon I tied around the kitchen chair.

"I think it's unfair that you guys already know and we're the ones being surprised. I thought the point of a gender reveal was for the parents to be surprised," Jace comments, grabbing a box of pizza from the top of the pile I hold.

"I don't know whether I should be impressed, or horrified, that you know what a gender reveal is." I chuckle.

Jace shrugs. "I'm full of surprises."

I set the rest of the boxes on the kitchen island and flip up all the lids.

"Dig in," I call, and step back to avoid the stampede.

Thea's the first one to grab a piece, and she's already stuffing it in her mouth before she walks away.

I finally manage to get a piece. It isn't long until most of the boxes are empty and we're all stuffed.

"Can you please pop the balloon now?" my mom asks, vibrating with energy. "I want to know."

I tilt my head at Thea and she looks back at me, nodding.

I grab a knife from the drawer and hand it to her. "Would you like to do the honors?"

She shakes her head. "No, you do it."

"All right, all right. Can everybody see?" I ask, grabbing the balloon string and pulling it to me.

"Yeah, we're all good," my dad calls out, grabbing my mom's hand. My sister stands to my mom's right and everyone else is spread out around them.

It makes me happy that despite how busy everybody is, they dropped everything to be here for this moment. Our daughter is already so loved and she doesn't even know it.

"Three, two, one," Thea and I count down.

I puncture the balloon and nothing happens.

I poke it again.

"What is this thing made of? Steel?" I mutter.

I poke it again and it pops with a loud explosion, showering us in pink confetti.

Everyone lets out hoots of joys and my mom bursts into tears, Thea's mom too, so no surprises there.

"Oh, my God, a little girl." My mom holds her arms out to me for a hug.

I squeeze her tight, and when we pull away, I tug a piece of confetti from her hair.

"I can't believe we're going to have a little girl running

around. She's going to be so beautiful." She touches her hand to my cheek. "I'm so happy for you both."

"Thanks, Mom."

"Congrats, son." My dad claps me on the back.

"I get first dibs on babysitting," Alexis tells me.

I laugh and nod, hugging her. "Sure thing."

Once hugs and congratulations are passed around, everyone leaves since it's getting late. I'm happy to finally be left alone with my girls, all three of them.

"I'll clean this up," I tell Thea, motioning to the mess of food and confetti. I can tell from looking at her that she's tired. "Why don't you go take a bath or something?"

She grins. "Are you telling me that I stink?"

"No, I'm saying it's been a long day and you need to relax."

She laughs and brushes some confetti from the counter onto the floor. "You're too good to me."

"Go," I urge her to the stairs. "Seriously, I can handle this."

"Thank you." She stands on her tiptoes and wraps her arms around my neck, kissing me. "I love you."

"I love you too," I whisper back, brushing my nose against hers. I drop to my knees and kiss her stomach too. "And I love this little girl too."

I smile up at Thea, amazed at how much our lives have changed, but how at the same time I wouldn't change a minute of it.

Chaotic madness, that's us.

We can't do anything simple, and that's okay.

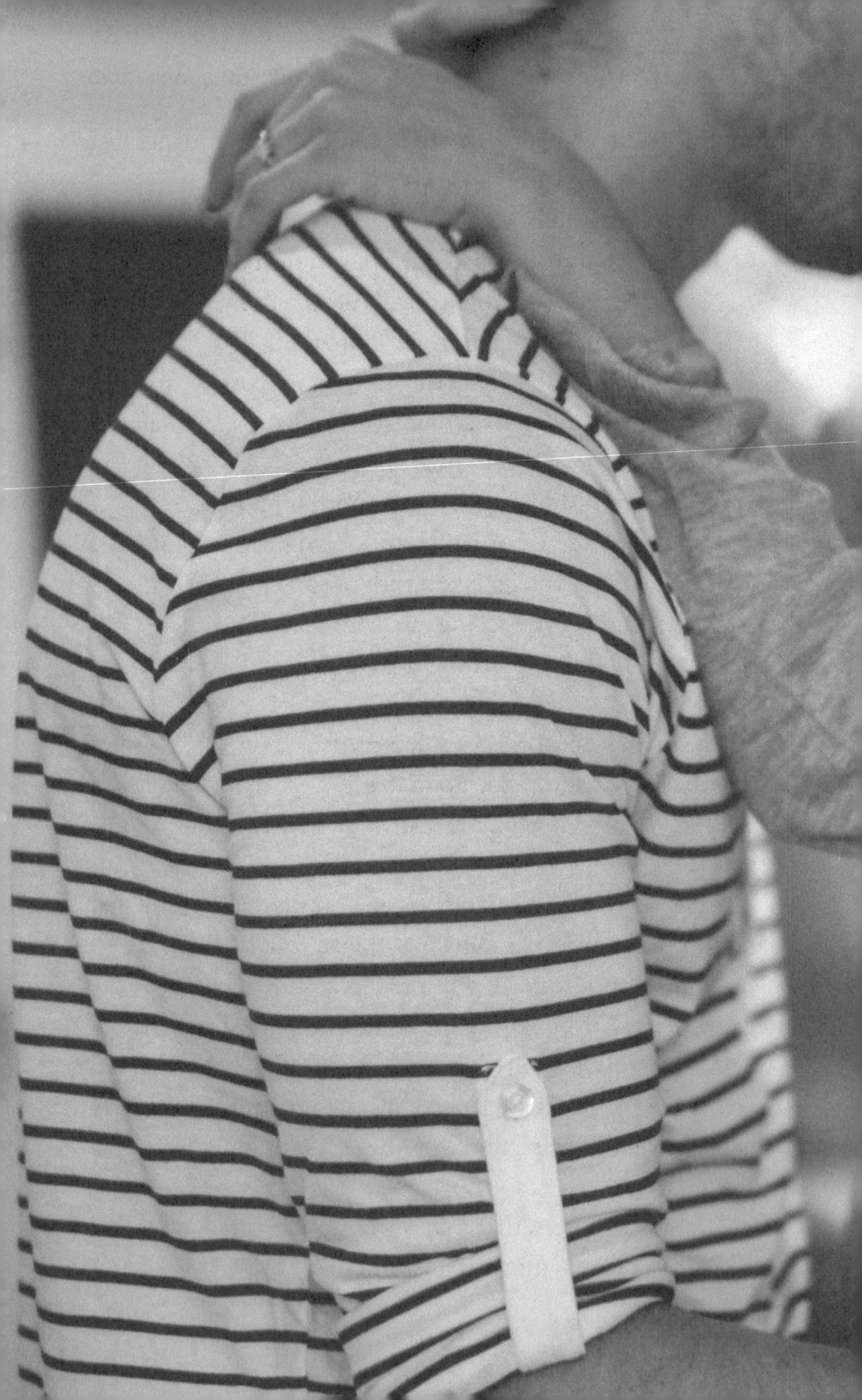

twenty-two
. . .

thea

20 weeks pregnant
Baby is the size of a small artichoke

Finally, after weeks of plans falling through, we're finally on our way to have dinner at Rae and Cade's apartment.

Xander holds my hand as he drives, and the baby does flips in my stomach. At least, it feels like that's what she's doing. Maybe she's going to be a gymnast.

Xander glances over at me and smiles.

"What?" I ask, looking back at him.

His smile grows. "I was just thinking about how lucky I am to have such a gorgeous, funny, amazing wife."

I snort. "You're not getting laid tonight."

He laughs. "Telling you you're beautiful has nothing to do with wanting to get laid, sweetheart. I'm just being honest."

"Well, in that case, lay on the compliments."

He shakes his head. "I love that I never know what's going to come out of your mouth."

"I can't have you getting bored," I joke.

We arrive at Rae and Cade's apartment and Xander parks the truck on the street.

I hop out and he comes around so we can head inside the building together.

Rae and Cade's apartment is a couple blocks from Jace and Nova's, so they live close enough to hang out regularly if they want, unlike Xander and me who live way out in the suburbs. At first I wondered if we made the right decision, but with the baby coming I know getting a house was *definitely* the best decision.

The inside of the building is simple and contemporary—lots of whites and low couches.

Xander takes my hand and leads me to the elevator. We step inside and he pushes the button for their level.

"I wouldn't like this," I mumble. "It's like living in a hotel."

He sighs, looking around at the shiny silver interior of the elevator. "Yeah, I don't like it either. I like having a home."

The doors slide open and we step out into the hall.

Xander leads me down it and we stop outside 403.

He knocks on the door and a moment later Cade swings it open. He holds a beer and he waves it around.

"Come in, welcome to our home."

We step inside and immediately to our right is a small galley kitchen. It has a gray cabinets and shiny white counters. An island extends into the living room with two stools. There's a small couch, one chair, a TV, and not much else.

There's a hall leading to a bathroom and their bedroom, and that's it.

"It's ... cute," I say, trying to interject some excitement into my voice.

Rae comes out of the bedroom, gathering her hair over one shoulder. "Oh, good, you guys are here. Nova just called and said they'd be here soon. Dinner's ready, so once they get here we can eat."

I want to ask *where* we're going to eat since there's not even a table, but I bite my tongue.

"The place is nice," I say instead.

I get it, while this is the way I'd want to live, it's what they wanted, so they must love it.

"Thanks." Rae smiles at Cade, and sometimes I wonder how my idiot of a brother managed to bag such an amazing girl. "We love it. It's small, but cozy."

Rae hugs me before she passes, heading into the kitchen. There's a big open window between the kitchen and living space, so we can all still see each other.

"Do you want anything to drink?" she asks, pulling a salad from the refrigerator.

"Water, please."

"I'm fine." Xander waves his hand in thanks and then sits down on the couch with Cade. There's a college football game playing in the background.

I pull out one of the stools and sit down so I can face Rae in the kitchen.

She busies herself making me a glass of water.

She scoops some ice into the glass and then uses the filtered water from the refrigerator.

"Do you have any lemons?" I ask jokingly, but I'm kind of serious.

She shakes her head. "Sorry. I should've thought and picked some up for you."

I shrug. "It's okay. I probably shouldn't have as many as I do," I admit. "I don't know why I'm craving them so bad."

She slides the glass across the counter to me. I take it and gulp down half in only a few seconds. I'm finding that while I'm pregnant, I'm *always* thirsty, which means I'm *always* peeing. It's quite the conundrum.

Rae stirs the salad in the bowl and then starts divvying it out onto six plates.

"How are you feeling?" she asks.

"Much better now—sometimes I still get nauseous, but it's not as bad as it was in the beginning so I'll take it. Still want to marry my idiot brother?" I ask her, leaning over and grabbing one of the small tomatoes and popping it in my mouth.

"I heard that," Cade mutters. "Little sisters are so annoying," he mumbles to Xander.

"I wouldn't know," Xander says back. "My sister is older."

Rae laughs and finishes dividing the salad. "Yes, I still want to marry him. I kind of like him." She winks.

"Kind of *like*?" Cade calls.

"I kind of *love* him," she amends. "Even when he's annoying."

There's a knock on the door and Rae jumps. "Ah, good, they're here."

She hurries to the door and lets Jace and Nova in. The apartment begins to feel extremely crowded now that there are six of us. Nova and Rae hug and Jace saunters past.

"What the fuck? Where am I supposed to sit?" he asks, looking around.

"The chair," I point out in a dull, unhelpful tone.

"That chair is made for a child. I think I'd get stuck."

I tilt my head, looking at the chair, and realize he's right. It is pretty small and he's a tall guy.

I pat the empty stool beside me. "I guess you're sitting with me, hot stuff."

Jace glances at Nova for help. "Nova, she frightens me."

She pats his chest and gives him a pouty look. "Don't be a baby."

He makes a face and finally sits down on the stool beside me. Nova stands in the space between his legs, practically on his lap.

"Hey." She smiles at me, her dark hair curling halfway down her back.

Sometimes, I miss all the different colors she'd dye her

hair, but brown really does suit her, which I guess it should since that's her natural color.

"What have you guys been doing today?" I ask, trying to make conversation.

Jace smirks, burying his face in the crook of her neck. "Having lots and *lots* of fun."

I snort and reach for another tomato. "I know all about that. That's why I'm currently in the predicament I'm in." I point to my round stomach. "Just say no, kids. And wrap it before you tap it."

Jace laughs and leans forward, biting his teeth slightly into Nova's shoulder.

"Are you guys ready to eat?" Rae asks. "We can start with the salad and then I made breaded chicken breasts, broccoli, and mashed potatoes."

"Sounds good. I'm starving," Jace says.

"You're *always* hungry," Nova interjects.

"I'm a growing boy." Jace smacks his flat stomach.

Rae passes out the salad and since there's no actual table we all just stay where we are. Rae ends up eating her food standing up in the kitchen. I feel bad, and would normally offer to trade places with her, but I'm pregnant, and my pregnant ass needs to sit.

The salad is delicious but it barely does anything to satisfy my hunger.

I need real food, not bird food.

I'm growing a human, after all.

We finish our salads and Rae clears away our plates,

sticking them in the sink, before dishing out the rest of the food.

When my plate is in front of me, I dig into the chicken.

"Mmm," I hum. "This is delicious, Rae."

"Actually, Cade made the chicken," she informs me, and Cade does a little bow.

"On second thought," I mutter, "it's disgusting and I don't want to eat it."

"Hey," Cade cries, "no take backs."

"I'm allowed to do whatever I want," I tell him, sticking out my tongue. "And I say it's gross."

He sighs. "Sisters," he mutters, eating his own food on the couch beside Xander.

Xander laughs and looks over at me, shaking his head. He doesn't even bother telling me to be nice to my brother; he knows it's pointless.

Cade and I might be adults now, but we're never ever going to grow out of making fun of each other. It's too entertaining.

Maybe that's how you know when you've surrounded yourself with the best kind of people—when you can make fun of each other, but at the end of the day you know you'd all drop anything to help the other.

Those people are the real deal.

They're the friends you have forever.

twenty-three

· · ·

thea

24 weeks pregnant
Baby is the size of an ear of corn

I haven't seen Xander in three weeks.

That's basically a lifetime.

Or close to it.

It feels that way, anyway.

He had several away games, so he and the team have been gone. I've occupied my time by working a couple days a week and helping Rae and Cade with their wedding planning. It's helped the days go by faster, but it's still sucked.

Let's just say, I've done a lot of shopping.

What can I say, it's my form of therapy.

It doesn't help that Halloween is in just a couple of days and it's my favorite holiday—so I had to buy stuff to decorate the house inside and out.

I might've gone overboard, but I can't help myself.

Cade and Jace helped me with the outside decorations since Xander isn't here.

Jace bitched the whole time. I'm pretty sure bitching is what he's best at in life.

Xander should be home any minute and I'm ecstatic to see him.

Prue whines and I reach down to pet her. "He'll be home soon," I tell her.

She looks up at me with her tongue hanging out of her mouth.

I head to the front of the house, looking out the window, waiting for his truck to come up the driveway.

Prue presses her nose against the front window, looking out too.

The baby kicks and I smile, pressing my hands to my stomach. She knows her daddy's close too.

I see his truck approach and the gates swing open.

I run from the front door to the garage door and swing it open, pushing the button to raise the main door.

Prue stays back until she sees the truck.

Xander ends up putting the truck in park so he doesn't hit her and hops out.

Prue jumps up and down, barking, ecstatic to see him.

"Hey, girl." He bends down to greet her and she licks his

face. He looks over at me, leaning in the doorway and his smile makes my stomach flip-flop. "How are my other two girls?" he asks.

I press my hand to my stomach. I'm more than halfway through my pregnancy now, and *huge*. I really got big while he was gone, at least it feels that way.

"We're good."

He grabs his bag and heads inside.

He bends and kisses me when he reaches me and then I wrap my arms around his chest, hugging him and inhaling his familiar scent. I missed him. So much.

"Do you ever feel like there's something between us?" he jokingly asks, looking down at my large stomach between us.

I roll my eyes and snort. "Yeah, your giant Viking baby."

He grins at me. "Our daughter's not a Viking."

"She's your kid. She's going to be a giant."

"Nothing wrong with that. She'll be able to reach her dreams easily then," he jokes and winks.

"That was so bad," I snort. "She's not even born yet and you're already starting with the bad dad jokes."

He shrugs and closes the garage door, locking it behind him.

He carries his bag over to the bench in the mudroom and places it there, then turns back to me.

He places his hands on my waist and pulls me into him—well, as much as he can, since my stomach gets in the way.

He lowers his head, brushing his lips softly over mine again. "I really missed you."

My heart soars. "I missed you too." I lift onto my tiptoes

and kiss him more fully, my fingers fisted into the fabric of his shirt. A soft moan escapes my lips.

I've missed him so, so, *so* much.

He cups my butt and lifts me up so I can wrap my legs around his waist.

"I'm too heavy," I protest.

"Shut up." He grins, carrying me out of the mudroom and through the house. "Even pregnant you're barely as heavy as a flea."

He carries me up the stairs and to our room, laying me gently on the bed.

His dark eyes flash with the promise of *all* the naughty things, and I'm all over that because it's been *weeks*.

He hooks his fingers into the back of his shirt and pulls it over his head, mussing his hair.

I sit up and start to pull my shirt off but he grabs my hands and shakes his head.

"No, let me."

I let him remove all of my clothes, and he takes his time, kissing each piece of skin he exposes.

I shiver, my need for him so strong I feel like I'm going to explode out of my skin.

When our bodies finally join I gasp, my toes curling and my eyes rolling into the back of my head.

Bliss.

"You know, we have to leave the bed eventually." Xander trails his fingers softly down my bare arm, and I shiver, curling into his chest.

"Five more minutes." I kiss his chest, determined to not leave the bed for the rest of the day.

He clears his throat. "You remember Jensen, right?"

I roll my eyes. "Xander, I'm a football-obsessed freak. I know everybody on your team. He's the halfback."

He chuckles, and my whole body shakes with it. "Anyway, I asked him a while back if I could borrow his kids for a day so we could babysit and he said yes. He and his wife want to go out tonight, so I said it was okay for him to bring the kids over."

I sit straight up, the sheets pooling at my waist. "How many kids do they have?" I ask, worried.

I don't really hang out with the other wives, so I don't know much about any of them or their kids, or anything like that. I had college and my own life, so I really only ever interacted with some of the guys on the team, and even that's rare. Xander likes all the guys on the team, but he prefers to keep that life separate from his so-called regular life.

He's weird like that.

"Uh … three I think."

My jaw drops, horrified. "We're going to die."

"It's going to be fine."

Xander's always been the go with the flow one, while I like a plan and structure. The idea of having three kids dropped on us this evening is horrifying to me, while he's so whatever about it.

"How old are they?" I ask, slipping from the bed so I can get dressed.

"One's a baby, then they have a little boy that's two, and a girl that's four."

"Oh, my God. We're going to die," I say again, because there's seriously no way we can survive this.

"Don't be dramatic."

I narrow my eyes on him. "Don't you dare call me dramatic, Xander Kincaid. That's three kids under four and I don't even know how to change a diaper."

"We'll be fine. They're kids. They can't be that difficult."

I snort. "We'll see."

Xander gets dressed too and then we start downstairs. I stop him on the stairs with a sheepish smile, thinking I should warn him.

"Don't be mad," I plead, giving him my best angelic look.

He tilts his head. "What did you do?"

I bat my eyes. "Nothing bad, I promise. But ... you know Halloween is my favorite holiday, and I wanted to decorate—"

"*What did you do?*" he interrupts again.

"I might have gone a *teensy* bit overboard." My voice spikes on the word and I hold up my fingers the tiniest bit apart.

He shakes his head and mutters, "This is going to be bad."

"Just remember, you volunteered me to babysit and didn't ask me, so this kind of makes us even."

He narrows his dark eyes, a wrinkle forming in his brows. "That's two totally different things."

I wave away his words. "Tomato, tomahto."

He sighs heavily. "Just show me the damages."

We finish the trek down the stairs. There are fake cobwebs and tombstones in the dining room across from us. Spiders hang from the ceiling. There are witches hats scattered about.

"Want to see my favorite thing?" I ask him.

He sighs. "Yeah, I guess so."

I lead him into the family room, where in the corner there's a lifelike mummy that's nearly as tall as he is. It's easily six feet tall.

"I call him Osiris—that's the god of the underworld."

He snorts. "Only you."

"So what do you think?"

He looks around and shrugs. "It's not as bad as I thought. I was expecting a coffin or something."

"Oh, that's in the front yard," I tell him honestly. "You must've been so excited to see me that you missed it." I wink.

He shakes his head. "God, I missed you. Talking on the phone every day wasn't enough."

"Is that your way of saying you love my crazy ass?"

He chuckles, looking around at the cobwebs above the TV. "Yeah, it is. There's never a dull moment with you, that's for sure."

His phone beeps and he pulls it out of his pocket, looking down at the screen. "That's Jensen. He says they'll drop the kids off in an hour. They want to do dinner and a movie and then they'll pick them back up."

"Oh, thank God. I *know* I wouldn't survive an overnighter."

He laughs. "What are you going to do with our baby? She's not going anywhere at the end of the day."

"Yeah, but she's ours so naturally, she'll be perfect and never cry, need to eat, or pee and poop," I joke.

He chuckles. "You wish."

Since we have an hour until the kids are dropped off, I spend the time cleaning up and then I make dinner. Since the kids are young I opt to do hotdogs and macaroni and cheese. That's kid friendly, right?

They finally arrive and I feel ... nervous.

Like somehow tonight is going to make or break whether or not I can handle this whole parenting thing—which is stupid, because ready or not, this little girl is coming.

Xander lets them in the gate and they park before bringing the kids inside.

"Thanks for doing this," Jensen says, shaking my hand and setting down the carrier.

He's a big guy, *huge*, really. I call Xander a Viking, but this guy is a tank.

He has floppy brown hair and bright blue eyes with a heavy beard. His wife is tall and curvy with sleek straight blond hair.

She smiles at me kindly and hugs me. "Thanks for doing this. I don't think we've ever been properly introduced. I'm Katrina."

"Thea," I reply with a smile, trying to be nice.

"Congratulations on your little one." She points to my stomach, like I don't know it's there.

"Thank you."

"Anyway—" she smiles, placing a hand on her daughter's shoulder "—this is Kira, and this is Ryland." She then points to the floppy haired little boy running in between her husband's legs. "And the tiniest one is little Finn."

The baby boy gurgles from his carrier and waves chubby fingers. I have no experience with babies, but I'd guess he's around four months.

"I've written down everything you need to know here." She hands me a piece of paper, and I promptly hand it to Xander because he's more responsible and I'll lose it. "We'll check in after dinner, and our movie is at eight, so we should be back here by ten-thirty. Thank you both so much for doing this. Jensen said you guys wanted to get some practice in, and I can't blame you. I wish we would've thought to have done that. Going home with a baby is the scariest thing ever."

"Babe, we need to go." Jensen urges her to the door.

"Okay, okay." She drops down and hugs and kisses both of the two older kids. "I love you both, be good for Xander and Thea, please?"

"Love you, Mommy." Kira hugs her mom back.

"Wuv you, Momma." Ryland wraps his chubby arms around her neck and smacks a loud kiss against her cheek.

Jensen hugs the kids goodbye and then they're gone.

Five seconds later Finn starts to cry and then all hell breaks loose.

Ryland runs through the house, shrieking like a banshee, and Kira begins to cry, asking when her mommy and daddy are coming back.

I glare at Xander. "This is your fault."

He holds his hands up in surrender. "We've got this."

"How do you turn them off?" I point at the crying baby and screaming Ryland.

"They're kids, Thea, you don't turn them off. You comfort them." He glares at me, like somehow it's my fault I have no motherly instincts whatsoever.

"Well, okay, mother hen." I purse my lips. "Tell me what to do."

"You take care of the baby, and I'll wrangle the toddler. That one looks most dangerous."

"What about the other one?" I ask, pointing to the crying four-year-old on the floor.

"She's stationary for the moment, so I think we're good."

Xander runs after Ryland, the toddler somehow having stripped naked, even his diaper gone.

I remove the baby from the car seat and rock him in my arms. He's drooling a lot and looks up at me with tear-filled blue eyes.

"Hi, Finn, how you doin'?" I ask, since I have no idea how to talk to a baby.

His pouty lips turn down in a frown and he only screams harder.

I bounce him on my hip and make a funny face. That seems to help some. At least he starts to cry less.

"You like that?" I ask. I stick my tongue out at him and wiggle it around. "What about that?"

He giggles and reaches for my tongue.

"Ah, we like that, huh?" I tickle his chubby belly and he laughs loudly. His cheeks are still damp with tears, but no fresh ones fall. "I can so do this whole parenting thing. I'm awesome."

Since the baby has quieted I bend down to Kira. "Hey, sweetie."

She looks at me between her fingers and hiccups. "Where's my mommy and daddy? I don't know you."

"They'll be back soon, I promise. You're hanging out with us right now. Do you like movies? Or want to play a game?"

"I like movies." She brightens.

I hold out my hand. "Come on, let's find a movie then."

I lead her out of the foyer and into the family room. When she sees the couch she scurries up onto it. I grab the remote and sit down, holding the baby.

I find the kids movies On Demand and let her pick. She goes with some recent animated movie and I click to let it begin playing.

"Do you want some popcorn?" I ask and her eyes light up like I've asked her if she wants to go shopping—at least, I imagine that's what I look like when someone mentions shopping.

She nods enthusiastically. I keep a hold on the baby and go to make the popcorn.

Xander is *still* chasing the naked toddler through the house.

How did the kid get naked? Seriously.

The popcorn finishes popping and I pour it into the extra large bowl we have. I carry it and the baby back into the family room and sit down next to Kira. She's completely sucked into the movie.

"Did you eat dinner?" I ask her.

She nods. "Yeah, I had dinosaur chicken nuggets."

"Oh, those are my favorite too," I tell her. "Dinosaurs are cool."

"Yeah, they are. Can you be quiet so I can watch my movie?"

I laugh and hand her the popcorn. "Yeah, sorry."

Minutes later, Xander collapses onto the couch with Ryland pinned in his arms with a dishtowel around his waist.

"Is that our dishtowel on the kid?"

Xander glares at me and blows out a breath, which fans his hair around his forehead. "He started to pee everywhere so I grabbed a dishtowel and tackled him to the ground."

"You tackled a two-year-old?" I snort.

He groans. "It was a soft tackle, I promise. I didn't hurt him. I'm pretty sure a tank couldn't take out this kid."

Ryland wiggles in Xander's arms and then he's on the loose again.

"You've got to be kidding me." Xander takes off after him.

It doesn't take him nearly as long to catch him this time. He comes back into the room with the kid over one shoulder and their bag in the other.

He then manages to wrangle Ryland back into some clothes and a diaper.

"Who would've thought," I begin.

"Huh?" He looks over at me.

"That I'd do better at this than you. I'm quite impressed with myself." I smile at him.

He chuckles, but the tone isn't all that humorous. "You got the easy ones."

"They were both crying, now they're not," I point out.

He bites out a gruff laugh. "I guess you're the baby whisperer then."

"*That's* what I wanted to hear."

Ryland wiggles away from Xander and moves over to me. He looks up at me with wide brown eyes and then plops beside me, sucking his thumb.

"I'm surrounded by children and I don't want to die, this is a miracle."

Xander chuckles. "They like you."

I look around at the kids. "I can do this, can't I?"

He nods. "You definitely can. I'm now questioning myself."

I laugh. "Oh, please, our child will probably hate me and love you."

He shrugs and glances at the movie playing. "I guess only time will tell."

"Even with all this screaming and crying you still want five kids?" I ask him, and it's a serious question.

He presses his lips together, thinking, and after a moment he nods. "Yeah, I want that. It's chaos, and non-stop insanity, but think of all the amazing memories we'd make along the way."

I can't believe I'm coming around to the idea, but I am. A big family is starting to seem less and less scary, and more and more like something I want too.

What is happening to me?

Jensen and Katrina check in with us after their dinner, and we let them know everything is fine. The kids are still watching the movie, and once it's over it's time for baths and bed.

Xander goes to start the bath while I somehow manage to get the three kids wrangled into the downstairs bathroom.

The baby, thankfully, doesn't need to be bathed.

Since he's taken a liking to me, I hold onto him while Xander undresses Kira and Ryland.

I sit on the closed toilet lid, bouncing a babbling Finn. He's actually kind of cute, in a wrinkly, drooly, sort of way.

Kira climbs into the tub on her own and Xander lifts Ryland in.

Ryland immediately starts splashing water *everywhere*.

"Don't do that, kid," Xander scolds, but Ryland only giggles. "Come on, sit down. Stop kicking the water," he pleads. "Here, you want a cup to play with?" Xander asks, grabbing a paper cup from under the sink.

Ryland takes it gladly, fills it with water, and dumps it on Xander's head.

Xander sighs and looks over at me. I bust out laughing because he looks like a drowned rat.

"That's a good look for you," I snort.

"Thanks," he mutters. "Give that back." He takes the cup from Ryland.

Ryland plops in the water and begins to cry. "You've done it now," I tell him.

He sighs. "Let's just get you washed," he mutters.

He washes Ryland first since he's making the bigger mess, and once he's clean sets him out and wraps him in a towel.

"Come on, Ryland." I stand up and guide the little boy out of the bathroom.

We left their pajamas in the family room so I lead him there and somehow, still holding the baby, I manage to dress the two-year-old in his Batman PJs.

Katrina packed their blankets from home so I set them out and fix the couch for them to sleep since it's bedtime for them.

Xander comes out of the bathroom with Kira a few minutes later and dresses her.

We then fix her and Ryland on separate places on the couch and read them a book together, both of us making voices for the characters, which the kids seem to like.

By some miracle, they both fall asleep quickly. I'm sure it's because they're exhausted from being in a strange environment.

Xander and I end up taking the baby upstairs to our

room and we lie on our bed with him in-between us.

It isn't long until little Finn falls asleep too.

"I'm going to shower," Xander tells me. "Are you okay here?"

I nod. "I've got this. But it looks like you've already showered," I joke, referring to the fact that he's still slightly damp from all the water poured on him.

He pulls his damp shirt away from his chest. "The kid tried."

He stands up and shucks his shirt, tossing it toward the basket.

I yawn, fighting my tiredness. It shouldn't be much longer until Katrina and Jensen come to pick up the kids.

Was it crazy there for a while? Yes, but overall it wasn't too bad.

Finn kicks his feet in his sleep and makes this adorable little purring sound.

I brush my finger over his chubby cheek. "You're not so bad. I think I can do this whole mom thing."

It's definitely not easy, that's for sure, but it doesn't seem so bleak anymore.

I might also be riding high still from the fact that I had an easier time than Xander.

I thought for sure Mr. Perfect would do just fine and I'd be the one floundering with this whole babysitting thing.

Xander finishes his shower and changes into a pair of sweatpants. He doesn't bother with a shirt—lucky me.

His phone rings and he answers quickly before it can wake Finn.

"Hello?" he whispers. "Yeah, they're all sleeping. Yep, all of them. Uh-uh. Okay. See you in a few. They'll be here in ten minutes. Should we try putting him in his car seat?"

I shake my head. "I think we should let them do it, they're probably used to doing it and can do it without waking him."

Xander nods in agreement. "That's true."

When Jensen and Katrina arrive, Xander lets them in. He comes back up with the carrier and Katrina behind him.

"Thank you so much for doing this," she whispers, so not to disturb the sleeping baby. "I hope they were good."

"They were great," I answer, and Xander snorts which makes Katrina raise a brow.

"There was one incident ... or two with Ryland."

She laughs. "Those terrible twos truly are terrible," she sighs. "What'd he do?"

"It wasn't too bad. Just some screaming and he stripped naked. There might've also been a bathtub incident."

She laughs, shaking her head. "That boy will be the end of me. Thank God, so far this one seems to be calm."

She gently lifts Finn and places him in the car seat without waking him up.

"Thank you again, guys, this meant a lot."

She buckles Finn into his seat and he lets out a small cry before stilling.

"I'll carry him down for you," Xander tells her. "This thing is heavy."

"Thank you," she tells him gratefully. He leaves and to me she says, "I'm busy with the kids a lot, I don't like to leave them with other people, but if you'd ever like to come over for lunch I'd love that."

I nod. "I'd actually like that. It'd be nice to have a mom my age to talk to."

"Great." She smiles. "I'll give you my number."

She points to my phone lying on the bed and I hand it over so she can put her number in.

"I sent myself a text so I'll have yours. I better go now. The kids will be grumpy we woke them up."

I wave goodbye and collapse on the bed, exhausted.

Xander joins me a few minutes later and we lay side by side, looking up at the ceiling.

"I guess this is a bad time to tell you I planned another party for Halloween."

He laughs. "I'm too exhausted to think about parties."

"That's what I figured." I roll over to face him. "Give me your hand."

He hands it to me and I press it to my belly. "Feel that?" I ask, looking over at him.

He nods, his eyes wide. "It amazes me more and more every time. She's so strong."

"She's the most active now. She's going to be a night owl, which doesn't bode well for us."

He rubs his thumb over my belly. "That's okay, night owls are cool."

I place my hand over his, my eyes growing heavy.

We both fall asleep, clutching my stomach and feeling the steady thrum of the baby's kicks, reminding us that she's there, and she's coming.

twenty-four

thea

24 weeks pregnant
Baby is the size of an ear of corn

We wake up in the same position we fell asleep, only now, the baby seems to have fallen asleep because there are no kicks.

I move Xander's hand off my belly and go to shower.

My aching back needs it. As much as my back hurts now I'm scared to imagine what it's like when I'm ready to pop. It's not going to be pleasant.

After my shower I dress and style my hair, doing my makeup as well.

Xander's awake by that time, already making breakfast, because he's awesome like that.

I head downstairs and slide onto one of the barstools.

"I smell something delicious."

He grins, his hair a mess from sleep. "Homemade pancakes and eggs."

"Mmm, my favorite."

I wait anxiously for him to finish making them and when he piles three pancakes onto my plate I barely add syrup before digging in.

"I think everybody's coming to your game this weekend."

Xander has a home game this weekend, which is why he's home for the time being. Then he'll he gone on the road again for a little while.

"Cool," he replies, shoveling food into his mouth. "It's fun when everybody comes. Is it crazy to say that the energy is better?"

I laugh. "No, not crazy. Home games are the best. It's your own turf."

"True," he agrees. "So ... another party?" He raises a brow. "You never mentioned that in any of our calls."

I snort. "Xander, we have a party every year. It's tradition. I might've purposely not said anything because I figured you wouldn't be that into it since you've been gone, but I was bored and the planning made me feel better."

He sighs. "How can I argue with that?" He sets his fork down. "What's our costumes?"

I smile slowly. "Don't be mad."

He throws his head back. "Thea, what'd you do?"

I take another bite of pancake and then scurry out of my seat and run to the hall closet, pulling out a shopping bag. I hand it to him and he inhales a deep breath, bracing himself.

He snorts when he pulls out the fabric and reads it. "Bun maker?"

"I have a shirt to wear that says Bun with an arrow pointing to my stomach."

"You're too much." He puts the apron back in the bag.

"There's also a hat in there," I warn him.

He sets the bag on the counter and I sit down to finish eating.

"Well, it could be worse," he sighs.

"Exactly."

Things are always so much easier when he sees things my way.

"What are we doing today?" he asks, finishing his breakfast.

"*I'm* going to work. I don't know what you're doing."

He makes a face. "Fuck, I forgot you had to work."

I glare at him. "Swear jar."

He sighs. "I'll put a quarter in there later. Is that thing full yet?"

"Just about," I laugh. "We're both lousy—but I'm worse."

Xander clears his throat. "Maybe I'll see if Jace is free to go to the gym or something."

"Sounds like fun." My voice is laced with sarcasm, because exercise is *not* fun at all.

"Maybe I should go out on my motorcycle. I didn't ride

it much this summer and it's pretty nice today."

"Yeah, that'd be good too," I mumble, half listening to him.

I finish my breakfast and clean our plates, Xander would do it, but I don't mind.

Once that's done I wipe the counters and check the time.

"I better be going," I sigh. I love my job, but I'm suddenly sad to leave since I've seen him so little. I should've thought and taken off.

"Right, okay. Do you want to meet somewhere after work for dinner?"

I shake my head. "I'm usually tired after being on my feet all day, so I just want to come home."

"Okay." He nods. "I'll have something ready then." He tilts his head, thinking. "Can I drop you off and pick you up?"

I shrug. "Sure, that'd be cool with me."

"What time do you get off?"

"Three."

"Okay, I'll be there then."

He grabs his truck keys off the counter and we head out to the garage.

Climbing inside his truck proves to be difficult, but somehow I manage.

The drive into the city is relatively peaceful, though we do hit some traffic once we get close to the store.

Xander knows the way, so I don't bother giving him directions. He drops me off in the back, where there's an alley for workers to park.

"I love you. See you later," I say, leaning over the console to kiss him goodbye.

He kisses me back, his fingers fisting in my hair. "Love you too."

I slip from the truck, feeling slightly light-headed. Xander waits for me get into the building before pulling away.

I clock in and greet Laurel, who's busy working in her office.

I straighten things a bit, though it doesn't much need it, and flip the sign to open.

It isn't long until people start wandering in.

I've learned that Sunshine's is a popular boutique. I had no idea what it was until I wandered in that day with Jace, but it stays busy all day with a variety of different aged women. They have a bit of everything, clothes, bags, watches, jewelry, candles, and little knickknacks for your house. I've already bought loads more stuff, with the excuse that I'm getting it for Christmas gifts, but let's face it, I'm keeping most of it for myself. And if Laurel ever starts selling baby things, then I'm really screwed.

The day passes quickly, and before I know it, it's time for Xander to pick me up. At two-fifty I see his truck pull up on the street out front.

Georgie, the girl that comes in after me, hasn't arrived yet, and since he's early I finish with the customers in the store and fold some clothes.

Georgie breezes in through the back a few minutes later with a smile and wave.

"I can take it from here," she assures me.

I know she can; she's been doing this longer than I have.

I clock out and say goodbye to Laurel before scurrying out to the truck.

I grin from ear to ear, so happy to see Xander. I never thought I'd be lucky enough to fall for a man that I genuinely want to spend every moment with.

"I missed you." I lean over to kiss him.

He smiles too. "I got you something today."

I grin back, bouncing in my seat. "What is it?"

"It's waiting at home," he tells me.

I narrow my eyes. "Xander Kincaid, I swear to God if you bought a crib I will throat punch you. You know I haven't made up my mind."

"It's not a crib," he assures me.

"Then what is it?"

"You'll have to wait and see." He has this little grin that tells me he's up to no good, so I'm instantly scared to death.

I spend the whole drive home racking my brain for what he could've possibly bought me.

When we arrive home I immediately get my answer.

"No." I shake my head.

His smile falls. "You don't like it?"

"It's a tank! How am I supposed to drive that?" I point at the big white Range Rover.

"It's an SUV not a tank, don't be dramatic."

He opens the garage door and my panic only increases.

"Where's my car?"

He smiles sheepishly and bites his lip. "I traded it."

"You're fucking kidding me, right, Xander? This is a joke. I'm being Punk'd. I have to be." I look around for the cameras.

"We needed a family car," he mumbles.

"Yeah, I get that, but you should've *talked* to me about it before going out and buying a … What is that, a seventy-thousand dollar car?" I clutch my chest. "Oh, my God!" I scream, staring at him horrified. "Where's your motorcycle?"

He looks away and won't meet my eyes.

"Where's. Your. Motorcycle."

He twists in his seat to face me. "I went to take it out today, and I got to thinking, I'm going to be a dad, which means I need to be responsible. So I sold it too."

I scream. Like an inhuman, blood-curdling scream.

I glare at him, warning him with my eyes that I'm *this* close to reaching over and strangling him. "I *love* the motorcycle and now it's gone? I can handle my car, but not that. And you know what, you said nothing would change when I got pregnant, and now *everything's changing*." I shout the last part at him at my wits end.

Normally, I agree that I'm being dramatic, but this is one instance where I think I'm being perfectly reasonable. He should've *talked* to me before he did this.

I begin to cry, unable to help myself.

I rub my chest where it feels tight.

"I think I'm having a heart attack," I mumble.

"Thea, you're not having a heart attack."

"I'm having some kind of attack!" I yell, unbuckling my seatbelt. I desperately need out of the truck.

I tumble outside and sit down on the middle of the driveway.

I hear Xander's door open and close, then he walks across to me.

He squats down, draping his arms over his knees.

"Thea, this isn't the end of the world. It's a car, and the motorcycle isn't as important as being safe."

I wipe at my tears. "This just sucks. I don't want everything to be different."

"Maybe you should stop thinking about it being different and think of it instead as the new normal."

I sniffle. "I'll try—but next time, don't by a fucking car and not tell me." I hold out my hands for him to help me up and he smirks, opening his mouth. "And *do not* tell me to put a quarter in the Swear Jar. I might stab you if you do."

He laughs. "All right, deal."

He helps me up and leads me over to the car. It's nice, I won't lie, I mean it's a freaking Range Rover, but I just keep seeing dollar signs.

He opens the door and motions for me to sit in the driver's seat.

"Look how much room is in the back. There's plenty of space for a car seat, and there's even a DVD player, granted she won't need that for a while but I thought it was a good thing to have," he rambles.

I shake my head, looking in the back, imagining a car seat and screaming kid there.

It's still slightly terrifying, but yesterday's babysitting adventures honestly helped a lot.

It's crazy to think she's going to be here in practically four months since October is almost over.

Xander continues to ramble about all the different features and why he chose this car out of all the other ones he could've gotten.

I interrupt him just as he sits down in the passenger seat. "Thank you."

"Really? You like it?"

I nod, rubbing the steering wheel. "Yeah, but I love the thought behind it more—that you cared enough about mine and our daughter's safety to incur my wrath."

He lights up, grinning at that. "I have to say, I'm impressed that you're not still mad."

I smile back at him. "What can I say, I'm maturing."

He laughs heartily at that. "I don't know if I'd go that far with it."

"Hey, I'm trying," I defend.

"You are," he agrees. "So you like it?"

I nod. "Yeah ... I couldn't have picked anything better."

Xander honestly did a really good job. I understand why he chose the car he did, and while I don't agree with him going behind my back, the deal is done so I might as well embrace it.

"Want to take it around the block?" he asks.

I nod enthusiastically. We buckle up and I adjust the mirrors before pulling out.

It's a smooth ride, and I instantly fall in love.

Yeah, the boy did good.

twenty-five

...

thea

24 weeks pregnant
Baby is the size of an ear of corn

"What are you doing?" I yell. "Get in there and take him down!"

"All that yelling can't be good for the baby, right?" I hear Jace ask someone. "All the jumping too ... I'm scared the thing is going to come sailing out."

"Trust me," Nova says, "childbirth is unfortunately not that easy."

"I feel like we need a doctor in here, though, in case she goes into labor. I don't want to deliver her baby."

"And I don't want you to see my vagina, Jacen, so stop worrying," I interrupt, but my attention is quickly pulled back to the game. "Hey! Hey! Hey!" I shout down to the field where we're losing terribly. "Throw the fucking ball, you shitstick ball hog." I glare at my friends in the box. "I fucking hate this game sometimes."

I collapse into my cushioned seat—a perk of having a box seats. I used to hate the box seats, preferring to actually be with the crowd, but now that I'm pregnant there's no way I'm passing this up.

"I need a drink. Where's my lemon water—and better yet, where's the lemons? I need one."

Cade hands me my glass of water and the plate of lemon wedges.

The lemons were meant for the water they provide us with, but I can't help but eat a few. Or all of them. But who's counting?

Cade and Jace watch me in horror as I eat the lemons.

"Is your tongue made of steel? Isn't that sour?" Jace asks me.

"Yes, and it's delicious."

Jace shakes his head. "That's the fucking craziest shit I've ever seen."

"I craved soap when I was pregnant," Nova tells him, and his jaw drops. She shrugs. "I didn't actually eat the soap, but I really wanted to."

"Man, pregnancy is weird," Jace groans.

"Don't talk to me about how weird it is." I glare at him.

"You're a guy, you don't even have to be pregnant or give birth to the thing."

He smirks at me, still tearing into my lemons. "At the rate you're going, the kid's going to be born a lemon."

I gasp. "That's just mean."

He laughs, and starts to hear something but I hear a roar in the crowd so I look back through the glass and jump up, nearly losing my lemons in the process.

"Yes! We finally scored!"

I scour the field, looking for Xander's jersey number.

He's the wide receiver and number 26. I wear a jersey that matches his. I had to get a new one for this game, since my old one was much too small and nearly ripped at the seams when I tried to put it on.

I finally spot him, and like always, I light up.

No feeling compares to seeing Xander playing on a NFL field.

I press my face to the glass like a little kid and wave. He's not even looking, but I always like to wave.

"Sit down, sis, you're blocking the view," Cade groans.

"Look around me then," I snap back. "I'm not a blimp."

"Yet."

Brothers are so annoying.

I turn, giving him my deadliest glare. "What did you say?"

He gulps, his eyes wide. "Nothing."

"Yeah, that's what I thought." I turn back to the glass.

The game starts to get exciting then. The other team was

ahead, but we finally start pulling our weight, which makes things interesting. We just might pull off a comeback, which would be awesome.

I can see Xander's coach down on the field yelling, red-faced, urging them on.

I sit back down, and sip at my water, needing a breather.

This game is making me way too stressed, and it's probably not good for the baby.

"I wish you'd change your mind and tell us the name," Rae pleads beside me, giving me puppy dog eyes.

I snort and shake my head. "You're my best friend, but no."

"Why?" She frowns.

"Because you guys will hate the name, and then I'll doubt it, and we'll be in trouble and I'm not going there because I actually really love it and it's perfect for her," I tell her the same thing we've already told them all.

"If it's perfect then you won't doubt it," she reasons.

"That might normally be true, but I'm pregnant, and pregnancy does weird things to your mind. Trust me."

"Like craving lemons?" Jace asks from where he's reclined in a chair. His eyes are closed and he's not even pretending to watch the game.

I snap my fingers together. "Exactly like craving lemons."

"I just really want to know her name." Rae frowns.

I laugh. "How do you think Xander's and my mom feels? They're driving me nuts. Xander's mom is worse. She texts me at least every day and she tries to be crafty about it."

"How?" Rae asks, her lips lifting in amusement.

I sigh heavily. "Well, first she said she was getting a monogramed blanket and I thought that was so sweet but then she said she needed the name and I saw what she was doing. Then she said, just the initials, but I didn't want to give those to her either. I think she's kind of mad at me about it, but this is a decision Xander and I made together. The name is special and we're waiting to reveal it until she's born. The way I see it, we could've kept the gender a secret too, but we didn't, so at least you all have that."

Rae grabs my hand then. "Nova and I were talking about it, and we want to throw you a shower. I'm sure you're already going crazy buying stuff, but a shower is like a rite of passage when you're having a baby."

I purse my lips, thinking it over. A baby shower isn't something I'd thought much about. "Yeah, I guess that'd be okay, but can you plan it for after the holidays? I can't handle all these holidays and a baby shower. *And* your wedding," I add. "I need time to breathe after all that."

Rae laughs and glances at Nova. "I think we can accommodate that. But Thea?"

"Yes?" I hedge, not liking her tone.

"*We're* planning this." She wags a finger between Nova and herself. "So that means, no texts about colors, or food, drinks, music, games. None of it. Understand?"

I frown. "It's like you're intent on sucking all the joy out of my life."

Rae narrows her eyes on me. "Promise me, Thea."

"Fine, I promise," I reluctantly agree.

I'm probably going to end up with a *Teenage Mutant Ninja Turtles* shower. That's something those two would do just to spite me and my love of pink.

My gaze wanders back to the game and I look down to see us in possession of the ball again.

I jump up. "Run! Run! Run!" I yell again. "You can do it! Almost there! Yes! Touchdown!" I collapse back in my chair and let out a heavy breath. "Man, I'm exhausted now."

Jace snorts. "Yeah, it's like you were down there running the ball or something."

I throw a lemon wedge at him, and it sticks to the side of his face.

"What the fuck is that?" he cries, since his eyes are closed, and he jumps, batting it away. "Oh, fuck, it's just a lemon."

The lemon wedge rolls away onto the floor and I sigh. It's a shame to waste it, but it was too funny.

The other team captures the ball again and I hold my breath, but we manage to get it back.

I spend the rest of the game alternating between screams, gasps, and peering between my fingers, but somehow we manage to pull off a win.

"You all are all coming on Tuesday for the Halloween party, right?" I ask my friends. It's more of a warning, but asking sounds better.

"Yeah, we'll be there," Cade promises.

"Even you guys?" I ask Jace and Nova.

"Wouldn't miss it," Nova vows.

"Is Joel coming?" I ask. "What about his girlfriend?"

"They broke up." She rolls her eyes. "But yes, he'll be there. He's coming as Zoro and he's ecstatic. He's such a dork." She laughs.

"All right, I'll see you guys then." I hug them each goodbye, amazed by how much my belly gets in the way now. The thing is basically a planet. I guess Cade wasn't too off base when he said I was a blimp.

We all head our separate ways and I wait in my car for Xander, knowing he'll be a while.

Oftentimes in the past, I'd wait for him near the lockers, but now that I'm pregnant there's no way I'm braving the psycho reporters.

Those assholes are crazier than me and that's saying something.

My phone pings with a text.

Xander: I have a couple of interviews. I'm sorry.

Me: It's fine.

Xander: It's going to be a while. You can leave. I'll get an uber or something.

Me: How about I go pick us up takeout and come back over? Think that'll be enough time?

Xander: Maybe...

I sigh.

Me: I'm in desperate need of a cheeseburger. I'll order some and pick them up and hope for the best.

Xander: K.

Me: You know I hate it when you just say K. That's the most annoying thing ever.

Me: Xander?
Me: XANDER?

I sigh again, figuring he's already started his interviews.

I call and order our food, my stomach already rumbling. The box had a variety of snacks, but nothing was appealing except lemons. I'm learning while I'm pregnant that there always seems to be one thing I want to eat, and nothing else sounds good. Like right now all I want is a big fat juicy cheeseburger.

Thanks to the stadium traffic it takes me a good forty minutes to get to the restaurant and pick up our burgers, fries, and drinks. Heading back doesn't take nearly as long, but I'm gone nearly an hour and a half.

Me: I'm back

I shoot Xander a text when I get back to where I park.

Xander: I'll be 5 more minutes.
Me: I had almost perfect timing then. Go me.

I don't tell him but I also stopped and picked up McFlurrys. Oreo for me and M&M for him since he's a freak.

It isn't long until I see the door open and he strolls out. His dark hair hangs over his forehead and the jeans and white dress shirt he's changed into clings to his muscles.

Damn, my husband is hot. I did good.

He opens the passenger door and slips inside. "That smells so good. I'm starving. Can we just eat here?"

"Picnic in the car? I like the sound of that," I agree. Plus, I'm starving so the idea of waiting until I get home to eat isn't appealing. I hand him the bag of food and he dishes it out. "I hope we don't make a mess in here," I comment, looking around at the pristine beige leather in the Range Rover.

"I'll have it detailed if we do," he reasons. "You got ice cream too?" He laughs, looking at the cups in the holder.

"I needed a McFlurry," I defend. "The baby loves them," I joke.

He chuckles. "Let's hope she doesn't have a sweet tooth like you."

I unwrap the foil from my burger and dig in, immediately moaning. "That's delicious. I'm so freaking hungry."

"Me too," he agrees.

We both grow quiet, to absorbed in our food to talk. I stuff a couple of fries in my mouth and moan again.

It doesn't take us long to finish our burgers and fries since we were starving and then we both start on the ice cream.

"Do you remember that time in your truck when we got McFlurries after our first official date and we argued about our fictional baby?" I ask him, swirling my tongue around the spoon.

He grins back at me. "How could I forget? We got ice cream all over my truck and ourselves."

"That was fun, and sticky." I laugh. "But can you believe this many years later, here we are again sitting in the car eating ice cream only this time I am pregnant and we're going to have a daughter."

He grins at me, his teeth perfectly straight and white. "A lot can change in the blink of an eye."

I think back to the two people we were then. I was so young, only nineteen, and all that we've been through since. We're much stronger, more mature people now. I guess sometimes you have to go through horrible things to come out a better person.

twenty-six

...

xander

25 weeks pregnant
Baby is the size of acorn squash

"What the hell is an acorn squash?" I mutter to myself, looking at the app on my phone that says at week twenty-five the baby is the size of an acorn squash. Thea has the same tracker on her phone, and I'm sure it's unusual for the guy to care so much, but I'm fascinated by the whole thing.

I read what it says beneath the size, and I'm shocked to learn that the baby is starting to grab things and can even grab her umbilical cord as well as stick out her tongue.

It really is the miracle of life.

"Xander, I need some help down here!" Thea calls and I head downstairs.

She's been a mad woman setting up for her Halloween party. I tried to help earlier but she got mad and told me to get out of her way so she could do it herself and do it right.

"Can you hang these?" she asks, pointing to some kind of bat looking thing she wants to dangle from the ceiling.

"Yeah, I'll grab the ladder."

I head to the garage and get it. When I get back inside, she's running around like a crazy person. This is what happens when she insists on doing everything on her own because she's a perfectionist.

I hang the bat things from the ceiling and then wait for her to ask me to do something else.

"Can you set all this stuff out on the dining room table? I already decorated it. It just needs the food and drink." She points to the spread of snacks and drinks on the kitchen island.

"Yep. Do I need to hang anything else? I'll put the ladder away first if you don't have anything else."

She presses her lips together, thinking. "No, that was it."

I put the ladder away, and then set out the drinks and food. I try to set it in a way that I think she'd like instead of just plopping it on the table.

I must do a good job because she walks by and gives an appreciative nod.

"Can you vacuum the family room?" she asks me next.

"Yeah." At least that's easy enough.

I'm in the middle of vacuuming when she lets out a war

cry. "This house is a mess. It's never going to be clean in time. We need to just throw everything out."

I look over at her and find that she's pressing her fingers to her temple like it's throbbing.

I cut off the vacuum and close the distance between us, wrapping my arms around her.

"Breathe, sweetheart. You're going to give yourself a headache."

"What was I thinking?" she cries with a frown. "I'm six months pregnant. This is too much."

I place my hands on her cheeks, forcing her to look at me. "You wanted to do something fun and spend time with friends and family on your favorite holiday. There's nothing wrong with that. Besides, nobody cares if the entertainment center is dusty or there's a crumb on the floor. That only matters to *you* because this is our home and you want it to look nice, but everybody else is going to be focused on all these crazy decorations, the food, and Osiris in the corner." I point to the scary realistic mummy she bought. I came down the other morning and screamed because I thought someone broke in.

She laughs at that and cracks a smile. "I see your point." She inhales a breath. "It's going to be fine."

I step back and finish vacuuming, winding up the cord and putting it back away in the closet.

An hour later, we're finished cleaning and setting out the decorations, so we get ready and change into our costumes.

I'm kind of thankful that this year they're simple. Last year Thea went as Maleficent and I was a dark prince.

Once I'm ready I'm tasked with the job of putting Prue in her costume.

"Ugh," I groan. "Thea, you know she hates wearing these things."

She parts her lips, applying mascara. "She has to wear a costume too. Those are the rules."

I sigh. "Fine, but she's going to hate me for the next month for this."

Wrangling Prue into her costume is a chore. She hates them and tries to take them off. But every year, Thea insists on her wearing one.

Next year, I'm burning the costume.

I grab the costume off the end of our bed and make a face. It's a fucking unicorn. Poor Prue.

"Come here, Prue," I call, clucking my tongue.

She runs up the stairs but when she sees the fabric in my hands she turns and runs like she already knows.

I sigh and chase after her, back down the stairs.

I find her under the dining room table and I call her name. "Prue. Come here, girl."

She's not budging, though.

I groan and stand up, heading into the kitchen so I can get a treat.

Normally, the sound of me opening the treat jar would send her running, but not this time.

"Prue, come on, please," I beg.

I crouch back down under the table and try to get her, but she refuses.

"Your mother is going to kill me," I warn her.

She looks up at me with big brown eyes and slowly creeps toward me.

"I'm sorry, girl," I tell her honestly as I put the costume on her.

She looks ridiculous, but I'm sure Thea will think it's adorable.

Sure enough, a few minutes later Thea comes down and goes, "Aw, Prue, you look adorable."

Prue shuffles around, taking one-inch steps with her head bowed. Now that I think about it, she kind acts like Eeyore from Winne the Pooh.

Thea pets Prue's head—well, the costume, and then takes off for the kitchen.

She puts some music on and then proceeds to start switching out all the light bulbs downstairs to purple ones.

When I just stare at her she shrugs and says, "I need to set the mood and make it more spooky."

Like she said, her costume matches mine in the fact that it says The Bun with an arrow pointing to her stomach, and she chose to wear jeans with it.

I'm wearing jeans, a white t-shirt, and the apron. I hid the hat, because it was ridiculous and there's no way in hell I'm actually wearing it. Thankfully, Thea's been too scattered to realize I don't have it on.

Yet.

The doorbell rings and I go to answer it.

"Don't tell me we're the first fucking ones here," Jace spits out before I barely have the door open.

"Afraid so."

He glares down at Nova. "I fucking told you she told us an early time. This is our punishment for being late last year."

I shrug. "It's Thea, she's crafty," I agree, stepping out of the way so they can come inside.

They're dressed as The Joker and Harley Quinn. They usually show up as villains, or just something scary. I don't think they can help themselves.

"Jacen!" I hear Thea call out and I shake my head.

She's the only person I know that regularly calls him Jacen. He hates it, so that's why she keeps doing it. She loves getting under his skin and even I have to admit it's hilarious. Jace isn't easily riled, but Thea usually knows the right buttons to push.

"The devil," Jace says back blandly.

I stroll into the room and find them all sitting on the couch.

"When does the party actually start?" Jace asks.

"Another hour." Thea smiles at him like the cat that ate the canary.

"Tell me you at least have food. I'm starving."

"Dining room," I tell him.

He jumps up to take off, but then stops and turns back to Nova. "You want anything?"

"No, I'm good."

Once he's gone, Nova smiles at Thea. "You just love messing with him, don't you?"

"Yep." Thea nods. "He makes it so easy. I can't help myself."

Jace saunters into the room with a plate of food. "What is this?" he asks, holding up something he's already half-eaten. I can't tell what it is.

"Donkey balls," Thea answers and he spits it out all over the floor.

"Fuck, get it out of my mouth."

Thea laughs, clutching her stomach. "God, you're so gullible. It's meatballs, you idiot, like the normal kind."

Jace glares at the mess on the floor. "It's probably your hairy fucking balls. I'm pretty sure you're a dude."

"Yes, that's why I'm pregnant—because I have a dick." She rolls her eyes, rubbing her stomach.

"Are you sure that's your kid?" Jace asks me. "It's probably a demon spawn or something."

I snort. "Could be, I suppose."

Thea's jaw drops and she throws a pillow off the couch at me. I laugh and catch it easily.

"Nice try, sweetheart." I toss the pillow back and it lands beside her.

"You're all a bunch of jerks." She frowns and crosses her arms over her chest, resting them on her stomach.

We end up hanging out and talking until more people start arriving. Thea kept it relatively small this year, only inviting Jace, Nova, Cade, Rae, Joel, and some girl she works with. She told me I could invite some guys from the team if I wanted so some of them might show up.

Joel arrives first, dressed as Zoro just like Nova said he'd planned. He even talks with a funny accent to complete the look.

Next is Rae and Cade, dressed as Salt and Pepper. Not the band, but the seasonings. I just shake my head at the weirdness and go on with my life.

A couple of the guys arrive next and we bump fists in greeting.

I know I should hang out with the guys more outside of work, but it's not my thing. Once I'm done with work, I like separating myself from it and hanging out with Thea. Plus, now that we have the baby coming that's where all my focus has been.

Clark comes dressed as Batman, Zack is some kind of steampunk looking character, and Drake is a Viking. I'm sure Thea will find that hysterical. I'm honestly surprised she hasn't made me dress up as a Viking yet. Though, she'll probably see him and that'll be next year's costume.

The girl Thea works with arrives last, and introduces herself as Georgie. She's dressed as a hippie.

Prue runs around with her unicorn costume half off and Thea chasing after her.

"Prue," she cries. "You're naked! Come back!"

Prue runs up the stairs and Thea pauses, hands on her hips as she struggles to catch her breath. "Ugh, fine. Go then."

I grab a plate of food, suddenly starving, but I avoid the meatballs. I can't eat them now.

For the most part the party is low key and more mellow than usual. It's actually kind of nice to hang out with everybody and not have so much chaos. The first year we had a party, when we were still living with Rae and Cade, it was *insane.* The music was loud, and the party bled outside. I'm sure our neighbors loved it.

I'm also fairly certain Jace and Nova had sex in the laundry room that time.

The party ends early, since it's really more of a get together than an actual party. Thea and I clean up as best we can and head to bed.

I pull the covers back and she hops inside, her face clear of makeup and her hair in a ponytail. She wears a tiny pair of underwear that barely covers anything and a loose tank top to sleep in.

I lie down beside her, covering us with the blanket and she rolls to me, laying her head on my chest.

Both of us are quiet and I hear her yawn.

"Xander?"

"Yeah?" My chin rubs her hair.

She traces a finger over my belly button. "When did we get old?"

I stifle a laugh. "What do you mean, sweetheart?"

She shrugs against me. "Just that ... I don't know, we're so boring now. This was the most mellow party ever, and I actually loved it."

"I guess things just change gradually. We become different people. We can't help it."

"Well, I can't believe I'm saying this, but I think I like being boring."

I smile and brush my lips over her forehead. "Sweetheart, you're the furthest thing from boring. Trust me."

She raises her head and smiles at that, then wiggles

around to get comfortable again. She ends up winding her leg through mine, with her head on my chest, and her hand splayed across my stomach.

Her round belly presses into my side and I feel the baby give a soft kick.

I smile to myself.

"Goodnight, Thea."

"Night," she murmurs, already half asleep.

twenty-seven

...

thea

28 weeks pregnant
Baby is the size of kabocha squash

What the hell was I thinking asking Xander to paint the nursery *days* before Thanksgiving? Thankfully, we're celebrating the holiday at his parents' house and not here, or I'd really lose my mind.

"Let me in!" I yell, banging on the door with an open hand. "I need to make sure the color is what I want."

"No," he yells back sternly. "You're pregnant and you can't inhale the fumes."

"Oh, my God, you're so annoying," I groan, sliding to

the floor. "It took me a month to pick the color and I want to make sure it's right before you paint the whole room."

"Can't you just trust me to know if it's okay or not?"

"No, you're a guy. Every shade of pink probably looks like orange to you."

Xander insisted on painting the nursery himself, instead of hiring professionals. I commend him for wanting to do it himself, but if he fucks it up I'm not talking to him for a week.

No, make that a month.

Heck, maybe even a year.

And let's face it, the chances of him fucking it up are high since over the pink paint he has to paint a silvery stenciled detail. I highly doubt he can get that right, but here's to hoping.

Ever since we found out we're having a girl I've been going crazy with plans for the nursery. I knew immediately it had to be girly and pink, because hey, that's me.

The crib, dresser, armoire, and glider arrived yesterday, so Xander wanted to get the room painted before he started putting things together.

"Xander," I plead through the door. "One small peek won't hurt me."

The door flies open behind me and I fall back. "Shit," he curses. "I didn't know you were there." He helps me up off the floor. "One peek, and then you're to go downstairs and leave me alone."

"Fine," I sigh, reluctant to agree to his terms but knowing it's the best I'm going to get.

I step through the doorway and nearly slip on the sheet he has laid over the hardwood. "Shit, Thea, be careful," he warns, grabbing my arm to steady me.

I look around the room, tears in my eyes.

"What do you think?" he asks nervously.

"It's perfect."

He hasn't done much, but it's enough for me to tell it's the exact right shade of pink.

"All right, now get out." He all but shoves me out of the room and slams the door closed.

"You're so rude!" I yell through the door, and all he does is laugh.

I head downstairs and fix a glass of lemon water. Prue prances along beside me, her tongue hanging out of her mouth.

Since Xander's occupied with nursery duty I busy myself with more shopping.

I still need to order her bedding. I was between two, but Xander hates the one, so I decided to be nice and veto it and go with the one we both like.

I order the bedding and then move on to other things for her room.

I purchase a fluffy rug and several paintings with gold accents to hang on the wall that'll match the chandelier. I also order a cute tufted pink ottoman that doubles as storage space, and a cute Parisian style chair.

Am I going overboard?

Hell yes.

But this is our first baby, and all the things are so cute I can't help myself.

Since I'm already shopping I go ahead and order the car seat and stroller we decided on.

It takes a lot to have one baby. I can't imagine having twins. I might die.

I feel baby girl kick and I smile, pressing my hand against the spot. "Hey, sweetie, what are doing?"

She gives two solid kicks at the sound of my voice, which makes me smile wider. I've definitely been able to tell that she responds to my voice, which is *awesome*. She responds to Xander too, which is cool. Sometimes when he's talking she starts to move around wildly, almost like she's dancing to the sound of his voice.

I'm officially in my third trimester now, which is just crazy to me. This is the home stretch now. Soon, we're going to have a baby.

Thankfully, I finally feel ... happy about the whole thing. Excited, even. I was worried I'd spend my whole pregnancy feeling miserable, but lately it's been great. Something tells me my grace period might be over soon, though, because from what I've read, your third trimester can make you feel miserable. It's understandable, too. There's a huge baby inside you and there's only so much room in your body.

I have an appointment with my doctor later today. At this point in my pregnancy I have to go in every two weeks, but they said the appointments should be in and out—so hallelujah to that.

Except I have to have my glucose test today, so this one will be longer. What sucks is I'm *starving* since I'm not allowed to eat before and I can only have small amounts of water.

I finish my online shopping and Xander comes down about an hour after that, waking me up since apparently I dozed off on the couch.

"Huh? What?" I sit up, my eyes dazed.

He chuckles at me, covered in flecks of pink paint. "I said I was jumping in the shower before your appointment. I have all the pink coats done and it'll have to dry before I do the rest."

"I can't wait to see it." I'm absolutely giddy thinking about the way the nursery is coming together.

"Don't even think about peeking," he warns me.

"I'll be good, I promise."

He eyes me like he doesn't believe me. Under normal circumstance I'd be up there in a flash checking it out, but at nearly seven months pregnant I'm exhausted and need a longer nap, so while he's showering, I fall back to sleep.

He comes down, changed into fresh clothes with his hair damp.

"Ready to go?" he asks, swiping the keys off the counter.

I stand up and stretch. "I hope I can eat a pizza after this. I'm *starving*."

He chuckles. "Come on, let's go."

He ushers me into the car and we make the short drive to the doctor's office.

I check in and it isn't long until they take me back to a room to take my blood and then hand me the glucose drink.

Xander sits down in the extra chair beside me while I brace myself for the super sweet liquid.

It's not as bad as I thought it'd be, but it's still not pleasant. The orange liquid is slightly thick and flat tasting, like old Sunkist.

I manage to drink it down, making a face of disgust at the end.

Thankfully, the test only takes an hour and they take a few vials of blood throughout.

Afterward, we meet with my doctor and everything's good, and I have no questions, so we're free to leave.

Xander doesn't bother asking me where I want to eat since I brought up pizza earlier. Instead, he heads straight to a local pizza place that wood fire grills their pizzas. My mouth is already watering at the thought of food.

We head inside and are seated quickly in a booth that overlooks the city streets. It's a bleak day, overcast, with a misty rain.

"Thank you for painting the nursery today."

He fights a grin, his lips twitching at the corners. "Even though you wanted to kill me for not letting you look?"

I glance down at the menu and shrug. "Yeah, even then, because soon we're going to be holding our daughter in that room and it'll mean more that you did all the work and not someone else."

He inhales a soft gasp. "I keep forgetting that she's going to be here soon."

"Only about twelve more weeks or so."

He rubs his jaw. "That's the blink of an eye."

It really is.

Once upon a time, three months felt like a lifetime, now it's a minute.

I fear that once she's born those minutes will turn into seconds.

I want to cherish every moment, because I know it'll be gone all too soon.

twenty-eight
...

thea

28 weeks pregnant
Baby is the size of kabocha squash

I gasp.

"What?" Xander looks at me innocently.

"What did you do?" I shriek.

He stares at me like I'm a crazy person—like buddy, you married me, you know my ass is psycho.

"Uh ... shaved?"

"Why?" I ask again, staring sadly at his bare face. "You look five."

He snorts. "Thanks, babe."

I wave my hand at his face. "Put it back. You look weird."

"It doesn't work like that, sorry." He begins cleaning the sink.

"Maybe you should save those." I point to the whiskers he's throwing away. "Maybe you can glue them to your face."

He tilts his head and sighs. "Thea, it's facial hair, it'll be back by tonight."

I let out a dramatic sigh. "It better be. I love your scruff." I frown, staring at his bare face. "But seriously, what possessed you to shave. You rarely have nothing."

"My mom asked me to."

I narrow my eyes. "I officially hate your mom."

He laughs. "You know you don't."

"Okay, I don't, but right now this feels a lot like hate, because my husband looks like a baby." I tilt my head, studying his face. I reach up, grabbing his chin so I can look at him from a different angle. "Is this what our daughter is going to look like?"

"Thea, stop." He removes my hand from his face.

"You didn't let me finish." I pout and he makes a face, urging me to continue. "I was going to say she'd be awfully cute."

"Great, so now I look like a baby and I'm cute. Exactly what every man wants to hear."

"Hey, if the shoe fits, wear it."

I slip my feet into a pair of heels, and I'm finally ready to go. Wearing heels at almost seven months pregnant is insane, but there's no way I can wear flats with this dress. I shudder at the thought. It'd be blasphemy.

We head downstairs and Xander lets Prue run outside to use the bathroom.

I slip my coat on and grab my purse. Xander comes back inside with Prue and gives her a treat.

Xander's mom didn't want us to bring anything for the meal, but I insisted, so she ended up asking me to do the macaroni and cheese. I'd never made it homemade before, but I think it turned out okay.

I grab the platter and look around, making sure we're not forgetting anything.

Xander chuckles and my gaze flicks to him. "What?" I ask.

"I was just thinking ..." He rubs his jaw, still laughing slightly under his breath. "I doubt we'll get out of the house this easy once we have the baby."

I pause, thinking, and laugh too. "I guess you're right. It'll be a lot harder to leave on time and we'll probably always forget something important."

He comes up to me, pressing his hand to my stomach. In the beginning, his hand swallowed my stomach whole, now not so much. "I can't wait to see her, though, and finally hold her."

"It's not much longer now," I breathe out.

I still feel scared when I think about the baby actually being *here*, but it's more the fear of the unknown and less a fear of her.

Xander removes his hand from my belly and steps back. "We have to go."

"Right," I mumble.

We load into the car, leaving Prue behind. I can hear her barking through the door and I feel bad for leaving her.

I gasp and Xander looks over at me before backing out of the garage. "What?" he asks. "Did you forget something?" He hits the brakes as I shake my head.

"No, but what about Prue?"

"What about her? She's fine. She just went out, and I gave her food and water."

I shake my head again. "No ... with the baby," I hiss. "What is she going to do with the baby? What if she hates her and is mean?"

He snorts and finishes backing out of the driveway. "Prue doesn't have a mean bone in her body."

"*Now*," I agree. "But she's never really been around babies before. What if she thinks it's some sort of strange puppy and tries to get the baby in her mouth."

Xander laughs at me.

"Stop laughing at me," I whine. "I'm being serious here. She could try to bite her."

"Thea," he says sternly, "you're worrying about nothing. Prue will be fine. You'll see."

"Ugh," I groan.

I hate it when he dismisses my worries like I'm being silly. There are horror stories of dogs being mean to babies—yes, I know most aren't, but you never know. We've had Prue for three years, and it's always only just been her, so what if she has some sort of ... oldest child syndrome and wants to take out the weakest link. Weakest link equals the baby, obviously.

We arrive at Xander's parent's house and find that we're the last ones there.

My mom and James are joining us here, but Cade and Rae are spending the holiday with her family. Jace and Nova were invited, but they opted to do something just the two of them. But it'll still be a larger crowd with both Xander's parents, his sister, and his brother in for the holiday.

Xander doesn't bother knocking since his mom gets mad when he does. He swings the door open and waves me inside first, even though he's holding the heavy macaroni dish.

I scurry inside and out of the cold.

It's going to snow soon—I can feel it. It's like something in the air changes, and you can't help but know that a big snow is coming.

"Ah, there you guys are," Sarah ushers us inside. "Oh, good, you shaved," she says when she sees Xander, standing on her tiptoes to kiss his cheek. "I asked your little brother to shave too and he didn't listen."

"Yeah, because I didn't want to look like a fetus!" we hear Xavier yell through the house.

Xander shakes his head. "Where do you want me to put this, Mom?" He nods at the dish in his hand.

"Just put it on the island on the counter. We decided to do buffet style this year. We figured that was easier than passing at the table."

Xander heads off with the food and I stay in the hall with his mom. I shrug out of my coat and she gasps at my belly.

"Oh, my God, look at you. Can I feel it?"

"Sure." I shrug. It's not like she's a stranger—though some strangers have no problem touching my belly *without* asking. A baby being in there doesn't suddenly give everyone the right to feel me up, but they do it anyway.

She presses her hand to my belly and smiles at me. "Wow. I can't believe I'm going to have my first grandbaby. I bought her something. Wait here."

"You didn't need to do that," I protest as she starts up the stairs.

She pauses and looks back. "Nonsense. She's my first grandbaby, and a girl at that. I have to spoil her rotten. She's a little princess."

She hurries up the last of the steps and I wait patiently at the bottom.

Xander comes back into the foyer, his brows drawn together.

"What are you doing?"

I point up the stairs. "Your mom said she had a gift for the baby."

He grins at me. "That was sweet of her."

He wraps his arm around me, drawing me into his body. It's hard to get as close as I used to with this big belly in the way, and I still have three months to go so I'm only going to get bigger.

Great.

Sarah comes down a moment later. "Oh, good, you're here."

She holds out an ornate decorative box. The box itself is a lacquered shiny off-white finish with pink and gold detailing.

"Open it," Sarah pleads, absolutely giddy.

Xander and I lift the lid together and I gasp, bursting into tears, because *hormones*.

A ballerina spins around to a song that I think is from *The Nutcracker*.

"This is beautiful."

"I ran across it in an antique store, and I had to get it because my grandmother gave me something similar when I was a little girl. It only seemed appropriate that I give my granddaughter something like it."

"It's perfect," I breathe, handing the box to Xander so I can wipe away my tears. "Can you put it in the car so we don't forget it?" I ask him.

"Sure thing. I'll be right back."

He grabs the car keys and dashes outside into the cold.

"Come on." Sarah tugs me toward the kitchen. "Now that you guys are here, we can eat."

An hour later, we're all stuffed and don't want to move.

"The dinner was delicious," I tell Sarah, helping to gather dishes.

"I don't know," Xavier interjects with an impish grin. "It could've been better."

Alexis smacks the back of her brother's head. "Don't be a dick," she scolds him.

"Kids," Sarah groans. "Can't you get along for *one* day. That's all I ask."

"No," they answer simultaneously.

Sarah sighs and shakes her head. "I tried."

Xander stands and helps me gather the dishes and together we carry them to the kitchen to start watching them.

"No, no, no, you guys are guests. You don't clean the dishes," Sarah cries, running into the kitchen. "And *you're* pregnant."

"Exactly," I snort. "I'm pregnant, not handicapped. I want to help."

She sighs.

"Mom, it's not a big deal. It's just dishes."

"Yeah, let my servants take care of it," Xavier jokes, carrying in some more dishes. "Thea, you know you're supposed to get the water *in* the sink not on the floor."

"What?" My brows furrow at his joke. "But we haven't even started washing dishes yet. *Oh*."

That's when I feel the trickle between my legs and I look down to see a puddle of water on the floor.

My horrified eyes fly up to meet Xander's. "Did my water just break?" I ask him stupidly.

He stares open mouthed from the puddle to me. "I ... I don't know. I guess. Are you having contractions?"

"No ... I don't think so. What do they feel like?"

Sarah snorts. "Trust me, you'd know if you were having contractions."

"But ... what is that?" I ask. "It has to be my water, right? But it's too early! Xander," I beg, panicking now, "it's too early."

"Calm down." Sarah takes my face between her hands, forcing me to look at her. "In my honest opinion, as a woman who's given birth to three children, I think you just peed yourself."

"What? No, that can't be it. I just peed not too long ago."

She shakes her head. "Trust me, something similar happened when I was pregnant with Alexis. I'd just peed but she kicked my bladder or something and I peed my pants in the middle of the grocery store."

Xavier busts out laughing. "Oh, my God, Thea peed her pants. This is great. I have to get a picture."

He whips out his phone and snaps a picture before any of us can blink. "Delete that," Xander tells him in a deathly calm voice, his eyes fire.

Xavier frowns. "It's not like I was going to post it."

"No, you were just going to save it to whip it out at every family occasion from now until the end of the time."

Xavier sighs and fiddles with his phone. "It's gone."

"Thank you."

Sarah grabs my hand. "I think you guys should go to the hospital for piece of mind, but I really don't think your water broke."

"What's going on in here?" my mom asks. "Is everything okay? You all disappeared."

"Thea peed her pants," Xavier tells her with a snicker.

"Just remember," Xander warns him, "I'm still bigger than you and I *will* take you down, little brother or not."

Xavier raises his hands innocently. "Just stating fact. Don't shoot the messenger."

"Yes," Sarah tells her, "I'm fairly certain she's peed her pants, but I told them they should go to the hospital anyway to make sure. If she *would* be in labor, it's way too early, so better to know than not."

"Do you want me to go with you?" my mom asks.

I shake my head. "I just want Xander."

"Okay." She frowns, so I can tell she's a little hurt, but she doesn't try to beg. I just know she'd make me more nervous in this kind of situation whereas Xander calms me down.

"Go, *go*," Sarah urges us, when Xander and I keep standing there. "And then call and let us know once you know something."

We say goodbye to his sister and dad, explaining the situation yet again, and then we put on our coats and leave.

Once in the car, I burst into tears.

"Thea," he breathes, backing out of the driveway. He reaches over and grabs my hand, using one to steer. "What's wrong?"

"I'm scared," I mumble through my tears. "What if it was my water and I go into labor early? It's too soon. I don't want to lose her. I love her."

Xander looks over at me with wide sad brown eyes. "I know you do. I'm scared too, but I'm trusting my mom right now. We'll be at the hospital soon and then we'll know for sure. Is she moving?" he asks me.

"I don't know," I admit reluctantly. "I haven't felt her in a little while." I start to cry harder. "What if something happened and she's gone?" He doesn't answer me. "Xander?" I prompt.

He looks over at me, tears in his own eyes. "That's not going to happen," he vows.

I want to believe him, but I know anything can happen.

And it sort of feels like this would be fates way of mocking me, since I was so ant-baby, and now I'm *finally* getting excited about the whole thing.

Since it's Thanksgiving and my doctor's office isn't open, we check-in at the emergency room. We explain the situation and it isn't long until they have me in a room and ask me to change into a gown.

I don't think I've stopped crying the entire time. My face is permanently wet.

Xander sits in the spare chair, his knee bouncing restlessly.

I change into the gown and climb onto the bed. Xander slides his chair closer and takes my hand, kissing my fingers.

"It's going to be okay." He keeps saying that over and over and I think it's more for himself than me.

There's a knock on the door and then it opens to reveal a nurse.

"Hi, I'm Alena. We want to get you hooked up to a fetal heart monitor since you said you weren't feeling much, if any, movement."

My terrified eyes dart to Xander and he looks as scared as I feel.

What if there is no heartbeat?

I pull up the gown for her, revealing my stomach and she comes over with the monitor.

As soon as it's on the steady *whoosh whoosh whooshing* sound fills the air and I burst into tears again.

"That's the greatest thing I've ever heard," I tell the nurse.

Xander stands at my side, rubbing my forehead and when I tilt my head back to look up at him I find him wiping away tears of relief.

"The doctor will be in soon to check your water. The heartbeat sounds great, though. *Breathe,* guys," she encourages.

Xander sits down in the chair again, wrapping our fingers together. His dark hair falls over his forehead into his eyes and I reach to push it back, gliding my fingers over his cheek in the process.

"I thought things were fine and I believed my mom, but when you said you weren't feeling her move …" he pauses, gathering a shaky breath. "Fuck, Thea, I've never felt fear like that before."

"I was scared too." My voice cracks since my throat's dry. "I thought maybe this was some cosmic way of mocking me for finally being happy about the baby."

"Oh, Thea," he breathes, and it's like I can see his heart break. "That would never be true. Some things just happen and there's no reason for them."

He leans over and kisses my forehead and then brushes his lips over mine.

"Please, never think like that," he begs.

I open my mouth to answer him but there's another knock on the door then.

"Hello, hello, I'm Dr. Keegan," a woman in her fifties says, her hair pulled back into a ponytail. "I hear you think your water might've broken."

I nod, sitting up in the bed. "My mother-in-law said she thinks it's more likely I peed my pants, which is embarrassing, but we'd rather be sure."

"You're not having any contractions, so that's a good sign." She points to a print out from the machine. "We're going to check to be sure, though."

Xander moves out of the way and she props my leg up. She slips some gloves on and looks me over.

"This is going to be uncomfortable," she warns.

"Ow." I bite my lip as she pushes her fingers inside, feeling around. I don't know what she's touching but it feels like brain.

After a moment she pulls her fingers out. "Your water is intact, so I think it's safe to say you peed your pants."

"Well ..." I blush. "That's embarrassing."

"Don't be," she assures me. "It happens to a lot of women. Most even poop during childbirth."

My eyes widen in horror. "That's disgusting. I better not do that. *Gross.*" I shudder at the very idea.

She laughs and removes her gloves, tossing them in the disposal box. "Well, if you do, just remember it's perfectly normal. Besides, you rarely even know you've done it."

I shake my head and look at Xander. "Don't even think about looking down there while I'm giving birth."

He raises his hands innocently.

"I'll send someone in with the discharge papers. You can go ahead and get dressed."

"Uh ... what about this?" I point to the monitor on my belly.

"Oh, silly me." She laughs and takes it off of me.

She leaves the room and I hop up, happy to get out of the itchy gown and back into my clothes.

"I can't believe I peed myself," I mutter.

Xander chuckles. "Better that than to go into labor three months early."

"Very true," I agree. "Can you call your mom so she can let everyone know it's okay?" I ask.

He nods. "Yeah, I'll do that now."

Xander calls her and the nurse from earlier comes back. I have to sign a mountain of papers before we can leave, but finally we're free to go. I shrug into my coat and grab my purse.

Xander guides me outside with his hand on my waist. He knows I don't need helping getting out, but I think he feels better to be touching me.

Today has been draining in so many ways, but eye opening in others.

I know now that I'm ready to be a mom. I didn't think I was, or ever would be, but I don't have any doubts now. This little girl is going to change my life, sure, but in the best possible way and I'm ready for whatever she brings.

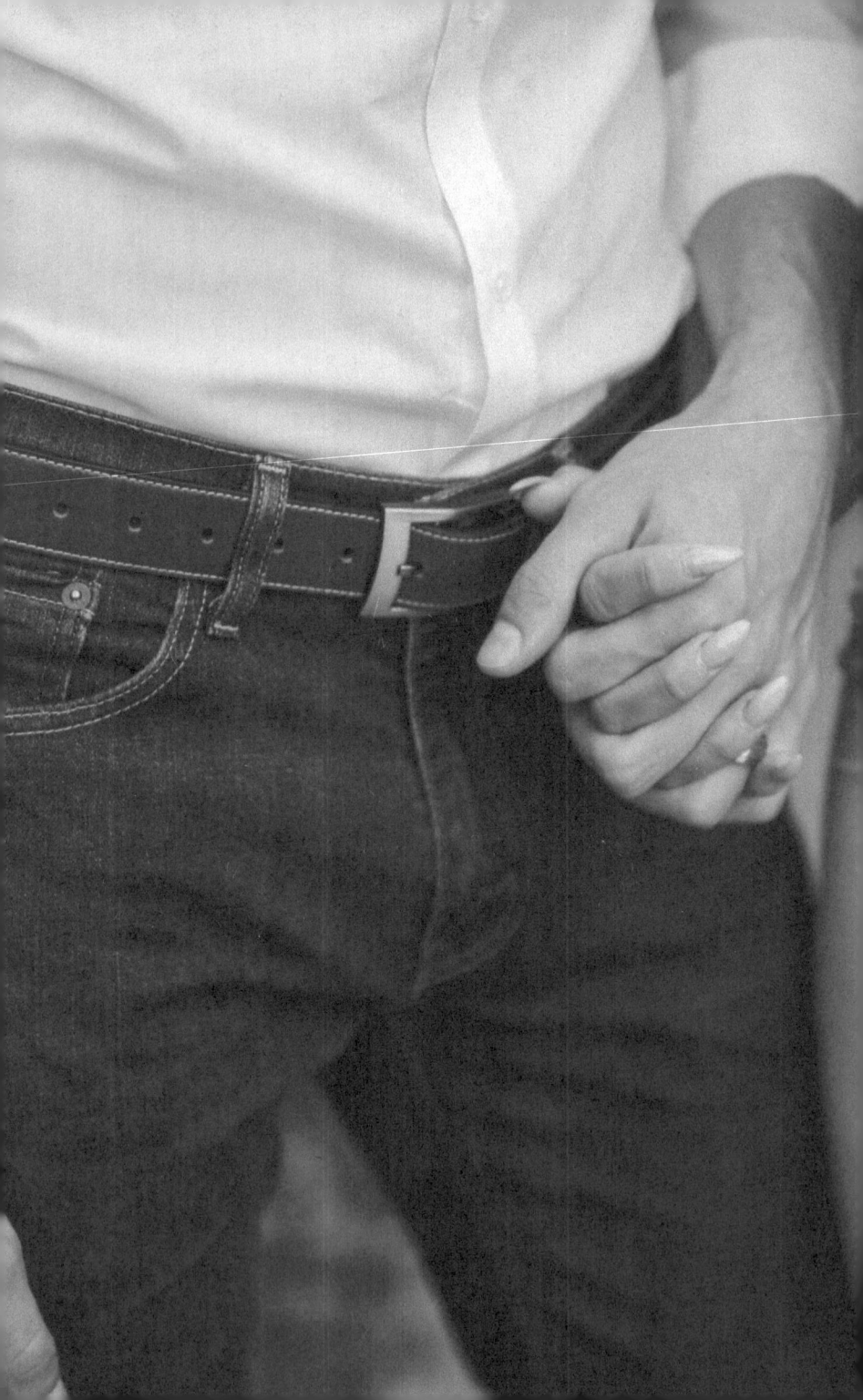

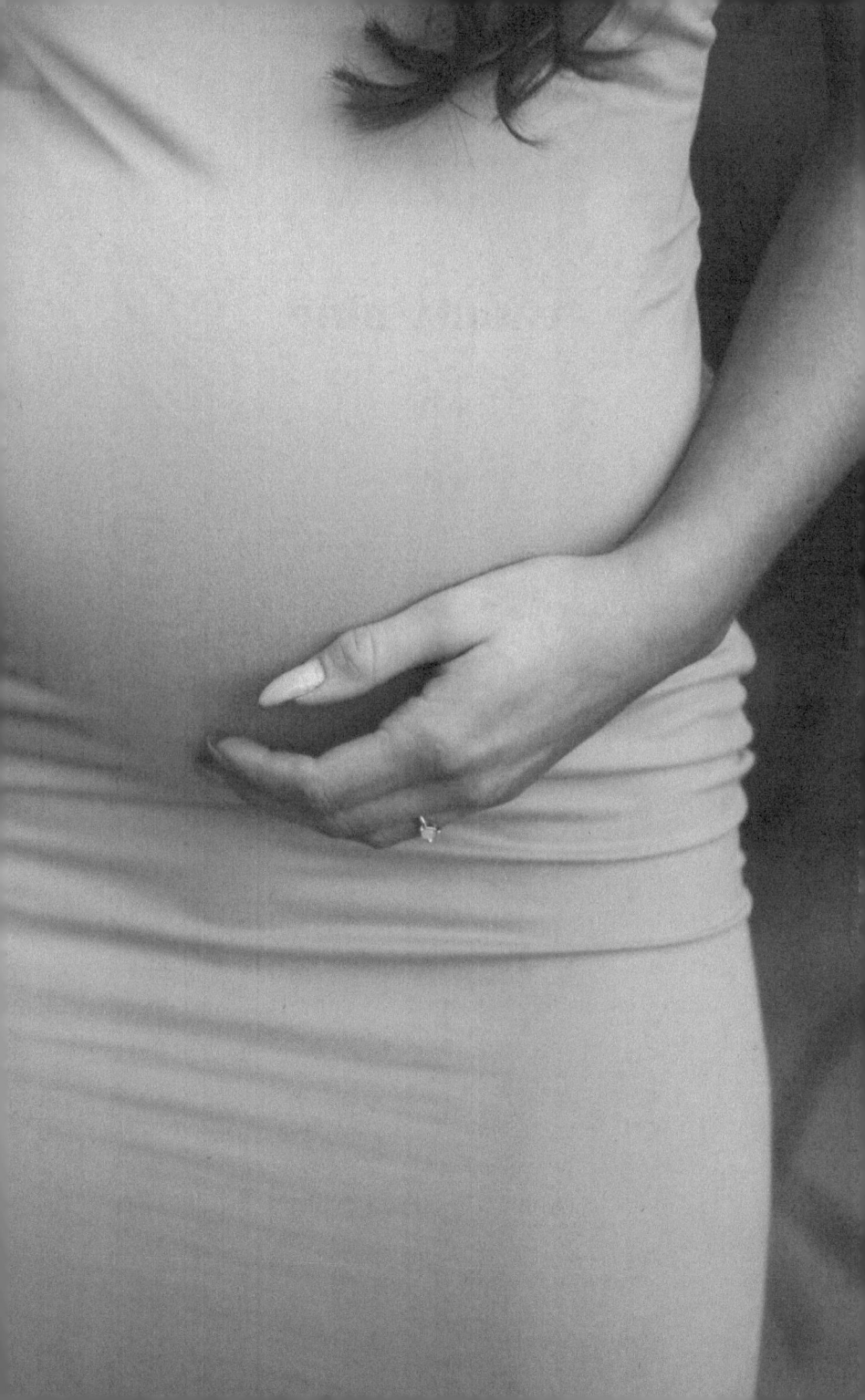

twenty-nine
. . .

thea

29 weeks pregnant
Baby is the size of butternut squash

"Xander!" I come running out of our closet horrified.

"What?" He looks up from his shoe he's slipping on.

I can't even take a moment to appreciate how nice he looks dressed up for Rae and Cade's wedding because I'm freaking the fuck out.

"I ripped my bridesmaid's dress trying to get into it. I need you to sew me in."

He looks at me like I'm crazy. "I play football, Thea. I don't sew."

I snap my fingers at his computer. "Then look up a video and *learn*. I need to get into this dress. I can't believe I've gained this much weight since my last fitting. This is ridiculous." I frown at the seam in the silvery gray dress.

"Do we even have a needle and thread?" he asks, standing up and making his sure his shirt is tucked in.

"Yes, it's a necessity when you have a house. You never know when you're going to have to sew something."

He sighs. "I'll look up a video," he promises. "Just give me a minute."

"Thank you," I tell him honestly. Rae's not a bridezilla, but I don't think she'd take too kindly if I show up in something that's not my bridesmaid dress. It'd throw off her whole color scheme.

I grab my sewing kit from the laundry room and head back to the bedroom. As promised, Xander is watching a tutorial on how to sew a seam.

He takes the sewing basket from me and finds a needle and thread that's a similar color, threading it through.

I stand beside him holding as still as possible.

"Don't move," he warns.

"If you poke me and get blood on this dress I might punch you."

He bites out a gruff laugh and pinches the fabric, restarting the video.

Thankfully it's not too big of a tear, just enough to be noticeable since my skin is peeking through. His tongue slides through his lips as he concentrates. I hold my breath as he works and ten minutes later it's completely closed. Is it the best job? Definitely not. But for his first time sewing I'll give him a pass.

"Thank you." I kiss him and he smiles against my lips.

I pack the sewing kit and put it away before I finish getting ready.

I keep my makeup light and simple and put my hair back in an up-do that's already approved by Rae.

Xander tends to Prue and then we leave for the wedding.

I can't believe my best friend is marrying my brother. She's going to be a permanent part of our family. It's awesome.

Rae and Cade are getting married in a historic hotel downtown. It's beautiful with amazing views of the city. I'm so happy they let me help plan the wedding as much as I could. Since Xander and I did things the way we did, I didn't plan ours. That's never bothered me, but it's fun to be a part of theirs.

Xander parks in the below ground parking garage and we take the elevator up to the ballroom level.

"Oh, good, there you are," Nova cries when she sees me. She's dressed in a matching dress with her hair pulled back similarly. "Rae's this way. And you—" she points at Xander "—need to go that way. Just start walking you'll hear Jace bitching soon enough."

Xander chuckles. "Okay—you both look beautiful, by the way."

"He had to sew me into my dress," I blurt.

Nova snorts, looking between the two of us. "Seriously?"

"Unfortunately," I mutter.

"That's hilarious," she giggles, looping her arm through mine and dragging me away.

She pulls me into a room that's been sequestered for getting ready.

Rae sits in a chair with a hairdresser styling her hair and someone else doing her makeup. Her mom bustles about the room, checking on various things.

"How are you feeling?" I ask Rae. "Nervous?"

She smiles up at me. "A little. Mostly excited."

"You can still run," I joke. "My brother's an idiot so I wouldn't blame you."

She laughs and shakes her head. "I love him. I'm sure."

"You know this means you're next," I warn Nova.

She snorts and dismisses my words with a wave of her hand. "No way. Jace and I don't want to get married."

I look at her like she's crazy. "Are you serious?"

She nods. "Yeah. We've both talked about it, and it's just not something we need. We don't feel like a piece of paper is going to prove we love each other. What we feel exists in our twisted broken hearts," she jokes with a shrug. "That's all we need."

"That's really kind of beautiful," I admit. "But being married is nice. I love being able to call Xander my husband."

Nova shrugs. "We have no plans to get married. That's all I can tell you."

Rae doesn't make any comment, but her eyes connect with mine and I know she thinks it's as crazy as I do. Don't get me wrong, I know you don't have to get married, and they're free to do what they want, but I don't want to them to miss out on something.

"You need to get in your dress," Rae's mom tells her. "It's almost time."

"I'll be done here in a minute," the hair stylist says. The makeup artist has already finished and packs up her stuff.

A few minutes later, her hair is done and it looks amazing. It's pulled back into a sleek bun, secured at the back of her neck.

She hops up and we help her into her dress, all the while the wedding photographer is snapping away.

When the veil is added and Rae looks in the mirror, she starts to cry.

She looks beautiful.

Truly.

Her makeup is done soft so that her natural beauty shines through, and the dress she chose is stunning. It's a tank-top style top that dips down into a V in the front, fitting until her waist with lace detailing, where it then billows out with an explosion of tulle.

"You look like a princess," I tell her, tears in my eyes. Being pregnant is turning me into a weepy mess.

She twirls around and around, letting out a tinkling laugh. She stops in front of us, her cheeks rosy and her eyes brimming with tears.

"I'm ready to marry my man now."

I laugh. "Cade's going to shit himself when he sees you."

"Let's not go *that* far." She laughs. "I'd love for him to cry, though."

We're ushered out of the room and down the hall and we line up outside the closed double doors.

Jace and Nova are walking first and then Xander and me, with the bride bringing up the rear with her dad.

"Hey, hot stuff." I loop my arm through the crook of Xander's and someone who I think is part of the hotel staff hands me my bouquet.

Xander bends his head and kisses my cheek.

"What was that for?" I ask.

He shrugs, straightening up. "Because I wanted to."

I smile. "I like that answer."

He chuckles.

"You look beautiful—really."

"Thanks." I smooth my hands down my dress. "It's a little tight, but ..."

"I like it." He presses his hand to my belly and the baby kicks in response.

"You're going to have to rip me out of it tonight."

He grins, stifling a laugh. "I like the sound of that."

"It's time," someone tells us. "Show time."

The doors open and Jace and Nova walk ahead of us.

Xander waits for our turn and then starts forward. He walks slow, matching my pace.

We separate taking our places and then the music changes.

Everybody stands, looking toward the entrance for Rae.

When she appears in the doorway on her dad's arm, I look to see Cade's reaction. He gasps, his lips parted, and tears fill his eyes. He takes a deep breath and grins at her. He's cut his hair and the atrocious beard is gone, replaced by some heavy scruff.

Rae reaches him and he takes her hand, whispering something in her ear that makes her blush.

I begin to cry, because it's a wedding, and that's my brother and best friend, and it's just beautiful.

I barely hear their vows over my struggles to regain myself.

Before I know it, they're announced as husband and wife, making their way back up the aisle.

We clear out of the room and the hotel staff hurries to get it ready for the reception.

In the meantime, we hang out outside the room. Rae and Cade have disappeared for pictures, and soon we're called to join them for the group ones.

When the pictures are done, the room is ready for the reception.

They've transformed the ballroom into a winter wonderland. Silver and white curtains hang down over all the walls, adding a softness. The tables are all covered in silver tablecloths. There's an area for dancing and a stage for the band.

We all take our seats for the sit down dinner of steak or fish.

I'm amazed by how many people are at the wedding. It's still small by most people's standards, but larger than some.

While they eat, Cade leans over periodically and whispers in Rae's ear. He must say something dirty once because she smacks his shoulder.

I'm so incredibly happy for them, though.

On a day like today I can't help but be reminded of the depressed girl I met when we were roommates our freshman year. She was so unhappy and didn't want to be friends with anybody, and look at her now. More than friends, she has a whole new *family*. Sometimes what we think we don't want is exactly what we need.

She laughs at something he says and I smile.

"Why are you smiling?" Xander asks me.

"I'm just happy," I tell him. "Everyone ... We all seem to be doing exactly what we're meant to be doing." I point at Cade and Rae laughing and admiring their new wedding rings, Jace staring at Nova as she photographs the wedding, and then finally, I indicate us and my very large bump.

Xander grins back at me and touches my belly. "Life's good," he agrees.

"It's perfect," I breathe.

"Not quite," he disagrees. "But it will be once she's here." He rubs my tummy.

I place my hand over his, smiling.

"I can't wait to meet her."

"Me too. I wonder who she looks like," he murmurs.

"I don't know. It doesn't matter."

"I hope she looks like you." He bends his head, kissing my shoulder.

"Funny, because I hope she looks like you," I admit, and he grins back.

"Two more months and we'll know."

"Did you hear that, little girl?" I ask my belly. "Two more

months and we'll know what you look like. We can't wait to see you."

I'm more than ready to meet her now.

Well, that's a lie. We still have to finish getting her nursery put together, but after that ... it's game on.

thirty
...

xander

33 weeks pregnant
Baby is the size of a pineapple

"Thea, would you stop breathing down my neck. I'm trying to concentrate."

"I don't think that goes there."

"Thea," I groan. "Don't you have something better to do?"

I've been trying to put together the crib for the last hour, and Thea picked the hardest fucking crib in the whole universe. This thing is impossible, but I'm determined to do it myself. I was planning to do this next week, but I think her flocking or nesting or whatever it's called has kicked in, because she's turned into a psychopath. It's Christmas Eve and she's insisting that everything in the nursery is ready, like the baby's going to drop from the sky tomorrow.

The baby isn't due until February twentieth, but at our last appointment the doctor warned he thinks she's going to come early since the baby is measuring big. Not by much, only by a week or two. Thea of course laughed hysterically at that, telling me she told me our child was a Viking like me.

But since then, she's gone into this mode where everything needs to be ready. I've already put the stroller together and installed the car seat in the car, and she's packed her hospital bag.

I keep reminding her we have plenty of time, but she won't fucking listen.

Stubborn woman.

"If you're going to stand there, make yourself useful and hand me that." I point to a screw that's rolled away.

She sighs. "You could at least ask nicely."

I sigh, removing my baseball cap and putting it on backward. "*Please*," I bite out.

"That still didn't sound very nice, but okay." She grabs the errant screw and hands it to me. "Do you want me to ask Cade to come over and help you? There's a lot to put together." She looks around at the items still in their boxes.

"I can do this," I assure her.

I already have the dresser together, which also functions as the changing table, and the armoire, but the crib, rocker, bookcase, and chest are still left.

Thea stretches her legs out on the floor, rubbing her stomach and groaning.

"She's kicking up a storm." She lifts up her shirt. "Look."

I look over and my jaw drops because she's not kidding. Her stomach ripples as the baby moves around and around.

"That's crazy." I shake my head, in awe of the whole thing.

"Ugh." She presses her hand to the spot and the movement disappears. "I feel like I've been pregnant forever. I wish she'd come already."

I chuckle. "She needs to cook some more. Leave her alone. We don't want her to come out until she's ready."

"True," she agrees. "But I'm going to really hate life the closer I get to my due date." She lowers her shirt and lets out another groan. "You know what else?"

I sigh, resolving myself to the fact that I'm going to be here all night putting this stuff together.

"What?"

"I want a refund, aren't you supposed to get bigger boobs when you're pregnant? What kind of sorcery is this? Mine are still small." She glares down at her chest.

"There's nothing wrong with your boobs, Thea."

"What if something's wrong though? I read this article the other day about this woman that accidentally starved her baby to death, because she was breastfeeding and thought the baby was eating but it wasn't. Maybe I should bottle feed."

"Do you believe everything you read on the internet?" I ask her, finally finishing the frame of the crib. I stand it up and move it to the spot she wants it, beneath the canopy on the wall.

"Well, no."

I grab the mattress and lift it over the railing. "If you want to breastfeed, go for it. If you want to do the bottle, do that. You wanna try both? Knock yourself out."

"The crib is perfect," she breathes, admiring it. She rubs her fingers over the wood finish. "I know she won't be sleeping here at first, but this ... this is the most beautiful nursery I've ever seen. It's perfect for her."

"She might be a tad bit spoiled," I admit, looking around the room. It's a fairy princess wonderland for a little girl.

Thea busies herself with fixing the bedding on the crib, which allows me to start on the glider uninterrupted.

This isn't how I imagined spending my Christmas Eve, but it's not so bad.

Seeing everything for her room come together makes it more real.

We're going to have a baby in a little over a month.

It takes Thea a while to get the bedding just right, so I manage to finish with the glider. I'm opening the box for the bookcase when she collapses on the fluffy rug in the middle of the room, staring up at the chandelier.

"She's doing somersaults," she complains, rolling up her shirt again so we can watch her stomach move. "Sweetie," she scolds, "you're going to make Mommy pee her pants again if you keep that up."

I snort and she laughs too, looking over at me. "Hey, handsome, I want to have your babies."

I shake my head, pulling out the pieces for the bookcase. "I'm pretty sure you're having one." I point at her belly.

She smiles, rubbing her stomach. "Lucky me."

"Really? I think you hated me in the beginning."

She fights a smile. "I may or may not have contemplated chopping off your dick and feeding it to the dog, but I've since forgiven you."

I bite out a laugh. "Thanks, I think."

She shrugs, biting her lip. "I won't lie, I wasn't happy. I didn't think I was cut out to be a mom yet, but now …" she pauses, rubbing her stomach absentmindedly. "I'm really excited to meet her. I don't feel scared. I can do this. Is it going to be hard? Yeah, of course. But I'm ready for the challenge."

"You're going to be a great mom," I tell her honestly. It isn't the first time I've said it, and I've meant it every time, but it means more now that she trusts that it's true.

"You're going to be an amazing daddy. This little girl is lucky to have you. Truly." I lean over and kiss her and she smiles. "What was that for?"

"Because I can. Merry Christmas Eve, Thea."

"Merry Christmas Eve, Xander."

"It's Christmas! It's Christmas! Wake up!" Thea bounces on the bed. "Xander, it's Christmas!" She shakes my arm.

I yawn, covering my eyes with the crook of my elbow. "What time is it?" I mumble sleepily.

"That's not important." She grabs my arm, shaking me. "Get up, get up, please. Let's open presents."

I groan and sit up, rubbing the sleep from my eyes, and she claps, pleased to have gotten me awake.

I look at the clock and the blinking numbers. "You have to be kidding me," I groan. It's only five-thirty in the morning. "I'm going back to bed." I roll over, hugging the pillow to my chest.

She rubs my bare back. "No, no, get up. I want to open presents."

"One more hour," I beg.

"Xander," she pleads. "Get up."

"You're not going to go away, are you?" I ask.

"Nope." She bounces on the bed.

I roll back over to face her. "All right. I'm showering first, though. Can you start some coffee for me?"

"You got it." She hops up and dashes out the door. She moves pretty quickly for someone so heavily pregnant. I'm impressed.

I roll out of bed and head across the room into the bathroom, starting the shower. It isn't long until the room is steamy. I shower, taking longer than normal, but it helps to wake me up.

Only my wife would be psychotic enough to wake me up at five-thirty on Christmas. I should be used to it. She does it every year. Something tells me next year she'll be even worse since it'll be the baby's first Christmas.

I finish in the shower and change into a pair of sweatpants and a t-shirt, since we're hanging out at the house today.

I start down the stairs, inhaling the scent of coffee.

I round the corner into the kitchen and Thea hands me a cup of coffee. In her other hand she holds a glass of lemon water. Shocker.

"Can we open presents now?" She dances on the tips of her toes.

I sweep my hand toward the tree. "Knock yourself out."

Our tree is decorated with white lights and pink, silver, and purple ornaments. It's a pretty girly tree, but seeing as I now have a wife and daughter, I figure I need to get used to it. My life is going to be surrounded by all things girl for a while. Though, our daughter could grow up to be a tomboy, which would be fine too. I want her to do and be whatever it is she wants to be. I'm looking forward to teaching her to play football and punch guys the right way—because my little girl is going to know how to defend herself if she needs to.

I sit down on the floor beside Thea, and she's already tearing through her stocking. It's filled mostly with bath products, like those bath bombs she loves and body wash and bubble bath. I take a long sip of coffee and then grab my stocking. It's filled with shaving stuff, a watch, socks, cologne, a portable phone charger, and other random items.

Thea sets her empty stocking aside and starts tearing through her gifts.

I'm not going to lie, shopping for her is *hard*. She's picky and she's not afraid to tell you if she hates something. Plus, the girl has a shopping addiction so sometimes she buys something before I have the chance to get it.

She opens her first gift and gasps. "I love it. This is beautiful." She holds up the new ivory leather purse I picked out for her.

"You really like it?" I ask, surprised.

"Yes, it's perfect. I can get so much stuff in this."

I open my first gift and bust out laughing. It's a boxed set of all the *Jaws* movies. "Can't have too many copies of these," I tell her, setting it aside.

She opens another gift, and then me, both of us alternating until there's nothing left.

"I have one last thing to give you, but it's actually for the baby," I explain.

"Oh?" She raises a brow and waits.

I hop up and grab the wrapped gift from the closet.

I'm nervous about the gift. I got it for the baby's room, but she might hate it. When I saw it, I couldn't resist having it made. I thought it was beautiful and different, like us.

I hand her the wrapped gift. It's thin and kind of long, maybe four feet.

She unwraps it, revealing the white box beneath and lifts the lid off. She pushes the tissue paper aside and gasps.

"Oh, my God. Xander ..." she breathes, pressing a shaking hand to her lips. "This is stunning."

I help her lift it out of the box.

"Do you think it'll go in her room?" I ask worriedly. "I had to get it, but I thought you might not like how it looks with everything else."

"No." She shakes her head. "It'll be beautiful."

I had the baby's first name spelled out on a piece of reclaimed wood with twigs and greenery intertwined around it so that it stands out boldly. I thought it was unique and different, but I wasn't sure if Thea would like the rustic style compared to the girly and pink look she has going on in the nursery.

"It'll be perfect above the door in her room. It's amazing, Xander." She rises on her knees and leans over to press a kiss to my lips.

I grin, pleased that she loves it. "I thought it would be special for her first Christmas since she isn't actually here yet."

Tears fill her eyes. "So special. This little girl is so lucky. You're already the best daddy and she's not even here yet."

Thea wraps her arms around my neck and hugs me, kissing the scruff on my cheek.

I close my eyes, content to stay wrapped in this moment a little bit longer.

I'd say Christmas was a success, and I finally allow myself to breathe a sigh of relief.

Now, we just have to make it through the baby shower.

thirty-one

thea

38 weeks pregnant
Baby is the size of a stalk of rhubarb

"Xander Kincaid, where are you taking me?" I groan, staring out the car window.

"Just be patient. You'll see," he urges.

I sigh, wiggling uncomfortably in the passenger seat of the Range Rover. I'm huge now. At thirty-eight weeks pregnant, I'm reaching the end of my pregnancy and with it all my patience for everything. I haven't slept in two weeks. I'm hot. I'm uncomfortable. I'm nauseous. I'm crampy. It's always something.

"I want to go home, eat snacks, and watch TV," I protest, figuring he's going to force me to socialize. I didn't even want to put pants on this morning, which is a big deal for me, because I love clothes and dressing up.

"Trust me, this is better," he assures me.

Ten minutes later, he pulls up outside a café I've never been to before. There's a sign with yellow and white balloons attached, swaying in the wind.

Xander parallel parks and then comes around to help me out. I don't really need the help, he's just paranoid the baby's going to fall out or something.

She's definitely dropped, that's for sure.

He takes my hand and helps me out, guiding me into the café. He seems to know where he's going, unlike me.

He reaches a back room and I gasp.

"Surprise!" yells our friends and family.

"Oh, my God." And then I burst into tears, because *hormones*.

The room is decorated with more yellow and white balloons with a sign when you first walk in that says, *Where troubles melt like lemon drops*. The tablecloths are all yellow and there are even cookies make to look like lemons.

"It's perfect," I confess, as my friends come around the table.

"Do you like it?" Rae asks, coming up to hug me. "I was worried it wouldn't be pink enough for you, but Xander said with your lemon craving we should do a lemon theme."

"This is better than I could've dreamed of," I admit. "It's ... wow."

I look around a table piled high with gifts and another with food. On the food table there are mason jars filled with lemon water and a yellow and white-striped straws.

Behind the table are streamers of yellow, pink, and white circles.

For decorations there are vases full of lemons and all kinds of lemon treats.

"I can't believe you guys did all this for me."

"We love you." Nova takes my hand and squeezes it. "And we love this little girl already. We wanted to do something special."

I wipe away my tears and look up at Xander. "You're forgiven for making me wear pants."

He chuckles. "Good to know."

I kiss him and look around the room again. "Where do we start?" I ask.

"Well, there's food, gifts, and games. You're the baby mama. What do you want to do?" my mom asks, already munching on a cookie.

"I'm starving," I admit.

"Food it is," Xander's mom declares.

An hour later, we're all stuffed and done with games, so we start on the presents.

"We know you guys have gotten pretty much everything

you need, so most of this stuff is clothes," Rae admits. "But no baby can have too many clothes."

Cade reaches over and rubs her shoulder and she smiles back at him. They're both tan and glowing from their Hawaiian honeymoon.

Rae hands me a bag. "This is from us." She indicates herself and Cade.

Xander sits beside me, watching as I open the bag.

I bust out laughing. "Continuing with the lemon theme, I see." I pull out a cute lemon jumper and a swaddle with lemons.

Rae shrugs. "It was too perfect to pass up."

"This is from us." Nova hands me a large bag

"Actually, it's just from Nova. I don't know what the fuck's in there so I shouldn't get any credit."

Nova shakes her head and sighs. "Boys," she mumbles.

I pull out the first item. "Aw, this is adorable." It's a cute floral romper with pom poms on the sleeves and legs that'll be adorable for summer. Next I pull out a pair of gray flats with pink bows on the feet. Then I pull out a shirt for me that says Boss Lady and there's a matching one for the baby that says Mini Boss. "These are great, Nova. Thank you."

She laughs. "You know I like my word shirts, so I thought you and the little lady could continue my tradition."

I fold everything again and put it back in the bag.

My mom points to a large box. "That's from me."

I try to lift it off the table but it's much too heavy. I stand up and rip the paper off, revealing the package beneath.

"Mom," I breathe in a scolding tone. "This is too much."

It's an infant seat that bounces, rocks, and sways. I'd looked them up and was planning to order one but since it's a more expensive item I'd been holding off.

"I wanted to," she insists. "I wanted my granddaughter to have something special from me."

"Aw, well thank you, Mom." I hug her and kiss her cheek.

I start to get a little weepy thinking about how loved this little girl already is and she's not even here yet. She's so incredibly lucky.

I open the gifts from Xander's mom and dad next. It's an assortment of clothes, swaddles, and diapers.

Xander's sister Alexis hands me her gift and I open it up to reveal a plaque that says, *First we had each other, then we had you, and now we have everything*.

"Alexis," I breathe, smiling up at my sister-in-law. "I love it."

"Really? I wasn't sure."

"No, it's amazing," I rush to assure her.

"The last gift is from Xavier," Rae informs me, handing Xander a little bag. "I had strict instructions that this was to go to you."

Xander sighs and takes the bag, looking at it like a snake is about to jump out and bite him. Knowing Xavier, it might.

He removes the tissue paper and laughs at what he holds.

"What is it?" I ask, trying to see it.

I laugh when he shows me. It's a onesie that says Dad You Got This in the center, and then has arrows pointing to where the arms, legs, and head go.

"Only Xavier," I mutter.

Xander shakes his head and puts the onesie back in the bag.

I lay my head on his shoulder.

"Can we have cake now?" I ask, eyeing the lemon cake we've yet to cut into. We all decided to wait and do that last.

"Oh, thank God, I've been wanting cake since I got here," Jace cries.

"I changed my mind," I chortle. "No cake. We'll pack it up and take it with us."

"No," Jace cries. "I need the cake." He pouts. I love getting under his skin way too much. It's a hobby.

The girls ignore me and begin cutting the cake. Rae hands me the first piece and Xander the second, which makes Jace frown. I stick my tongue out at him. Childish? Yes. But you know what, the minute we stop picking fun is the minute we all start walking around with sticks up our asses. Sometimes you just have to be silly and that's okay.

I take a bite of cake and moan.

This takes my lemon craving to a whole new level, because lemon cake is officially the greatest thing I've ever tasted.

"Oh, my God," I moan.

Xander snickers beside me. "That good, huh?"

"Better," I mumble, shoving another bite of food in my mouth.

Jace finally gets a plate and starts digging in. "This is really fucking good," he declares, mouth full of lemon cake.

I finish my cake, and as much as I want a second piece, I

refrain. I'm still full from the lunch, and I don't want to overdue it. I'm already stuffed feeling enough as it is with this giant Viking baby. If she gets much bigger she's going to get stuck in there.

"So," Xander starts, brushing his lips over the side of my forehead, "did we do good?"

I smile at him and then Rae and Nova. "You guys did great. Truly. Best baby shower a girl could ask for. All I need now is my baby," I joke.

He chuckles. "One step at a time."

thirty-two
. . .

thea

39 weeks and 1 day pregnant
Baby is the size of a watermelon

Everything is ready.

The car seat is in the car.

The crib is put together.

The basinet is in our room.

The playpen is taking up space in the family room.

The hospital bag is packed and by the door.

All I need is my freaking baby.

"Get out," I beg, squatting down. "Please, get out already."

"What are you doing?" Xander asks as I raise and squat again. "That can't be good for the baby. What if it falls out?"

"Trust me," I tell him, blowing out a breath. "It isn't that easy."

"We need to go. Can you stop whatever it is you're doing," he begs, looking at me like he's ready to brace himself to catch the baby if he needs to.

"I suppose. Put the hospital bag in the car, though. I want it to be in there for when we're ready."

He sighs, and puts his coat on to head outside. I do the same.

It's February fourteenth—Valentine's Day, but instead of celebrating the day with my husband we're going to a charity football game. Xander's team is playing the local college team for fun to raise money for the local children's hospital. It's an amazing cause and the sale of tickets has already raised a ton of money for the hospital, which is awesome. As much as I'd love to spend the day with Xander to ourselves, this is an amazing opportunity.

Both teams are wearing special made jerseys to represent the hospital.

It's a sweet thing they're doing.

Rae, Cade, Jace, and Nova are meeting us there because Xander didn't want me to be in the box by myself.

Xander I load into the car and head over to the field.

He parks in the garage and takes me to the box, because he's paranoid, before he leaves to go get ready.

It isn't long until Rae and Cade join me in the box and then shortly after that Jace and Nova.

"Are you sure it's okay for you to be here?" Cade asks, munching on some apple slices provided. "That kid looks like it's going to come sailing out any minute."

I sigh, rubbing my stomach. I've been feeling uncomfortable since last night, but I don't think it's labor. I wish, though.

"I'm fine," I assure my brother. He looks doubtful and keeps a watchful eye on me.

I pour myself a glass of water and sit down again. I sip at my water and Rae reaches over, tapping my arm.

"What'd your doctor say? Are you dilated any?"

I had an appointment two days ago. "He said I was three centimeters and he mumbled some other kind of doctor mumbo-jumbo. He thinks I'm going to go into labor by Friday." It's Wednesday, and even though two days isn't that far away, when you're this pregnant it feels like forever.

"You look like you're ready to pop," Jace interjects. "Maybe we should poke you with a needle and see if that helps."

I give him my best withering glare. "Not helpful, Jacen."

His lip curls at my use of his full first name.

"How are you feeling?" Nova asks.

"Tired," I reply honestly. "I haven't slept in weeks and I just want her to get out."

She laughs but gives me an understanding smile. "That's how I was. The last two weeks *sucked*. You're miserable, and tired, but so excited to meet them."

I frown, wondering how it must've felt to be her, to be so

young, and carry a child for nine months, and then give birth and immediately have to give it away.

That would suck hardcore.

Nova's a stronger person than I am, because I know that would break me.

The game begins and our idle chat dwindles. I get sucked into the game, and start cheering like a crazy person.

"Woohoo! Come on! Yes! That's how you do it!"

You'd think this game actually counted for something and wasn't just for fun.

"Yes! Ahhh!"

"Can you stop that?" Cade asks. "I don't think all the jumping is necessary, and it can't be good for the baby."

"Shut up," I groan.

Boys are so annoying.

The game progresses, and I start to sweat from all the jumping and dancing I'm doing. I can't help it, I'm a hyper person.

"Here, drink some water," Rae coaxes, handing me a fresh glass.

I take it gratefully, sipping at the ice-cold water. I clear my throat, feeling a little pain in my abdomen.

"Are you okay?" Nova asks, her eyes clouded with concern.

"Yeah, I'm fine," I promise.

I definitely don't think it's contractions. It hurts, but it's not painful, more uncomfortable like a lot of pressure. More than likely this little girl is pushing against my bladder and I'm going to end up peeing my pants again.

"You're not having contractions are you?" Cade asks. "Don't fucking lie, sis."

"You guys worry too much." I roll my eyes, dismissing their concern, but I notice them all, even Jace, watch me a little closer.

The game continues, and I'm amazed how well the college guys are doing against the NFL team. It's nice seeing the camaraderie on the field though—the older guys actually stopping to give them pointers. It's a more relaxed and fun environment.

I stand up, peering out of the glass.

I gasp, feeling wetness trickle down my leg. I look down at the tiny stream dampening my jeans.

My gaze darts to Nova since she's closest. "Um ... Nova, what's it like when your water breaks?"

"I don't know, they had to break mine so I think it was different than if it breaks on its own." Her jaw drops. "Oh, my God, do you think yours broke?" she asks, looking down at my pants.

"I don't know. I've peed my pants a couple times since the first time and it's always a puddle, this is ... it's not much but it's something." I take a deep breath.

"Are you having contractions yet? We need to time them if you are."

"I don't know. I guess what I've been feeling is contractions, but I didn't know."

"Should we get her to a hospital?" Cade asks.

"Of course we fucking should, dipshit." Jace smacks the

back of his head and I'm shocked of all people that he's coming to my defense.

"When you think you're having a contraction, tell me," Nova instructs. "I'll time them. Let's get you to the hospital. Did you drive? We can't all fit in Jace's truck."

"Xander drove the Range Rover, but he has the keys with him."

"Dammit," Nova curses. "Cade, we'll have to go in your Jeep."

We start to head out of the box, but I feel what I guess is a contraction. "Stop, stop, stop," I plead, pressing a hand on my back. "Contraction."

Nova presses a button on her phone to keep track. The contraction only lasts a minute and then we're on our way again.

"Someone's going to have to tell Xander!" I cry when we're almost to Cade's car. "He doesn't know! Oh, my God we have to go back!" I start to go back into the stadium, but they tighten their grip on me and urge me forward.

Cade hands his car keys to Jace. "You get her to the hospital. I'm going to go get Xander."

"What are you going to do?" I cry, near tears, because this shit hurts and I want my husband.

"I'll climb onto the damn field if I have to," he mutters, before jogging off and disappearing from sight.

Nova climbs into the back with me, coaching me through my contractions, which at the moment seem to be ten minutes apart.

Rae sits up front with Jace and he quickly makes adjustments with the seat, before speeding out of the parking garage.

"You're going to meet your little girl today," Nova tells me, holding my hand. "A Valentine's baby."

"This hurts," I whine, squeezing her hand.

"I know, I know. Believe me. Just breathe through it. Mirror my breaths," she coaxes, doing exaggerated slow breaths.

I copy her and it helps some but not a lot.

"I want Xander," I beg.

He keeps me calm and sane ... somewhat.

With the city traffic it takes us thirty minutes to get to the hospital and in that time my contractions move to five minutes apart. I'm drenched in sweat by the time we reach the hospital. I already called my doctor on the way, so they're expecting us.

Jace parks at the front and hops out, getting a wheelchair and bringing it to the car. He helps me into it.

"Thank you, Jace."

He grins. "It didn't even kill you to call me Jace that time, did it?"

"Oh, shut up," I groan through a laugh. "Nova," I beg. "Will you go in with me until Xander gets here?" Rae looks a little green, so I think it's best if she's not in the room right now, besides Nova's been through this so she knows what to tell me.

"Sure, whatever you want." She unbuckles her seatbelt and hops out.

"Grab my purse," I plead, pointing to the inside of the car. "I need my phone."

Jace grabs it before she can get it and places it in my lap.

"I'll park the car and then Rae and I will hang out in the waiting room," Jace tells her.

Nova wheels me inside and we head to labor and delivery.

When we reach the level they take one look at me and get us into a room.

I change into the gown and then sign their papers. Once all that's done I finally get ahold of my phone.

I have twenty missed calls from Xander. I call him back and he answers on the first ring.

"Thea?" He breathes a sigh of relief. "Please tell me I didn't miss it."

"You didn't miss it. They haven't checked me yet so I don't know how far I am, but hurry. I need you. Where are you?"

I hear him hit his hand against the steering wheel. "I got out of there as fast as I could. Cade ran onto the fucking field and I barely caught sight of security dragging him away. Once I saw him I *knew* you were in labor. We're on our way there, sweetheart, but traffic is a bitch. Tell her to stay in there a little longer, okay?"

"I'll try, but it doesn't work like that."

"I love you."

I sigh happily. "I love you too."

"We're going to have a baby, Thea."

I start to tear up. "I know."

"I'll be there. I will," he vows and hangs up.

A nurse comes in, hooks me up to monitors, and checks me saying I'm six centimeters dilated. "You're getting close," she tells me, covering me with the sheet again. "Do you want an epidural?"

I look at Nova. "Do I?" I ask.

She shrugs. "That's up to you—do you want to go natural or have drugs?"

I laugh. "I don't know … it's not so bad right now, so no epidural for now."

The nurse looks at me like she thinks I'm going to regret that decision, but shrugs and heads out of the room.

"Do you want anything?" Nova asks me.

"Can I have some ice?"

"Sure thing. I'll be right back."

She heads out into the hall to get it, and of course as soon as she leaves I get a contraction.

I breathe through it like she told me and that helps, but I'm sweating like a pig.

I lay my head back and close my eyes.

I comfort myself with the fact that soon I'm going to see my little girl, finally, after nine long months.

The door opens and Nova comes in with a plastic cup full of crushed ice. She pulls the chair up beside me and sits down, handing me the cup.

I hold the cup and grab a couple of pieces, popping them into my mouth.

Crunching on the ice helps, because it cools me down and gives me something to do to distract from the pain.

Nova rubs my arm, trying to comfort me, but her eyes are far away.

"Thank you for staying with me. I know this can't be easy."

She smiles but it doesn't quite reach her eyes. "It's strange being here like this."

"Did you have someone with you when you had Greyson?" I ask. I've never talked to her all that much about her son she gave up for adoption, I know she has a good relationship with him and his adoptive parents, but that's only recently. Before then, he was a stranger to her. I can't imagine going through this whole process and having my baby taken from me.

She shakes her head. "No, I was alone."

My heart breaks, picturing a sixteen-year-old Nova scared and alone in a hospital giving birth to her son. "That's horrible."

She shrugs, still absentmindedly rubbing my arm. "It's okay."

"I can't imagine going through this without Xander," I murmur, and if he doesn't get his ass here that's a very real possibility.

We hear a commotion in the hallway and then a moment later the door swings open.

Xander bursts into the room ... Well, shoves is a more accurate description since he's wearing his uniform with big shoulder pads and he barely fits through the door.

I breathe a sigh of relief the moment I see him.

"Fuck, Thea, I was so scared I wouldn't make it in time." He collapses at the foot of the bed.

"I'm so happy you're here," I tell him, and promptly burst into tears of relief. I can't seem to help it. Pregnancy makes me a weepy mess.

He picks himself up and comes to stand over me, kissing me desperately.

He pulls away and smiles at Nova. "Thank you for staying with her."

"It's not a problem. Do you want us to go to your house and bring you some clothes?"

He looks down at himself. "Shit. Yeah, I need something."

"We'll take care of it," she promises and squeezes my hand before leaving. When she opens the door I see my brother tiptoeing outside it.

"Go tell my brother I'm okay?" I ask Xander.

He nods. "I can do that."

I take a deep breath, growing more uncomfortable since my contractions are getting closer together.

Xander finished speaking with my brother and comes back.

"Can you at least get rid of the shoulder pads?" I ask. "You look like the Hulk."

He chuckles. "Yeah, give me a minute." He peels off the jersey and then takes off the rest of the gear. By the time he's done he's shirtless and I'm regretting my request, because at the moment the nurse comes back in.

"Oh." She jumps, and then her jaw drops, staring at my husband.

"Yeah, yeah, I get it." I wave a hand. "He has a nice body, that's why I'm currently knocked up, now can you stop staring at my husband?" I plead.

She shakes her head, her cheeks flaming.

"Thea," Xander scolds.

"I'm having a baby here," I defend. "I can do and say whatever I want."

"I wanted to check you again," the nurse says. "Since things seemed to be moving fast I wanted to stay on top of it."

I prop my legs up once more and she checks me.

"Looks like you're at eight centimeters now, so we're having a baby soon, and I hate to tell you but you're moving so fast they won't give you an epidural now." She gives me an apologetic smile. "I'm going to go hunt down your doctor. I think we're going to have a baby in the next hour."

My jaw drops and Xander's surprised eyes meet mine.

In an hour we could be meeting our daughter.

The nurse leaves us alone. Xander pulls the chair closer to my bed and sits down. His hair and chest is still damp with sweat but he doesn't seem to care.

He grabs my hand, kissing my knuckles. "I can't wait to meet her."

"Me either."

I feel absolutely giddy at the idea of meeting our little girl.

"I hope she likes me," I murmur.

He shakes his head. "Silly girl, she already loves you. You're her mom."

My lower lip quivers. "I'm scared again."

"That's okay. I am too. Our lives are about to change forever." He leans over and kisses me. "I love you, and there's no one else I'd rather take this journey with than you."

I lean closer to him. "Back at ya."

"Can I get you anything?" he asks, combing his fingers through my damp hair.

"Water please, and more ice chips."

The cup I'd set aside is mostly melted now.

"I'll be right back," he promises, and heads out of the room.

Shirtless.

He's probably going to give all the nurses a heart attack.

He's not gone long and I take the water from him gratefully. I sip it slowly, afraid if I gulp it I might get sick.

"Oh, fuck," I cry, nearly dropping the cup of water. "This shit hurts."

I reach for his hand and he gives it to me gladly. I squeeze the life out of it, breathing through the pain.

"Why'd I tell them no drugs?" I ask him. "I'm an idiot."

I breathe through the pain and when it subsides I let go of his hand. I don't miss him shaking his hand out. I didn't squeeze it *that* hard.

There's a knock on the door and Nova pokes her head in. "Here are your clothes. Jace grabbed them, and I didn't check, so hopefully they're okay. Is there anything else we can do?"

Xander crosses the room and takes the clothes from her. "Would you mind asking Cade to run out the car and get Thea's bag? It has stuff for her and the baby. It's in the backseat of the car. He has my keys."

"Sure thing."

She disappears again and Xander heads into the bathroom attached to my room to change.

"Oh, shit," I cry. "Here comes another contraction."

I grab my stomach, breathing as deeply as I can, but my instinct is to hold my breath.

"I feel like I need to push!" I yell. "Xander, hurry up. Go get *someone*."

He busts out of the bathroom, his jeans not buttoned yet and yanking on his shirt.

"I'll get someone ... just hang on." He flies out into the hallway and I hear him calling for help.

The nurse from earlier comes in and I'm near tears again. "This baby is coming *out*," I warn her. "Get the doctor."

"Let me check you," she protests.

"*Now*," I seethe.

Her eyes widen and she runs out in search of the doctor.

Xander stands at my side, and I can feel his nerves radiating off of him. He's trying to remain calm for me, but he's barely keeping his cool.

"You're doing great, sweetheart." He brushes my damp forehead off my forehead.

Dr. Hawkins and two nurses burst into the room.

He quickly gets his scrubs and gloves on.

"You're ready to push?"

I nod. "Yeah, she's coming quick."

"All right, Dad, why don't you hold her leg up and will get this show on the road."

One of the nurses grabs my other leg and Dr. Hawkins gets ready.

"On your next contraction I want you to start pushing," he tells me.

"I'm so hot," I whine. My body is already drenched in sweat.

He says something to one of the other nurses and she heads out of the room.

"I feel one coming," I warn, sitting up.

Xander tightens his hold on my leg.

"Push," the doctor instructs.

I bear down and I totally and completely understand now why you'd shit yourself giving birth, because that's exactly what it feels like you're doing.

"It burns," I complain, collapsing against the pillow.

"You're doing beautifully," Dr. Hawkins assures me.

The nurse comes back into the room and drapes a cold cloth over my brow. It helps immensely.

I push again and again and *again*.

"The head's almost out," Dr. Hawkins informs us. "Do you want to look?" he asks Xander.

"Don't you dare," I warn.

He looks anyway.

His face lights up and he looks at me with awe in his eyes. "She has dark hair, Thea. She has my hair."

Before I can respond another contraction comes and I have to push again.

I know my labor is going faster than normal, but this shit is still hard. I'm exhausted already, but all I want is to see my little girl.

"Here comes another contraction," Dr. Hawkins warns.

"I can tell when one's coming!" I yell.

I push with everything I have, desperate to get her out.

"It hurts," I whine. "Get her out," I beg.

"One more push," Dr. Hawkins tells me. "One more and she's here."

I begin to sob. "It hurts. I can't do it."

Xander grabs my hand and I turn to look at him. "You *can* do this. You're a warrior. You're the strongest person I know." He presses his forehead to mine. "Lean on me. You can do this."

Another contraction comes and I take a deep breath, bracing myself.

I push as hard as I can, my eyes squished closed.

And then ...

Her crying fills the air and they press her warm body to my chest. My eyes pop open and I instantly start sobbing as my eyes land on my daughter.

My daughter.

She's tiny and pink and wrinkled and perfect.

So damn perfect.

She reaches out with an open fist and grabs Xander's finger. I look up at him in awe, and tears are streaming down his face.

"You did so good, sweetheart," he confesses. "She's perfect."

She lets out another cry, blinking wide blue eyes up at us. She opens and closes her mouth and I laugh.

"She looks exactly like you," I tell him. From her dark hair, to her pouty lips, she's one-hundred percent Xander's daughter.

"She has your nose, though, thank God for that," he jokes.

"I like your nose." He broke it when he was younger and it's never been the same since. I think the crookedness gives him character.

She stretches out her hand and he chuckles. "She has big hands. Maybe she's going to be a football player like her daddy."

I narrow my eyes on him. "And maybe she'll want to be a stripper? Did you ever think about that?"

He glares back at me. "My daughter is not going to be a stripper—anything but that."

I shrug and kiss her warm head. "Mommy says she can be anything she wants. Even a stripper."

"And Daddy says we'll discuss this more later."

I laugh, rubbing her plump cheek. "She's so chunky and perfect," I murmur.

"Come here, Dad," Dr. Hawkins instructs. "Why don't you cut the cord?"

Xander takes the strange looking scissors, looking at them quizzically. "I don't want to hurt her."

"It's fine. Just cut there." Dr. Hawkins points to the area and Xander cuts the umbilical cord.

The baby gives a little cry and Xander rubs her head. "I'm sorry, baby girl. I know it's probably so scary here."

"We need to clean her up," one of the nurses says, covering the baby with a blanket and plucking her off my chest.

I instantly feel cold and reach out weakly for her.

"We'll bring her back," the nurse promises.

"You did so good." Xander kisses me, his lips pleasantly warm. "I've never seen anything like that. It was incredible."

"I'm so tired," I confess.

He brushes my hair out of my eyes, his fingers lingering on my cheek. "You can rest soon."

"Thea?" Dr. Hawkins interrupts.

"Yeah?" I ask, bringing my tired eyes to his.

"You're going to have to birth the placenta now. You shouldn't have to do much work, but I just want you to know what's going on, okay?"

I nod.

Xander rubs my arm, drawing my attention back to him. "You seriously did so good, sweetheart. You're a rock star."

I smile tiredly at him as our baby lets out a cry in the background. "Go to her," I plead.

"Thea?" Dr. Hawkins says again, worry in his tone that instantly puts Xander and I on alert. "Your placenta's not detaching."

"W-what?" I stutter, my eyes flicking from the doctor to Xander. "What's wrong? Is something wrong?"

"It's okay," he rushes to assure me. "Your placenta is stuck and we're going to have to go in to get it out. It's nothing to panic over."

"Nothing to panic over?" I cry. "That doesn't sound like nothing? Xander? What's happening?" I plead with him, like he can make this go away somehow.

He looks pale and helpless.

"Shh," Dr. Hawkins consoles me. "Really, this is fine, Thea. You'll be in and out in no time."

The nurses immediately start to wheel me from the room.

"What do I do?" Xander asks, looking helpless.

I grab his hand. "Stay with her," I beg. "She needs you. Please don't leave her."

"But, Thea—"

"*No*," my tone is final. "Stay with the baby. I'll be okay," I vow.

He watches me leave helplessly. They slap something over my face and everything becomes fuzzy.

The last thing I hear is the baby crying and then ...

Nothing.

thirty-three

xander

I WATCH as they take Thea away, my hands clasped behind my head. I still don't quite understand what's going on and I feel so weak and useless. I just want to be there for her, but she wanted me to stay with the baby, and I understand.

We both no longer live solely for each other.

Now we live for this tiny little girl.

I walk over to her and the nurse cleaning her off. She now has a tiny diaper on. She flails her arms, looking up at me with big eyes.

"You want to follow me over here?" Tthe nurse asks. "We're going to wash her hair."

I nod, at a loss for words as I stare at my daughter.

I can't get over how small and perfect she is. Thea's right, she looks exactly like me.

The nurse carries her over to the sink and regulates the temperature of the water. She gets it right and then holds the baby so that only her hair gets wet. She uses a brush to come through her fine dark hair. I'm amazed by how much hair she has. It's not an obscene amount, but it's enough.

When her hair is clean she dries off her head and brushes her hair. She slips a little blue and pink hat on her head and then swaddles her.

"Okay, Daddy, are you ready to hold her?"

It hits me then, that I haven't even held her yet. I nod, unable to find the words to tell this woman yes.

She smiles and hands her over.

She looks up at me with big blue eyes. I'm sure those will change, since I have brown and Thea's are hazel, but for now they're beautiful.

"She's hungry. Do you know if you're wife wanted to try to breastfeed?"

"She wanted to try."

The baby opens and closes her mouth making a sucking noise.

"She should be back soon, so as soon as she is we'll try to get the baby to latch."

"Okay, thank you," I mutter, but all my focus is on the baby.

She leaves and finally I'm alone with my daughter.

I smile at her in my arms. She looks like a burrito or a really fluffy football.

I rock her back and forth and she lets out a little cry.

"I know you're hungry, sweetie," I croon. "Mommy will be back soon."

She manages to get her little fists free of the swaddle and swings the wildly.

I sit down in the chair, and I find myself just staring at her.

She truly is the most beautiful baby I've ever seen and I can't believe she's ours.

"I'm your daddy," I tell her, kissing her forehead.

She yawns and starts making the sucking noise again.

It isn't long until Thea's wheeled back into the room. Her eyes are heavy, like she's tired, but she manages to smile.

"You look good holding a baby," she tells me.

I chuckle. "Are you coming on to me?"

"A hot guy with a baby? Hell yeah I'm coming on to you."

I laugh. Only my wife.

"Give me my daughter," she begs, holding out her arms.

"The nurse wants you to try to feed her."

"I'm sure she's hungry," she agrees, taking the baby from me.

The baby flails around wildly, searching for a boob.

Thea tugs down her gown and gets her into position. The nurse comes in then and smiles.

"Well, here I thought you might need my help and you've already got it. Is she sucking?"

"I think so," Thea says, rubbing her finger over the baby's soft cheek.

"If you need me, just hit the button on your bed," she tells us.

She closes the door and finally it's the three of us alone.

"Look at us." Thea smiles over at me, and I swear even having just given birth she's the most beautiful woman I've ever seen. "We're really a family now."

I kiss her and then I bend and kiss the baby. "I didn't think I could possibly love you more than I did yesterday, but after watching that, and seeing her ... I love you so much."

She smiles at me. "I love you too."

We both watch the baby again, unable to stop staring at her. I'm sure all new parents feel the same way—like if you blink this moment will be gone forever.

An hour later, the baby's fed, burped, and with a clean diaper.

"Can I let everybody back now?" I ask.

Thea rocks the baby in her arms and nods. "Yeah, let them in. She's ready to meet her crazy lovable family."

I kiss them both before I leave the room and then I head down the hall to the waiting room.

Inside the waiting room, it's packed with family and friends.

Jace, Nova, Cade, and Rae haven't left, and my parents, and Thea's mom have since joined them.

"Do you guys want to come meet her?" I ask.

I'm probably not supposed to let this many people go back, but some rules are meant to be broken.

They all jump up, eager to meet the newest addition to our family.

I lead them down the hallway into the room. They crowd around the bed and my mom, being the sap that she is bursts into tears.

There's room for me on the bed with my girls so I rest there.

"Everyone," I begin, and they hold their breath waiting for us to *finally* reveal the name. "We would like you to meet Xael Therese Kindcaid. Xael, meet everyone." I pronounce the name like *Zale*.

"What the kind of name is *Xael*?" Cade blurts.

"Shut it, Cade," Thea scolds her brother, glaring at him. "The greatest thing you've ever done is throw a football, I just birthed life. Life trumps balls."

"Xael," my mom repeats. "I like it. It's different."

"We wanted her to have a different, strong name, and we thought Xael did that." I smile at my daughter, rubbing her small cap covered head.

Thea smiles up at me, and despite how exhausted I know she must feel she's stunning. "Xander, Thea, and baby Xael Therese."

Our family.

thirty-four
...

thea

TWO DAYS later and it's time to go home.

With a baby.

I brush my teeth and change my clothes. I need a shower, desperately, but I'm waiting until I get home. I pull my dirty hair into a ponytail and call it a job well done.

I enter the room and find Xander dressing Xael in her going home outfit—a cute sleeper with unicorns on it, and then swaddling her in the lemon swaddle Rae got her.

I sit down on the bed as he picks her back up, rocking her in his arms.

The nurse comes in with the discharge papers. "You can't send me home with her," I plead. "I killed a hamster once. You can't send me home with a baby. Tell her, Xander."

He chuckles, rocking the baby. "We've got this," he tells the nurse. "Ignore her."

My jaw drops. "You're no help."

"You're going to be fine," the nurse assures me, patting my hand.

She goes over the papers I need to sign and then she helps us put the baby in the car seat so that we know we have her buckled in properly.

She brings in a wheelchair to take me out, which I find completely unnecessary but she insists it's protocol.

That leaves Xander to carry the baby carrier and our stuff.

Thankfully, I didn't over pack ... for once.

Once outside, Xander sets down the carrier with Xael and goes to get the car.

She fusses and I bend down, popping her binky back in her mouth. She sucks on it, but I know she's getting hungry. Breastfeeding is hard, and even though it's only been two days I'm close to giving up. My nipples *hurt*.

Xander brings the car up to the front and hops out. He grabs the carrier and the nurse helps him make sure it's locked into the base properly. Once Xael is in he helps me to sit beside her.

"Good luck, guys." The nurse waves goodbye.

Xander gets in the car and looks at me in the rearview mirror. "We're going home with a baby. This is crazy."

"It does feel weird," I agree as he pulls out.

He drives way more cautious than normal and it takes a full forty minutes to get home instead of twenty.

When we get there he pulls into the garage and kills the engine. Normally, we'd hear Prue barking but Jace and

Nova took her for the last couple of days, and they'll be dropping her off later. We gave them one of the baby's blankets that she's been using so that Prue could get used to the smell. I have no idea if it'll actually help, but it made me feel better.

Xander opens my door and helps me out and then gets the baby.

Watching him carry our baby into the house makes me fall in love with him all over again. Anytime he does anything new with our daughter I love him more. It's such a unique thing, seeing him with her.

He sets the carrier down on the floor and bends, getting her out. I sit on the couch and he hands her to me so I can feed her.

"Are you okay?" he asks and I nod. "I'm going to go shower. I won't be gone long."

"We'll be fine here, won't we, pretty girl?" I ask Xael. She looks up at me, already eating. I give him a thumbs up. "Go. But I'm next," I warn. "I smell gross."

He chuckles and smacks a kiss on my cheek. "I'll be quick, promise."

He bounds up the stairs and Xael and I are left alone.

I brush my finger over her cheek and she hums. I keep staring at her, amazed that we created this tiny perfect thing. I kiss the top of her head and she reaches for my hair. I give her my finger instead and she holds on with a surprising amount of strength.

Xander finishes his shower and since Xael's still eating he makes us both a sandwich for lunch. I eat mine while I feed her. Something tells me I'm going to be doing that a lot from now on.

Xael finally finishes eating and after I'm done with my sandwich I transfer her to Xander's arms. She wiggles around on his chest, getting comfortable.

I hate leaving her, even for a second, but I *need* a shower. I can barely stand smelling myself.

I wash my hair and scrub my body.

Cleaning myself makes me feel *loads* better. I change into a pair of yoga pants and a tank top, letting my hair dry on its own.

I pad downstairs quietly in case the baby is sleeping and I smile when I enter the family room and find that Xander's fallen asleep on the couch and Xael's asleep on his chest. I grab my phone and snap a photo, knowing it's something I don't want to forget. Our baby sleeping on Xander's chest is the sweetest thing I've ever seen.

I make myself a cup of decaf coffee and move around the kitchen as quietly as I can.

I get a text from Nova saying that they're bringing Prue back so I head to the front to watch for them so I can let them in.

They arrive and I push the button to open the gate and let them up the driveway. I unlock the front door and open it, which makes the security system beep.

"Thea?" Xander calls out sleepily.

"I'm letting Jace and Nova in," I explain.

He pads into the room carrying Xael, his hair sticking up everywhere.

Prue comes running into the house then, Jace and Nova behind her.

"Hey, girl." I bend down to pet her. She licks my face and then goes to smell Xander's feet.

Jace and Nova come in, so I close the door behind them.

"How long have you guys been home?" Nova asks.

"Not long." I shrug. "Maybe an hour or two."

Xander bends down, introducing Prue to the baby. She smells her and wags her tail and then runs over to her toy box. Xander stands and shrugs.

"I guess Prue doesn't care," he chuckles.

"Can I hold the baby?" Jace asks, holding out his arms.

Xander shrugs. "Sure." He hands her over.

Jace holds her delicately, like he's afraid if he breathes on her he'll break her. His face splits into a grin and he rocks her. He smiles over at Nova. "I'd like to place an order for one of these."

Nova is clearly taken aback by his words. "We'll talk later," she says.

Xander and I exchange a look. I'm not sure the world is ready for Jace babies, but neither of us says anything.

Jace and Nova end up hanging out for the next hour until Xander's mom and dad shows up. They leave then so the grandparents can have a moment with the baby.

Sarah is completely enamored with the baby, and Cooper is too.

I think it's safe to say that Xael is the most loved baby ever ... but I'm sure all parents think that.

The day fades into evening and Sarah and Cooper leave.

Xander makes dinner and I tend to the baby. We begin to fall into an easy pattern, and I'm surprised at how well we're adapting to parent life.

After dinner we're both tired so we head up to bed.

With a baby.

This is crazy.

I fix Xael in her rocker bassinet in our room and she cries at leaving my arms.

"I hate it when she cries," Xander confesses.

"Me too," I murmur, watching her. "It breaks my heart."

Xael flails her arms, and cries. We both stand back and watch her, ready to grab her if we need to. After a couple minutes her cries quiet and she falls asleep.

I smile at Xander and give him a high five.

I'm sure the quiet is short-lived, but I'm learning to revel in the good moments when we have them.

Xander and I climb into bed and turn the lights off. I snuggle against his chest and he runs his fingers through my hair.

It isn't long until I fall asleep listening to the soft sounds of Xael's breaths.

I wake up a short time later, jolting awake and running over to make sure she's breathing.

"Thea?" Xander asks sleepily. "What are you doing?"

"I had to check on her," I explain. "I was worried."

I count her breaths, pleased every time her little chest rises and falls.

"Thea, come back to bed," he pleads.

"Just a minute," I beg.

I count her breaths for a solid minute before climbing back into bed.

"You can't be so paranoid," Xander warns me.

"I know." I frown. "It's hard being a new mom."

"It's hard being a new dad," he echoes. "But we'll do it, one day at a time."

He brushes his lips softly over my forehead and I force my eyes closed.

It isn't long until I fall asleep again.

thirty-five

...

xander

TWO WEEKS.

Thea and I have managed to survive two full weeks as parents.

It's hard as fuck, that's for sure, but I love being a dad. I love it more than I thought I would, and I know that as she gets older that love is only going to grow with all the things I can teach her.

"I don't want to leave her," Thea confesses, as she puts on her makeup. She watches me in the mirror where I hold the baby, rocking Xael back and forth.

"My mom wants to watch her, and we need a break. It's a win-win," I reason. "We'll just do dinner and be right back. We'll be gone an hour, two at the most," I tell her.

I don't want to leave Xael, either, if I'm being honest, but we've barely left the house these two weeks and I know we need a breather before we lose our minds.

Thea sighs, circling her lips as she applies mascara.

I smile down at Xael in my arms and she yawns. She's always yawning. I think it's adorable.

"Hey, cutie." I kiss the top of her downy soft head. Her dark hair is soft against my lips.

She yawns again in response and I laugh.

Thea finishes with her makeup and moves on to her hair. She brushes through the long strands and then curls them. I bounce Xael in my arms when she stars to get cranky.

"She's hungry," Thea sighs, finishing her hair. "Hand her over."

I give her Xael and she takes her, carrying her over to the bed so she can lie comfortably while she feeds her.

I'm ready, but I slip my shoes on. I dressed up, opting for a pair of nice jeans and a blue button down shirt tucked into them with a belt. Thea plans to dress up too. She has a dress laid out to put on.

"She's not wanting to eat," Thea complains. "Your mom might have to give her a bottle."

"I'm sure she won't mind a bit," I laugh.

Thea's been breastfeeding as much as she can, but it's a struggle, so Xael has been having to drink from a bottle some. I know that makes Thea feel a little like a failure, but I tell her she shouldn't feel that way at all. As long as Xael's eating, that's what matters, not *how* she gets it.

My mom arrives and Thea tries a little longer, but when she's unsuccessful she ends up calling it quits.

We both take turns kissing the baby goodbye. It takes us a solid ten minutes to leave because we won't stop kissing her.

We finally manage to get in the car, and I leave before either of us can change our minds.

It's hard leaving your baby for the first time, and I'm the dad, so I can't imagine how Thea must feel.

"You look beautiful," I tell her, it's the truth but I'm also hoping to distract her.

She forces a smile. "Thanks, you don't look so bad yourself."

I made reservations at a nicer place downtown that we haven't been in a long time. It's actually the place we went to on our first official date, and now it'll be the first place we went to eat after having Xael.

We reach the restaurant and leave the car for valet parking.

I guide Thea inside with a hand on her waist. She looks uncomfortable and I know she'd much rather be home with the baby, so would I, but we need a breather and we'll be home before we know it.

"Reservation for Kincaid," I tell the hostess.

She smiles and grabs two menus. "This way, Mr. and Mrs. Kincaid."

She guides us to a table in the corner. The restaurant is packed, and I asked for private, but I guess this is as private as it's going to get.

"Would you like me to take your coats?" she asks as we shrug out of them.

"Sure," I reply, handing her mine. She takes Thea's as well and we sit down.

Thea picks up her menu, skimming it. She bites her lip, tapping her fingers on the table.

I can tell she's nervous about something, but I can't figure out what it is.

Normally, I can read her easily, but tonight, I can't get into her head.

I furrow my brow as I watch her, trying to figure her out, but nothing is making any sense beyond her being uncomfortable about leaving the baby.

I turn my attention to the menu and our waiter comes for our drink order.

We both order water.

Thea looks at her menu like it's the most interesting thing she's ever encountered.

I decide what I want to order and set mine aside.

Thea decides too and lays her menu down. Our waiter comes with our waters and a basket of bread. He takes our orders before leaving again.

Thea sighs, crossing her fingers together.

I lean closer to her. "What's on your mind, sweetheart?"

She bites her lip. "You're going to laugh."

"I won't laugh," I vow.

"You're going to say, I told you so, then." She frowns, tilting her head.

I shake my head, totally confused now. "You've lost me."

She sighs heavily. "I don't want to go back to work."

She's been on maternity leave sine a few weeks before she had Xael, and she still has time left, obviously.

"Okay," I say slowly.

She rolls her eyes. "I don't want to go back to work," she repeats. "I want to quit and stay home with Xael. I know I was so anti-stay-at-home mom at first, but that was before I had her and realized ... this is what I'm meant to do with my life. Being a mom is everything I was ever made to do." She starts to tear up and my jaw drops in surprise.

"Thea," I breathe. "Whatever you want, you know I'm on board."

"This is what I want," she promises. "More than anything."

I feel proud, that her mind changed and she was adult enough to own it. Sometimes we think one way and then learn that it's not the best. It's okay to change your mind.

"You know I'm on board with whatever you want."

She smiles, pleased with my answer.

I'm definitely relieved that we don't have to look for a nanny or put Xael into daycare. Not that there aren't plenty of good nannies and daycares, but it's hard to think about leaving your child with a stranger.

Thea's shoulders sag with relief at having told me. The silly girl shouldn't have been nervous. Why would I be mad that she wants to stay home and raise our child? It's what I wanted from the beginning. I never said anything because I didn't want her to feel like it was forced onto her.

And if a year or so down the road she decided that she *did* want to go back to work, I'd support that too, because when you love someone you stand beside them and hold them up, you don't fight them.

Marriage is all about compromise, in my opinion.

Sometimes you're both going to be on the same page, and sometimes not, but you have to be willing to open up and see the other person's side.

I reach across the table and take her hand, entwining our fingers together.

"I love you." I love that girl more than I ever thought it was possible to love someone else. I think back to how I knew her when we were both only children, and how far we've come. We've been through so much, but we're both stronger, better, people for it.

"I love you too," she sighs happily.

Our food is brought out and we both dig in. I got a steak while she opted for a salmon salad.

Our meals have mostly consisted of things we can eat quickly while holding a baby, so most hasn't been of the healthiest variety. So it's nice to eat *real* food for a change.

Thea sits back. "Oh, no."

"What?" I ask around a mouthful of food.

She looks down and I slowly follow her gaze watching as her boobs leak.

"Shit, oh, no." She bites her lip, looking at me with panic in her eyes.

I don't have my coat, since they took it when we sat down.

She begins to cry, which draws more attention than her leaking boobs.

I can tell she embarrassed and uncomfortable, so I stand up and start stripping out of my shirt. I don't have anything on underneath, but my wife is uncomfortable and I'll be damned if I keep letting her feel that way.

I undo all the buttons and once I have it off I help her put it on, pulling it around her chest.

"Thank you," she mouths, wiping at her eyes.

She looks around at the people staring and then averts her eyes to her food.

"There's nothing to see here," I bite out to the staring people.

I sit down and Thea raises her eyes to mine. "You're the best."

"I didn't do anything special, sweetheart."

We finish our meal in peace, and I'm surprised. It's a nice restaurant so I expected them to kick me out for my strip show.

When we collect our coats, Thea gives me my shirt back. The ring of milk has dried on her dress. I'm not sure it'll come out, but what do I know?

Thea zips up her coat and we wait for the car to be brought around.

Once inside, I expect her to want to go straight home, but instead she surprises me by saying, "Can we get McFlurryies?"

"We can get anything you want sweetheart."

There's a McDonald's not too far, so I head there.

"I'll let your mom know we'll be home soon," Thea tells me, fiddling with her phone.

Her phone dings. "Aw, she sent me a picture of Xael. She's sleeping in her bouncer and Prue has her head on her feet."

Prue has taken surprisingly well to Xael. I thought she'd be fine, but I didn't expect her to love her so much. I think Prue thinks she's a helpless, hairless puppy.

When I pull into the McDonald's drive-thru line, Thea shows me the photo and I grin.

"My girls," I whisper.

The urge to get home is nearly overwhelming. I just want to get home so I can hug and kiss her and tell her goodnight.

I made a vow with myself that no matter what, no matter where I am, every night I'll say goodnight to my daughter.

I place an order for our ice cream and move forward in line.

I get to the window and pay, and then to the next window to actually get our ice cream.

Normally, we'd park and eat it, but tonight Thea says, "Can we wait and eat this at home?"

"You read my mind, sweetheart."

I head home, and when I pull into the garage Thea's out of the car before it's in park.

I grab our ice cream and head in after her.

I find her bent over Xael in the rocker, kissing the top of her head.

"Thanks, Mom." I kiss my mom on the cheek.

"She was a perfect angel."

"Did she take her bottle?" Thea asks.

"Like a champ."

I set our ice cream on the counter and go to look at Xael. I smile when she wiggles in her sleep, kicking her little feet. I bend and kiss her head. I'm always amazed at how soft and fine her black hair is.

"I hope you guys had fun," my mom says, squeezing Thea's hand. "I'll head out. I'm tired."

"Thanks for doing this, Mom." I kiss her cheek again and she smiles. "I'll walk you out."

I head outside with her to her car. There's a small dusting of snow on the ground, but not much, thankfully.

"I love you," she tells me. "I'll see you later."

"Bye." I wave, watching her slip into the car.

I head inside and find Thea with Xael in her arms, waiting to go upstairs.

Prue runs up ahead of us and I take the baby from Thea while she changes and cleans up. She then takes the baby from me so I can do the same.

When I come out of the bathroom I find her in bed with Xael, and the baby's awake, feeding.

I lie in the bed, stretching out, watching my girls.

Xael looks around as she eats. Always the curious one.

I lean over and kiss her head.

"Goodnight," I murmur.

It's just one night, among many, but they all matter.

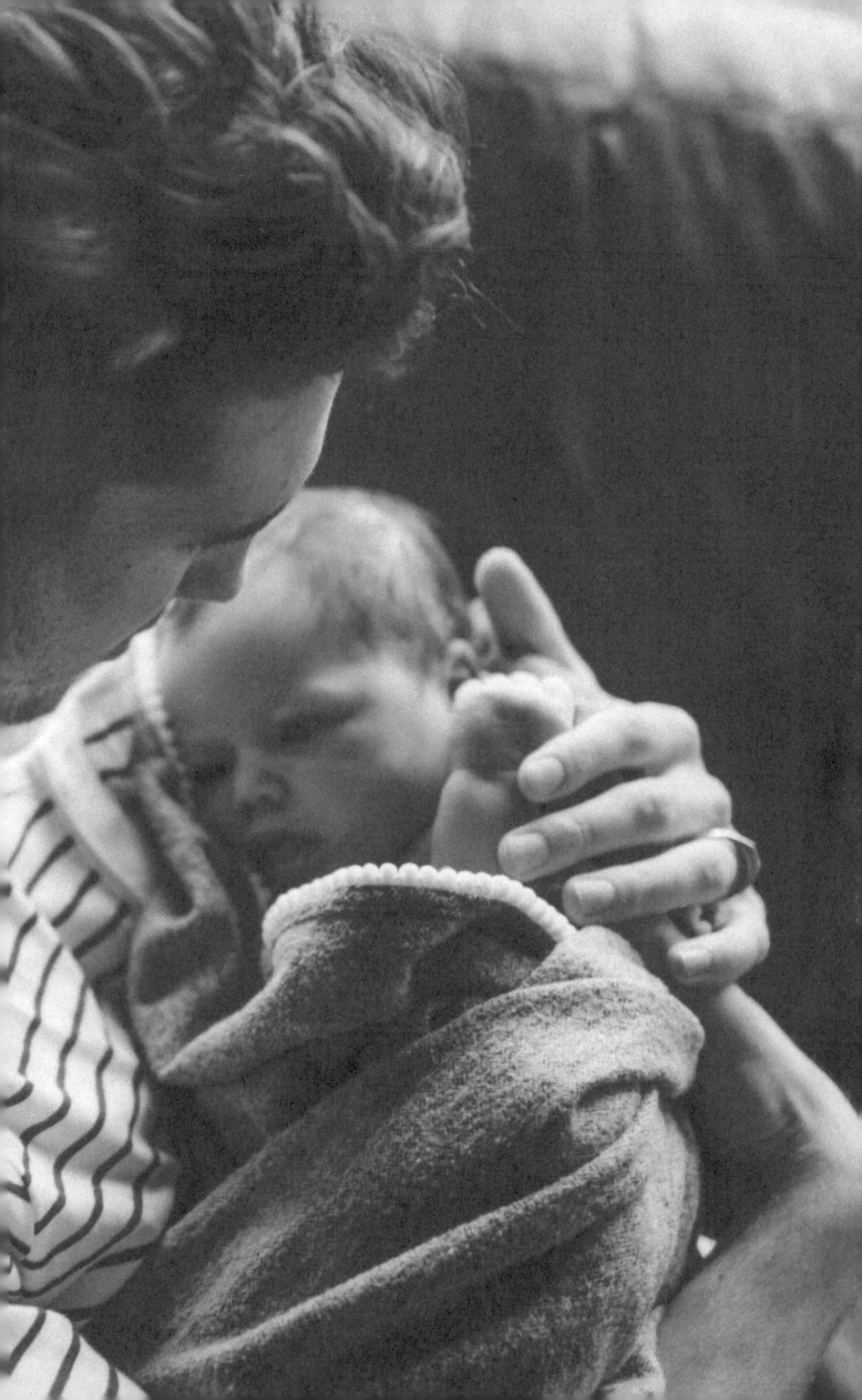

epilogue
...

thea

Four months later

It's been one whole year since I found out I was pregnant.

That's crazy to me.

So much has changed in that year.

For starters, I got pregnant, then I got a job, we bought a second house, a new car, had the baby, I decided to quit my job, and all the other little things in-between. It's been one wild ride, but if I could do it over again I wouldn't change a thing. Not one minute of it.

I'm learning that life doesn't give us more than we can

handle, and sometimes what we think is impossible is exactly what we need.

I didn't want a baby.

I didn't think I was cut out to be a mom.

But I couldn't have been more wrong.

Being Xael's mom is what I was born to do. This little girl has brought me more joy than almost anything.

She's perfect. She's everything I love most about Xander and me, rolled into one tiny human being.

I step outside onto the deck and smile when I see my husband holding our daughter. Her chubby little legs stick out of her ruffle bottom bathing suit and a bucket hat sits on her head, shieling her eyes from the sun—eyes that were once blue and are now as brown as her daddy's.

She's his clone, I've resolved myself to that fact.

Xael giggles when she sees me and reaches for me.

The rest of our family mingles around the yard of our second home, hanging out. We all decided to come out here for the weekend and just decompress together.

But while I love all of them, I only have eyes for these two.

They've stolen my heart, and I don't want it back.

Ever.

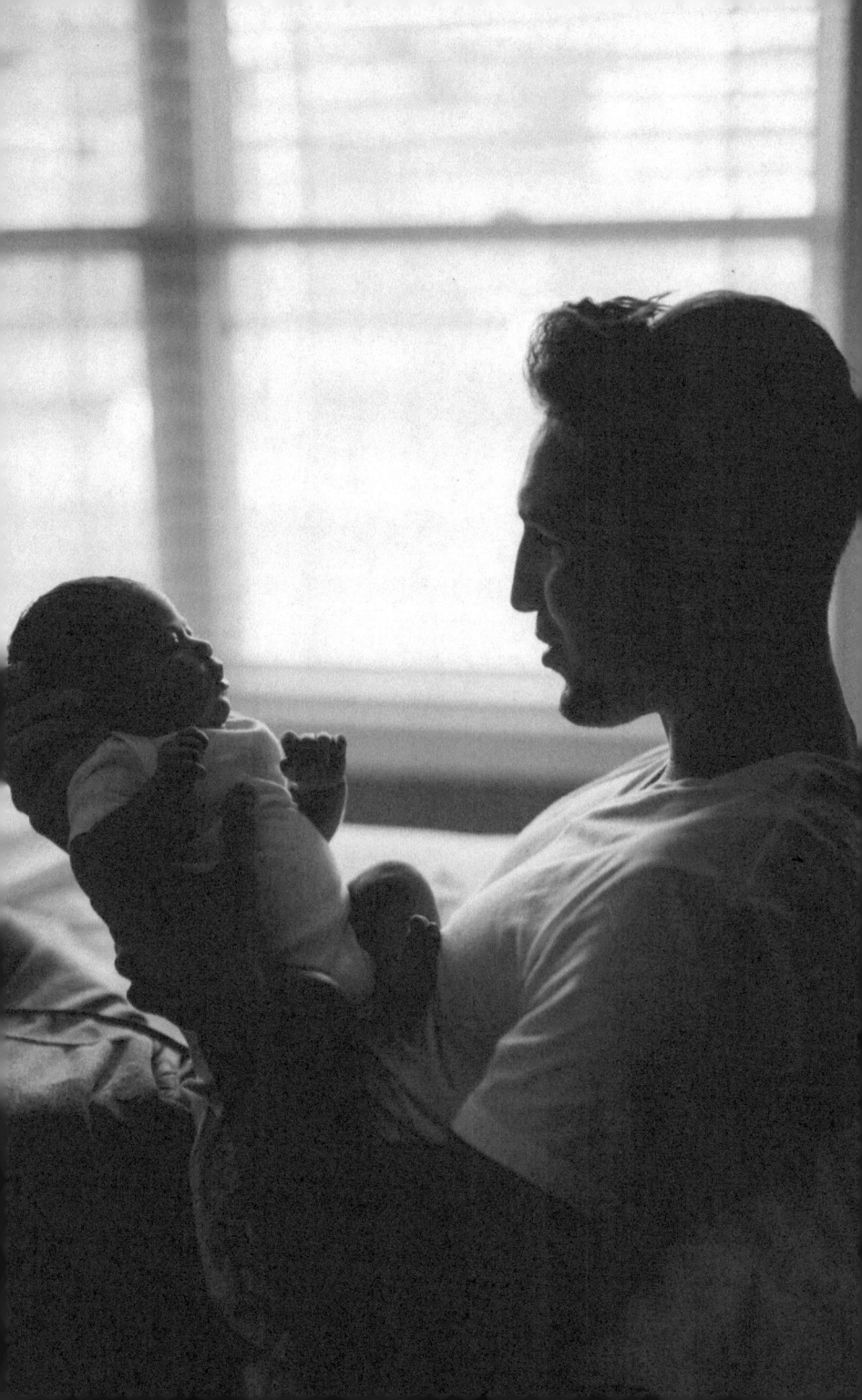

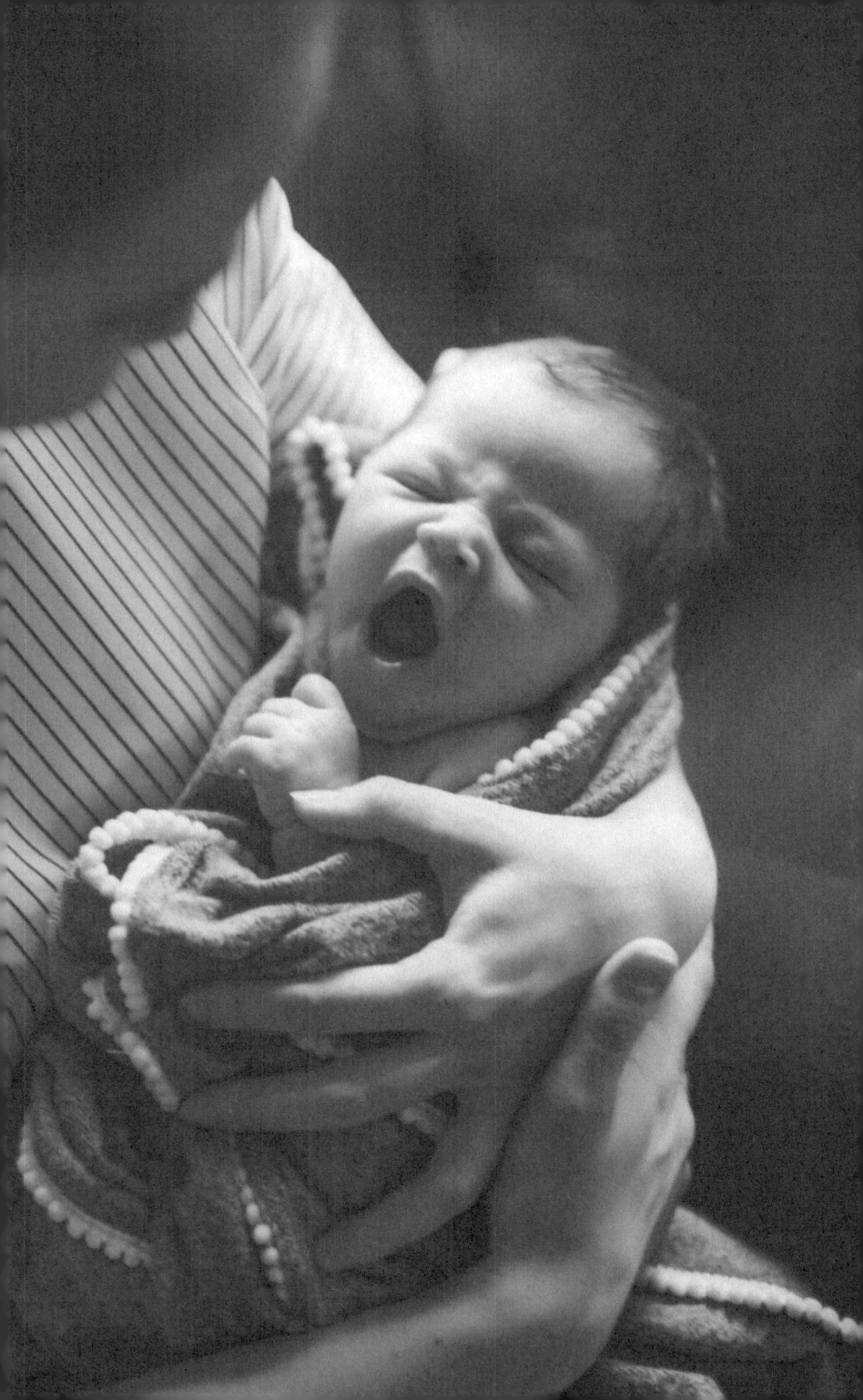

www.ingramcontent.com/pod-product-compliance
Lightning Source LLC
LaVergne TN
LVHW030054090526
838199LV00127B/6455